BURIED

M Greenhill

© 2020 by M. Greenhill

BURIED

All Rights Reserved.

2 Little Monkeys Limited

Auckland, New Zealand

No part of this book may be reproduced, scanned, or distributed in any printed or electronic form without express permission. Please do not participate or encourage piracy of copyrighted materials in violation of the author's rights.

This is a work of fiction. Names, characters, business, places, events and incidents are either the product of the author's imagination or used in a fictitious manner. Any resemblance to actual persons, living or dead, or actual events is purely coincidental.

For More Information:

www.mgreenhill.com

Cover By: L1graphics

First Edition February 2020

*To everyone who knows what it's like to have a bad
day last a year.*

And to you my dear reader.
Thank you for coming along on the journey

ONE

Monsters Live Among Us

Philadelphia, PA

Kowaiski appeared a pillar of the community. In reality, he had butchered five little girls.

Murphy O'Neill clenched his jaw and pushed down his wolf's growl. If only the local FBI team had brought him in earlier, he might have stopped Kowaiski months ago, and saved some of those girls. Now five sets of parents were suffocating under crushing grief, and they would carry the weight of it every day for the rest of their lives.

He knew that kind of grief all too well.

Murphy was damned if he'd let Kowaiski take the life of another child. Not on his watch. He pulled out the photo tucked into his bulletproof vest and took another look at Brooke Connors, Kowaiski's latest victim. Memories, long dead, rose to the surface and he closed his eyes. His heart withered and died the moment June was brutally taken from him, but what little was left ached for the poor girl's parents. Their panic, anguish, and the overwhelming stress had visibly aged them in the short time since Brooke's abduction. They would never recover if he couldn't save the child.

He crouched behind a dumpster and counted to three before raising his head to scan the outside of the abandoned meat-packing factory. The building had seen better days. Paint peeled off the walls, and rust had leached through the window frames. The air was thick with the scent of animal blood and rancid meat. He'd carried out a quick reconnaissance earlier, and despite its derelict state, the factory was locked tight. A dim light shining from a small window on the first floor was the only indication someone was inside. He calculated the distance to the loading docks. One hundred and fifty-two feet, give or take a few inches. He needed to be fast enough to make the distance without being seen by Kowaiski, but not so fast to garner unwanted attention from his team.

He needed to be careful. One wrong move and Kowaiski would kill the girl before he could reach her. And the bastard didn't need to be in the room to do it. Horrifying images flashed through his mind of when Kowaiski slaughtered the other girls. Rage surged through his veins. There must be a special place in hell for someone who could do that to a child. He wanted to tear Kowaiski limb from limb. He wanted to let Kowaiski know what it was like to be set upon by someone bigger and stronger.

Give me five minutes with him, and he will know. His wolf's anger was close to the surface. *Five minutes, that's all I need.*

He mentally shook himself and refocused on the job ahead, but his wolf kept pushing for action. He needed to calm down. Neither he, nor his wolf, wanted another innocent's death on their hands.

Murphy jumped at a small metallic click and suppressed an annoyed growl.

Gabe, one of the agents in his unit, grimaced beside him. "Sorry, just checking the safety was off." He inched closer and peered over the dumpster then checked his watch. "We're cutting this one close. Real close."

He said nothing. Gabe was right. Kowaiski had abducted the eleven-year-old girl on her way home from school three days ago. If he stayed true to form, she only had a few more hours before Kowaiski ended his sick ritual and killed her.

Gabe ducked his head and his brows furrowed together. "You positive he's got her in there?"

He gave a curt nod.

Gabe shook his head. "I've known you for years, and I still don't know how you do it. You swoop in, work the case alone, then wham bam you've solved it. And the rest of us get to share in the glory of catching the unsub, but we're none the wiser on how you actually did it. You're like superman. Only with bigger muscles."

He squirmed. Gabe was better off not knowing.

Gabe rechecked his gun. "But I tell you this for nothing, it's going to take me a long time to get over this sick S.O.B. The sooner he's off the street the better. I don't care how you tracked him down, I'm just happy you did."

Gabe fell silent, and Murphy glanced at his watch. They had another minute before the rest of the team was in place. His lips pursed into a thin line. If only he didn't need to hide behind the badge.

That badge gave you access to the information to track Kowaiski down, his wolf reminded him as he paced. He, too, was agitated at the wait.

The muscles along his jaw tightened. This case was getting to him. But why? He worked these types of cases all the time.

His wolf snorted. *You know why. Kowaiski reminds us of Elijah.*

He held back a growl. He had deliberately avoided this conversation, but his wolf was right. Kowaiski and Elijah shared the same perverse pleasure from butchering those weaker than them. For Kowaiski it was young girls, for Elijah it was anyone who got in his way. Like June.

A hollow ache filled his chest, and he dug his nails into his palms. The ache filled with a simmering anger, but he would not allow his inner storm to swell to the surface. He closed his eyes and focused his rage on where it belonged. Elijah. This was the only way he'd managed to survive all these years without June. Hate fueled him and gave him the will to carry on.

He had been so close.

The veins in his temple throbbed. Why hadn't he gone down into the prison with Daniel when they rescued Parker Johnson? He had asked himself that question many times in the past eight months. If he had gone into the prison, he would have recognized the pretend prisoner for what he really was—the stone-cold killer who had eluded him for fifty years.

Now Elijah had vanished again, and he was left cooling his heels, waiting for him to resurface. It was only a matter of time. That monster would not stay low for too long. He would kill again. And when Elijah did, he would be there to hunt him down.

Gabe nudged him. "It's time."

He got into position, then depressed a small button hidden in his vest. "Team Alpha in place."

Clive, the special agent in charge of the local team, paused for a moment, then responded. "We had a problem getting in, Murphy. Give us two minutes."

Gabe rolled his eyes. "His team's too green," he said once Clive had signed off. "Three probies in one team is two too many. And it doesn't help two of them have been eyeing you up like cotton candy instead of doing their job." He chuckled. "When you ignored Amy's advances, I think Peter imagined he was in with a chance."

Instead of taking the bait at Gabe's teasing tone, he glanced up at the night sky.

His wolf paced. *Why must he talk so much? Ignore the others. Let's go, we don't need them.*

The wait is killing me as well, but we need to be patient.

At least the moon was behind a blanket of clouds. They would be hidden right up until the moment they breached.

A fat rat raced past them and Gabe swore under his breath.

Murphy's gaze followed the rodent as it scuttled across the asphalt and through a stormwater grate. If only the animal could tell them where in the factory to target. He pulled out his phone to recheck the few photos of the factory they had managed to find, but they weren't much help.

A suffocating weight pushed at him, and he fought back. He'd lived with it for so long he sometimes forgot it was there, but the feeling was his constant companion. Tired. That was the word for it. Who would have thought tired was heavy, like a coat lined with lead, dragging him down with every step he took? He drew in a deep breath and glanced over the rim of the dumpster to recheck for movements. What was it Marilyn Monroe once said? Don't stop when you're tired. Stop when you're done.

His mouth set into a grim line. Well, he wouldn't be done until Elijah was dead by his hands. Then, and only then, would June's soul be at peace, and he would be free to retreat from the world and join her. Sometimes, if he closed his eyes in a moment of peace, he imagined her with him. Her joyful laughter as she ran through the meadow, her hand softly caressing the tall wild flowers she loved so much.

But the peaceful moments were rare. Instead, his body ached from the pain. The pain of missing her, the pain of anger, and the pain of wondering if he had done things differently that day, would she still be alive.

Dwelling on what is no more will not bring her back.

His wolf was right. He was torturing them both. He swallowed hard, ran a hand through his short hair, and cursed Elijah and fate for taking her from him. He only prayed that Brooke Connors' soul had a lot longer on this earth.

The light in the building flickered and his patience snapped. They couldn't wait any longer. The girl's time was almost up. "Moving in. Breaching through the north entrance. Remember, wait for my signal."

Gabe patted his gun. "Norma and I are ready."

He pulled out his service weapon and flicked off the safety. He wouldn't need it, but if he didn't look the part people would ask questions. "Stay here until I confirm he's in there and we know Brooke's condition."

Gabe nodded. "I know the drill. Just make sure you stay on comms."

He stood and, careful to keep out of any light, raced across the distance to the main door of the meat-packing factory. He slowed his pace. If he moved any faster, there would definitely be questions from the team. Mindful to not make a noise, he tested the padlock on the door. Locked. Someone had replaced it. And recently. He glanced over his shoulder and stepped up so his body blocked the team's direct line of sight to the door, then pulled on the padlock. The shackle broke with ease. "I'm in. Lock's rusted," he said in a low voice. With any luck no one would bother to take a closer look at the destroyed padlock.

He stepped inside and surveyed the room. A countertop covered with empty boxes, old toner cartridges, and trays took up most of the room. The sharp smell of thousands of animal carcasses was more pronounced inside the building, and he winced. The stench had leached into the walls and would make finding Kowaiski that much harder. He stilled and tilted his head. The faint sound of Marvin Gaye's *Sexual Healing* was playing from somewhere beyond the door into the main body of the factory. He closed his eyes and focused. The far right. And it wasn't on the ground floor.

A soft scrape and footsteps too heavy to be a child's confirmed Kowaiski's location upstairs.

He was across the room and through the door in a heartbeat. When the sound of a shower being turned on echoed down the stairs, he picked up his pace. They were just in time. Kowaiski was purifying himself before finishing with his latest victim. He hesitated, his foot on the bottom step. He could storm the room and take Kowaiski out, but that would be too much of a risk. Brooke needed to be secured first. She would be booby-trapped in some way, and he couldn't risk Kowaiski setting the detonation device off.

"Inside and performing an initial sweep."

He raced up the stairs, his footfall making little noise on the metal steps. Brooke would be in a separate room Kowaiski had prepared for her. The question was, where? He tried the first door. It opened easily, and he was standing in the middle of a dark and empty room. Shadows danced off the walls from the dim light he let into the room. The next two, while not as empty, held no sign of Brooke.

Downstairs, urged his wolf. *Quick.*

Despite the speed and his large frame, he made no sound as he returned to the ground floor. She could only be in one other place. The fridges. His pulse thudded in his chest as he placed a hand on the door. The metal was cold under his fingers, and he hesitated. What would he find behind it?

The latch opened with a dull click, and he stepped inside the walk-in fridge. A small lightbulb hanging from the ceiling cast a yellowish glow on everything it touched. He winced at the stench that wafted up from the grate in the concrete floor. When his gaze rested on the large meat-chopping table in the middle of the cooler, his chest tightened. *I'm going to kill him.*

His wolf barred his sharp teeth and a menacing growl echoed between them. *Not before I tear him to shreds first.*

The young girl lying on the table was barely recognizable as the child from the photo. Her face was caked with layers of makeup. Unnatural red cheeks, painted eyelashes, and scarlet button lips gave her the appearance of an old-fashioned porcelain doll. She was lying on her back, her arms down by her sides. Kowaiski, that bastard, had given her a paralytic that made it impossible for her to move or to speak. She was trapped in her own body, unable to run or cry out for help. But her eyes were open and full of fear.

He reached out and touched her face gently. "It's alright Brooke, don't be afraid. My name is Murphy O'Neill, and I'm with the FBI. I'm here to take you home to your mommy and daddy. Everything is going to be alright, honey, I promise you that."

Brooke's eyes teared up and the fear turned to relief.

He struggled to hold back the desire to tear Kowaiski's stomach out through his throat. The monster didn't deserve to live. In addition to Brooke's painted face, she'd been forced to wear an ill-fitting dress that reminded him of a Spanish flamenco dancer. His pulse jolted. She was wearing an oversized choker around her neck. The same one they had reconstructed from the other victims. Kowaiski, true to form, dressed his victim as a doll, then blew her head off. The same way he blew up his stepsister's dolls when they were kids.

He took photos and forwarded them to Gabe before pulling out the small tools he'd tucked into his back pocket. He hovered over Brooke's face so she could see him. "Before I can get you out, I need to take off your necklace."

His wolf emitted a low whine. *Careful.*

His jaw set as he unscrewed the small panel that held the detonation device. At least Kowaiski had been consistent. It meant he knew what to expect and how to disarm the explosives. He reopened a channel to Gabe. "Tell the paramedics to be ready."

Gabe's voice boomed through his earpiece. "They're prepped. Just looking at the images. Crazy motherfucker, it's a wonder he hasn't blown himself up."

"Disarming it now."

Less than two minutes later he separated the explosive from the electronics, then snipped the choker off her small neck. When it came away, a faint growl escaped his lips before he could stop it. He'd been so focused on her immediate danger, he'd missed the rainbow set of bruises on her neck and, from what he could tell, down her arms and torso.

His wolf rose to the surface and growled. He wanted out. He wanted to make Kowaiski pay for hurting an innocent child.

No. He fought to keep his wolf at bay. *She has already gone through too much. If I allow you to take over, it will break her.*

The air went out of his wolf's sails in a heartbeat. No matter how angry they were at Kowaiski, keeping the girl safe was their first priority.

He gently picked up Brooke's limp body. She was small for her age. Petite and frail. Instinctively, he cradled her in his arms and attempted to give her a smile. Smiling was something he hadn't done in a very long time, and it took some effort. Brooke's eyes wavered between hope and fear, and her heart was racing. Any faster and she would pass out. Not sure how to calm her down, he pulled her against his chest and lightly kissed the top of her head. "It's alright, Brooke, everything will be alright. I'm going to get you out of here and back to your parents. But I need to you to calm down first. Can you do that for me?"

He pulled her away from his chest and looked her in the eyes. "Take some slow breaths."

Her pulse slowed a fraction, and her fear eased.

"That's a good girl." He glanced to the door. "Now I need you to do one more thing. I need for you to close your eyes tight and not open them again until I tell you. It's really important. I know you can't talk, but I want you to blink once for no and twice for yes. Do you think you can do that for me?"

She blinked twice.

"Okay, here we go."

He rested her head on his shoulder and tried to cuddle her, but his body was rigid and ready to snap in half. How could anyone do this to a child? The Werewolf race had their own set of problems, but he would never understand how Humans did this to each other.

He pressed the button and opened the comms link. "We're coming out. Kowaiski is all yours, come and get him. He's in the north corner office on the mezzanine floor."

He held Brooke against his chest as he made his way out of the death chamber. From the placement of the black plastic bags folded by the table, Kowaiski was ready for the last stage in his sick ritual. Rage rose in his throat again, and he struggled to shove it down. He was about to push through the door when footsteps clomped down the metal stairs.

"Bollocks." He'd hoped to spare her any further interaction with Kowaiski, but there was no avoiding it. He readied himself and prayed the small child in his arms would forgive him. With lightning speed, he was through the door, across the floor, and in front of Kowaiski as he reached the bottom of the stairs.

Kowaiski's face froze in a comical mix of shock and horror.

Before Kowaiski could open his mouth, Murphy wrapped his hand around the murderer's neck and pinned him against the nearest wall, his legs flailing five inches from the floor. He lowered his voice and whispered in Brooke's ear. "Remember, honey, keep your eyes closed no matter what."

He turned back to Kowaiski and squeezed harder. His voice came out harsh and cold. "If it were up to me, I would bury you alive and let you rot."

Kowaiski, struggling to breathe, clawed at the iron grip. His face had turned red and was heading toward purple.

His wolf nudged at him. *He deserves a slow painful death. But the others are too close. Get the child into her mother's arms. She is more important than our anger right now.*

He hesitated when a shout from the north entrance announced the first team's arrival. At any moment, they would see them. He hurled Kowaiski across the factory floor.

Kowaiski screamed as his body slammed into a concrete post like a rag doll, and he collapsed to the floor with a dull thud.

Murphy turned away from the bastard who deserved everything that was coming to him and patted Brooke's back. "Easy honey, we're almost home free."

He was headed to the exit when the two teams of agents swarmed into the main factory floor. Shouts from the agents joined Kowaiski's screams as they secured their prisoner.

Gabe nodded at Kowaiski as he was being hauled up by two of Clive's agents. "What happened to him?"

He shrugged. "Fell down the stairs."

Murphy stood in the anteroom and glared at Kowaiski through the one-way glass. The killer stared at his own reflection with a wide smirk plastered across his face. He showed no remorse.

His wolf snarled. *He cannot be allowed to go free. Did you see what he did to that poor child? To all of those babes.*

Calm down. The case is airtight. Everything was by the book. It will hold up in court.

He could not shake the similarities between Kowaiski and Elijah, and that was probably why his wolf was so agitated. He glanced at his photo of Brooke. She was in recovery at Jefferson Health Hospital. The drugs would take a few hours to wear off. Until then, her parents were surgically attached to her. He didn't blame them. They'd almost lost their only child to their worst nightmare. He shivered. What if he hadn't found her in time?

A sharp knock on the door snapped his thoughts away from just how different this could have turned out. He donned the mask he wore for other people: gruff, unapproachable, and stoic.

He didn't need to turn around to know who walked in. They had been FBI recruits together at the academy, and his scent announced Gabe well before he interrupted his solitude.

Gabe stood next to him, and they both gazed through the window as Quinton, one of the local FBI agents, set a paper cup of water in front of Kowaiski.

"Is it just me, or are agents getting younger each year?" Gabe said.

He crossed his arms over his chest. "Seems that way."

"DA's on her way. Said not to start before she gets here."

He remained quiet. He already knew this, but from Gabe's pensive expression he would get to the real thing on his mind soon enough.

Gabe pushed his hands into his pockets and continued to observe Kowaiski. "I hear you're taking early retirement."

And there it was.

"It seems like only yesterday that we were wet behind the ears. Now look at us, a little wiser, a lot more jaded, and somewhat older." Gabe chuckled. "Me anyway. I don't know how you do it, but you look the same as the day I met you. Still blonde with not a speck of gray."

He barely held back the flinch. This was why he had to leave the FBI. Too many people were noticing his appearance hadn't changed over the years. Unlike Gabe, whose receding hair was graying and whose forehead was marked with worry lines from a high-pressure career, teenage kids, and natural aging, he looked virtually the same. A Werewolf's lifespan exceeded a Human's tenfold, and caused all sorts of problems. The excuse of good genes took him only so far.

He changed the subject before Gabe dwelled too much on that particular topic. "Who told you?"

"Anderson. He was a little too excited. I think he's gunning for your position at CIRG."

He held his tongue. While he still had months before his final day, he could well imagine the flurry of activity when word he was leaving got out. The Critical Incident Response Group was highly sought after, and with a vacancy on the horizon, many would be eyeing up the post. He would miss the job. Not only did it put him in a position to mitigate exposure of his race and allow him to pursue Elijah, but it also gave him a sense of purpose. The work the unit was doing was important to the Human world. And even though his motives weren't completely aligned with the FBI's, he would make sure his replacement had respect for the dignity of all those the bureau protected. Anderson was not that person.

Gabe checked his watch then headed for the door. "I'll message you when the DA arrives."

Two minutes later his phone vibrated across the table and bumped into his laptop. He raised a brow. That was quick. At least with the DA arriving he could finally interview Kowaiski and be done with the case. He reached for his phone, scanned the message, and the air left his lungs.

> Elijah's returned to Boston.

He tightened his grip on the phone and reread the message from Tim, an officer with the Boston police department. Tim was one of the Alliance's watchdogs assigned to ensure their race remained a myth.

Why?

Why would Elijah go back to Boston?

A boulder plummeted to the bottom of his stomach as a sudden coldness chilled him to his core. Was Elijah taunting him?

He forwarded the link Tim had sent, along with the message, to his laptop and opened the lid. When the message arrived, he clicked and the link opened to a browser. He watched the news clip with growing unease. When it finished, the room was silent again. Yet it wasn't. To him, the noise was deafening, a cacophony of chaos. Above, a low-pitched hum sang out from the air-conditioning duct. Outside, jumbled voices seeped through the walls. A ping from his laptop announced an incoming email, and to his right, the incessant buzz of a fly as it touched down on a small shelf. His wolf, demanding to be let loose, added to the bedlam. He wanted to scream at them to be quiet. To stop the infernal racket so he could think. He slammed his fists into his eyes. Shut the fuck up.

Whether the universe listened to him and granted his wish, or he managed to cut himself off from the world, he didn't know and didn't care. All that mattered was the peace. If not in his mind and soul, then at least in his ears.

Why had Elijah gone back to Boston?

His pulse raced. He had no choice but to follow Elijah. But could he? Boston held too many bad memories. He turned his hands over and stared at them. His heart had died in Tudor Falls along with June. And Boston was where he lost the last remaining slither of humanity within him. When Elijah took Ryan, too, it was the last time he'd allowed himself any form of weakness, the last time he'd allowed himself to care about anyone.

He re-watched the video. His fingers squeezed around the computer mouse as the knot in his stomach grew tighter.

He. Was. Back.

The mouse splintered in his hands. This was what he had been waiting for. He pushed his shoulders back. It had to end. Elijah had taken too many good people. This time would be different. This time he would not be hunting Elijah down just to hand him over to the Alliance. No, this time he would be judge, jury, and executioner. He was going to deliver Elijah to the gates of hell. Personally. He pushed away from the laptop. His computer mouse lay in tiny pieces across the desk.

Yes, he was tired, but the weight of his coat was suddenly lighter.

TWO
Open Wounds

FBI Field Office, Boston

Kaitlyn Quinn was ready to scream. Not the Oh-I-just-saw-a-mouse kind of scream. She was prepared to emit the type of scream that keeps the dead up at night. The kind that could make paint peel off the walls and the drug-trafficker she'd arrested last week cross herself five times before heading to church.

Two days tied to a desk doing paperwork had her climbing the walls. She clicked twice to open yet another I65–32A form and pressed her lips together. Served her right for resolving three damn cases in the same week. She was never going to repeat that mistake again. Not if she could help it.

Mike, who sat across from her, finished his call and began to rummage through his top drawer. She looked up and gave him a hopeful smile. "I'll pay you a thousand dollars to finish my reports."

He closed his drawer, stood up, and grinned. "Sorry Quinn, can't. Off to Hartford—lead on the Bryce case."

Her eyes darted to her monitor then back at Mike. "Two thousand," she called as he grabbed his suit jacket. He disappeared out the door. She scrunched her nose and flicked a paperclip at his desk.

"You still not finished with those closure reports?"

She froze and a hot flush crept across her cheeks. How had she not noticed her boss's return? "Working on it, Doug."

He headed for his office. "Bribing colleagues, Agent Quinn, is the opposite of working on it."

She glared at the stack of evidence bags on her desk, and picked up the one on top. Short of the building blowing up, she had no chance of getting in the field until the relevant case reports were filed with Doug.

In triplicate.

She dropped her forehead onto her hands and groaned.

Kaitlyn grabbed her phone when it went off. Anika was probably phoning to vent her frustration. Her young friend was finding it difficult to be taken seriously at work. Not surprising, considering her lab coat couldn't hide the Hello Kitty T-shirts and bright matching shoes she wore underneath. She wouldn't be shocked if Anika turned up in a pink tutu to finish off the ensemble.

"I don't suppose you want to do my paperwork, either?"

"Huh?"

She accidentally clicked undo instead of save and swore under her breath. "Nothing. How was last night?"

"Great, it gave me all the feels. It would have been better if the jerk behind us didn't mansplain the whole movie to his date, but I couldn't believe Tans took me out even though all she wanted to do was watch Netflix and chillax at home. No wonder I'm so in love with her."

She typed as she half-listened to Anika rave on about an anime movie. How anyone could get that excited about a cartoon was beyond her. She had to hand it to Tania, it would be the last thing she wanted to do after a double shift at a hospital.

Anika took a micro breath. "But that's not why I phoned."

She stopped typing. A tingle at the back of her neck began to pulse. "Oh?"

"Now, before you say no, just hear me out. I have no one else to turn to, and you're like … one of my BFF's. It would just crush me, I can't even … not to mention the emotional devastation to my psyche."

Her brow rose. In another life, her friend would have been a soap opera queen. Everything she said and did was overly dramatic. "Are we getting to the point any time soon?"

"Can't you just say yes? I mean, it would mean so much to me."

She drummed her fingers on the desk. Evasion on Anika's behalf could only mean one thing. This was not going to go well for her. "Out with it."

"It's my cousin's wedding next month and Tania's out of town at a conference that weekend."

She rubbed her forehead. The tingle was now more of a throb.

"You can't expect me to front up on my own. The great aunts would descend on me like vultures. You don't know what they're like. Show fear and they're like pack animals. They have the disappointed tsk down to an art form. Add that to their head bobble and it's downright freaky."

"I don't know what the problem is. You're going out with a doctor, isn't that what all Hindi families want for their daughters?"

"They generally expect the doctor to be a man."

She shrugged. "Don't go then."

"What? And miss out on being in their wedding story movie? I would never hear the end of that. Priyanshi would never speak to me again. Please, just say you'll be my plus one."

She dropped her head onto her desk. "There must be someone else you can ask."

Anika's voice rose an octave. "There's going to be a lot of single men. You might even meet someone, and these weddings are cool. Uncle Reyansh is dropping nearly a hundred grand into this thing. Please say you'll come. I'll even lend you my best sari."

Anika paused to change tack, her voice coming back whiny and pitiful. "Please don't make me suffer on my own. Use your superpowers for good. You can just tower over the aunts and glare at them. You're the only one I know who wouldn't be scared of them. I'll even let you bring your gun, that'll shut them up."

She counted to ten. "You're not going to let this go, are you?"

"Nope."

She almost heard the grin when Anika realized she was about to get her way. "Fine. But you owe me."

Anika squealed. "You're the best." She dropped her voice down a notch. "Whoops. Angry McKrusty just looked this way. I'm supposed to be finishing up the probabilistic genotyping of a DNA sample. Better go, talk to you later."

She stared at her phone. She would rather have bamboo shoved under her nails than go to a wedding. Why? Why didn't she just say no?

Anika was Kimmy Schmidt on steroids. With any luck Tania would decide not to attend the conference and go with Anika instead. Her shoulders dropped and she groaned. Who was she kidding? There was a wedding in her future. One where she would tower over ninety percent of the guests. "I couldn't have just said no."

She looked up. The floor was deserted. Where had everyone gone? Her eyes darted to the time on her computer. Three fifteen. Too early for them to go home. A half-eaten brownie sat on Darren's desk, and the hairs on the back of her neck bristled. The man spent two weeks begging her to bring in her signature batch of chocolate brownies. He would not have left it half-eaten without reason.

Soft footfalls from behind caught her attention, and one of the support staff rushed past her desk. "Jordin, what's going on?"

"Not sure." The young woman readjusted the pile of folders she carried. "Something about a story that just broke."

She followed Jordin into the break room. A small crowd had gathered around the screen, blocking her view. She frowned and moved closer. Being just shy of six feet, she towered over many of the other agents. Plastered across the screen was a local news reporter. Behind him, the familiar sight of police tape cordoned off a crime scene. The key points of the story scrolled across the bottom as the reporter described the crime that had played out in the background.

When the words, Has the Boston Wolf Killer Returned? flashed across the screen, a chill ran down her spine and she felt all color drain from her face. She backed away from the screen.

No, it couldn't be.

A weight pressed on her stomach, and the air rushed from her lungs. Her heartbeat thrashed in her ears. She couldn't hear the journalist or her colleagues as they voiced their opinions. Just the thump-thump-thump of foreboding drums in her chest. Fine beads of perspiration broke out across her forehead, and her eyes darted around the room. She had to escape before they noticed she was spinning out of control. She raced to the bathroom, locked the door behind her, and leaned against the wall.

Her chest heaved as she took a series of painful gasps of air. Memories hidden for years erupted like molten lava ejected from an angry volcano. She pushed them down and pulled out her phone. She needed to reconfirm what she had just seen. Maybe she was mistaken? Maybe she had only imagined those three words, Boston Wolf Killer? It wasn't possible. Not after all this time. The same headlines repeated as she flicked through the mainstream media channels. Her stomach tightened with each flick.

"God, no, please no." Her voice came out in a tortured whimper.

The walls of the small cubicle closed in. Nightmares, that moments ago were long hidden, pushed to the surface. At the time she didn't understand. All she had heard was, "Vivian, I am very sorry but—"

Nine was too young to truly understand the six words that changed their lives forever.

When her mother screamed and collapsed to the floor, she dropped and wrapped her arms around her mother's heaving shoulders. Terrified, but not knowing why, she tried pulling her mother up from the floor. *Daddy had left her in charge. Mommy was not to get upset and stressed. It wouldn't do the baby any good. How could daddy's boss upset mommy like that? Just wait until daddy got home.*

For weeks after they laid her father to rest, she and her mother were reminded of their loss on a daily basis. The media, in a feeding frenzy over the inability of the Boston PD to apprehend the murderer who had taunted and killed one of their own, were all too willing to exploit her and her mother as victims. Her father's face was on the front page of the papers, on the television news, and in her nightmares. But despite the media shitstorm, Detective Ryan Quinn was also the last victim of the Boston Wolf Killer before he disappeared without a trace.

She closed her eyes. Second to last.

Kaitlyn clenched her fists and ground her teeth. Come on, pull yourself together. This was just some copycat whack job. It couldn't possibly be him. Stone-cold killers did not take a holiday and then resume their killing spree two decades later. Slowly but surely, she rebuilt her carefully constructed protection. Brick by brick, until the last piece slipped into place. She wasn't going to show any weakness. Not today, not ever. She stood up, took a deep breath, unlocked the bathroom door, and checked her face in the mirror. The media had it wrong. Fake news. They did it all the time. He wasn't back. He couldn't be.

For the next hour, she sat at her desk and stared at her screen. Much as she denied the possibility, a question gnawed at her. What if it was him? Unable to sit still any longer, she marched across the floor and stormed into Doug's office without knocking.

"Is it him?"

He checked his watch and looked at her over the top of his reading glasses. "That's got to be a new world record. Even for you."

He wasn't going to get away with deflecting her question. She crossed her arms over her chest. "I want in on that case."

Doug took his glasses off and pinched the bridge of his nose. "No."

Her eyes widened. "No? What do you mean no?"

"No, as in, the opposite of yes." He sighed. "Quinn, you may be one of my best agents, but I couldn't put you on this case even if I wanted to. You're too close."

"I—that's bullshit and you know it."

"I'm not going to let you loose on a case you have a personal interest in. And Shaw wouldn't approve it without a supervisory special agent's endorsement."

Shaw, the special agent in charge of the Boston field office, was a stickler for the rules. "Then get one."

He let out a sarcastic chuckle. "Martin's away on maternity leave, Gonzales's caseload is already full, which only leaves Sean."

Her shoulders dropped.

"You pissed him off so much on that last case, he's refused to partner with you again."

"B-but I was right. We were looking at the wrong suspect, and Dillon nearly got away with it."

"Even so, calling your team leader a jackass in front of the director of the FBI didn't score you any points."

She snorted. "I don't know why he got his nose bent out of joint. He's too dumb to know what it means."

The corner of Doug's mouth twitched upwards. "But not so stupid he didn't know you were insulting him." He shrugged. "It's moot anyway. The case is with Boston PD. Until they kick it to us, it's their party."

Doug waived at the TV in the far corner of his office. "For all we know, the media's blown it out of proportion to sell airtime." He picked up his glasses and focused back on his monitor. "Close the door on your way out."

Her brows drew together. This was not going the way she hoped. Before she could close the door, Doug's voice boomed across the room. "And don't forget to get those closure reports on my desk by the end of today."

Kaitlyn got home late. She locked her sidearm in the safe, kicked off her shoes, and headed to the kitchen where she dumped her Chinese takeout on the counter. Her phone rang just as she sat down. She turned it over and winced. On Wednesday nights her mother should be teaching art to a bunch of borderline criminals, not phoning her. The moment the unkind words rushed through her mind, she regretted them. Her mom, a nurse during the day, worked a few nights a week with the local community to rehabilitate and educate teenagers who had gotten on the wrong side of the law.

Vivian was currently working with a group of young taggers. Her art classes taught them to appreciate art and understand the difference between art and vandalism. Her mother's motto was,

"If they are going to deface public property, it should at least have some artistic value."

While they were similar in many ways, she and her mother were polar opposites when it came to those who broke the law. Her idea of rehabilitation was to lock them up overnight and scare the living daylights out of them.

She braced as she pressed the accept button, very much doubting her mom was calling to give her an update on the latest news from Miami. "Hi, Mom."

"Is it true?"

Her mom had been crying. She winced at her mom's tone. On the face of it, Vivian sounded fine, but there was a slight tremor in her voice. She longed to reach out and hug her mother. "I don't know, mom. Right now, I know as much as you."

"It can't be him, not after all this time, can it?" Vivian said.

She wandered over to her wall-to-wall bookshelf. Five framed photos took up a corner of one of the shelves. The newest was of her and her mother at her graduation from Harvard. Next to it, a photo of her grandfather, Joshua Quinn, a decorated officer with the Boston PD. She had never met him, but both she and her father had followed in his footsteps.

She still remembered her mother's horrified expression when she announced after her graduation that she had joined the FBI.

"I'm not sure. It's been twenty years. The profiler back then had the unsub between thirty-five and fifty. I really can't see a seventy-year-old doing this sort of damage."

She reached out and reverently touched the third photo on the shelf. Her father, in full dress uniform, cut a striking figure. A hollow ached filled her heart.

"Kaitlyn, honey, I just … please be careful."

Her fingers trailed from her father's photo to the framed child's drawing nestled behind it. She had drawn it after their last father-daughter fishing trip.

A local dog always knew when they were staying at the cabin and followed them around the entire weekend. She smiled at the memory. No matter how much she begged to take Princess home, her father just chuckled and told her it wouldn't be fair to lock up a wild animal. He reminded her, once again, that the animal was a boy, not a girl. Nonetheless, she insisted on drawing Princess with a pink tutu and tiara.

She exhaled loudly. "Mom, you know I love you, but you have got to stop worrying about me all the time. I'm a grown woman for goodness sake. I kick butt for a living and put away the bad guys. I'm more than capable of looking after myself."

"But you're not superwoman. You're my little girl. I worry. I'm supposed to worry. It's my job."

She groaned inwardly. Here it came.

"Have you been eating properly? With those long hours you work it's even more important."

She cringed. "Yes, Mom."

"What about exercise? And not that fake exercise in the gym. Are you getting out into the sun?"

"Mom, you already know the answer to that."

"What about your social life? Are you seeing anyone? You know, sex is also an acceptable form of exercise."

Her free hand flew up to her forehead. "Mom! Enough, I am not going to have a conversation with you about that particular subject."

Vivian did not do subtle, though that was something she and her mother shared.

Vivian sniffed. "Fine. But you work too hard. You need to find a balance. That's all I'm going to say. You know I worry."

"I know." She wandered back to the kitchen and poked her head in the fridge. "So, what's the latest with Lee?"

Lee, her mom's eccentric friend, was in a war with her neighbors over recycling, or their lack thereof. She pulled out a bottle of Pinot Gris and poured herself a wine. Anything involving Lee was going to take a while.

Her fried rice was well and truly finished, and she was on to her second cup of hot chocolate when her mom turned the conversation back to her original reason for phoning.

"Promise me, baby, that you won't do anything silly. We've given enough lives to this monster. I don't think I'd survive another."

She placed her plate in the dishwasher and grimaced. Her mom would go ballistic if she found out she had already tried to get on the case. What she didn't know wouldn't hurt her. "Mom, I've been doing this a while now."

The line fell silent, her mother's light breath the only indicator she was still there.

"You know, Kaitlyn, sometimes late at night I look up at the stars and wonder what it would be like if he were still here."

Her throat constricted. While Vivian never dwelled on the subject, not a day went by when her mother didn't miss him, too. He was the love of her life, and no matter how many times her friends tried to get her back into the dating scene, she was adamant she wouldn't. Her mother still loved her father. Neither death, nor time had diminished her mother's feelings. And while she longed to find the same enduring love her parents had, she doubted it would ever be in the cards for her.

"He … he would be so proud."

Vivian's words hung in the room long after the call ended. Her mom worried for her, but she also accepted her career choice. Not once had she asked her to leave the bureau. Her only request was that she try to stay safe.

She suppressed a yawn. After spending two hours on the phone with her mother, coupled with the news of the potential reappearance of the Boston Wolf Killer, she was both physically and mentally exhausted. She picked up a stray cup left on the bookshelf and the fifth framed photo caught her eye. Her vision blurred as she reached out and caressed the photo. The image brought her both great sorrow and contentment. In it, she was being tickled by both her parents. The three of them were laughing, pure joy reflected on their faces as the camera caught such an intimate moment of love.

Pain ripped through her soul. Life wasn't supposed to work out this way. Her mom wasn't supposed to lose her husband. They were supposed to grow old together and drive her insane with their forgetfulness by repeating every conversation three times.

She straightened up to her full height and steeled her resolve. Regardless of whether he was back, or a copycat had taken up the baton, more lives were about to be destroyed. This was something she wouldn't allow. It was why she had followed in her father's footsteps. Someone had to stand between the innocent and those that would harm them. She placed the photo back on its spot with a thump. The force of it shook the contents of the shelf, and Dan Brown's *Inferno* toppled to its side.

Enough was enough. It ended here.

<u>THREE</u>

Be Careful What You Wish For

Four weeks later

"Kaitlyn!"

Her brows drew together as she looked around the crowded lobby outside the courtroom.

Mike stood in front of a coffee cart and called out to her again. "Hey Quinn, want a hot chocolate?"

The people in line behind him glared at her.

She grinned. "Sure, why not."

He handed her a hot paper cup. "You finished with your testimony?"

"Just. It was all pretty routine, so I don't think I'll be called back."

Mike nodded at the door she had come through. "I heard you've been stuck in there since yesterday."

She raised an eyebrow and threw a glassy stare at the courtroom door. "Defense called an unexpected witness. By the time they got around to me, Judge Winston decided to call it a night, and I wasted an entire day cooling my heels. Then I wasted all morning answering stupid questions about how we found that weapons stash. At least it's over with now."

"So, you wouldn't have heard?"

His apprehensive expression sent goosebumps running up her arm like the scales on a piano. She cocked her head. "Heard what?"

"They found another body. The Boston Wolf Killer struck again."

She froze, but resisted the urge to hold on to something. This was the fourth death in three weeks. The city was in a panic, and the media were once again having a field day with the Boston Police Department and its inability to keep the city safe. She had stopped watching the news when her father's face flashed up behind the news anchor one too many times.

Mike stirred his coffee. "The way I hear it, this one's particularly nasty. And it sounds like the BPD has come to its senses and asked the FBI for help."

At last. The police department would have reluctantly handed the case over to the head of the FBI's Boston division, who would, in turn, hand the case to Doug's unit.

Careful not to look over-eager, she sipped her chocolate. "Has Doug met with Shaw yet?"

She had found a loophole in the policy. Doug had no grounds to keep her off the case. She knew it, and she had made sure he knew it.

Mike nodded. "Yep. Way I heard it, they've put a team together and flown in some hotshot from the Critical Incident Response Group."

She nearly choked on her drink. He'd what? That mother— "When did Shaw meet with Doug?"

"They've been in and out of each other's offices all morning. Why?"

She ground her teeth together. That case was hers. She had worked too hard to be sidelined now. "No reason." She glanced down at her half-empty cup. "Thanks for the chocolate by the way. Better go, I have a thing."

She cringed as she rushed out of the courthouse. She had a thing? Couldn't she think of a better excuse than that?

She threw her bag on her desk and raced to Doug's corner office. She burst through the doorway without knocking, marched straight to his desk, and threw him a death stare.

Doug remained quiet.

"How dare you? That case is mine."

Doug sat back in his chair and placed his hands over his middle-age spread.

"I've had to work twice as hard as the guys just to be considered half as good. I've earned that case. Not only that, but you bring in outsiders. How does that look to your own people? It makes us look incompetent, that's what. You have no faith in your own teams, so you bring in one from the CIRG."

She brought her fist down on the desk. "This is my case. Not only do I have the highest closure rates on the team, I know every inch of the original case. You're going to fix this now, and I don't want to hear any bullshit about being too close."

Her jaw clenched, and heat radiated off her cheeks. She could only guess how red they had become.

Doug raised an eyebrow and sat up. "Are you quite finished?"

She nodded and crossed her arms over her chest. "Yes, that about covers it."

"Good." He stood. "I would like you to meet your new partner, on loan to us from the Critical Incident Response Group. Supervisory Special Agent Murphy O'Neill. You'll be working the Boston Wolf Killer case together."

Doug smirked and nodded behind her.

She froze. Kill. Me. Now.

She glared at her boss, friend, and mentor. He must have known exactly how she would react in this situation and had most likely put her in this position just for a laugh. Or at least, that's what she gathered from the smirk that progressed to a full blown, all-knowing smile on his face. She lifted her chin, squared her shoulders to stand at full height, and turned, almost colliding with a row of small cream-colored buttons attached to a crisp white shirt.

Fudge-knuckle.

She took a step back from the massive frame and took in her opponent. Time slowed to a snail's pace, and a faint gasp slipped from between her clenched teeth. The perfectly tailored dark suit couldn't hide the broadness of his chest, and he towered over her like a giant. Now she understood how other people felt around her height. Forcing her features to appear calm and unaffected by his nearness, she moved her gaze upward. The top two buttons of his shirt were unbuttoned, and the tie she expected with his attire was missing. She took in his determined jawline, covered in a dusting of stubble. His jaw was clenched, muscles tense, and his lips pursed in a tight line. When her gaze finally rose to meet his, she gasped again. His eyes both shocked and captivated her. They were the color of night. Two pools of ebony ink.

Adonis. Sinfully so. And the way he filled out his suit could only mean he had the body of a Greek god, too. She dragged her gaze away from his eyes before she became physically trapped in the darkness, the sensuous maleness of him. Her face heated up. This was not the time or place to have fantasies about a man she'd only just met.

She forced her erratic heartbeat under control and took a proper look at him. There was more to him than met the eye. With her years of experience in the field, she recognized the danger in this man. She couldn't place it, but there was a raw and primal magnetism in his stance, as though he had a tenuous hold on something that could erupt at any moment.

He had not moved an inch. He just stared through her coldly, unblinking as he stood his ground. "As I was saying ..."

His voice, rich with a hint of aged whisky, sent a shiver down her spine. Jumpin' Jesus Jones, his voice was just as commanding as a Greek god.

"I can work this case alone. I don't need one of your agents slowing me down."

His words sunk in, and she faltered from the sucker punch. "I beg your pardon?" She squinted at him. Good looking or not, if he wanted this case for his own, he'd have to pry it from her cold, dead fingers. "Who the hell do you think you are?" Her fists clenched, nails cutting into her skin, as she barely held back from an overwhelming desire to slap his very masculine face.

Something triggered in the back of her brain, and she hesitated. She couldn't place it but she'd seen him before, and yet, she was equally sure they had never met. But then why did he seem so familiar?

Before she knew what had happened, he stepped around her and headed for the door. "I work alone. Don't need or want a partner."

She gasped. How the hell did such a large man move so fast and stealth-like?

Doug halted him in his tracks. "Oh no, you don't. You wanted on this case, and upstairs agreed, but one of the local special agents must be on your team. End of story."

The giant man turned around slowly, a flash of disbelief plastered across his face. He looked between her and Doug.

She held back a grin. You show him who's boss, Doug.

Doug turned to her. "And that goes for you, too." Doug smirked. "It looks like both of you will have to learn to work together."

Her face dropped. This wasn't going the way she planned. "Oh, I'll just go and practice my levitating skills too, shall I?" she said. "Because both have about the same chance of happening."

Her new partner remained silent, his expression cold and unreadable. The subtle bulge of a vein in his neck was the only indication of his current state of mind. That and the micro flare of his nostrils.

Doug smiled. "And just to add to your happy little family, the police commissioner is adding three of his own people to your team."

"What?" both she and the senior supervisory special agent said in unison.

"See?" Doug slapped a hand onto his desk. "You're already working together. That came out in perfect stereo." He turned to her. "The dynamic duo of Murphy O'Neill and Kaitlyn Quinn has a certain ring to it, doesn't it?"

Her mouth fell open. O'Neill? She'd failed to register it fully when Doug first introduced him. "You're the Murphy O'Neill?"

She groaned inwardly. Blue cheese in the oven. No way this was O'Neill. He couldn't be more than, what? Thirty-five?

He grunted and gave her a curt nod.

Murphy O'Neill was a legend within the FBI. He had worked nearly every high-profile serial killer case in the past fifteen years, and his success rate was astounding. In addition to being part of the bureau's elite CIRG, he also guest lectured at Quantico. He pretty much singlehandedly rewrote the book on violent crimes and serial killers.

"As I was saying," Doug said. "The police commissioner is running this case as a joint effort with his people. He has assigned detectives Garcia and Ruby to work the case with you, as well as a point person from the Massachusetts State Police Crime Laboratory."

She frowned. She couldn't believe the FBI had agreed to this.

Doug raised his hands, palms up. "Look, just play nice with the commissioner's people, will you? The city is about to panic and implode on itself. We don't need any further animosity between us. Remember, if this goes south, the FBI will bear the brunt of the fallout."

"And when it succeeds, the commissioner will take the full glory," she muttered.

The office fell quiet as she considered her options. She had to be on this case. Fear welled within her at the thought that her future could be set by a man who clearly didn't want her on his team.

After a thick and unpalatable silence, Murphy grunted. "Fine."

She released the breath she didn't know she was holding. Relief flooded through her.

"But if she trips up once, she's off the team."

What the hell was the matter with this jerk?

"Uh, hello, I'm standing here," she said.

Her irritation escalated as he continued to disregard her. Why the hell she had thought he was good looking was beyond her. He was way too grumpy to be attractive.

Doug picked up a folder from his desk and held it out to Murphy. "If you're worried about commitment and ability, don't. Kaitlyn is my best agent. A bit headstrong, but she's usually on point. Just be careful of her temper. She bites."

Her eyes darted around the office. Someone must be playing a sick joke. She yanked the folder from Doug's grasp. "She's also the best sharpshooter you have, and I'd be careful about pissing her off."

She ignored Doug and deciding that she should at least pretend to want to work with Murphy, she held out her hand. "How about we start again? Special Agent Kaitlyn Quinn."

His ebony eyes searched her face. "Any relation to Detective Ryan Quinn?"

She froze. How did he make the connection? Quinn was a very common name, especially in Boston. And the subject was not something she talked about. Ever.

"Uh, yes, he was my father."

His left eyebrow twitched upward. "I see. Is that why you're so hell bent on being assigned to the case?"

She clenched her jaw, and lifted her chin. "No. I want the case because I'm the best person for the job. My personal feelings don't come into it." She hoped fervently that he did not see through her lie.

Murphy stared at her, making her squirm inwardly. His dark orbs, unblinking and all seeing, gave her a strange mix of comfort and anxiety.

"We'll see. But the moment you get too close to the case, you're off it in a heartbeat."

She squared her shoulders. "That won't happen."

He grunted and shrugged his shoulders.

Before she could snap at him again, Doug weighed in. "The latest scene hasn't been cleared yet and they're waiting for you, so you'd better high-tail out of here before I'm on the business end of a call from the commissioner demanding an update."

Without saying a word, Murphy nodded to Doug and left the room, ignoring her as he did so.

Her boss noticed her expression.

"And Quinn, try to keep your temper under control with this one. He normally works these cases alone, so it's going to take a bit for him to get used to working with a partner. And don't forget, you report to him." Doug smirked. "Try and not piss off another SSA."

Bollocks. What the hell had just happened?

As Murphy stormed across the department, agents moved out of his way, careful to not look him in the eye. A reaction he was used to. People instinctively made themselves scarce when he was around. He knew better than to let his wolf so close to the surface, but his thoughts were jumbled and erratic. He pushed his wolf down. If he gave him any more leeway he might take over.

His wolf resisted. *Turn around, I want to see her. She's Ryan's daughter.*

I know. He ignored the urge and continued to the elevator lobby.

She has his fire.

I know.

But a lot nicer to look at. Magnificent. Did you see how she stood up to us? We like her.

No, we don't. We can't. He let out a growl. *I don't want to discuss this, now settle down.*

This was not how the meeting was supposed to go. He'd done this hundreds of times. He'd take over the case, work it alone, then hand it back to the local team to tie up any loose ends. The first part of the meeting with Doug ran as expected. But a familiar scent from someone about to burst through the door hit him in the gut and stopped him mid-sentence. For a moment, just the briefest of moments, he'd almost believed his long-dead friend was about to walk into the office. And it wasn't just him who'd noticed. His wolf stood to attention, too.

She lit up the room with her presence when she stormed in. Confident, determined, and ready to blow a fuse. He knew the instant she appeared who she was. The familial scent, the familiar features, and even the way she spoke left him thinking a ghost had walk through the door. She was Ryan's daughter without a doubt. Memories of his friend tore at his soul. The snot-nosed kid had grown up to be one of the finest men he had ever known. June would have liked him.

The loss of his best friend still hurt, and remembering had wrinkled his stoic composure. He became distracted. So distracted, he had landed her as a partner before he knew what happened. Of all people, Ryan's daughter was the last person he should be partnered with. He stabbed at the down button just as she caught up to him. Her scent filled his nostrils. Ryan, yet not Ryan. There were subtle differences, but enough similarities to throw him. The elevator doors slid open and he stepped in and pressed the basement button before they had fully opened. From her stiff posture and stormy features, she was still angry with him. The silence drew out. What could he say? I'm sorry. It's my fault your father is dead. She'd have something to really be angry about then. He stared at the small screen that indicated the floor number. Why was it taking so long to go down a few floors? He could have taken the stairs and already been there.

His wolf nudged at him. *Turn around so we can see her.*

No.

The ding of the elevator announced their arrival at the basement. This time she pushed through the doors before they had completely opened. She turned left and marched down a row of parked cars.

He glanced to where he'd left his Cadillac Escalade. Why was she headed in the wrong direction? "Where do you think you're going?"

She slowed and threw him a frustrated glare over her shoulder. "Well, I don't fancy walking to the crime scene, so I'm heading to my car. If that's okay with you, and unless you have the required stickers on your vehicle, I suggest you come with me."

His shoulders tensed. Had she forgotten who was in charge? He stormed across the parking garage and caught up to her as she pulled a keychain from her pocket, pointed it, and depressed a button. He groaned inwardly. In a line of gray sedans, of course, hers had to be shiny red. The doors clicked as the car unlocked. "What the hell is that?"

Her hand reached for her holstered gun as she tensed and glanced around the carpark. "What?"

He pointed to her car. "That."

Her brows furrowed together. "It's what we generally like to call a car," she said, slowly and evenly, as if he were a child.

He shook his head. She wasn't actually expecting him to ride in that? Was she? "That's not a car, it's a battery on wheels. I'm not getting into that death trap."

Her eyes narrowed. "I'll have you know, Prius's have been given the highest rating for the least carbon emissions."

He folded his arms over his chest and stood impassively as she continued her tirade about vehicular pollution. How could anyone get so worked up about a hybrid? "Are you quite finished?" he said once she stopped for a breath.

Not waiting for an answer, he opened the front passenger door, reached in, snatched the two police and FBI permits that were stuck to her windscreen, exited the vehicle, and headed in the opposite direction. "I'm driving."

He strode down the aisle of vehicles, not once looking back to see if she was following. This was his case. Elijah was his problem, and he didn't need complications. Unfortunately, he had one. A big one who was currently mumbling under her breath, threatening to shoot his ass and covering it up as an accidental discharge.

We like her, his wolf repeated.

His lips pursed into a thin line. *No, we most certainly do not.*

<u>FOUR</u>

Face to Face with Death

The drive in Murphy's Cadillac Escalade was silent. After her initial internal battle and overwhelming desire to shoot him, Kaitlyn reluctantly followed him to his car. The man outranked her, and for the duration of the case, he would be her superior. It probably would not look good on her FBI record if she was cited for insubordination.

Again.

Not to mention the paperwork involved in a not-so-accidental discharge.

They were already out of the parking garage and maneuvering through the heavy traffic by the time she put on her seatbelt. She was surprised at his obvious familiarity with the city's streets. He navigated them quickly and efficiently out of Central Boston, through the Sumner Tunnel, and along the 1A toward Lynn. She leafed through the file Murphy had taken from Doug. The folder contained a summary of the previous deaths. The first victim had yet to be identified, and the medical examiner had not yet determined cause of death for the second one. She scanned the details of Vince Marke, vic number two. Thirty-eight. High School Teacher. Husband and the father of a ten-year-old boy.

38

The pain they would be going through was all too familiar. As she flicked through the police file on the bodies, each new detail hit her like a punch to the gut. She swallowed, closed the folder, and threw it onto the back seat. A light sheen of perspiration covered her forehead, and her chest ached. She stared at the passing cars. She mustn't let O'Neill see how this was affecting her. She had been so focused on getting the case, she had not contemplated much beyond it, and now it was suddenly all too real. Her hands grew clammy. Damn it, she needed to get her emotions in check. Otherwise, Murphy would kick her off the team. He was practically waiting for an excuse to do so.

The traffic was heavy, and it took nearly fifty minutes to reach their destination. They were the fifty quietest minutes of her life. Her new partner was not the talkative type, but if she were honest, she was thankful for the silence. It gave her time to prepare. She needed to bring her A-game to this investigation. Everything was riding on it.

A small crowd had gathered along the distinct yellow police tape. She and Murphy approached the scene officer and presented their identification before being granted entry into the secured area. The building boom in Boston meant the once abandoned warehouse was being given a second life as high-priced apartments. The original building had been gutted, and only the concrete frame remained.

She approached a police officer who was standing watch just inside the building. "Special Agents Quinn and O'Neill." She held up her identification. "We're after Detectives Garcia and Ruby."

The officer pointed to two men standing a short way off. "That's Garcia there interviewing the security guard. Detective Ruby is canvasing the neighborhood."

Without acknowledging the officer, Murphy headed into the inner sanctum of the crime scene.

The scene officer frowned.

Was there no end to his rudeness? She smiled apologetically, thanked him, and raced to catch up to Murphy. A natural animosity existed between the FBI and local police departments, but why get on their bad side before they even started?

As she hurried after Murphy, she took stock of her surroundings. Exposed wooden beams were fashioned into frames that would eventually be drywalled. Builder's tables littered with plans, empty cups, and an odd assortment of tools were positioned throughout the area. Ladders, scaffolding, and plastic drop sheets hung from some of the beams. Large sheets of builder's plastic hung from the upper beams and obscured the crime scene. Blurry silhouettes of the forensic staff showed through the translucent material, and cameras flashed over the scene.

Murphy opened the plastic flap and disappeared through the opening. She moved to follow, but her legs turned to lead. She gulped to dislodge the lump in her throat, but it wouldn't budge. Breathe, just breathe, Kaitlyn. Not only was this case make or break for her career, but it was also, no matter how much she argued, personal. Twenty years ago, her father lay behind the milky white translucent wall. She shuddered as a gust of wind ruffled the plastic and lifted the hair on the nape of her neck and arms. Ignoring the anxiety, she reached out and touched the plastic sheet. It was smooth and warm under her fingertips. She could do this. This case was no different from any other murder scene.

"Grow a pair," she said under her breath.

She stepped through the opening just as a flash went off, temporarily blinding her. When her vision cleared, her heart slammed against her ribcage, then stopped. Her pulse froze in her veins, and her fingers turned to icicles. Every cold ounce of blood drained from her face as she stood, rooted to the spot, and took in the horrific scene. No matter how many disturbing crime scenes she'd witnessed over the years, this would be etched on her brain forever.

A wooden chair was tipped over on its side, one of its legs broken. Behind the chair a plastic drop-cloth coated in red fluttered in the breeze. Everything was soaked with blood. Trickles of blood permeated the rough concrete so that it resembled an intricate map of haphazard streets. A man's body, at least parts of him, lay strewn across the floor. She winced at the putrid metallic odor shooting up her nostrils. Her stomach, usually stoic, churned. She swallowed the bile, and pushed down her emotions and hid them away. For now. Later, when she was safely at home, she'd have time to heave up every terrifying detail. Right now, she needed to be a professional, not fall apart the moment she stepped onto the path of her father's killer. She would not let him win that easily.

Body parts lay scattered everywhere. The man's arms had been sliced so badly her stomach churned. Portions of a shredded and bloodied shirt still clung to the lacerated torso as if attempting to provide some level of privacy. She struggled to keep her expression neutral as she stared at what must have been a right leg. It still hung on to the torso, barely. Flesh had been ripped and chunks of skin, muscle, and sinew lay on the bloodied floor. Distinct gouges from teeth marks cut into exposed cartilage and bone. Even a crazed grizzly would have trouble exacting this level of damage. How could a canine have inflicted this much mutilation?

A yellow marker lay beside each fragment. She did a quick count, and her stomach churned again. Seven. Seven pieces from the victim's body were scattered over a twenty-foot radius, including the man's ears, which had been sliced off. She took a step back to let a photographer by. He checked his last few shots then wiped a bead of sweat off his brow before kneeling down to take a closer shot of an arm. The room was eerily hushed, a far cry from the mood of a standard crime scene where officers and analysts maintained a certain level of joviality and conversation. Not that she blamed them. Processing a normal murder scene would be sobering. But one like this? She shuddered. None of them would sleep well for weeks.

Detective Garcia pushed back the plastic and stepped into the crime scene.

"You're the feds the commissioner has assigned?" Garcia held out his hand. "Antonio Garcia, but you can call me Tony."

"Special Agent Kaitlyn Quinn," she said before taking his hand and nodding toward Murphy. "And this is Supervisory Special Agent Murphy O'Neill."

Garcia smiled. "Your reputations proceed you."

She warmed to the smiling detective. Unlike others she had worked with over the years, he didn't appear to harbor any animosity at having his case taken over by federal agents.

Murphy, clearly not one for small talk, proceeded straight to business. "Has the medical examiner determined time of death yet?"

Garcia nodded, then checked his watch. "The ME determined time of death to be between twelve and eighteen hours ago. She's sending out her assistants to supervise the uplift to the morgue. They're about half an hour away."

While Garcia briefed them on what he knew, she scanned the personnel on scene. Some of the female analysts and officers were throwing glances their way. Turning to see what they were looking at, she realized what they were focusing on and groaned. She would have to be blind or dead not to appreciate the sight of the testosterone-laden men they were eyeing up.

Garcia, while not as large or tall as Murphy, was definitely easy on the eye. His Latino background was evident in his olive complexion and his thick dark mane, which did not have a hair out of place. In fact, Garcia looked as though he'd just stepped out of a salon. In comparison, Murphy made the police detective look like a boy. He exuded raw masculinity. His dirty blond hair was ruffled, and his scruffy face reflected his disinterest in how he was perceived. But she could not fault him on the way in which he filled out his suit. If she didn't already know how grumpy and rude he was, she might be curious about what was hiding under his white shirt, too.

Garcia, not immune to the looks thrown their way, winked at one of the analysts. For his part, Murphy seemed not to notice, or if he did, he ignored the glances directed at him.

She rolled her eyes.

When she moved toward them, she was on the receiving end of a warning glare from Murphy. Her ears grew warm. Busted.

Murphy reached for a pair of gloves. "If you're quite done with your ocular exercises, Special Agent Quinn, how about we walk the scene?"

She scowled at him. "Yes, sir."

Garcia reached into his coat pocket. "No need. I already did, you can have my notes."

Murphy shot the detective a glance that left him in no doubt about what he could do with his notes.

Garcia raised his hands in mock surrender. "Suit yourself." He took a step back. "I'll just wait here."

Murphy turned to the analysts. "I want this scene cleared now."

His voice boomed across the empty building, halting everyone in their tracks.

She suppressed a smile when a couple of them physically recoiled as his voice broke through their hushed tones. She had to learn that trick.

Within a few seconds, the scene was cleared of all personnel. Yes, she definitely had to learn how to do that. She pulled a set of disposable gloves from her pocket and donned crime scene booties.

Murphy glanced at her and pointed to the far left of the room. "Zone pattern, I'll start at one."

She nodded and made her way to the far right. "Confirmed, I'll take four."

For the next hour, they carefully inspected the scene, quadrant by quadrant, inch by inch. The enormous amount of evidence made it slow going, and they had to make sure they did not taint anything. Who knew what evidence they might need to rely on later? She inspected a broken phone and a pair of loafers then moved to the man's left foot. Compared to the rest of the body parts, this one was relatively intact, or as intact as a severed foot could be. When she moved to the leg it had been ripped from, her hands grew clammy. The leg joint had been ripped to shreds, with teeth marks cutting right to the bone.

She glanced around the leg, squinted, and looked closer at the floor. Though faint, she could just make out an animal's bloody paw print that hadn't been recorded. "Need a marker here."

Once she had shown an analyst her discovery she continued with her inspection. While there were differences between this scene and scenes she had studied, there were far too many similarities between this killing and the ones from twenty years ago. But was it really the same man? And how did he train a canine to do that?

She had half-filled a notepad by the time she took a moment to steady her nerves. With each piece of evidence, her suspicions became firmer. Along with the rank smell of blood, there was another odor she couldn't place. She looked over to Murphy to check if he had any idea what it might be and froze.

"What the—?"

Half crouched near the wall of blood, Murphy was sniffing the evidence. Or at least that's what it looked like he was doing. He bent down nearer the body and again inhaled. She cast a quick glance at the analysts standing off to one side. None of them seemed concerned about Murphy's strange techniques. And when she looked back at him, he was taking notes. Shaking it off as pure fantasy, she focused on her own arduous task.

She was crouched down studying a nearly unrecognizable severed ear when Murphy cleared his throat. "So, do you think this is a copycat?"

She nearly jumped out of her skin at his sudden appearance. "Son of a nutcracker."

Instead of apologizing for startling her, Murphy just continued to look at her expectantly. She shook her head. "I'm not one hundred percent sure yet, but I suspect we are dealing with the original," she said in a low voice.

"What makes you say that?"

"Well, for starters ..." She pointed to the small puddles she'd finally identified as the source of the unknown smell. "He's urinated around the entire circumference of the area. The killer's key trademark from the original crimes was never released to the media."

He grunted.

"And the cuts on the torso, as well as on the face and arms, are consistent with the knife marks from the earlier crimes. The removal of some of the extremities, and not to mention the fact that he fed the parts of the body to some type of canine—"

"Why almost one hundred percent?"

She frowned as she continued to survey the macabre scene. "Something's different though. Two things, really."

Murphy's only response was a slight raise of his eyebrow. She couldn't be sure, but she detected surprise in his expression.

"You noticed it, too?" he said.

"The cuts are deeper, especially on the face. They're closer together. It's almost like ..." she trailed off trying to find the words.

"Like he's perfected the art of cutting?"

She nodded. "Exactly. The incisions are precise and so close together. That only comes with practice." She looked around the room. "But what the hell has he been practicing on?"

Her focus returned to the severed ear she had been inspecting before Murphy interrupted her train of thought. "In addition to the missing fingers, there's also something not right with this."

She called out to one of the young criminalists who was chatting away with Garcia. "Hey you, get a camera over here."

She tilted the severed ear lobe with her pen and studied it in more detail. She nodded to the photographer to take some closeup shots of the ear and glanced up at Garcia. "With the exception of the missing fingers, have they accounted for all parts of the body?"

Garcia shrugged. "We won't know that until the ME puts it all back together."

"What about the other two bodies? Were all parts accounted for?"

"Examiner hasn't finished the jigsaw puzzle yet. Why?"

She pointed to the filleted arm. "The damage is severe, but that's definitely a Marine tattoo."

"And?" said Garcia.

She pointed to the severed ear. "What ex-Marines do you know who would be caught dead with a Tiffany's cultured pearl stud earring?"

Murphy leaned in closer to the ear and inhaled.

She recoiled in surprise. Did he really just sniff that ear?

Murphy looked up at her with an unreadable expression then moved across to the torso, knelt down, and peered closely as he breathed in.

Good Lord. He did. He sniffed the evidence.

She watched as he reexamined everything. His movements were precise but gave nothing away as to his inner thoughts. It took all her effort not to question his bizarre techniques. Perhaps they were something new that had come out of Quantico?

He returned to stand next to her. "You are correct. That ear isn't from our vic."

Garcia crouched down to get a better look. "Who does it belong to?"

She had to stop her mouth from falling open. Surely the question should be how in fartleberries did he know? She glanced at Murphy and gulped. He was looking directly at her. A micro expression flitted across his face. He knew exactly what she was thinking. Something was definitely off with her new partner.

Murphy stood up, pulled off his gloves, reached for his phone, and took a photo of the dead man's face. "We'll need to take a look at the other bodies. But first, we need to follow the lead."

Lead? Her brows shot up almost to her hairline.

Garcia scratched the back of his head. "I don't understand. What did you find?"

She was as bewildered as the detective. This was heading into the twilight zone. What had she missed? Apart from the blood-spattered scene she'd scoured inch by inch, there was nothing left behind that could even remotely be classified as a clue.

Murphy headed out. "Wait for the ME's people. Make sure to let them know they need to check that ear against the other vics. We need confirmation ASAP." He halted and turned back to glare at her. "You coming?"

Murphy strode through the building without waiting for her. His focus was on his phone as he tapped away at it.

She scrambled to catch up to him, just as the press surrounded them demanding information. "What lead? What did I miss?"

Murphy cut through the crowd to his Cadillac Escalade and pushed away a microphone that had been thrust at his face. "No comment."

The reporter backed off. She had to hand it to him. A gruff, no comment, was enough to frighten off all but the bravest of the reporters. However, she couldn't help but wonder if his words were in response to her question. She followed her new partner in silence. Too many questions crowded her already overactive mind. She was a trained agent with advanced interrogation skills, and she couldn't, get him to answer a few simple questions. What the hell was this lead, and what was he doing sniffing the evidence?

FIVE

Just a Hunch

Kaitlyn climbed into the Cadillac Escalade and reached for the seatbelt. "So, where are we going?"

"I've already said."

She snorted. "No, you didn't. You said you were chasing a lead. You haven't mentioned what the lead is, where it is, or even how you worked out there was a lead."

She glared at him and tapped at the leather console between them. She hated to be kept in the dark, and his lack of communication skills frustrated her to no end. After counting to ten, still nothing. Not even an acknowledgement he had heard her. Her tapping intensified, if she clenched her jaw any tighter her back teeth would crack. This was ridiculous. What was it about her that made people feel she could be walked over? She had spent the majority of her life dealing with people who underestimated her just because she was a woman. Well, she had never backed down, and she wasn't about to start now. She swung her head around to face him, ready to let rip, when she stopped short. His profile triggered a feeling of déjà vu, and the nagging suspicion there was something familiar about him returned. Why? Why did he seem so familiar? Confused, she stared out the window and resumed her tapping.

She had well and truly given up hope of any type of response when he finally broke the silence. "We're heading to the docks."

He glanced at her, and his eyes narrowed as they rested on her drumming fingers.

She suppressed a grin. The tapping irritated him enough to cave. She filed that away for later. "Why the docks?"

The muscles along his jaw rippled. "Because our vic spent time there."

Her brows shot up. "And how exactly did you work that out?"

Murphy's hands tightened on the steering wheel.

What was he not telling her?

He shrugged his tense shoulders and focused on the road. "Just a hunch."

Hunch my ass. Before she could push him further, Murphy's phone rang. She couldn't catch a glimpse of who was calling. His short, sharp answers gave away nothing of the conversation, and once he'd hung up, the vehicle returned to silence. Determined not to let him get the better of her temper, she sifted through her memory of what she knew about the man. Before she got very far, Murphy surprised her by instigating a conversation.

"I assume you are familiar with the case files from twenty years ago?"

She nodded slowly, unsure of where he was going. "Intimately."

Murphy cleared his throat. "He was a good man."

This time there was nothing gruff in his manner.

"P-pardon?"

"Your father. He was a good detective. And an exceptional Human."

He spoke in a gentle and sincere way. Neither of which were traits she associated with him. She rarely spoke about her father to anyone other than her mother. She'd long since adopted avoidance as her best policy.

She drew in a hesitant breath. It was hampered by the sudden lump in her throat. "That's what they say." She dropped her head and focused on a small, faint scar on her finger. Anything to stop her from dwelling on wounds that had never really healed. "I mean, I usually get that from people who knew him. How do you know what he was like?"

Murphy focused on the road ahead, but if his fingers tightened around the steering wheel any more, the thing would snap. "People talk, I guess. Is that why you went into the same line of business—you wanted to follow in his footsteps?"

She bit the inside of her cheek and considered her response. If they had any chance of working together, they needed to trust each other. Normal human communication was clearly not his strong point, but he appeared to be trying. She at least needed to attempt to reciprocate. "I guess you could say that." She sighed. "As I got older, I understood more about the damage the killer inflicted on the other victims' families. I was lucky, Dad didn't suffer like they did."

She fell silent, wrestling with the same demons that had plagued her dreams since she first understood the path of destruction carved by a madman all those years ago. She only knew about the events from that night through the official police files and what she had found in old newspaper clippings. Many of her father's colleagues refused to talk about the period the Boston Wolf Killer was active, so she had to rely on other avenues of information gathering. From what she pieced together, her father managed to track down the killer, but unable to risk waiting for backup, he disobeyed orders and went in alone. Many believed he went in to save the life of the victim he heard screaming. When backup arrived a short time later, they found her father already dead. His neck was broken, and a section of his throat was torn where the powerful jaws of a canine attacked him. And the body of the man he tried to save was found on the next floor up.

Rage rose to the surface, and her body became so tense she shook. "I can't wait to get that bastard, and make him pay for everything that he's done."

Murphy's wall dropped, and he flashed her a concerned look. "Be careful. That feeling is dangerous. Believe me, you don't want to wake up one day a shadow of the person you once were. Your father would not want that for you." He paused. "And your mother has already lost a husband and a child to this. Don't let her lose you, too."

A tightness clenched deep within her chest. That ... that was something they never spoke about. An open wound that had never healed. "How did you know she lost ...?"

A fire tore through her throat, effectively cutting off the ability to finish the sentence, and she stared out the window. Her vision blurred, and she blinked rapidly to quell the tears and the pain that threatened to crack open her chest. Her mother had been pregnant at the time of her father's death. The grief was too much. Within twenty-four hours of losing her father, she had lost her unborn brother, too. She resisted the urge to reach up and wipe away the single tear that crept down her cheek. She couldn't let him know how deeply all this affected her.

"People talk," Murphy murmured.

Was that almost a tender and sympathetic tone in his voice? But when she glanced up at him, any temporary veil of kindness was gone, and in its place was the Murphy she was beginning to know. All business, non-talkative, and grumpy as hell. She squirmed in her seat. Something still was not adding up. How did he know this intimate part of her history? She had never mentioned it to her colleagues, and it was most definitely not common knowledge.

The chance to interrogate him disappeared when they arrived at their destination. Murphy flashed his identification at the Port Police, then proceeded through the gates of the Conely Container Terminal and pulled into the staff carpark. Before she had a chance to step out of the vehicle, he was heading for the pier clerk, and by the time she caught up to him, he was already asking questions.

He held up his phone to a slightly overweight port worker dressed in a yellow fluorescent jacket. "We are investigating the death of this man."

She cringed. What had possessed him to show the clerk a grim photo of a brutalized victim? They were not allowed to do that, especially since the image had been taken straight from the crime scene.

The port worker squinted at the small screen, but he didn't bat an eyelid.

"We have reason to believe this individual was employed here at the Container Terminal. He most probably worked in maintaining the cranes and other machinery," Murphy said.

She struggled to keep her expression neutral. She couldn't believe what she was hearing. What was he up to? What had she missed at the crime scene? More importantly, how could he be so specific?

The burly man reached into his pocket for his reading glasses. The moment they were on, his face paled. "What the hell happened to him?" He took a step back and shook his head. "Sorry, don't recognize the face. I focus on the container movements in and out on the trucks, you'd be better off talking to Phil."

Confused, she glanced at Murphy's phone screen before he pocketed it. It was their victim alright, except his face wasn't torn to shreds. Instead, he looked like he'd been in a fight and come out the other end a little battered and bruised. Her head began to spin. How was that possible?

The clerk gave them directions, and she followed along behind Murphy, but her mind was awhirl. There had to be a valid explanation for how he magically conjured up a photo of their vic with his face still intact. Garcia. That had to be it. Garcia identified the vic and sent Murphy the image. They rounded a corner of stacked forty-foot containers as she checked the messages on her phone. If Garcia had sent the photo to Murphy, he must have sent it to her as well. She scrolled through the list and frowned. Where was the mess—

Air ripped from her lungs as strong arms wrapped around her midriff and unceremoniously wrenched her back into a warm, firm body. A forklift flew around the corner, dangerously close to where she had stood. Her heart pumped wildly as the ten-ton vehicle careened past them. She gulped. If not for Murphy, she would be roadkill about now. Her body was pinned against Murphy's muscular chest. A fire spread from where his hands splayed across her midriff and burned the length of her body. Electric sparks shot through every nerve ending, many of which she didn't know she had. He was far too close and personal for her to think straight.

She gulped. What the hell just happened?

His lips lightly brushed the tiny hairs on the shell of her ear and set off volcanic goosebumps across her exposed skin. "How about you watch where you're going next time. Unlike your roller skates, most vehicles are dangerous."

Murphy grunted, let go of her like she had a contagious disease, and headed off as though nothing had happened.

His words threw cold water over her, and the heat coursing through her body dissipated in a heartbeat. She stood in the middle of the thoroughfare, confused and flushed. How ridiculous, getting hot and bothered over nothing. Over Murphy.

"Are you coming?" he called back, clearly agitated.

She flinched, and pulled herself together.

By the time they found Phil, she had hidden her muddled emotions behind her professional mask. She couldn't risk being thrown off the case. No matter what, she would not let him get the better of her. If he avoided mentioning the incident, she would, too.

"How can I help you?" Phil said, after Murphy identified them both.

Murphy held up his phone. "Do you recognize this man?"

The man's eyes flew open wide. "Jesus Christ, what happened to him?"

She shot a glance at the seriously photoshopped crime scene image. The back of her neck tingled. No way had Murphy received the photo from Tony Garcia. Where the hell did he get it?

"Do you recognize him?" Murphy said again.

"Well, I can't say for certain, on account of the funny looking bruises and all, but that sort a looks like Jacob Haladlo, one of the mechanics for the STS cranes. He works the night shifts." Phil scratched the back of his neck as his gaze slid from the photo. "Ya know, I'm not really sure."

The muscles in Murphy's jaw twitched and his eyes narrowed.

She shot Murphy a warning glare. If he got any more agitated, they might be thrown off Port grounds. She forced a bright smile and stepped into the conversation. "Is he due in today?"

Phil checked his clipboard and shook his head. "He's rostered on tonight, but it looks like he didn't show last night." He craned his neck out the window. "But you're in luck, that's his boss."

He opened the window and bellowed to a wiry man in a hard hat and overalls. "Denzil, get your butt in here. You ain't gonna like this."

A few minutes later, Denzil confirmed Phil's guess. She took copious notes as they questioned the two men. It wasn't lost on her that less than an hour ago they had an unidentified body. Even if the killer had left any of the victim's fingers behind, the results of the fingerprints would take forty-eight to seventy-two hours to process. Half that, if the job was approved for a rush. Yet, without any physical evidence, Murphy had narrowed down where the vic worked and they now had a name, address, and social security number.

How was that possible?

"And what about people on the other shifts? Did Mr. Haladlo associate with any of them outside of work?" she said as a follow-up to Murphy's question.

Their initial meeting was strained to say the least, but their examination of the crime scene, and now their effortless tag team in questioning Phil and Denzel was smooth. Anyone would think they had been working together for years. She shook out of her over analysis and focused on taking notes. While the day was becoming stranger and stranger, she was a professional and needed to act like it. A serial killer was on the loose. No matter how much she was determined to get to the bottom of Murphy's weird behavior, they needed to stop a madman before he had the chance to kill again.

Boston PD Headquarters

The police superintendent's assistant, Lenny Something or other, pushed on the large glass door and revealed a hive of activity. He waited for her and Murphy to pass through. "We've repurposed one of the meeting rooms, and IT will connect you to our network when you're ready," he said.

Lenny Something led the way across the floor and briefed them on the layout, and their new home while they were on the case.

Kaitlyn resisted the urge to poke her tongue out at the stunned PD staff as she and Murphy made their way across the floor. From the looks the staff was shooting their way, anyone would think they had suddenly sprouted two heads.

Lenny pointed to a half-closed door and handed them two white cards. "This is you. If you need anything, let me know."

Murphy nodded and strode into the room.

She thanked Lenny, took the access cards, and raced to catch up with Murphy. Garcia and two others, an older man and a young woman in a bright pink Hello Kitty T-shirt, were already waiting for them.

The girl rocketed up from her chair and grinned at her. "Surprise."

She clamped her jaw tight to keep it from dropping to the floor. "Anika, what are you doing here?"

Anika clapped her hands together. "I'm on the case. How cool is that? We'll be working together. I can't wait to tell Maggie, you should have seen your face. She was so jelly I got the gig instead of her."

Murphy glared at Anika.

For once she stopped talking, and her face paled when she looked directly at him.

"Where are we with Haladlo?" Murphy said to Garcia.

Garcia closed the lid of his laptop, reached for a folder, and handed it to Murphy. "Not much to tell. He's worked on the docks for the past fifteen years. Forty-two, divorced, two kids, lives in Revere. A couple of misdemeanors when he was younger, but apart from that, nothing much stands out."

The other man, whom she guessed was Tony Garcia's partner, cleared his throat and shifted forward in his chair. "Yah-huh, pretty much the same with the locals. No one saw or heard nut'in." He stood and held out his hand to Murphy. "Ruby. Saul Ruby."

They shook hands and Saul turned to her. "I've only got three months to retirement, so don't you expect me to go climbing no walls or chasing perps across town." He pointed a thumb at Garcia and frowned. "I didn't want this case, but with eager beaver over there, I didn't have much of a say."

She smiled and shook his hand. "Kaitlyn Quinn."

Garcia sighed heavily. "God help me if I've got to hear how many more days, weeks or months until your retirement again.

Just chillax old man and enjoy the ride. What other case could you possibly want for your swansong?"

Saul raised a bushy gray eyebrow, and his forehead crinkled even more. "Oh, I don't know, something like a lost cat, or a stolen garden gnome, maybe?"

Garcia slapped Saul on the back and laughed. "At least this way, you can have your Dunkin's in peace without Mildred finding out."

Saul cocked his head and grinned. "There is that. She's got spies everywhere. I swear if she puts me on one more diet, I'll divorce her."

Murphy let out a low growl. Garcia and Saul snapped their mouths closed.

She held back a grin. Despite their age gap and personality differences, the two partners respected each other and worked well together.

Murphy's stoic gaze fell on Anika.

She fidgeted from one foot to another, like her entire body was pent-up with unused energy. The light reflected on the stud in her nose each time she moved, making it look like a tiny disco ball was stuck to her face.

"A-anika Kumar, I'm a criminalist with the State Police Crime Laboratory. I'm lit to be on the team. I couldn't believe it when I was called in to see the superintendent. I mean, it's goals AF. You learn about these sorts of cases at college, but to actually be on it. I had to pinch myself. Then just to be sure, I got Maggie to pinch me." Anika shuffled from one foot to the other. "I won't let you down. Whatever you need, I'm your man … woman … you know what I mean. I just—"

Anika stopped mid-sentence when Murphy let out another low growl. She retreated to the chair she had just vacated.

Kaitlyn threw her a sympathetic glance. She knew from experience holding her tongue would be killing Anika.

Murphy scooped up the blown-up photos from the table and stuck them to a large whiteboard. "The police commissioner has scheduled a press conference for the six o'clock news. He's expecting answers and so are the media. So, if you are quite done with discussions around retirement and inflicting self-injury, can we please get back to working the case."

Anika snapped her mouth shut, and her face turned a dark shade of pink. Saul shifted uncomfortably in his chair.

Good grief. Not only did Murphy not do small talk, he expected the team to follow suit. She held back a grin. With Anika in the room, that was never going to happen.

Murphy faced them. "So we can all get up to speed, we're going to go back to the first vic and walk our way forward."

Over the next two hours, Garcia and Saul walked the team through the first three scenes.

Anika added to the conversation where it related to the evidence or preliminary autopsy reports. She wandered over to the photos and sighed. "We found so much trace evidence at the scenes it's going to take a while to process. So far, the only unique thing we can attribute to the crime is the animal paw prints, and we really don't have a database for that."

Saul pulled at his moustache. "The fucker knew what he was doing. All the kill sites have dozens of people traipsing through it every day. It's going to take a month of Sundays for the geeks to identify and eliminate the prints collected at the scene. We have a shit show in hell of striking lucky down that avenue."

Garcia shrugged. "I agree. Trying to ID the perp through fingerprints is a waste of time. His lawyer would have a field day in court."

"Did they ever find fingerprints at the original killer's sites back in the dark ages of the late nineties?" Anika said.

She shook her head. "No. At the time, they believed his locations were chosen because they were open, and the collection of evidence was always going to prove difficult. He's maintained that same MO."

Garcia leaned forward in his chair. "Okay. How about we address the elephant in the room? Are you saying for certain that you think we are dealing with the original perp?"

She glanced up at Murphy. While she had voiced her thoughts, she had no idea about his take on the subject.

"Yes."

His grim tone shot to the bottom of her stomach. There was no hesitation in his answer. From the expressions on the others' faces they took his word as gospel. She implicitly trusted the judgement of a man she had just met. No doubt she would argue the point with him on many things, but with this, she had no hesitation. She was finally on the hunt for her father's killer.

Garcia rubbed his forehead and shook his head from side to side. "I don't know whether to be relieved there's only one screwed up psycho who could do this sort of thing, or terrified that the psycho's back with a vengeance."

Saul grinned and held out his hand to Garcia. "Pay up. I told you it wasn't a copycat."

Murphy tapped a finger on the crime scene photo of Haladlo. "The victims. If we can determine who he's targeting and why, we might be able to work out who is next."

Garcia handed Saul a twenty dollar note and frowned. "But you just said it's the same perp as last time. Back then, there was no pattern. It was random."

"Well, there is this time."

She shot up from leaning against the wall. Why hadn't she seen it before? "The hands. Vics one and two were sliced. Vic four, the fingers taken. He doesn't want us identifying the victims."

Garcia's brows crinkled together. "How do you explain the high school teacher, vic number three?"

Murphy shrugged. "His injuries weren't as severe as the other two. I suspect he was in the wrong place at the wrong time. Either that, or he's a red herring to throw us off the unsub's scent."

Murphy moved across to the board again and stared at the gruesome images of the victims. "There was something more personal about one, two and four. We just need to work out what that is."

Anika pulled on one of her many earrings. "We know the ID of four. Without prints or a decent photo of the woman, vic one, it's going to be difficult, same with two. We've sent a swab away for a DNA match, but short of them being on any of the registers, we have very little hope of identifying them that way."

"What about one of them fandangled computer reconstruction-thingys?" Saul said.

Garcia chuckled and shook his head. "I don't know why the captain sends you on those courses with me, it's not like you actually listen."

"Were you the one who photoshopped Haladlo's face?" she asked.

Garcia's brows puckered together. "Huh?"

Murphy stiffened. "No, he wasn't."

Before she could push the matter, he carried on with the briefing.

"Image reconstruction is not a viable option for the first vic. She was a lot more cut up than Haladlo. It'd be virtually impossible to establish her identity that way." Murphy tapped on the image of the first victim. "We need to ID her. Anika, I want you to work with the ME to find anything on that body that will tell us who she was."

Saul placed his coffee cup on the table. "Without prints or knowing what she looked like, I don't see how we're going to do that."

Anika's eyes flew open wide. She raced back to the table for the pile of photos and flicked through it. Finding what she was looking for, she waved an image in the air. "But we may be able to do something with the fingers. I remember reading an article in the *International Journal of Computer Science and Mobile Computing* about altered fingerprint detection, recognition, and verification.

I could use some of their techniques. No wait, it used a different algorithm." She pulled on her long braid and fingered the elastic holding the ends together. "Maybe if I contacted them, they might give me access. Or I could try a phase model–based approach to interpolate the missing regions—"

Murphy growled and Anika jumped out of her skin.

"Can you do it or not?"

Anika bit her bottom lip, deep in thought. She nodded. "It will take time, but I think I could get at least one solid print."

"Get on it then." Murphy turned to the others. "Garcia, Ruby, get a warrant to search Haladlo's place. I want to know everything there is about him, down to the brand of toothpaste he uses and the type of coffee he drinks. Quinn, you're with me."

She frowned. "Where are we going?"

"To the first scene. I want to take a look for myself."

She checked her watch. It was getting late. They'd better hurry or it would be too dark to see anything properly.

The scene at the abandoned warehouse was still cordoned off. All evidence had been removed, and the coating of blood on the walls and floor was the only indication that something terrible had taken place. With very little light, they used their torches to see in the murky shadows, which reinforced how chilling the crime would have looked to the first responders. As with the scene earlier in the day, they separated into quadrants and inspected every nook and cranny. Murphy sniffed his way through the zone. Although his actions were only slight, the minuscule intake of breath and the slight flaring of his nostrils was a dead giveaway to her trained eye. What he deduced by doing so was still beyond her, but something was not quite right with her new partner.

She turned her torch to a blood splatter and followed it down the wall. The severed arm that had been flung against it was long gone. The marker at her feet, however, was still there, and a stark reminder of the chilling and brutal death of an, as yet, nameless woman.

Murphy had moved to his second quadrant and was still sniffing. She envied how quick he worked the evidence and scene. If she didn't know better, she'd think he had eidetic memory, something valuable to have in their line of business.

She squatted down and lifted a scrunched-up piece of paper. The more she thought about the incident with the forklift at the port, the more she was convinced she needed to keep a close eye on him. The speed at which he had whipped her away from the imminent disaster was not natural. No one had that type of agility, or strength. And yet, he hadn't even broken a sweat. Her face burned hot at the memory of his arms wrapped around her and pushed all other thoughts aside. How good his arms felt had her pulse skipping a beat.

Blue cheese. She was losing it. How could she be getting hot and bothered over nothing? She seriously needed to get a grip. Kaitlyn stalked over to the far side of the scene and kept her back to Murphy. He was far too astute. His all-knowing eyes missed nothing. If he knew what was going through her mind, she would be mortified. Blatantly ignoring her involuntary physical reaction, she tallied up the other strange things she had noticed about him. Evidence sniffing, magic photos, victim divining skills, the list went on. If she thought he was this weird after a day, what would she think by the end of the week?

<u>SIX</u>

Jack the Who?

Boston City

A makeshift stage had been set up on the far side of the crowded pub. What could loosely be called music blared from a live band, and a large group of fans euphorically chanted along with the lead singer.

Elijah, bored at the lack of skill from any of the musicians, turned his back on them and watched from his corner of the bar as patrons came and went. Over the years, he had learned that patience was most definitely a virtue. Tonight was no exception, especially with having to listen to the off-key and off-beat sorry excuse for a song.

A beautiful woman leaned over the bar to get the bartender's attention. While she waited for her drink, she gave him a bright smile and looked him over. She leaned toward him, providing an ample view down her low-cut top.

"Can I buy you a drink, handsome?"

His gaze slowly raked in the woman offering, from her tone, something far more than a drink. Lazily admiring the ample cleavage threatening to spill out of her top, he sighed, recalling a time when he did not need to be careful. During his years in

London in the late 1800s, he had chosen his victims based solely on the amount of breast they showed as they propositioned him for money. A smile flickered at the corners of his lips. Such a thrill to watch their expressions change when he sated his hunger and then slit their throats as his seed flowed down their thighs. Oh, how Scotland Yard was useless. They didn't find half of the bodies he had piled up.

About to accept her offer, he paused when the reason he was there walked through the door. He frowned, disappointed at the timing. The woman's smooth alabaster skin would have looked so beautiful under his blade. His loins stirred at the thought of slicing through the flesh across her young, nubile body.

"Sorry lovey, I'm expecting someone. Maybe next time."

He moved across the crowded room and resisted the urge to finger his blade. The locals here had an issue with people carrying weapons. Not like the good old days when he could carry what he wanted, where he wanted. He kept his eyes on his target. His plan was genius. Why he had not thought of it before was beyond him. Pissing off both the Alliance and Elise at the same time? He grinned. Payback's a bitch.

Since arriving in America, he had evaded the Alliance, whom he detested with a vengeance. That pathetic group of alphas who thought they could make the rules were at the top of a short and heavy list sitting on his shoulders. Recently, he had added to this list.

Elise.

He was going to make that bitch pay for abandoning him after he had served her all these years. Then she discarded him in a heartbeat when the Alliance scum invaded their compound. The bitch escaped, leaving him behind to fend for himself.

His fingers retracted, turning claw-like. *When I'm finished, she won't be able to get to me. Even if she succeeds with her plans, I'll be untouchable.*

His wolf paced and saliva dripped from his powerful jaws. *Us you mean?*

He was of two minds about tonight's prey. While he needed answers the Human had, he hoped that like the others, he held out. He and his wolf were quite enjoying the game. Their cries for mercy as he sliced them through to the bone conjured up his fondest memories of this city. He let out a heavy sigh. Too much time had passed since he called the shots. Since he'd decided who lived and who died. That was about to change. He leaned against the pillar and watched as his mark, Eric Weiss, better known as Moe, ordered a drink.

Moe the Schmoe.

That name suited him better. He was weak. Pathetic, even for a Human. He frowned. Only one week left until his end game, give or take a few days. Time was running out. And if he didn't find what he'd lost, things might start to get a little tricky. He yawned as he studied the poor excuse for a Human that was about to become tonight's distraction.

Moe the Schmoe slipped a bulky envelope across the table to his associate. Elijah's pulse began to race. It looked like Moe was finishing up.

About time.

He glanced at the blonde bitch in heat. He'd get this over with and come back to sate his thirst. Just the thought of slicing her made his blood run hot, and desire ripple through every nerve ending. Lovey, I'll be back for y—

The large TV monitor behind her caught his attention. His mouth curled into a sneer, and his muscles tensed as he gazed at the all too familiar face. The thorn in his side had finally turned up. Murphy O'Neill was a blight. One he would get rid of as soon as he put his plans in motion. He needed to set the ledger straight. No one, but no one bested him. Especially not an upstart pup with bogtrotter Irish blood. Everywhere he went, the man wasn't far behind, and he was tired of looking over his shoulder. Having the do-gooder pit-bull chase him around the country had been amusing for a time, but after a few years, the novelty wore off.

Murphy had not changed much over the years. If his curt reply to the reporter was anything to go by, even his disposition was the same. A woman in a dark suit and Rayban sunglasses followed Murphy to his car.

His wolf stirred. *Hmmm … What do we have here?*

His face relaxed, and his lips turned up in a sadistic grin. Murphy's FBI partner, while not the willowy blond type he was partial to, was easy on the eye. A bit tall maybe, but still fuckable. Perhaps he'd play a little before putting an end to the Irish bastard. He licked his lips at the thought of carving through her silky skin, and his groin twitched. Yes, he would enjoy filleting her and leaving her for Murphy to find. It wouldn't be the first time he'd taken something from the mutt. A genuine twinge of excitement surged through his body.

He chugged back his drink and skulked out the door after Moe the Schmoe. "Playtime's about to begin."

SEVEN

Not All as It Seems

Kaitlyn dragged her body home after a long and tiring day keeping up with Murphy, who was constantly stuck on fast mode. The case had also taken its toll on her state of mind. As much as she hated admitting it, Murphy was right. What she was really after was revenge, not justice. Her ingrained hatred for the man who had viciously taken her father from her had festered through the years. Now, it was almost all-consuming.

Kicking off her shoes, she ventured into the kitchen. She threw some ingredients into a pan, let them simmer, then reached for a bottle of red wine. She needed wine before she spoke to her mother. Vivian should hear the news from her, not the media.

She had consumed half a bottle of cabernet sauvignon by the time she put down the phone. The conversation had been difficult for both of them. At first her mother was devastated, then she became frantic that Kaitlyn would meet the same end as her husband.

"Sweetheart, if you're not going to leave the case," her mother said, "at least be careful, for my sake. I don't think ... I don't think I could recover if I lost you, too."

Her gut squirmed as she tried to reassure her mother. "I need you to not worry. Besides, I'm working with a partner." She shook her head and muttered, "If I've managed to survive so far with him, I can get through anything."

Vivian took in a shuddering breath over the phone.

"To be honest, Mom, he's the best in the business. And I suspect he is more than capable of holding his own against anyone—or anything."

Tears flowed down her face for a long while after she ended the call. Times like this, she desperately missed her mom. Boston wasn't the same without her, but she understood the reason for her mother's decision. The city held too many bad memories. Her mother struggled for years to crawl out of the depths of depression. If she had stayed in Boston, perhaps she never would have found the strength.

The combination of wine and their conversation put her in a melancholy state of mind. She sat back and stared at the photo of her father on the bookshelf. What would he make of all this? How different was it back then? She stiffened and bolted upright. "I'm an idiot, how did I forget?"

Her mom left all of her husband's old files, including his personal case notes when she moved to Florida. They were hidden away at the back of the lockup in the basement of her apartment building. Something in the files might help them understand how he tracked down the killer. No one had ever been able to figure out how he knew the killer was in that building.

She hauled the boxes upstairs and blew away the dust on the first box. Her stomach churned as she placed the box on the coffee table, and she broke out in a cold sweat. She hesitated, her hands on the first box. Was she ready for whatever was hidden in them? A part of her was on the brink of taking them back downstairs.

"Grow a pair."

She poured another glass of wine, sat on the couch cross-legged, and carefully opened the lid. The musty smell burned her throat and lungs. She closed her eyes. It was harder than she thought it would be. Her father was in these boxes. "People's lives are at stake. You needed to treat this like any other case."

She gathered up her courage and reached for the first file. It contained the case notes of the first victim from twenty years ago. Her finger traced over her father's neat handwriting. Tears stung the back of her eyes as she scanned through the pages. It had been years since she looked at them. Even then she had been too emotional to read through all the files. Much of the information she already knew, but there were passages in her father's careful hand she had not noticed before. She reverently placed the folder to one side, reached for the next file, and pored over its contents. For the next hour she was fully immersed in a time warp. Her father's notes were extensive, and gave her incredible insight into the policing methods at the time. Each time he needed a warrant check he had to radio into the station and wait for someone to get back to him. All she had to do was type the information into her phone.

Kaitlyn was halfway through the box when a faded yellow envelope fell off the side of the box. She turned it over. Her fingers tingled and the sensation swept up her arm and over the rest of her body. No markings on either side indicated what was hidden inside. Only one way to find out. Her heart raced as she opened the top flap and peeked inside.

Photos?

She pulled out the large stack, and the wind went out of her lungs. The photo on top could have easily been from the most recent crime scene. She flipped it over. De Vissher. One of the first victims from twenty years ago. The next image was taken from a different angle, and again showed an eerily similar scene. When she got to the fourth photo in the stack, her hands shook. This photo was of a group of Boston PD officers outside the precinct. Many of whom she recognized. They were posed in front of one of the squad cars and looked relaxed as they laughed together. Her eyes were riveted on the image of her father smiling and staring straight at the camera.

She closed her eyes, opened them again, and looked at each photo in turn. Unlike the top few, they were all personal photos. She clutched the stack tightly and bit down on her bottom lip as she stared at an image of her father. The anguish of having missed out on him surfaced once again. Her dance recitals, her graduation, her acceptance into the FBI. Every defining moment of her life was experienced knowing that one person was missing.

Tears welled in her eyes as she recognized a younger version of her father staring back at her. His father stood beside him. They were both happy and smiling as if they had just shared a joke. Her grandfather, in dress blues, tall and striking, stood proudly beside his son. From the background and the brass on his lapel, she guessed the photo was taken at an award ceremony where her grandfather was presented with a commendation. She regretted never having met him. An accident had taken his life years before she was born.

She flipped to the next photo, and her brows drew together. What was that doing there?

A small folded slip of yellowed paper rested among the stack of photos. Careful not to rip it, she opened it slowly. Tears welled again when she realized what was hidden within the folds. A child's drawing. For the life of her, she couldn't remember drawing it, but it was definitely her artwork. She had drawn her family. She was standing between her parents, holding their hands. An oversized sun was shining in the background, and Princess was chasing a ball. She smiled at the dog in the drawing and remembered how much she had pestered her father to allow her to take her home.

Him.

Her emotions swayed between sad and happy and all the variations in between as she slowly leafed through each memory. Images of her dad and a few officers she recognized stared back at her, and she grinned at some of the haircuts they sported. McArthur, how did they let you have a moustache like that?

When she turned to the next photo, her breath caught in her throat. The candid image was of her father with another man whose face she recognized.

It couldn't be ....

She peered closer then recoiled as if burnt, and the stack slipped from her fingers. That couldn't be right. There must be an explanation. A doppelgänger, maybe? She leaned forward and picked up the photo, and uncertainty washed over her. No way could it be possible. She squeezed her eyes closed then opened them again. It was still the same image. Nothing had changed. Staring back at her were two men deep in conversation. The photographer seemed to have surprised them, and they looked to the camera the moment the picture was captured. Goosebumps spread over her skin. What the ...?

Reasons, explanations, they all ran through her mind. From A to Z, then back again. She put the photo face down on the coffee table and flipped through the rest of the images, unease growing in her stomach. Perhaps if she ignored it, it would go away. Her muscles tensed, and her skin grew clammy when she discovered a second image of her father and the doppelgänger. It was not him. It couldn't be. She wiped cold sweat away from her brow and brought the photo closer. His eyes. How many people had those eyes?

A shiver raced down her spine. There was no mistaking who she was looking at. Staring at her in full faded color was Murphy O'Neill. And he looked exactly the same now as he did in the photograph. The man had not aged a day in twenty-odd years. Her brows furrowed together. Think, think, think.

Her father's handwriting on the back of the first photograph caught her eye. In her haste to forget the image, she'd not noticed it before. Scrawled across the back of the photo were the words, "Me and Murphy. *Nihil prius familia.*"

Relief flooded through her veins, and her shoulders dropped. That was it. The man must be Murphy's father. Yes, that was it. Our fathers worked together. Positive she was working with Murphy Junior, she reached for her laptop.

Thirty minutes later, she was no closer to proving Murphy's father worked the Boston Wolf Killer case twenty years ago. Outside the FBI, Murphy O'Neill junior was an enigma. Nothing. No Facebook, Twitter, Instagram … no social media whatsoever. The only digital footprint he had was the online FBI records of the cases he worked. Beyond the walls of the FBI, he did not exist. But how was that possible?

She picked up the two photos. At first, she couldn't bring herself to look directly at Murphy. Her hand shook at the effort to sit still. She focused on her father. From his relaxed posture and wide smile, she could only surmise that he and this … this doppelgänger were friends. She forced her gaze to the Murphy clone and studied him. That's when she noticed it. A hint of a smile brightened those dark eyes. She let out a shaky laugh and sagged back into the couch. Well, there she had it. It couldn't be Murphy. That grumpy bastard didn't know how to smile. Or relax for that matter. She sat back up and smoothed the front of her shirt. See … Not him. She returned the photos to the envelope and placed them back in the box. Her drawing lay on the coffee table. She picked it up and placed it on her bookshelf alongside the photo of her father. She touched the cold glass, and her smile faded. "I'm going to get justice for you, dad. I promise."

She yawned and checked her watch. It was late. No wonder her mind was playing tricks on her.

A menacing growl ripped through the darkness. Not sure of the direction it came from, Kaitlyn spun around. Her hand reached for her gun, only to discover it wasn't there.

Crap.

The guttural sound repeated. This time, it was accompanied by the soft pad of paws as they stalked across the hard surface. From the darkness, a figure flew at her. Razor-sharp teeth glistened as powerful jaws snapped closed then opened again.

Wolf.

She screamed and turned. She needed to run.

"Katy, honey, this way. This way."

The male voice was familiar, but she couldn't work out why. She ran toward it. Perhaps he had a gun?

The voice called to her. "This way. *Nihil ant mi familiam.* This way, Katy."

Suddenly, Murphy materialized out of nowhere, and she ran into his arms.

"Wolf. There's a wolf chasing me. We have to stop it."

She looked back. A giant wolf with red glowing eyes flew at her, its jaws dripping with blood and saliva.

She was too terrified to scream.

Kaitlyn opened her eyes and stared at the ceiling. Her body was covered in perspiration, and the damp sheets clung to her body like a second skin.

"Oh my god, that was the definition of fucked up."

She'd thought the wolf nightmares were a thing of the past. Her brain clearly hadn't got the message. She rose and wandered her apartment. Paced it, really. But at two a.m., she wasn't about to argue with herself too much. It might wake up the neighbors. Instead, she headed to the kitchen and scanned the contents of her pantry. Raspberry white chocolate muffins. That might do the trick.

She always thought better when she was doing something productive. What could be more productive at two a.m. than baking a new recipe? As she pulled out the ingredients, the photo of her father and Murphy's father repeated in her mind like a bad record stuck at the same riff in a bad song. While her rational mind was convinced the man in the photo was Murphy's father, her tired, overworked one was not so sure.

Silly, but she had to prove herself right, if only to get some sleep. But how was she going to do that? She found the answer the moment she put the tray of muffins into the oven. She would show the photo to Murphy. He'd grunt, call her an idiot, and they'd laugh over the uncanny likeness.

She stopped in her tracks. Wait … did he even know how to laugh?

She smiled as she reached for her phone. For the sake of her sanity, this couldn't wait. Thirty minutes later, she was in her car and on the road to Groton, though damned if she knew what the hell Murphy was doing that far from Boston.

By the time she turned up his long, secluded driveway, she was having second thoughts. Perhaps this wasn't such a great idea. If he was so crabby during the day, he might not appreciate being woken up at three-thirty in the morning. Light from inside the house alleviated her guilt. Murphy was still up. He would solve her puzzle so she could go home and get some sleep.

No one answered the door. Should she be relieved or worried? After banging loud enough to wake the dead, she wandered around to the back of the house. His Escalade was in the driveway, which meant he must be home. She climbed the two steps onto a large verandah facing the forest. The back door was open. Her muscles twitched. Murphy was the last person she imagined would keep his doors unlocked. "O'Neill, you in there?"

No response. Something was not right. She reached for her gun and groaned inwardly when her hand slapped against her hip. Her gun was locked in her safe. She looked around the verandah, but nothing looked out of the ordinary except for a bottle of Jack Daniels and an almost empty glass sitting on a side table. A sliver of ice clung to life at the bottom. He couldn't have gone too far.

She took a seat on the porch swing. The cacophony of crickets and owls kept her company, and she found the lack of street noise soothing, but the air was chilly and she shivered. She wrapped a blanket left hanging on the swing around her shoulders. The masculine, earthy scent was both comforting and intoxicating as she relaxed and snuggled back into the pillows. Every now and then, she stole a glance at the photo clutched in her fingers. Why wouldn't he come out and tell her their fathers worked together? The likeness was amazing. Not only did they share the same intense and unusual eye color, but Murphy had inherited the same smoldering good looks. The only difference was Murphy Senior looked approachable, whereas it'd be best to keep well away from the junior version.

She yawned. Perhaps his grumpy attitude came from his mom. A shiver ran down her body as a cool breeze washed over her. She glanced to the back door. Would Murphy mind if she ransacked his kitchen to make a cup of tea? Or better yet, hot chocolate.

She was about to investigate when a movement near the trees caught her eye. The luminous three-quarter moon gave off enough light to see across the yard and into the shadowy trees at the edge of the forest. She peered over the railings. Her body tensed and her eyes narrowed as she struggled to make out the figure. Instinctively, she looked around for a weapon in case she needed it. A large wolf emerged from the tree line.

Shit, shit, shit.

She froze. Any sudden movement would draw its attention.

Her obsession with her father's murder meant she had become an expert on all things related to the Wolf Killer cases. That included all matters relating to his accomplice, too. Her steadfast determination to learn everything about wolves extended to visiting Wolf Hollow in Ipswich, a wolf sanctuary an hour and a half north of Boston. She studied the habits as well as the nature of the animal, and tried to figure out how the killer would have trained his wolf. How a wild wolf could be tamed enough to participate in the brutal slayings still astounded her. Even after becoming a frequent visitor to Wolf Hollow, she was none the wiser. From all accounts, it should not be possible.

She risked another peek at the animal. The magnificent creature stealthily sauntering across the clearing was definitely a wolf. What was odd, though, was its stature. From this distance, it looked like the animal was almost twice the size of the gray wolves at Ipswich.

She frowned. Wolves did not roam free in this part of the state. "You look too healthy to be a wild animal," she whispered as she scrutinized the large lupine.

Her pulse raced as her brain considered the remote possibility that this was the animal they were after. That being the case, surely its savage owner would not be too far behind. And here she was, a seasoned FBI agent without a weapon. She pulled her phone from her pocket, all the while scanning the darkened tree line, ready to dial for backup if the need arose.

The wolf stopped midway between the tree line and the house. The wolf's body rippled as it began a series of jerky motions, each more extreme than the last, like something inside the wolf's body was itching to get out.

She covered her mouth to hold back a whimper. Everything moved in slow motion. Her legs had gone numb and she could not move. She was forced to watch in mute silence. Skin replaced hair, hands replaced forepaws, paws became feet, and the powerful streamlined upper body of the wolf disappeared. In its place was the defined muscles and broad shoulders of a naked man who stood gracefully from his crouched position.

Murphy.

Murphy O'Neill, her partner, and the person she had come here to demand answers from, had just turned from a goddam wolf into … into …

Fraggle rock. This was not happening. Think.

Her brain attempted to make sense of what had just happened. Wolf. Man. Wolf. Man. Fuck, she was losing it. She slapped her cheeks with a shaky hand. She was not going insane. She did not imagine what just happened. Like a dealer flicking through a large deck of cards, her mind raced through other credible explanations, each time coming to the same conclusion:

Occam's razor. The simplest explanation was usually the right one.

A chill coursed through her veins, and her ears began to ring. A flurry of questions followed as she considered the ramifications of an animal transforming into a man. Snippets from the Boston Wolf Killer case reports now started to make more sense. She gulped. One of the biggest unanswered questions was how a wolf roamed the streets of the city unnoticed. She had her answer. A wolf wasn't roaming the streets. At least one person who could be an animal one moment, and a human the next roamed Boston. Her chest tightened. A terrifying thought struck her, and she pulled the blanket closer. The photo clutched in her hand burned into her brain. What if there was only one?

Murphy stepped onto the porch, and she let out a squeak. Blood pumped through her veins and her heart raced so violently she heard and felt the roar of her pulse in her eardrums.

Was Wolf, now a Man. Not just a man ... O'Neill. Frack it. Maybe she was losing her mind.

The look on Murphy's face told her he was just as shocked as she was, and that consoled her a bit. Self-preservation kicked in as he took a step toward her. She reached for her sidearm, but again her hand felt nothing but air. Crap, no gun.

"I am not going to hurt you," he said in a voice more a growl.

She looked around for a weapon or an avenue of escape. "Yeah? Well, wolf man, I'm not staying to find out."

She pushed down the panic, but she had nothing to defend herself save for a blanket, and what's more, he'd blocked both exits, effectively cutting off her escape routes. She cleared her throat. She had to know. No matter what the outcome. Was she looking not only at her partner, but at the Boston Wolf Killer? "Are you ... him?"

His head flinched back as if he'd been singed. "Fuck no!"

She tensed at the sudden venom in his tone, and he held up his hands. "I didn't mean to scare you." He slowly dropped his arms to his sides. "Like you, I'm trying to stop him."

His words sounded sincere, and she stood her ground when he took a step closer. She stared into his dark eyes. Eyes that held so much power and determination. She had been around criminals and degenerates long enough to recognize a killer when she saw one. The ebony depths of his eyes pulled her in, as if something was calling to her. No, the man standing before her was not a cold-blooded killer. He may be many things, but he was not the person she was after. Oh, he was capable of killing. Of that, she had no doubt. Something raw and primal exuded from him, but Murphy was not the Boston Wolf Killer. "But … he's just like you."

"If you mean not quite Human, then yes, we are the same." His eyes narrowed as he icily spat out his disgust at her implication. "But make no mistake, I am nothing like that cold-blooded bastard."

His bitter response left her in no doubt that the powerful man in front of her had also been wronged by her father's murderer. Her brain reengaged, and her vision cleared. She had been so focused on the implications of the change, she had missed the fact that a very impressive-looking naked man was standing less than two feet from her. His broad shoulders framed his chiseled and well-defined chest. His strong athletic arms begged her to touch them, and tapered down to hands that were definitely not afraid of hard work. If she thought the wolf was impressive, the human in front of her equally matched.

Her face grew warm. Before her train of thought embarrassed her any further, she stopped her gaze from moving down his body. She let out a deep breath and flicked her heated gaze away. "Okay, okay. I believe you. But can you please, for the love of Mike, put on some clothes?"

Murphy grunted and vanished through the door.

The moment he disappeared, she commenced pacing the length of the verandah. Wolf. Man. Animal. Human. Big Wolf. Big, naked man.

The two sides of her over-active mind did battle until a creak of the door stopped her in her tracks and Murphy, now dressed in jeans and a form-fitting T-shirt, approached her.

Without saying a word, he offered her a small object.

She glanced down at a handgun. "What's … what's this for?"

Murphy shrugged. "It might make you feel safer."

She hesitated.

He placed the gun on the table and made his way to the far side of the veranda.

Minutes went by before she broke the silence. She had so many questions desperately needing answers. She raised her face to look directly at him. "Do you change into any other animals?"

His posture did not change nor did his face give her any indication of his thoughts.

Minutes ticked by. He answered, finally. "No."

"Apart from you and him, are there more of you?"

Murphy gave a single nod.

She closed her eyes and swallowed. "Are you … an alien?"

A flicker of a smile haunted his lips. "No."

Not sure if she really wanted the answer, she asked anyway. "What are you, then?"

He sighed, uncrossed his arms, turned and leaned over the railing. He stared at the trees. "We refer to ourselves as Werewolves."

Her eyebrows rose and she briefly glanced up at the night sky. "How? I mean, that's not a full moon. Don't you only change on a full moon?"

He shook his head. "That's just a Hollywood myth."

"So you can …" She trailed off, not quite knowing the right words. "You know, change, or whatever, whenever you want?"

He nodded.

She shrugged off the blanket, walked over to him, and placed the photo on the railing. "Is that your father?"

He glanced down and stiffened slightly. "No."

"Then w-why does he look like you?" She swallowed hard, but did not look away.

He let out a long sigh. "That's because that is me." He picked up the photograph and studied it. He handed it back to her after a moment. "Like I said, he was a good man."

Her mouth fell open and her brows shot up. "But, why do you still look the same? This photo was taken over twenty years ago."

He shrugged. "We age differently."

"And you knew my father?"

His face darkened. "That's a story for another day."

She clutched the photo and blurted out her question before she could stop it. "Was he like you?"

He stood up straight and ran a hand through his short hair. "I think that's enough questions for tonight. There's a reason you and your mother were kept in the dark."

Murphy strode over to the table, picked up her car keys, and held them out to her. "You need to forget what you saw here tonight."

Like that was going to happen. He was not getting out of this that easily. Turning the photo over, she held it up and pointed to the words. "Why did he write that on the back?"

His gaze flicked over the message, and he flinched slightly. An expression of pain washed over his face, then it was gone. His hands clenched into fists. "Kaitlyn, I said that's enough. You already know too much. And there are consequences."

She took a step back. He had shut down. She could see it in his stance and the way he spoke. Despite being desperate to know more, she wasn't getting any more out of him tonight.

But he didn't say he wouldn't answer questions tomorrow.

She placed the photo in her pocket. "Fine, but you'll need to answer my questions at some point. I want answers and mark my words, you will be giving them to me."

He let out a low growl. "Be careful what you wish for. You may not like what you find."

"Well, that's up to me to decide, isn't it?"

Murphy sighed. "Unfortunately, it's out of both our hands."

"I very much doubt that."

She grabbed her keys from his hand and stormed out, muttering. Her footsteps crunched so loudly on the gravel driveway she failed to notice him trailing behind. She jumped when he spoke as she unlocked her car door.

"You do know that if you say anything about what you saw, no one will believe you."

She held her hand over her chest to keep her heart from leaping out. "Where the hell did you come from?"

His eyes bore into hers. "Maybe if you didn't walk so loudly, you might have heard me."

"I do not walk loudly. You just have noisy gravel." She scowled as she got into her car. "And, for your information, I have no intention of outing you or your little secret."

For one, he was kind of right. They'd lock her up at Belview and throw away the key.

"Fine." He leaned on the car door.

"Fine." With a flourish, she slammed the door closed and started the car. "But I want my answers."

Murphy snorted. "Humans."

He crossed his arms over his chest and watched her Prius quietly roll down the driveway. "Maybe that car's not so bad after all, at least it's quieter than you."

"I heard that."

The entire drive home, her mind kept replaying Murphy's transformation from wolf to human and the words her father had printed on the back of the image.

Nihil prius familia.

Although her Latin was a bit rusty, she was almost positive it translated to nothing before my family.

EIGHT

Can This Get Any Worse?

Bollocks.

The week started out as a mess and ended as a complete and unmitigated disaster.

"Damnú air."

Murphy swore in his native Gaelic, something he tended to do in extreme situations. And this qualified for that in spades.

Sure, he was a man of few words. Ask anyone. Actions were the standard he lived by, because conversations with others led to illusions of trust and friendship. Both of which he had in short supply, by choice more than necessity. His drive home earlier this evening gave him ample opportunity to reflect on the fiasco that began the moment she walked through the door of Doug's office, and had inadvertently continued throughout the three days since.

He trudged back to the house. This was precisely why he worked alone.

This mess was his own fault. He should have kept tabs on the family, and not been blindsided. He let out a low growl. There were a lot of things he should have done, but now no amount of wishing would make it so. He stared at the amber liquid in his glass. How many times did he need to tell them he worked alone?

So how in bollocks' name did he end up with Ryan's offspring, two detectives, and a strange woman obsessed with pink everything and out of whose mouth he only understood every third word?

His fingers curled around the crystal and squeezed. He did not want to be responsible for any other deaths. He most certainly did not want Ryan's daughter's blood on his hands. He already had enough blood on him to drown a lesser man. He emptied the remainder of the drink in a single chug. The whiskey burned as it blazed a trail down his throat.

Ryan would be proud though.

True enough. The apple did not fall far from the tree. She had her father's inane instinct and did not miss a thing. Her discovery of the ear was something even he had failed to notice. The scent from Elijah and the victim had been so overpowering, he had missed the trace scent from the other vic. Her resemblance to her father in attitude and determination was uncanny. Like picking up on him sniffing the scenes for clues. No one ever noticed, but she did. He would be impressed if not for the guilt and worry over the chance that history might repeat itself. Despite her obvious capabilities, he was still unprepared for the responsibility of a team, let alone a partner.

He swept up the bottle and headed inside. The heavy weight he had carried for years had grown heavier. He turned off the lights. Maybe sleep would bring him a few hours of peace.

Or maybe not.

He tossed and turned, then lay on his back and stared at the ceiling. How had his life gotten so complicated within such a short period? Disparate emotions, long suppressed, were surfacing and he was unsure how to process them, let alone understand what to do with his feelings.

We need to help her.

His wolf, part of the reason for his restlessness, had been chipping away at his conscience. Why his wolf was adamant about them helping the loud and headstrong Kaitlyn Quinn was beyond him.

Because you have no idea how to deal with this.

He growled at his wolf. "Just shut up, will you?"

He ran a hand through his hair. He had been in denial since the moment she was partnered with him. She wanted answers, most of which weren't his to tell. And even though he wasn't a fan of the Alliance, there were some rules he agreed with. He knew what he needed to do. His wolf knew. He just didn't want to do it.

Giving up on sleep, he rolled over and reached for his phone.

An agitated male answered. "It's four thirty in the fucking morning, this better be good."

He pinched the bridge of his nose. "Depends on your definition of good."

A slight pause then something dropped in the background.

"Murphy, is that you? How the hell are you? It's been years."

This conversation was not going to go well. "This is not a social call."

"I heard Elijah's back."

"Yeah, but that's not why I'm phoning."

"Oh?"

He had to come out and just say it. "Ryan's daughter is on the case."

A sharp intake of breath came through the other end of the phone, followed by a disapproving growl. "No. Absolutely no fucking way. You get her off it right now, or I swear on my son's grave I will end you."

He sighed. "Yeah … well that's a bit of a problem."

The panicked rustle stopped. "Why?"

"She's found out about us."

The voice on the other end of the phone erupted swiftly and without mercy.

He ran his free hand through his hair and waited for the tirade to stop. This was why he worked alone. No complications. And certainly no partner who reminded him of how dangerous it was to be around him.

Because where ever he went, death followed.

NINE

Who is the Elusive Mr. O'Neill?

Kaitlyn paced her living room. She was too wired to sleep. How could she after discovering W—. She winced. Even her brain would not say the word, let alone speak it.

Seven billion humans shared the world with another race.

She hesitated. Just how many were there? Murphy could change back and forth from wolf to human. She had seen it with her own eyes. He was a wolf one minute and a man the next. Yet, to the rest of the population he was a normal FBI agent. Check that, a grumpy FBI agent. Her pulse sped up. How many others walked around pretending to be normal people? Her eyes narrowed. The loner in apartment 3a always did act weird. Bet he was one. She chewed on her thumbnail. She needed to tell someone. But who? Murphy had not broken any federal laws. And as far as she knew, there wasn't a local law preventing people from changing from one thing to another and then back again. Otherwise RuPaul and Dame Edna Everage would have been locked up long ago.

She headed to her computer for answers. Her earlier attempt at searching for information on Murphy had revealed nothing. But maybe she would get lucky with … She grimaced, still unable to say the word in her head. After opening a browser and opening Google search, she typed in Werewolves. At least her fingers had the guts her mind didn't.

Seventy million results?

A few hundred sites later, she gave up any hope of getting accurate information from that avenue. Now that she had been exposed to the real thing, it was obvious how Murphy and his kind had remained hidden. Millions of complete and utter lunatics with conspiracy theories up the wazoo lurked on the net. They hid the real thing.

"How about this." She typed in *nihil prius familia*, the words her father had written on the back of the photo. Sure enough, her Latin was not that rusty. Nothing before family.

She rubbed her forehead. What did that mean? Were Murphy and her father related? She stared at her phone. Unable to sit still without having some way forward, she messaged him.

>How did you know my dad?

She'd almost dozed off before he responded.

<Complicated.

She rubbed her eyes and pursed her lips. "Complicated my butt."

>That's not an answer!!! Or a reference to time!!!

This time she did not need to wait long for his reply.

<Monday.

She reread the message. Before she could question him further, her phone beeped again.

<GO TO SLEEP.

Well, Mr. Grumpy was clearly in need of some shut eye. And her mind, now with a purpose and a way forward, let go of the adrenaline that had pumped through her veins. She yawned and slumped on the couch. Her body gave in to fatigue, and she fell asleep before she could make it to her bed.

By the time Monday morning rolled around, Kaitlyn was well and truly ready to get out of her apartment. She had spent her entire weekend scrolling through conspiracy sites. And if she were to believe half of them, Elvis was still alive, singing *Jailhouse Rock* to adoring fans on some outer planet in the next galaxy. Vampires were real, but people were conflicted on whether they could come out in the daylight. And to top it off, cockroaches were the most intelligent race on earth and were just waiting for humans to kill themselves off so they could have their planet back again. The way things were going, she would not discount the possibility.

But even with hours of surfing the information superhighway, she was none the wiser about the thing that Murphy was. The only common thread was his kind had been spoken about in myths and folklore in most cultures for two thousand years. That's where the similarities ended. On at least five separate occasions, she'd nearly jumped into her car and driven straight to Groton. Murphy wasn't answering any of her calls or messages, and she had so many questions. Was her father the same, and if not, had he known what Murphy was?

In turn, she ignored calls from her mom and Anika. What would she say to them? "Sorry can't talk, having a nervous breakdown. Saw a sexy naked man. Pity he's not Human."

The elevator stopped at her floor in the station, and the doors slid open. She straightened her jacket and rechecked her buttons before she exited. She needed to be emotionally ready to see Murphy. That way, she could refocus on the case and be prepared to face him when he came in. She needed to separate the case from Murphy's secret or she wouldn't get through the day in one piece.

When she walked into the office she shared with the others, she stopped short. "Fudge nuggets."

Murphy was already in and on the phone, so at least she didn't need to speak to him yet.

"Good morning," she murmured to Garcia and Saul and made her way to her desk. She avoided looking in Murphy's direction. The image of him as he changed form flashed through her mind, and her face grew hot.

She threw a quick glance in his direction. As on Friday, he wore a perfectly fitted suit. She struggled to erase the memory of what he looked like underneath the suit. The more she attempted to forget it, the more vivid the images became. The man was sex on legs. She would have to be blind not to recognize his physical appeal. The warm flush rushed from her cheeks and through her body. Her neck was likely scarlet and could possibly fry an egg.

She cleared her throat and turned on her computer. She needed a distraction and smiled at Saul, who was flipping through a stack of holiday brochures. "Good weekend?"

"So-so." Saul pushed a half-eaten box of donuts across the table. "You want?"

"No, thanks. I've already eaten." She nodded at the pamphlet in his hand. "Going somewhere?"

Saul grimaced. "Mildred's on a mission. She's determined we're going on a trip to celebrate my retirement." He snorted. "I have to read all this crap and decide which trip. I don't know what the point is, though. When I pick one, she'll only ignore it, and we'll end up going on the one she's already chosen."

She couldn't help the laugh that tumbled out. Saul's expression said he was caught between a rock and a hard place.

Garcia yawned, folded the newspaper he had been reading, and tossed it onto the table.

Saul tsk-tsked and glanced over his Carnival Cruises brochure. "You been moonlighting again?"

"Yeah, didn't get in till four-thirty this morning."

Saul buried his nose in his pamphlet. "Well, that's what happens when you go out on raids with organized crime. No sleep."

She raised a brow. "Are you leading a double life?"

Garcia laughed. "I wish. There was a raid on a suspected arms shipment, and they needed extra hands, so I volunteered."

"Successful?"

Garcia snorted. "Nope. Complete clusterfuck. Somehow, they'd been tipped off, and by the time we turned up, the warehouse was empty."

Saul frowned and flicked his pamphlet. "There's been a lot of that lately."

She had heard the same thing from colleagues who worked organized crime cases at the bureau. "The way I hear it, over the past couple of years we've had to redefine what we know about the organization."

Garcia nodded slowly. "With Gionellii, Di Nunzio, Manocchio, and Rossetti now either behind bars or in a coffin, we thought we had cut them off at the knees. Di Nunzio was the sixth consecutive head of the New England Mafia to be charged and all his predecessors were convicted. When Gionellii Junior got ill, we thought that would be the end of them."

"I told you at the time, cut off the head of the snake and it'll replicate like breading rabbits," Saul said.

"What I don't understand is how that's possible? Their control has been diminishing over the years, not increasing," she said.

Saul threw all the brochures in the bin, and his gaze flicked upward. "Please don't get him started."

Garcia leaned forward in his chair. "Whoever is the new don has reorganized the entire operation into cells. They are mimicking terrorist organizations. We're struggling to even get a picture of who the captains and lieutenants are, let alone who the don is. And we haven't seen a don hold as much power since Patriarca. They're gaining a phenomenal grip on both the illegal drug market and racketeering."

She raised both brows. "You sound as though you admire him."

Saul laughed. "Ahh, my young partner here has been trying to get into that division for years. Seems to think it's the quickest way to earn his lieutenant's bar. But as they keep downsizing the team, he's got as much chance of getting in as I have of having a peaceful retirement."

Garcia rubbed his hands together. "But that's all changing, I hear they have no choice but to grow the team again. And when they do, I'm in. After all, I'm called in for most of their major busts as an extra resource." Garcia leaned back on his chair. "Why wouldn't they come to me first?"

They all jumped when Murphy's voice boomed across the room. "What you do on your own time is your own business, but if I get one inkling that it's interfering with this case, I'll drop you faster than you can say lieutenant."

Garcia sat up straight and grimaced. "Sorry boss, didn't mean anything by it. We were just talking."

Murphy ignored the apology and stood up. "How's the warrant going?"

"Just waiting for court to open. We found a judge who will sign it," Garcia said.

Murphy stared at Garcia and Saul. "What are you still doing here, then?"

Garcia darted a glanced at Saul. "Err, court's not due to open for an hour and a half."

Murphy's expression grew thunderous, and Garcia jumped up and reached for his coat. "Or we could just wait outside the judge's door."

She groaned inwardly. With Saul and Garcia gone, she'd be alone with Murphy. What the hell would she say to him? Hi, how was your weekend? Did you catch any stray rabbits?

Murphy grabbed his keys and headed for the door. "Let's go."

Her leg fidgeted, and she thrust her hand down to stop it. "Where are we going?"

"Medical Examiner, she's finished the autopsy."

Murphy's phone rang. The conversation was one-sided, and he remained silent through most of it.

When he ended the call, he frowned. "Change of plans."

"Why, what's happened?"

Murphy looked her dead in the eyes, and her blood ran cold. "They found another victim."

<u>TEN</u>

Ghost of Christmas Past

The day passed in a blood-soaked blur.

Late in the afternoon, they returned to police headquarters. Kaitlyn sat down at her desk and stared at her monitor. She needed to unscramble her thoughts. She shivered involuntarily. The scene, very much like the previous one, would have her rechecking her locks for many nights to come.

Garcia threw himself into his chair. "Am never going to get used to that."

Saul, who held two cans of coke, threw one to Garcia. "You wanted on the case." He pulled open the tab and shook his head from side to side. "Retirement can't come soon enough."

"I still can't work out how the limbs are separated like that. No tool marks and there's no way an animal did it." Garcia sipped on his coke. "Two of them must be working together."

She knew better, but she couldn't come out and say it. Now that she was aware of the nature of the thing carrying out the macabre crimes, questions buzzed through her head, but she couldn't voice any of them. How would the team react if she suddenly asked Murphy whether their unsub arrived at the scene looking like a human or if he was already in wolf form? And if he was in wolf form, where did he keep his knife or clothes for that matter?

She rubbed her aching temples. Stop it Kaitlyn, you're losing it.

She sighed. Her only relief for the day? The conversation with Murphy throughout the day was limited to work-related matters. He was just as grumpy and gruff as ever. Which was perfect, because it meant she could focus on the work and pay proper attention to the scene. Too many cases had gone belly-up over the years when agents missed vital clues.

Murphy walked in just as she received a skype call. She pressed accept and Anika's face took up the entire screen. She gave her kooky friend a weary smile. "The evidence is on its way. It took the team a little longer than expected to bag and tag."

"No worries. Is Murphy with you?" Anika smile grew and she wiggled in her chair. "Oh, there you are."

She glanced up to discover Murphy standing directly behind her. Her heart leapt to her throat. Blue Cheese. Someone give the man a bell.

Anika leaned forward and dropped her voice. "I got the first set you sent through and did a rush job, just like you asked. You were right, a different blood group." Her brows furrowed together. "How did you know? The fingers were so mangled up there was no way to tell the difference. But you'll never guess the blood type, it can't be a coincidence. Maggie is grabbing the stuff for me to compare." She sat back and clapped her hands together. "This is so exciting. I'm just so—"

She jumped when Murphy cut Anika off with a growl. "Anika."

Anika shuffled in her chair and her face reddened. "Sorry. I know I can get a bit carried away."

When Garcia snorted, she threw him a glare. "The finger," she said to Anika, "who does it belong to?"

Anika looked ready to burst. "Haladlo, I think. Same blood type, B positive. Which only accounts for nine percent of the population. And he's the only B positive victim. I'll know for sure when I run a comparison."

"What about Haladlo's missing ear?" Saul said. "Are we sure both ears on today's vic belong to him?"

Murphy nodded. "Yes." He rubbed his jaw. "Anika, once you have confirmation, let me know. And we need a positive ID on today's vic. It's a long shot, but run his DNA through the system."

"On it."

Hopefully, that avenue would prove productive, otherwise identifying the victim would be a challenge. The man's face was disfigured beyond recognition, and his fingers were sliced from his hands, then mutilated.

Murphy printed off an image from the scene and pinned it to the wall along with the others. "The ME is going to fast track a determination of time of death. Once we have it, we need to—"

The duty sergeant knocked and stepped in the room. "Which one of you is Quinn?"

Garcia and Saul pointed at her.

"This arrived for you today." He dumped a box on her desk and threw down a single gift wrapped rose. "In case you hadn't noticed, this is not the post office, nor is it a dating service." With that, he turned and stomped out the door.

Saul sniffed. "Brown always was a frickin' gump."

Garcia pointed to her packages. "If it's your birthday, the rule is you're buying us drinks after work." He grinned and smoothed down his tie. "And I only drink top shelf."

She stared at the blood red rose, and a knot formed in her stomach. No, Kaitlyn, stop being paranoid. She reached for the envelope tucked into the rose and shook her head. "My birthday is not for months."

She opened the envelope and frowned. Instead of the expected card, it contained a folded slip of paper. The hair on her nape and arms rose, and the knot was back with a vengeance as she read the card. With each word, her heartbeat increased, to the point where it seemed ready to explode through her chest.

My Dear Caitlin,

What lies behind the shield that obscures the window to your soul? It is a question I have been asking since I first laid eyes on you. I am intrigued. Is it as black as your partner's, or is it as bright as your father's?

I think red will suit you well. Red is the color of pleasure, of life, and of passion.

Just the thought of you beneath me as I worship your delicate skin has my body on fire. The kiss of my blade as it caresses your face, your neck, and your bountiful bosom will provide you with such ecstasy you will forget all who came before me. As your life blood rolls from your nakedness to paint the earth below, and we entangle like new vines at night, I will forever have the satisfaction of knowing I will be your last.

The thrill of the chase will only be surpassed by the pleasure and passion of the catching. Yes, I think red will suit you well.

Until we meet, this gift is for you.

E.

Her hands began to shake and the room swirled. Someone was playing a cruel joke. They must be.

Murphy's hands wrapped around hers to steady them. "Are you alright? What's happened?"

She took a shaky breath. A psycho butcher serial killer, non-Human, sadist was taunting her, that's what happened. They were trained for this sort of thing. Only, she was finding it difficult to concentrate. They had not covered how to deal with W—non-Human stalking at Quantico.

She pulled her hands from his and held out the letter. "Y-you'd better read it."

Murphy's expression grew thunderous as he read the message. Even Garcia, who had come over, took a few steps back. A vein in Murphy's neck bulged, and his jaw clenched. She flinched when a low growl rumbled deep in his chest.

He looked at the box, and his eyes narrowed. "Garcia, get me some gloves and a box cutter."

Garcia quickly complied.

Saul let out a whistle as he read the letter. "You got a love letter. I've heard 'bout these sort a things. Never seen it with my own eyes till now." He held it out to Garcia. "And I ain't never seen handwriting like that, except on those fancy schmancy wedding invitations."

Murphy cut through the tape that held the lid in place.

"You sure you should be doing that?" Garcia said. "It could be a bomb."

She moved closer. There was no danger of it being a bomb. X-ray screening in the building would have detected it. Besides he had other plans for her. Her stomach churned. She didn't want to think about the greater implications of the letter right now. The contents of the box should be her focus. She glanced at Saul and Garcia, who had both edged closer.

Murphy flipped the flaps open and pulled out the polystyrene to reveal …

She frowned. A jar?

Murphy reached in and gently pulled out the glass jar before setting it down on the table.

"Now that's fucked up."

She had to agree with Saul. The jar was full of a clear liquid. Floating in the liquid was a severed ear.

She gulped. She would have preferred jewelry.

Murphy crossed his arms over his chest. "You're off the case. No discussion."

She counted to ten. Her blood pressure was already shooting for the sky, but she wasn't backing down. This was her case, and he had no right to remove her from it just because of one measly letter. "I'm staying."

Murphy ran a hand through his hair. "It's too dangerous. You're in his crosshairs now. I will not risk it."

Hands on her hips, she glared at him. "It's not your risk, it's mine. Besides, the package was redirected from the FBI field office, and he spelt my name the same way Boston 25 News did the other night. They got it wrong and so did he."

"Just because he doesn't know where you are right now, doesn't mean he won't be looking for you."

A part of her wanted to flee, but she had to stand firm. If she didn't, she wouldn't be able to continue as an FBI agent. Danger went with the territory. She sighed. "I'm prepared to take that risk. We just need to make sure we get to him before he gets to us."

Murphy's eyes bore a hole through her forehead, and she broke out in a sweat under the pressure of his gaze. Finally, his shoulders relaxed, and he grunted before pulling out his phone and heading for the door.

She followed him. "What are you doing?" What if he was going over her head to get her removed?

"Getting you protection. If you're staying on the case, you're going to need it."

"Protection? What do you mean by protection? I can protect myself, thank you very much." She squinted at him. "Just who are you phoning?"

Murphy ignored her.

She crossed her arms over her chest. "What is it with you and answering questions? You still haven't answered the ones from Friday."

He grunted. "I told you already. I can't."

"Can't or won't?"

"Damnú air." He clenched his jaw and spoke into the phone. "No. Not you. Hold on." Murphy turned to her and let out a low growl. "It's not my place to give you the answers."

"If it's not yours, then whose is it? And when am I going to get them?"

"Tonight."

She halted in her tracks. An actual timeframe was the last thing she had expected.

Pacing her living room that night, she had almost given up hope he would keep his word when her doorbell rang. She stormed to the door and yanked it open. "It's about fricken ti—" Her voice caught as she stared at the man on her doorstep. Her eyes widened, her throat constricted, and she brought a hand up to her mouth to stop a stunned cry. "No, it's not possible. It can't be."

She shook her head and clutched her stomach with her free hand. Very little had shocked her over the years, but within a few short days her understanding of the world had been shattered not once, but now twice. She stared at the man standing in her doorway. His brown eyes were familiar and yet unfamiliar.

His expression was grim. "I'm guessing you know who I am?"

Unable to move, blink, or think for that matter, she was rooted to the spot. A hard lump grew and consumed her throat. This wasn't possible. A movement from behind the man caught her eye. Murphy stood a short way off. She anchored her gaze to him. If she ignored this other person, she might be able to hold on to her sanity.

Her lungs, unable to survive much longer without air, forced her to breathe in a rush. Blood circulated throughout her body, and warmth returned to her face. She shook her hands as if casting off water. "I … I need a drink."

She turned and headed for the kitchen, leaving the two men standing in the doorway. She reached for a glass and a bottle, but her hands were shaking so much she couldn't uncork the wine.

Someone gently removed the bottle opener from her grip. He reached out and lightly squeezed her hand. "Here, let me."

Her eyes locked onto his face. In place of his ever-present scowl was a gentle, encouraging smile. For once, she didn't waver and look away. His intense, dark eyes were almost comforting.

A shuffle from the living area burst her comfort bubble. She tore her gaze away from Murphy and watched as the other man wandered the living area, picking up and studying some of the photos lying around. She closed her eyes and turned back to Murphy. She was not ready to face that man just yet.

Murphy handed her the glass of wine. "Here."

She grabbed the glass and drank the contents in one long gulp. She closed her eyes again, then slowly opened them and looked straight at Murphy. He was pouring her a second glass. She lowered her voice. "Is he still here?"

"Yes, he is," said the man she couldn't look at.

He was standing by the bookshelf inspecting her framed photos.

Murphy's firm hand rested on the small of her back and guided her across the room. "I think you had better sit."

She did as instructed but reached for Murphy's hand. When she sat, he followed suit, and she held on to him like a lifeline.

The man smiled at her. "So you recognize me?"

She nodded. "Uh ... you're my ... my ..." She couldn't get the words out.

He cleared his throat. "I think the word you are looking for is grandfather."

The man standing larger than life, less than four feet away, was the exact same man as the one in the photo on the bookshelf.

She frowned. "I don't understand, you're supposed to be dead."

Her brain reengaged, and she sucked in a deep breath. She turned to Murphy, frowned, and lurched her hand away. "Please don't tell me ghosts are real, too?"

Murphy chuckled. "Joshua is very much alive."

The realization hit her hard. "Oh ... Oh. That—that means he's a ... you know ... like you."

Murphy nodded confirmation.

Joshua snorted. "He's in the room, you know."

She turned to face Joshua. Her grandfather. Her father's father. How was this possible? He only looked a few years older than her. "Does that mean my father was like you?"

Joshua sat down on the couch opposite. "No, sorry Katy, he was Human."

She took another sip of wine to allow her thoughts to unscramble. "How is it that you and Murphy are the same, but your son—my father—wasn't? Why, why did everyone think you were dead? And why are you here now?" She sat up in her chair. "Does this have to do with the killer we're after? I know he's one of you. Just how many of you are there, anyway?"

Joshua raised his hands. "Perhaps I should tell you a little about myself first, and then you can ask questions."

He raised his eyebrows at her, and she nodded.

"How much has Murphy told you about us?"

She threw an accusing glance at Murphy. "He's been an absolute fountain of knowledge. He's told me nothing."

Joshua sighed and rubbed his forehead. "Well, before I begin, I need you to understand. As much as it has pained me over the years, you were never supposed to learn about us."

She frowned. "But why?"

"For your own safety, as well as ours." He hesitated, and his light brown eyes darted toward Murphy. "As you've discovered, there are some of us that can change back and forth from wolf to Human. Across time, we've kept our existence a secret from Humans."

"Why?"

He smiled, and a sharp emotion punched her gut. He had the same warm and gentle smile as her father.

"You were always a curious one. Always wanting answers." He shook his head and a sad expression fell across his face. "We've discovered, all too tragically, what happens when Humans find out about us."

Now that she was recovering from the initial shock, she looked closer. He shared many features with her father. His hair was just as brown and thick. Something she would never have guessed since as the peaked cap in the photo on the shelf hid it from view. Unlike her father, his jaw was square, and there was a light dusting of whiskers across it, which she guessed was normally kept clean shaven.

Joshua settled back in his chair. "In the Middle Ages, Werewolf packs were caught up in the religious persecutions raging across Europe. Those pogroms decimated the packs. We needed to do something before we became extinct. In the mid-1800s, a few Werewolf communities who were living in Europe and England banded together and travelled to the New World. When we arrived, we migrated west. You have to understand, back then very few Europeans had settled in the land beyond the Mississippi. The farther west we travelled, the harsher the frontier, but that was perfect for us. We were not afraid of hard work, and the isolation from other settlers was just what we needed."

"So you were pioneers?"

Joshua chuckled. "You could say that. Like most others at the time, we abandoned our homelands in hope of a better and more peaceful life here. Once we reached the Missouri Territory, the packs disbursed. Some headed to Oregon Country, others moved across the Spanish Treaty line."

Her mind was spinning. This American history was not taught in school. "But it was so dangerous back then. What about the local Native American tribes? Weren't they attacking every wagon train that came through?"

Joshua shook his head. "No. The books and newspapers back then skewed reality. In the early days, they pretty much left everyone alone. I heard tales about them helping to pull out stuck wagons, rescue drowning settlers, and even rounding up lost cattle. It wasn't until their way of life was under threat that the violence started."

"How did you not get caught over the years? Didn't some of you eventually just say screw it, lets out ourselves. It's getting too hard to hide."

Joshua shifted positions. "Before we separated, the packs realized the truce and joint leadership that held us together for the migration proved we would be more powerful together than apart, and the Alliance was formed. This council still serves as our governing body."

He paused, and she waited for him to continue. This version of events was a lot to take in.

Joshua rubbed his jaw. "The main council is made up of the Alphas from each of the original packs. As new packs were created over time, they aligned themselves with the Alliance. They were afforded the same protection and rights as the other member packs, and they also must abide by the rules. A great deal of change was implemented, but many of the old laws from Europe were brought across with us. The main rule, the one that all packs abide by, centers around the need to be invisible."

She leaned forward. "I can't believe that everyone toes that line."

Joshua nodded. "As with the Human population, not everyone is happy with the way things are done. We have troublemakers and malcontents as much as you do. Often their actions spill over into the Human world causing problems, including exposure.

"Daniel Locke is the Alliance's alpha who is in charge of ensuring the protection and security of all the Werewolves in North America. He quickly learned the best way to find out if a Werewolf was causing trouble was to have other Werewolves in frontline law enforcement."

She rested her head on the back of the couch and fixated on the ceiling. Her chest tightened as the ramifications of his revelations hit her hard. "So, you weren't really trying to protect the people of Boston. You were only in it to look after yourselves."

He shook his head. "No, Katy. We do better than you realize. While we keep an eye on the Werewolf population, we equally serve and protect the Humans under our charge. We consider it a great honor to serve our people, and yours."

"How does my dad fit into all this?"

"I had already been in the Boston PD for over ten years when I met your grandmother. One thing led to another, and one day she announced she was pregnant. Unlike many of my kind caught in that situation, I made the decision to marry her even though she wasn't my true mate. I couldn't bring myself to abandon my unborn child or allow him or her to grow up with the stigma of having an unwed mother. Times were different back then."

He rested his arms on his knees and stared at the ground. Sorrow etched his features. He cleared his throat and continued. "Just after your father's tenth birthday, Sally was killed in a hit-and-run. It devastated him. And in my own way, I grieved, too. While she was not my mate, I grew to love her. Around this time people were starting to talk. I'd been with the Boston PD for nearly twenty years and colleagues were noticing I hadn't aged. They were beginning to ask questions. I had already stayed in one place longer than I was supposed to, so I resigned and took Ryan back to Tudor Falls. That was when he found out what I was."

Joshua smiled sadly. "It's amazing what a child will accept unconditionally, and my pack accepted him wholeheartedly, even though he was not a Werewolf. He spent the next few years surrounded by family. Alpha Locke found me a post at the local sheriff's department so I could be close to my son, and Ryan grew up knowing who and what his father was."

Murphy stood, and a flash of panic shot through her. He wasn't leaving, was he? Relief flooded her mind when he simply picked up her empty glass and wandered into the kitchen. For some reason, he had become her anchor in all this mess. He might be many things, but she trusted him. And if she were to survive this reunion, she needed him. But her mind refused to delve into the deeper reasons why, so she focused on Joshua.

Joshua's voice lowered, snagging on a deep sadness. "Your father was the joy in my life. I treasured each and every day I had with him, despite knowing we were on borrowed time with our ageing difference."

He paused and studied a spot on the carpet. "Ryan wanted to play his part, and understanding the number of years we were able to be posted to a city was limited, he decided to join the police force. His reasoning was that he could be our eyes and ears much longer than a Werewolf was able."

Joshua smiled as he glanced across at her. "I can't tell you how proud I was the day he graduated from the police academy." He paused, and his fleeting smile disappeared again. "In order to protect him, we needed to fake my death in the Human world, but that meant we would no longer be able to spend time together, and I couldn't return to Boston on the off-chance of being recognized."

"So you never saw him again?"

"No, I didn't say that. Once a month, Ryan and I would go on a fishing trip." He chortled as he shook his head. "The first few years I don't think those rods were used once. We spent the entire weekend catching up. Every now and then, one of Ryan's friends from the pack would join us, too."

Joshua leaned forward on the couch. "I'll never forget the day he phoned to tell me Vivian was pregnant. He loved your mother so very much. And you, you were such a beautiful baby."

She arched an eyebrow. "How would you know that?"

Joshua frowned. "Do you seriously think I would miss the birth of my own grandchild?" His eyes shone with unshed tears. "I was there the day you were born. My, the lungs on you. You made sure the nurses knew you had arrived."

Murphy placed a topped-up glass of wine in front of her and handed Joshua a beer. "Nothing has changed much since," he said.

Joshua stood up and walked over to the bookcase. "Once you were old enough, Ryan brought you along on our fishing weekends. As far as Vivian was concerned, that was his monthly father-daughter bonding. For me, well, they were some of the happiest moments of my life."

She frowned. "I don't understand. How could it be happy for you? You weren't there."

He grinned and reached for the framed child's drawing. "Oh, but I was."

When the penny dropped, she jerked back on the couch. "Princess? You were Princess?"

Murphy smirked. "That one kills me every time."

Her head was buzzing. The stray dog she'd played with as a child was her grandfather?

Joshua picked up the framed photo of her father. "The day your father died ..." His voice broke, and his head dropped as he silently shook.

Joshua turned back to her and her chest grew heavy at the anguish and hurt in his eyes.

"I couldn't even pay my last respects. I had to say goodbye to my only child from the other side of the cemetery. I knew I would only ever have a few years with him. I knew we were on borrowed time compared to what we'd have if he were a Werewolf. I just, I didn't realize how short it would be."

Joshua placed the photo of his son back on the shelf. His spine stiffened, and he balled one of his fists by his side. "Elijah took my only son from me. I went through it once, and I will not allow it to happen again."

His voice was firm and resolute. He strode across the room and crouched in front of her so that they were eye-to-eye. "Please remove yourself from the case, and let Murphy deal with it. You were never supposed to know about us. And you certainly were never supposed to be on that bastard's radar." His voice was now angry, demanding.

She stared at Joshua, his brown eyes begging her to comply with his wishes. Her mind had been thrust into turmoil the moment he stepped foot in the door. Now, it escalated into mania. But something in her demanded she hold back.

"No."

Joshua's brows shot up, and he rose from his crouching position. "No?"

"No."

She stood and faced him head on. "My father was a good man. Or so I've heard from my mother, his old colleagues, the people he knew, and now you." She couldn't keep the bitterness out of her voice. "But I never got the chance to learn that for myself. This … this butcher you call Elijah, he took him from me, from us. I have a chance to bring him to justice, and I am going to do it."

Putting some distance between them, her fists pulsed with anger. "You have no right to tell me what to do just because you turn up claiming to be my grandfather."

A thick, unpalatable silence descended on the room.

Joshua reached out to her, but she took a step back.

He sighed. "Look, I realize you're angry, and you have a right to be. But I only want what's best for you. I want you to be safe. And right now, you are not safe from those who would harm you because you are aware of our secret. And you are definitely not safe from Elijah. That letter he sent should tell you that, at least."

She crossed her arms over her chest. "That's my call to make, don't you think?"

Murphy stepped in. His voice boomed across the room, forcing Joshua and her to stop in their tracks. "Okay, that's enough both of you."

He walked over and laid a hand on Joshua's shoulder. "I think Kaitlyn has had enough this evening without you pushing your agenda."

He turned to her. "But don't you try to over analyze it. Joshua is your grandfather, you have my word on that. You need to hear him out, but not any more tonight."

She was about to respond when Murphy cut her off. "I'd advise you not to argue with me on this one. You will lose."

His voice held enough danger and forcefulness that she wisely kept quiet.

Murphy ran his fingers through his hair before addressing them both. "Josh, tomorrow Kaitlyn and I are going to have a chat with some of Elijah's old acquaintances. You can join us. Kaitlyn, this will give your grandfather a chance to speak with you further. You need to hear what he has to say, and you need to understand this situation is not safe for you."

Joshua sent a look of apology in her direction and cleared his throat. "I appreciate this is going to sound strange, but before I go, I have a small request."

She cocked her head. "What is it?"

"It … it has been twenty years since I hugged my grandchild," he said haltingly. "I was hoping I wouldn't need to go another day without, without holding her again."

She wasn't sure whether it was the way the words were said, or the haunted way his eyes met hers, but in that moment she silently broke, and quickly closed the distance between them. Joshua held her in a bear hug. One that left her without a doubt that he was who he said he was.

As she stood, her face resting on his chest, her body in his large and comforting embrace, a missing piece of her fit back into place. The feeling was both strange and familiar, and it settled as though it had been there before.

Tears were welling in his eyes when she stepped back. The same tears as in her own eyes.

"I'll see you tomorrow." He placed a gentle kiss on her forehead and headed for the door. "Make sure you lock up tight."

A moment later, she was left standing in the middle of her living room. Not really sure of what to think, do, or say. She glanced over at the drawing she'd made so very long ago. No wonder her dad always chuckled when she called the dog Princess.

ELEVEN

Is That a Dagger I See Before Me?

Elijah traced his blade across the delicate skin on his prey's neck. Humans were pathetic. This one, particularly so. He clenched his teeth together. While he enjoyed the chase, he longed for the kill. His blade moved lower. But no, it was too soon. He needed to restrain his inner needs.

"Where is he?"

The sniveling man struggled against his restraints. Blood mixed with his spittle as he struggled to get the words out. "I-I-I've already told you, I don't know."

He pressed his blade with enough force to slice through to muscle. The fresh aroma of blood sent a wave of desire coursing through his veins as he savored the man's screams. This must be what heaven felt like. He moved his blade half an inch lower and made another incision. A mirror of the one before, and the one before that. Wounds lined up along his prey's chest like rungs on a ladder.

He frowned. What was the Human's name again? Sven? Glenn? No, Ben. That was it. Ben.

He circled Ben and admired his handiwork. The thick plastic cable ties that secured Ben's arms above his head cut deep into his skin, drawing blood and adding further peaks to the pain. Four hours of delicious pain.

He made a vertical slice into the canvas on Ben's back. His mouth split into a grin as the razor-sharp knife continued its languishing path downwards. The skin separated, leaving raw tissue and sinew exposed. Blood seeped from the wound and flowed behind the metallic blade. The lacerations were even and uniform on both front and back. His slashes were deep enough to allow sufficient loss of blood, but shallow enough to allow him a fun time with his new play thing.

Yes, he was a true artist.

"Tell me how to find Ambrose Giordano."

This time, Elijah did not wait for an answer before he sliced again.

A blood curdling scream tore from Ben's throat as the knife cut deeper into an existing wound.

He sniffed, the sharp aroma of urine threatened to overpower the sweet bouquet of metallic blood.

Ben dropped his chin to his chest, his body wracked with sobs. He murmured an almost inaudible plea for mercy.

His voice as cold as ice, he asked again, "Where is he?"

He brought the knife up to Ben's eye and grinned. Oh, yes. He'd found the soft Human's weak spot.

Ben clamped his lids closed and screamed. "No. No, please don't. I don't know."

Elijah forced Ben's eye open and brought the sharp tip of the knife to rest delicately on his lower lid. "Did you know that eyeballs pop like grapes when you push a blade into them?"

Ben's eyes widened as the knife continued to dance and weave across his skin. "N-no one knows. W-we only know who we report to, I swear."

By the time he finished slicing into the man's face, Ben's voice was hoarse, and he was unable to draw the strength to struggle or even moan.

A bit more resistance would sweeten his victory. His prey was giving up too easily. "Who do you report to?"

The only response was the labored breathing of his victim.

"I said who do you report to?"

The name came out in a mumble. Ben had lost too much blood to speak clearly.

Elijah smirked. "And where can I find this Al?"

Again, Ben provided the required information without hesitation.

He yawned. Now that he had the details, he was bored. Just as well, really, with this much blood loss, he hadn't much play time left. His wolf wanted his share of the fun, and he wasn't prepared to wait any longer.

He cut the restraints and Ben fell to the floor, too weak to hold his own weight.

He slowly disrobed and allowed his wolf to take control. Oh, how his wolf loved to watch the life drain out of their prey's eyes. And who was he to stand in the way of such a noble desire?

He did not break eye contact with Ben the entire shift. The blood curdling scream from Ben's lips sent a rush of adrenaline throughout his wolf's body.

Perhaps we should play a little more? he said to his wolf.

TWELVE

The Burden of Knowledge

Kaitlyn checked her watch. So much for being early.

She willed the elevator to speed up. She had awakened before dawn in a cold sweat. Her dreams were so vivid. And while the nightmarish parts were chilling, they weren't wholly unexpected given they had been with her since childhood. This time, however, she had a name to give to the horror in her nightmares.

Elijah. His name on her tongue left a bitter, twisted taste.

But the parts of her dream that weren't so nightmarish … Murphy. Her face grew hot as sensual images from her dreams pushed through. What was her brain up to? In a few short days, her life had been turned upside down. Her new partner had turned from a wolf into a man in front of her disbelieving eyes. She met her long-dead grandfather who wasn't dead at all, and now she was tracking down her father's killer with the help of a … a …

She grit her teeth together. God. Why couldn't she say the word aloud?

One more try. She blurted out the first word that popped into her head. "Pioneer."

That would have to do until she overcame her mental block. This whole situation was frying her brains. If she never met another Pioneer, it would be too soon.

The elevator doors whooshed open and before she stepped out, Murphy stepped in, jabbed the ground floor button, then the subbasement button. Without looking at her, he turned and waited for the doors to close. "Joshua's waiting outside. I'll bring the car up."

She raised a brow. "Good morning to you, too."

He glanced at her sideways. "Why are you late?"

She stared at the shiny metal doors. She didn't dare look at him. When she managed to fall asleep again, Murphy had taken up most of her dreams. Well, technically, she and Murphy had taken center stage. She counted to ten. It wouldn't do to have hot flushes next to the subject of her erotic dreams. Or her partner, for that matter. When she got to seven, she pressed her lips together and bit the inside of her cheek. Why in God's name did she have those sorts of dreams about Murphy of all guys? He was grumpy, non-talkative, and to top it off, a Pioneer. Sure, he was easy on the eye, and the body that hid under his dark suits was perfection, but really?

Frack it. She had to get her mind out of the gutter.

When the elevator pinged and the doors opened, she quickly strode through the lobby and out the main doors. Joshua was leaning against one of the brick columns, a warm smile on his face as he watched her approach. Dressed in jeans, T-shirt, and a leather jacket, he looked amazingly modern and cool. How the hell could that be her grandfather? Grandfathers were old. And wrinkled. With dentures or at least hearing aids.

He enveloped her in a bear hug. "Katy, honey, how are you this morning?"

"Uh, fine," she said as she pulled away. "To be honest, I'm still a little stunned."

"It's to be expected."

They both jumped when Murphy pulled up in his Cadillac and blared the horn.

"I suspect that means he wants us to get in," Joshua whispered loudly as he held the door open for her to get in the back seat.

When they pulled onto the road, she leaned forward. "I'm assuming we're going to see Elijah's associate?"

Her eyes met Murphy's as he glanced through the rearview mirror. He nodded.

Joshua rested an arm on the middle console. "If Elijah's contacted anyone, it will be him. They originated from the same pack in Romania."

Curiosity got the better of her. "How old are you, exactly?"

Joshua laughed and shook his head. "I was wondering how long it would take for you to ask that one." He turned in his seat to face her. "Let me see. I think I'm around two hundred, give or take a few years."

Her head jerked back as she gasped. "You've got to be kidding me. I would have guessed late thirties."

Joshua smiled at her outburst. "Werewolves age at the same rate as Humans until our bodies and wolves mature. Typically, we can reach maturity anywhere from our early to mid-twenties. From that point onward, we age much slower. For every ten years, we age around one."

"Murphy, does that mean you're two hundred, too?"

Murphy's shoulders stiffened. "I am nowhere near as old as your grandfather."

She glanced at Joshua, a grin on her face. So, she could ruffle him. She sat back in her seat. "Oh, I'm sorry, I didn't realize age was such a touchy subject."

Murphy mumbled something she couldn't make out.

She leaned forward again. "Sorry, were you talking to me?"

He glanced through the rearview mirror. "Eighteen sixty-three."

She raised an eyebrow.

"That's when I was born. Eighteen sixty-three."

She stifled a smirk.

Murphy stopped the car outside a pawn shop. "You two stay here. I need to brief Daniel's men."

She glared at Murphy's retreating back. "I do not need protection."

Joshua sighed. "That's a matter of opinion."

"Don't you start."

They sat in silence, each staring at the shop door Murphy had disappeared through.

Silent maybe, but her brain was boiling. She was livid with both of them. No matter how much she protested, they were both adamant someone would watch her around the clock.

"Don't be so hard on him," Joshua said.

"Pardon?" After all the shit Murphy had given her, she couldn't quite believe what she was hearing.

"Murphy. This is difficult for him. Don't take what he says and how he acts to heart. There is more to this for him than you know."

She frowned. Something in the way Joshua was talking made her lean forward.

Joshua gazed out the window. "The three of us have something in common. Elijah. He took someone precious from each of us. You lost a father, I a son." His voice dropped low and he sighed. "And about forty-five years ago, Elijah killed Murphy's mate. Not only that, but he butchered one of the local deputies. The deputy was Murphy's partner. He's been seeking revenge ever since."

Her heart constricted. She had no idea. Not that she would. Murphy was not exactly a fount of information at the best of times. The family dynamics of the wolves she had studied at the Wolf Sanctuary in Ipswich came back to her. "A mate is like a spouse?"

"Yes. And no. Unlike Humans, Wolves, once mated, are monogamous for life. Our mate, if we are lucky enough to find them, is our other half. Our soul mate, if you will. The person that both our human and wolf half agree we cannot live without. The person who will make our life complete. We are with our mates forever."

The sadness reflected in his every word had her reaching out and squeezing his shoulder gently.

"Mates who have been together for a few hundred years are unable to live without the other. Often if one dies, the other will, too," he said.

"What if they haven't been together that long?"

"It depends on their inner strength. The remaining Werewolf will recover slowly over time or go mad with the loss. Those poor souls who go mad often leave their packs and become rogue."

"Do they ever find another mate?"

"Not typically. However, it has been known to happen on rare occasions."

Her brows furrowed together, recalling the conversation from the previous evening. "My grandmother Sally wasn't your mate?"

He shook his head.

"Do you have one now?"

He shook his head again. "Though to be honest, I don't know. I had hoped by now, if she was out there, I would have found her. But sometimes things don't turn out the way we expect."

Joshua fell quiet and she detected his hesitation.

"You should know that I have known Murphy his entire life. Your father and Murphy were friends. When I moved back to the pack with Ryan after Sally died, Ryan and Murphy bonded in their grief. That was only a few months after Elijah passed through town on a killing spree."

He rubbed the back of his neck. "None of us know how, but my child and Murphy drew a measure of strength from each other. By the time Ryan reached adulthood, they were friends, brothers, even. Murphy had retreated into himself, and no one but Ryan could get through to him."

Joshua's voice dropped. "Ryan was the one who alerted Murphy when Elijah turned up in Boston twenty years ago. You've probably surmised by now they worked the case together. But what you don't know is that after Ryan died, Murphy vowed he would never work with another partner."

She looked down to discover her fingers digging into her thighs. Her throat ached, and it wouldn't take much for her to break down. "Why?"

Joshua looked her straight in the eyes. "He didn't want to be responsible for any more deaths. That's why I imagine working with you has brought up a lot of history he wants to forget."

She sat back, her mind and body emotionally drained. No wonder Murphy was reluctant to work with her. How could he not have told her this before? She stared out the window, a little shell shocked.

Nihil prius familia.

That at least answered the question of how her father and Murphy knew each other. She bit the inside of her lip and focused on the physical pain to ignore the emotional one pricking at the back of her eyes and tearing at her heart. They had each suffered so much by Elijah's hands. Murphy, more so than most.

Murphy got in and threw a small keychain fob onto her lap. "Keep that on you at all times."

She picked it up. "What is it?"

He turned the engine over and pulled into traffic. "Insurance. If you're in danger, slide open the cover and push the red button. Help will be seconds away."

She opened her mouth to protest. The idea of bodyguards was ridiculous. Even if they were hidden, she would know they were there. She thought better of protesting and snapped her mouth shut. Knowing Murphy's history with Elijah, she understood his paranoia. No matter what she said, he was an immovable rock. She slipped the fob into a pocket and crossed her arms over her chest. But on one thing, she would fight him all the way to hell. She was staying on the case. He had another thing coming if he thought pioneers watching her apartment every night was going to stop her from doing her job.

"Where are we headed?" she said.

"Downtown."

Less than ten minutes later, they were making their way down a narrow alleyway full of garbage cans and dumpsters. The smell was so overpowering she had to hold her breath as they passed by. She groaned as they neared a dumpster, full to overflowing. "God, this place stinks."

Joshua's skin had turned a slight shade of green. "Try being us, with our noses, then you wouldn't complain."

A dirty red door was recessed into a building at the end of the alleyway.

Murphy halted as he reached for the handle. "Abe and Elijah go way back, and Abe has no affiliation to a pack. He can't be trusted. With these types of Weres, you never know where their loyalties lie." He looked at her. "I want you to stay close to me in case anything happens."

She was a federal agent and a good one, not some weakling. She pursed her lips into a thin line and glared at him. "I'm a big girl, Murphy. I can take care of myself."

She moved to enter the building, but Murphy let out a low growl. "Don't test me, Kaitlyn. You're not equipped to deal with this."

She patted her gun and smiled smugly. "Actually, I'm pretty sure I am."

Murphy looked ready to snap. He glanced at Joshua, as if seeking support on the issue.

Joshua shrugged his shoulders. "If you won't open the link, I can't warn you when to shut up."

Link? What link? Her eyes darted between the two men and she frowned. Neither of them wore earpieces.

Murphy glared at them, grunted, then disappeared through the door.

She followed behind them, but stopped in the entrance. The turn-of-the-century exterior of the building was dirty and falling apart, but the inside was modern and spacious. Her eyes fixated on a large neon sign above the bar. They had entered through the back entrance of one of the most popular nightclubs in Boston.

A movement on the mezzanine floor caught her eye, and she swung to face the figure who materialized on the landing. He raised his voice as he made his way down the stairs. "We're closed."

Halfway down, recognition dawned on his face. "Fuck, it's you."

"Friend of yours?" she mumbled to her partner.

Murphy glared at Abe. "Get down here, we need to talk."

As Abe approached them, he nodded to her grandfather. "Joshua. Long time, no see." He turned back to Murphy. "You, I could do with a few more years of absence."

A smile lit up Abe's face as his eyes roved over her. "Aren't ya going to introduce me to this beauty?"

Murphy bristled. "No."

She resisted the urge to roll her eyes.

"Where's Elijah?" Murphy said.

In an instant, Abe's expression changed. His eyes darted nervously between Murphy, Joshua, and her.

"She knows about us," Joshua said.

A wide smile spread across Abe's face as he took a closer look. "Well, what do ya know, and a Fed to boot."

Murphy cleared his throat. "Yes. Now answer the damn question. Have you seen him?"

Abe snorted and spun on his heels. He headed for the bar. "I wish I hadn't. That motherfucker cost me a truckload of customers and money."

"What happened?"

Abe lined up four shot glasses and reached for a bottle of tequila. "You mean who happened?" He began to pour. "Elijah turned up one night 'bout three months ago. He was looking to party hard. I told him to stay the fuck away from my staff, but he didn't listen and nearly killed my best shift manager. Ya think he could have just fucked one of the strippers. At least they're a dime a dozen. Do ya know how hard it is to find a trustworthy employee these days? Lola's only just come back to work."

Abe shook his head and downed one of the shots in a single gulp. He slammed the glass down on the counter, then picked up the next one and held it out to Joshua.

Joshua raised his hands. "We're good, thanks."

Abe shrugged. "Suit yourself." He emptied the second shot.

Murphy let out another low growl.

Abe scowled at him. "Keep ya fucking pants on. This ain't a conversation I wanna have, especially with the likes of you. If it gets back to Elijah, I'm as good as dead."

They were going to get nowhere if Murphy kept goading him. She stepped in. "We appreciate the risk you're taking. But the only way to keep you and your employees safe is to get him off the streets. I'm sure Lola will feel safer if he's taken care of. Anything you can remember about that night might be helpful."

The club fell silent as they waited for Abe. She schooled her expression to stay neutral. Otherwise her inner shock might out itself. Besides everything else going on, it turned out the owner of one of the most popular nightclubs in Boston was a Pioneer.

Just how many were there?

Abe pushed a hand into his jean pocket while the other one rubbed the back of his neck. "When he turned up, he was ranting on about Elise. How she'd screwed him after everything he'd done for her, and how he was gonna make her pay. I was only half listening. The place was getting packed, and Elijah was always unpredictable at the best of times."

He cleared his throat. "But the moment he referred to himself as a god giving birth to the path of his new dominion, I knew he'd fucking lost it. I mean, he was always on edge, but to think of himself as some sort a all mighty being? That's fucked up no matter which way you look at it."

She raised a brow. Neither Murphy nor Joshua had mentioned the psycho was delusional. "What did you do?"

Abe shrugged. "I did what anyone in my position would do. I called in rein-fucking-forcements." He downed another tequila. "But it was too late, the shit hit the fucking fan before they arrived."

"Do you know where he is now?" Murphy said.

"Nup. And I don't wanna. He cost me over a hundred grand in damages. But I'll tell you something for free, the man always was a slimy motherfucker. Whatever shit he's got going on, it scares the pelt off a me. He was way too confident, almost like he's onto a sure thing. He has a bone to pick with Elise and the Alliance. I don't know what it is, but mark my words, this plan of his has zero chance of failing."

Her heart thudded in her chest. Abe's words had fallen over her like a dead weight. What the hell was Elijah up to that had the guy so scared?

Abe pulled a card from his top pocket and pushed it across the counter to her.

She raised a brow and reached for the card. "What's this?"

Before she could pull it back, Abe's hand covered hers, and he raked his gaze over her. "It's a VIP pass for the club. How 'bout you ditch these two, come back tonight, and I can show you how a real Werewolf parties."

The hairs on the back of her arms bristled at his touch. And he called Elijah slimy.

Before she could refuse his overtly lewd proposition, Murphy grabbed Abe's hand and slammed it on the counter. He grit his teeth and snarled at the club owner. "She doesn't need your kind of hospitality."

Abe took a step backward. "Sorry, I didn't know she belonged to you."

She pushed Murphy aside and tossed a glare his way. "I can take care of myself. I don't need you to intervene on my behalf." She turned on Abe, who was very much on the defensive. "Secondly, I do not belong to anyone." She threw the card at Abe. "And I'm pretty sure I don't need to tell you where you can put this."

Fear rippled in Abe's eyes as a low, angry growl rumbled from Murphy's throat. He tossed Joshua a set of keys. "Go get the car."

Murphy turned back to Abe, who cowered with his head dropped. "If I hear one whisper that you do know where he is or what he's up to, I'm coming back for you."

Abe, too frightened to speak, bobbed his head even lower.

Murphy turned to her. "Let's go." He reached for her arm and half dragged her out of the bar.

She pulled away from him the moment they were in the alleyway. "Who the hell do you think you are? I can damn well look after myself. I do not need you, or anyone else for that matter, to defend me. Especially not from some scrawny nightclub owner."

Murphy's expression was unreadable, his clenched fists the only indication that he was no longer calm. He grabbed her wrists and bent her arms behind her back. Securing both of her hands in one of his own, he used his free hand to pull her head back to look up at him. Her body, flush with his, was caught, pressed against his rock-hard chest.

She struggled to break free, but it was no use. She couldn't move an inch. She was trapped, at his mercy. And his eyes were blazing with a deep, penetrating rage that sent cold dread shivering down her spine.

"What you don't seem to understand is that you are physically weaker than Werewolves. You have no chance whatsoever of overpowering one."

He pulled her closer to him, if that was even possible. Her pulse thundered in her neck as his warm breath washed over her. The pure maleness of him was dominating not only her body, but her senses. Shards of electricity leaped through her veins as her blood heated and betrayed her. Warmth grew in the pit of her stomach and radiated to her limbs. Her breathing came in stops and starts, her pulse wild, as he bent his head closer to hers.

As his lips brushed her earlobe, the hairs on the back of her neck stood to attention. "You seem to think your weapon will save you. Tell me. How is a gun going to save you now?"

She struggled against his restraint. She was fuming, but she was angrier with herself than with him. How had she managed to get in this situation? How had he overpowered her so quickly?

"Let me go," she said. "You've made your point."

All too soon, he pulled away, his eyes still locked with hers. An unfathomable expression marked his features as they glared at each other. As quickly as he had trapped her, she was freed.

"Let's go," he growled. He stormed out to the main road, not once looking back.

But she stood where he had left her, and valiantly attempted to gather her frazzled wits together and bring her thumping pulse back to acceptable levels.

What the hell just happened?

THIRTEEN

Fox on the Run

Bollocks. What the hell was he thinking?

Murphy held back the storm that brewed just below the surface. How could one Human get him so worked up? Didn't she know how dangerous his kind could be?

That was not the way to show her.

Guilt tugged at him. He knew he'd stepped over the line. But how else could he make her understand how vulnerable she was? He didn't trust Abe. The Were had an overinflated ego, and went from one conquest to another. He didn't want her anywhere near the maggot.

I do not think it is that predator you need to worry about

His stomach churned. He'd been trying to under play it, but Elijah's letter terrified him. Elijah had already taken two Quinns. He couldn't let him take another. He reached the end of the alleyway just as Joshua pulled the Cadillac up to the curb.

Joshua got out, his brow furrowed together. "Where's Kaitlyn?"

He nodded behind him and got into the driver's seat, slamming the door harder than intended. She was Joshua's kin, let him worry about her. Her headstrong ways were going to get her in trouble if Joshua wasn't careful.

He groaned inwardly. Who was he kidding?

To keep her safe, he couldn't let her out of his or her minders' sight. Daniel wasn't thrilled about the extra security, but he didn't care. While he'd only known her a few days, going into hiding until he tracked down Elijah was not an option she would entertain. She would fight him tooth and nail on that.

He avoided looking at her as she stopped to speak to Joshua. Her cheeks were flushed. He shifted uncomfortably in his seat.

You did that to her.

She did it to herself. She needed to be shown.

A growl from the back of his throat escaped at the memory of her bright eyes and smooth cheeks with a dusting of freckles. His body had reacted to their nearness. He swore under his breath. All it had shown was neither was as strong as they believed. He pressed the horn. Why the hell were they taking so long? They needed to get back to work. Elijah wasn't about to hand himself over to the authorities.

She glanced in his direction and rolled her eyes at him. A small weight lifted from his shoulders. If his rash action had made her wary of him, she wouldn't be pushing his buttons now. The corners of his lips twitched. No. She was made of sterner stuff than that.

As they were getting in, his phone beeped. Anika had an ID on their victim. He pressed down on the horn again to hurry them up. Was this the break he was waiting for? The moment the doors closed he pulled into traffic and made a sudden U-turn in the busy street.

Kaitlyn let out a minuscule yelp. "I know you probably got your license with a horse and buggy, but these days, we generally like to get where we are going in one piece."

He glanced in the rear-view mirror. She had clutched the door to keep from sliding across the car. "We need to head back to the office. Anika has an ID on our first vic."

They dropped off Joshua at Downtown Crossing and made it back to police headquarters in double time.

"What did you find?" he said before he was fully through the door. Saul, Garcia, and Anika were already in their temporary office.

Anika jumped up. "Well, it took a bit to get the algorithm adjusted, and Dr Swanson slayed the clean-up of the hands and fingers. When I saw the raw data, I wasn't sure it was going to work. After all, we've not really done this sort of thing at the lab before. Most fingers printed have prints, and—"

Why did she use twenty words when one would do? "Did you, or did you not, get a hit?" he said.

Anika's eyes darted to her monitor, then back to him. Her head bobbed up and down.

He raised a brow. "And?"

"I got a hit on a woman named Tania Potter."

Saul pushed a printout across the table to him. "Real piece of work, that one. She skirted the law for years. Never was convicted, but according to the people I spoke to, she put the shark into loan sharking."

"Any link to our other vic's?"

Garcia scratched the back of his neck. "Nothing so far, but that doesn't mean there isn't."

"Okay, I want to know everything there is about Potter. Search for a link to Haladlo." He scanned through the printout. "I'm assuming you've started the ball rolling for a warrant?"

"Yep, for her home and place of business," Garcia said.

He looked over at Anika. "What about the latest vic?"

"Still waiting on a match to come back from Tatt-C."

While their latest victim had a fairly intact prison tattoo on his arm, he wasn't as convinced it would be in the database. An uproar from the prison inmates about their right to privacy had made recording tattoos and entering them into the Tattoo Recognition Database more difficult. "How likely are we to get a match?"

Anika bit a thumbnail, and her brows crunched together as she glanced at her monitor. "Well, it looks like it's been there a while. And it's only in the last few years we've started to get gaps. We should get a hit, but it's going to take as long as it takes."

He grinned inwardly. Anika was stranger than most, and that was saying something considering how long he'd been around. But she was good at what she did. What she failed to mention to the others was that she'd worked around the clock to get the fingers digitally reconstructed.

He tossed the printout on the table. "Garcia, Saul, as soon as the warrant comes through, you two take Potter's home. Kaitlyn and I will take her office. In the meantime, how are we doing with interviewing Haladlo's colleagues and family?"

The warrants came through just before midday. Within a minute of notification, he and Kaitlyn were driving to Tania Potter's office.

Kaitlyn glanced around the small office space. "Do you think we'll find anything?"

He pointed to the laptop on Potter's desk. "I want that bagged and to Anika ASAP."

The crime scene analyst nearest him nodded and complied.

She pulled open the top draw of a filing cabinet full of files. "So much for a paperless society."

An hour of rifling through Potter's files led to nowhere. "How does this business get any customers? Some of these contracts are for twenty percent interest per month." She scanned the next file and her brows shot up. "Since when is a cordless drill valued at five thousand dollars?"

She dumped the stack of folders on the desk and smiled at the crime scene tech. "Those ones, too. I may not be an accountant, but even I can tell they don't add up."

His phone vibrated, and he quickly checked the message.

Fuck.

His fingers curled around his phone. He forced his muscles to relax before he broke it. He was tired of resetting new phones every two months. He pressed Tim Maxford's number. The Boston PD officer, and Daniel Locke's leader for the local Werewolf first responders, was a straight shooter and wasn't prone to exaggeration. In this instance, he hoped Tim was embellishing the story.

Tim answered on the first ring.

He listened as Tim provided him with additional details of the new disaster. But couldn't help the growl that erupted from deep within his chest. "Will be there in thirty."

When the call ended he fixated on the nearest wall. Bollocks. Couldn't anything be simple? He typed up a message to Joshua and a moment later turned on his heels and strode out the door. He needed his tablet. Yesterday. He climbed into the front seat of his Cadillac, reached for his computer, and stabbed at the keyboard.

Kaitlyn caught up to him and slid into the seat beside him. "Problem?"

"That was Tim Maxford, he's stationed at the C-six. A tanker has jackknifed on the I-93 at the beginning of Bunker Hill Bridge. It plunged over the edge into oncoming traffic below." He paused. "The death toll is sitting at eleven, four in critical condition, with a lot more injured."

Her hand reached up to her throat. "Joshua. Is Joshua okay?"

"He's fine. He was going to St. Joseph's to visit Ryan's grave."

Her face relaxed for a moment before her head jerked back. "Wait. Why would a cop from the C-six phone you about an accident?"

He ran his fingers through his hair. "The reason the tanker jackknifed was to avoid a wolf. After the truck went over, the wolf took advantage of the chaos and attacked several motorists attempting to flee their vehicles."

Her face lost color. "Wolf wolf, or Pioneer wolf?"

"That's what we're trying to work out. Tim and the others are getting up to speed with the situation."

Her lips set into a grim line. He knew her mind had gone to the same place as his.

Elijah. Elijah had something to do with this. He had no doubt on whose shoulder the blame for this new disaster fell. How many more innocent lives would that psycho take before they tracked him down?

A panicked voice blared from his tablet, and they leaned over to watch the video. A motorist caught in the middle of the drama had posted the disaster online. In less than thirty minutes, it had two hundred and fifty thousand views. Everything was happening so fast, it was hard to work out the order of the chaos. Cars veered to avoid others screeching to a halt, and slammed into barriers, or other cars like in an action movie. Unlike a Hollywood movie, though, the people behind the wheels were civilians, and the blood on the people who stumbled out of their wrecks wasn't fake.

While it was hard to make out one mangled vehicle from another, the wolf was another story. It darted in and out of traffic, causing chaos on both sides of the causeway.

When the truck tipped over the side of the bridge, her hand came up to cover her mouth. "Good lord."

The girl videoing the disaster began to chant, "Oh my God, oh my God."

His stomach knotted. The large gray wolf attacked motorists who left their cars. This was going to be a problem. They already had Elijah running around putting the city in a panic. Now one more of his kind was in the limelight.

She cleared her throat a few times before she spoke. "Is, is it him? Is it Elijah?"

He paused the video. "No. Elijah's wolf is a darker gray and a lot bigger. But it is a Werewolf."

She grimaced. "Frackleback."

He held back a grin. For someone who avoided swearing, she certainly found interesting alternatives. He started the car. "I'll drop you at headquarters."

"Where are you going?" she asked.

"That Werewolf needs to be found before it has the chance to wreak more havoc."

The Werewolf first responders, including Joshua, were already gathered by the Amphitheatre in Paul Revere Park when Murphy arrived. His argument with Kaitlyn had delayed him longer than it should have.

She waved at Joshua, who was deep in conversation with Tim. The rest of the team turned to watch their approach. Most of them stiffened and looked at each other with raised eyebrows and questions in their eyes. This wasn't a good idea, but Kaitlyn had refused to get out of the car, insisting this was her city and it was her job to protect it. He momentarily contemplated physically removing her, but there were too many witnesses, and he didn't fancy the paperwork that went with one of the crime scene techs reporting him.

Joshua glared at him. "What the hell is she doing here? She shouldn't be caught up in this mess."

"Had no choice, she wouldn't get out of the car."

Joshua exhaled and gawked at him. "Then you make her get out of the car."

He folded his arms over his chest. "You're her grandfather, how about you send her home?"

Joshua whirled on her and opened his mouth to speak.

Hands on her hips, she glared at him. "You've got another thing coming if you think I'm not going to help. I'm not a child, and I can take care of myself."

He snort-laughed. Hadn't they already proven that she couldn't?

She whipped her head around and leveled an angry stare at him. "And don't you start. I was caught off guard, that's all."

Tim cleared his throat. "Would someone like to explain to me who she is, and why she's here?"

She pushed her way around Joshua, peered at the shield on Tim's shirt, and stuck out her hand. "Sargent Maxford, I'm Special Agent Kaitlyn Quinn. I'm working the Boston Wolf Killer case with Murphy. I'm also Joshua's granddaughter."

Tim's eyebrows nearly disappeared into his hairline. His mouth fell open, and he glanced between Murphy and Joshua for confirmation.

Joshua shrugged. "Cat's out of the bag now, I suppose."

A shorter, stockier man than Tim slapped Joshua on the back. "You sly old devil, you. I had no idea you had family here." He leaned closer to Kaitlyn and grinned. "Danny Fulchello, I work out of the A seven."

She gave him a bright smile as she shook his hand.

Danny pointed to the man on the left of Tim. "That over there is Jose. He's Boston Fire Department, so we tend to talk a little slower 'round him."

Jose sighed and shook his head. "Ignore him, he's just jealous cause he didn't have what it takes to get into the fire department."

Danny introduced Kaitlyn to Wendy, a paramedic, Rachel, a supervisor at the city morgue, and Adam, another firefighter.

Murphy frowned. This wasn't a social gathering, and they were being way too nice to Kaitlyn the interloper. He had to refocus them on the reason they were gathered. "What's the plan?"

Tim pointed to the bridge. "We need to track him before he surfaces again. The serious crash unit is still mopping up the scene, so there's no way we're getting anywhere near it."

"Without a scent, how do we know what we're after?" Jose said.

Wendy reached into her backpack. "I took clothing items from the poor sods he attacked. It should be enough to give us a start." She handed a sealed plastic bag to each of the Werewolves. "There's a common scent on each."

Kaitlyn's brows furrowed together and she stared at the bags. He could almost see the wheels in her brain turning.

Joshua took pity at her obvious confusion. "Our sense of smell is far greater than a Human's. We can track who did this by his scent.

She glanced at Murphy and raised a brow. "So that explains your crime scene sniffing."

He grunted.

The plastic ruffled as they took in the scent so each one of them could commit to memory the scent they were after.

Wendy glanced over her shoulder at the chaos in the distance, and her face turned pensive. "The freeway is backed up for miles, and so many people need help. I can't stay. We just got word of an elderly couple trapped in their car."

Tim nodded. "I know you're stuck in the thick of it, and I appreciate you bringing the clothes to us."

Wendy shrugged. "No problem. Just do me a favor and find this rogue." She waved to the team then jogged off, leaving the rest of the team familiarizing themselves with the scent of the freeway wolf.

Tim checked his phone. "This thing has gone viral. We need to find the Were before the authorities do, or this could become an even bigger disaster. Team up, and if you find him, alert the rest of us. Whatever you do, do not engage alone. We have no idea how strong he is or what resources he has."

Murphy's jaw locked. They needed to deal with not only the Were, but the evidence as well. "Have you let Parker Johnson know she needs to take down the video?"

"She's on it." Tim pulled a map out of his back pocket, and opened it flat on the ground. He glanced up at the others. "Okay, here's the plan."

Tim meticulously outlined the areas to be covered and who would be assigned to each area. Murphy had to hand it to Daniel, he had a knack for putting the right people in charge. Once they were clear on what needed to be done, Daniel's team headed out to start the search.

"I'll leave my car here and catch a ride with you," said Joshua.

He glanced towards the bridge still caught in chaos. They needed to find the Were behind it before there was another disaster.

"Do you think he's gone rogue?" Joshua said.

He rubbed his jaw. "Not sure. I've re-watched the videos but none of them are clear enough to get a read. If I had to guess, he was terrified."

"Of what?"

He shrugged. "When we find him, we'll ask."

When they reached the Cadillac, Kaitlyn pulled the door open. "Where do we start?"

He stared at her without blinking. Surely he'd misheard? "Unless you've suddenly developed superior smell capabilities, you're going nowhere with us. You'll just slow us down."

She frowned. "If you think—"

Joshua's hand rested on her shoulder. "Katy, honey, he's right. We need to find him before he has a chance to do something like this again. You don't have the skills to keep up with us, and I don't think it would sit well with you if this resulted in more lost lives, would it?"

Her shoulders sagged and her expression flitted from defiance to resignation then to something he couldn't put his finger on. "Fine."

He frowned. That was way too quick. What the hell was she up to?

FOURTEEN

The Gatecrasher

Somewhere in New Hampshire

From his vantage point, Elijah counted nine soldiers. Two shooters on the roof, three near the front entrance, two roaming the perimeter, and two more standing guard at the dock. What a joke. Did they really think their pathetic attempt at security would stop him? He resumed his assessment of the property. Finding the place had taken him longer than expected. He smirked. But at least he had a little fun along the way.

If only that bitch could see him now.

His time with Elise had not been all in vain. She taught him the value of knowing thy enemy. He was more than prepared. He knew everything about the property, as well as the people in it. The sprawling Mediterranean-style villa was a rich man's paradise, and a far cry from the hovels he'd found himself in over the years. No expense had been spared, from the expansive granite terrace, to the grand two-story arched doorways, and the spectacular marble-floored, groin-vaulted gallery. The local real estate agent had been most knowledgeable about the estate. Pity she would not be listing any more properties, but at least her last moments were satisfying. For him.

The waterfront estate was well hidden in dense woods, and he had spent nearly seven weeks finding it. He sniggered. He had to admit, the dozen or so humans he played with to get here had more than made up for the delay. And those dumb cops only found a fraction of his playthings. If Humans knew the true number of his victims, they would really have something to write about in their silly little newspapers.

He surveyed the area once again to ensure lurking soldiers would not disrupt his grand entrance, then he settled into his hiding place to wait for the right moment. Timing was everything, and everything had its time. His was now. And oh, how he was going to enjoy it. Each Human he encountered along the path to where he was now provided pieces of the puzzle. The last one was a gold mine of information. He was going to fit in quite nicely. The people living in the mansion were similar to him in many ways. They had very little regard for human life, and they flourished on the misery of others. And, like him, they hid who they truly were from the public.

He studied the carpark and counted the vehicles. Cars had been arriving at regular intervals for the past hour. The latest had just pulled up the driveway, and the sole occupant disappeared into the house. They would be waiting a good while for the next guest. Joey Skinny Boy Marino. To be fair, he held out until his granddaughter was hauled in by her hair and a finger removed. It was amazing how quickly he had given up any and all information after that.

Consigliere. Advisor to the Don. He smiled. Yes, that would suit him just fine.

One of the soldiers hopped into the car and parked it along with the others. He had to admire their constraint. Rather than flashy sports cars and the high-end luxury vehicles their money could buy, they drove nondescript middle-class sedans and SUVs. The driveway was littered with Ford Escapes, Dodge Durango SUVs, Chevrolets, and Cadillacs with a couple of Lexus thrown in for good measure.

He waited another thirty minutes to make sure everyone invited was present and accounted for. A shiver of excitement ran down his spine as he prepared for his grand entrance. But first, he needed to deal with the pesky soldiers. He made his way to the side of the house, careful to keep out of their line of sight. Quickly climbing to one of the first-floor decks, he crossed the short distance to the roof. He stalked the soldier perched on the opposite side of the large brick chimney, and before the poor sap knew what happened, he snapped the man's neck. He placed the man back in his position, and made his way to the second man guarding the roof, who was watching for approaching cars.

Second one down, with little fuss and no noise. He sighed. Breaking necks was underwhelming and not at all fun. He was an artist, and as such, he wanted to remain true to his art. He reached for his blade and his heart grew lighter. If one couldn't be true to oneself, what was the point? With a spring to his step, he plotted a path to the remaining soldiers. Three minutes later, and he was reveling in the metallic scent of his masterpiece. Five men lay dead, their necks sliced from ear to ear. He licked his lips, savoring the beauty of the notes from the streams of blood ejecting into the air. Music to his ears.

Grinning, he made his way to the front door. The soldier posted in the foyer died with a surprised expression on his face, and so did the one who turned the corner at just the wrong time. His heightened sense of hearing provided him with enough information to detect another soldier standing vigil in front of a set of closed doors. From what he could make out, an intense discussion was going on in the sequestered room.

His wolf pushed to take part in their favorite pastime.

No, you can't come out yet. But we will have our fun later. I promise.

He disposed of the man quickly then burst through the double doors to the large meeting room, his arms outstretched. "I have arrived. We can start the meeting now."

Eleven sets of eyes turned to face him, each as shocked as the others.

A stocky man sitting nearest to where he stood, moved his chair back and rose. "Who the—"

He stepped over to the man and broke his neck, then did the same to the man on his right. He returned to his original position and pointed to an empty chair near the top of the shiny wooden table. "I assume that's where the consigliere sits?"

The stunned onlookers, too shocked to utter a sound, were frozen to the spot. They looked from their dead companions to him, then back again.

He tutted at the next man who was brave enough to rise. "Oh, no, no, no. I wouldn't try that if I were you. Unless you have a death wish, that is."

The man sat down.

He turned to the man sitting at the head of the table and grinned. Finally.

Ambrose, the man he had spent the past two months chasing down, stood up slowly. "I don't know who the fuck you are, but you have just taken your last breath."

Ambrose nodded slightly and three of the men at the table rushed him.

He'd hoped something like this would happen. He needed to show them just how fruitless their actions were. Before the men reached him, he bounded to the fireplace, reached up above it and grabbed a ceremonial Japanese Katana. The sword was a thing of beauty, and now was the time to take it for a test drive. A moment later, all in the room heard a rustle of displaced air followed by the hollow zing of the blade, as it sliced through its mark.

He stepped back and waited.

The man's legs were the first to give out. In slow motion, his body swayed and his head tilted backwards. The woman to Ambrose's right screamed as the man's severed head toppled to the marble floor seconds before the rest of his body. With a small bounce, the head rolled away and came to rest against the leg of a chair.

Elijah pursed his lips. What was the screamer's name? Oh, that's right. Briana.

A violent stream of blood erupted from what remained of the man's neck. The pure force and volume coated everyone in the warm sticky substance.

Ambrose pushed Briana behind him. "Stand down."

The two soldiers on guard he hadn't killed took a series of pitiful steps backward. A moment later, all but Ambrose and the woman had retreated to the safety of the opposite side of the table.

Ambrose raised his chin defiantly. "What do you want from us?"

He grinned as he gazed at his handiwork. "It's more what I can do for you."

He sniffed the air. They were so close to their first turn. He could taste it. Their first awakening as a Werewolf. His army was about to be born. Was this how parents felt just before the big event?

His wolf salivated at the blood scattered across the room and pooling under dead bodies. *Why did you stop?*

Because we need them alive for our plan to work.

He took a seat at the table and ran a hand over the reflective top. Only the best for him now. The table was worth a small fortune. He leaned back in the chair, placed his hands behind his head, and swung his feet up on the table. "How would you like to take over not only the five families but also the Russian mafia, the Mexican cartels, and the Triads?"

<u>FIFTEEN</u>
History Lesson

Boston PD Headquarters

Murphy's mood was as severe as the Boston weather. He scowled at the elevator button and stabbed it for the third time. Was it too much to expect things to work smoothly?

In hindsight, taking the stairs from the sub-basement level of the Boston PD Headquarters to the fifth floor was probably faster. He rechecked his phone. Still no reply. He resisted the urge to hit something and flicked a glance down the row of cars instead. Sure enough, her red roller skate was parked front and center. He shook his head. Six-thirty in the morning on a weekday, most people were just rolling out of bed, but she was already at work.

He frowned. So why wasn't she answering?

His jaw tightened. They had a crime scene to get to. The mutilated remains of a woman had been found in the back alley of a pub, and they needed to process the scene before the storm set in.

The moment the elevator dinged its arrival, he was in and stabbing at the close button. He crossed his arms over his chest. What the hell was Elijah up to? To make matter worse, they still hadn't found the Were that caused the freeway disaster. He and Joshua were splitting their nights to assist the local team with their search for the rogue Were. And to top off an exceptionally shitty week, they had two more close calls with newly turned Were's. Why was not clear, but if he wasn't killing, Elijah was actively turning people. Tim's team was tracking down every possible lead, but so far, nothing. He could only hope this new vic gave them the break they needed.

When he finally entered the main bull pen leading to the team's temporary office, he wasn't surprised to find it empty given the time. The department of paper pushers his team shared a floor with would not be in for at least another hour. He strode across the office and rechecked his phone. Still no answer. He grunted. She better have a good excuse. They were wasting valuable time. Who knew what condition the scene would be in by the time they got there? That's if they got to the scene this side of Christmas.

He entered their shared office and frowned. Where was she?

His facial muscles twitched as he reached for his phone. Were Daniel's men so incompetent they couldn't keep track of one woman?

Changes to their main board stopped him short. He cast his eye across it. She had been busy. His pulse sped up. She'd made some headway with their first vic. His lips twitched and a sense of pride overtook him, but her success didn't surprise him. In addition to being good, she was determined. He glanced across at her desk and groaned inwardly. Her phone peeked out from under a pile of papers, taunting him. No wonder she wasn't returning his messages. From the state of her desk she'd been at work a while. Her laptop was switched on, and she'd tossed her bag under the table.

When did that woman sleep?

She was always the first to arrive and the last to leave. Since the incident with Abe she had been getting very little sleep. And it was his fault. He regretted his show of force when they were in the alleyway. Why he did it was still a mystery to him. He kept going over it and justifying it in his head, arguing that she needed to understand the type of person she was up against. Her captivating beauty, along with her perfectly proportioned body, would be too much for Abe to ignore.

He grunted. Hell, she was too much of a temptation for any red-blooded man.

And does that include you?

He froze at his wolf's sly question. Admittedly, his mind had wandered. More than once he had speculated about what lay beneath the suits she wore like an armor. What would her skin feel like under his fingers as he molded himself to her curves? Would her curls be as soft as they looked? His body temperature rose along with his wandering mind. He stopped short. Guilt, then shame, washed over him like a bucket of ice. How could he have disrespected June's memory so easily?

We didn't, his wolf said.

He clenched his jaw. *What the hell is the matter with you? Of course, we did. We have no right to desire a woman not our mate.*

His wolf snorted.

He rubbed his forehead. Between this case, Kaitlyn, and his wolf, life had become a lot more complicated. He needed to uncomplicate it. This was Joshua's fault for not convincing Kaitlyn to remove herself from the case. He needed to focus on the case and only the case. The rest was just noise he didn't need right now. And right now, he had a scene to get to.

"Where the hell is she?"

Guessing she would be getting a hot chocolate, he made his way to the kitchen. A low hum at the back of his mind vibrated and set his teeth on edge.

Out with it. His Wolf's not-so-subtle hints were becoming annoying.

Joshua's not the only one to blame.

She's not my responsibility, he said.

Are you sure about that?

Murphy clenched his fists. *What are you talking about? What's gotten into you lately, you've been acting do-lally.*

He rubbed the back of his neck. His wolf was more agitated than normal, and he needed more runs than he had in years. In the beginning, he had put the restlessness down to Elijah being back, but his Wolf was telling him otherwise, and keeping something from his Human half. He couldn't put his finger on what.

His thoughts returned to Kaitlyn. He should have known she wouldn't back down and allow Joshua and him to get the job done. No, she had resolved to catch her father's killer. The stubborn woman was even attending mixed martial arts classes at night. And when time permitted during the day, she was at the gun range. He snorted. She was under the delusion that her renewed training efforts would help her go head to head with a Werewolf.

His wolf sat up as they walked through the door to find her pouring a hot chocolate. What was his problem?

"Coffee?" she said, without looking to see who was in the room behind her.

Murphy's nose twitched. This was another thing that irritated him. She instinctively knew when he was near her. He had not made a sound audible to the human ear, yet she detected his presence. "No time. Get your stuff. Another body has turned up."

Her head snapped up. "William Shatner's pants." She tossed the contents of her cup into the sink and joined him. "Well, what are you waiting for? Let's go."

Murphy closed his mouth and resisted the urge to point out the delay was due to her. Instead, he headed for the elevator and made a call to check in with the officer at the scene. On the way to the parking garage, he briefed her. She slipped her handgun into the Cant holster attached to her waistband. "And she was left out in the open?"

He nodded. "Came as a surprise to me, too." This was definitely not Elijah's MO.

"Maybe he was spooked before he could take her to a secluded place?"

Murphy glanced up at the small screen. Could an elevator go any slower? "No. He doesn't leave things to chance. If that's where she died, that's where he wanted her to die."

She glanced at the surveillance camera and then lowered her voice. "Any luck last night?

He held back a smile. She knew as well as he did, the CCTV's did not include audio. "No."

A small sense of relief hit him as the doors slid open. They could not afford these delays, even if only ten minutes. He bolted out the door and headed for his Cadillac.

Like a dog with a bone, she raced to catch up. "Is that normal? I mean, Elijah's been in the city for that long, and he hasn't made contact with anyone?"

He found it hard to believe, too. Joshua and he had questioned nearly every Werewolf Elijah might have had contact with, as well as others. All dead ends. No one had seen him in weeks, and no one knew what he was up to. But they all agreed on one thing. Elijah was too unpredictable, and the sooner he left Boston the better. He stopped at the driver's door and hesitated. "He's up to something. I just don't know what."

"I'm afraid to find out.'

He got in, but he couldn't shake the prickling at the back of his neck. Elijah's actions over the past few months were best described as manic. Which worried him. Elijah was calculating. While he was unpredictable, he did it with a singular goal. Rarely did he deviate. So why was he killing some, while turning others?

She buckled her seat belt. "Why is everyone so surprised he's turning Humans into Pioneers?"

His breath hitched and he stiffened. How did she know where his train of thought had gone?

Once they were winding their way through the early morning traffic, he pursed his lips and glanced at her hand, which was steadily thrumming nails on the middle console. That bad habit was another thing that unnerved him.

She caught his eye and grinned. "Sorry, did that bother you?" She stopped. "I was just waiting on my answer."

His fingers tightened around the steering wheel. Why had he not kicked her off the team yet? She was a pain in the butt. She knew far more about them than she ought to. Why, in the short time since she met Tim and the other members of his first responders team, she had even lunched with most of them. She was becoming part of their team. He could well imagine how many stories about Were life she had elicited from those loose-tongued, eager beavers.

"So why is everyone surprised he's turning people?" she said again.

"Because of who he's spent the last two decades with."

"You mean Elise? The alpha that's got everyone freaked out?"

His stomach tightened.

She grinned. "What? Just because you want to keep us weak Humans in the dark, doesn't mean that I'm going to stay that way. You may have a problem communicating, but Tim certainly doesn't."

He ground his teeth together, and his pulse moved into overdrive. Tim was an idiot who didn't know when to keep his mouth shut. Why would Joshua even allow her near that Lothario?

His wolf slyly cocked its head. *And why would that worry you?*

He growled in the back of his throat. *Shut up.*

"According to Tim, this Elise has everyone running scared," Kaitlyn said.

His wolf's guard hair bristled. *It must be comforting for Joshua, knowing Daniel's people have accepted her as pack. How kind of Tim to take a special interest.*

His blood boiled. *I told you to shut up.*

What the hell had gotten into his wolf? He didn't care what Kaitlyn got up to in her spare time. As long as it didn't affect her work on the case, it was none of his business.

"What else did he tell you?" It came out more of a demand than a question.

She shrugged. "Not much else. I got the feeling they're all still recovering from whatever happened. I didn't want to push it."

His shoulders relaxed. Tim had been with him and Joshua most nights. She couldn't have gotten a lot of information from him. He mentally shook himself. Of course, she would go fishing for answers. When she wanted to know something, nothing stopped her. He sighed. No point in keeping her in the dark, and better she heard it from him. "Do you remember the FDA alert a while back on the virus placed in a caffeine additive?"

She nodded. "I don't think any of us will forget it. The deaths around the country mounted, and for a while, we thought it was a terrorist attack. Why do you ask?"

He glanced in the rearview mirror before overtaking another vehicle. "The virus was placed in the food additive by a group of extremist Werewolves."

She fumbled with her phone, and her head shot up. "I beg your pardon?"

He considered the best way to explain. It was never easy talking about such a shameful blight. "Some Werewolves, like Humans, carry a number of prejudices. These extremists believe we should only have pure bloodlines."

She frowned. "I don't think I'm following you."

"There is a pack in France that goes by the name Sandulf. It's a very old pack and is run by a bloodline called Lauzon. The name Sandulf means True Wolf. Historically, they were the loudest and most vocal about putting an end to what they called mixed breeding. Their Alpha, Elise Lauzon, was so entrenched in her belief that over the past two decades she, and a small army of her acolytes, developed a disease that can kill non pure-blooded Werewolves."

Her brows furrowed together and her expression turned grave. "But I thought you don't get sick?"

"We don't. But somehow, she managed to work out how to suppress our immune systems and introduce a deadly disease into our bloodstream. The disease was originally targeted at Werewolves who were born to a turned parent, or who were turned themselves."

He gave her a moment to mull over what he was telling her. For a Human, she was very much in control of how her body reacted to emotions. He was grateful for her tells because unless she was experiencing an extreme reaction, he had difficulty figuring out what she was feeling through her scent. Something he wasn't used to. Trust Joshua to teach her how to control her reactions.

"If all these dead people were Pioneers, how did they end up in hospital? I thought you tended to shy away from possible exposure. You know, hide in plain sight and pretend to be normal, like say grumpy FBI agents."

His face relaxed into a half smile as he rubbed his forehead. Even when he couldn't read her emotions through scent, her mouth would give him the information he needed. "That's the problem. Her hatred extended to all Humans who could possibly be turned. She found a way to target any Human that had a dormant Werewolf gene, so those who died in the hospital were like you. Somewhere in their ancestry, they all could be traced back to a Werewolf."

As the words escaped his lips, his breath caught. Kaitlyn was one of Elise's intended victims. Until now, it had never occurred to him.

Her face paled, and he resisted the urge to reach out and smooth away the sudden anxiety. "Is, is that why Joshua keeps on going through my kitchen?"

He nodded. Thank goodness Joshua had the wherewithal to check.

"I threw out any coffee I had weeks ago, straight after we were briefed on the biological attack in the food." She paused and her brows drew together. "But what does Elijah have to do with the caffeine additive? I'm not seeing the connection."

His stomach clenched. This was his fault. If he had gone with his gut back then, maybe all of this could have been avoided. "He was with Elise and her little army for the past two decades. And from what we can tell, she kept him in full supply of victims."

Her face lost all color, and his guilt increased.

"Does that mean he has the same beliefs?"

Thankfully, they had arrived. He double parked next to a squad car and leaned forward to look up at the black clouds ready to burst. They were running out of time. "No one is really sure. He hates everyone. Humans and Werewolves alike."

He froze when her hand rested on his arm.

"We will get him."

Her voice, while soft, was determined. It gave him a measure of comfort, even if the risk to her ate at him.

He turned his head back to face her. The color had returned to her freckled cheeks. His gaze fell to her hand on his arm, and his eyes narrowed. "What the hell?"

He grabbed her arm and pushed up her sleeve to expose a bruised wrist. "What's that?"

She pulled her arm away and pushed the fabric down to cover the purple injury. Refusing to meet his gaze, she mumbled, "Nothing." She reached for the door handle. "We need to go."

His blood boiled and pounded in his ears. Before she could open the door, he reached over and locked it. "That's not nothing. You need to stop spending hours every night at the gym. It's not going to help. You have no hope of overpowering us. Or of defending yourself, if you're stupid enough to get involved in something you shouldn't."

She jabbed a finger at him. "Don't you tell me what to do. You're the one who pointed out Humans are weaker than

Pioneers. I'm just trying to even the playing field. Besides, next time you won't be so lucky. I'll be ready for you."

He fought to control the rage rushing through his veins. Every part of him shook with the effort. How could she harm herself this way? This had to stop. He grabbed her by the arm and hauled her across the seat to him. The light-colored freckles scattered across the bridge of her nose and cheekbones made her look so young, so vibrant. And so vulnerable. "How can you be so naive? You know what we are. Do you think Elijah is the only one capable of doing that sort of damage? Kaitlyn, we're your worst nightmare. You need to stop thinking this is a fair fight."

His breath was erratic, and he saw red.

She struggled to pull free. Unable to budge, she met his anger head on. "And if I don't stand up and fight, who will? A whole city out there has no idea what is happening. Who is going to keep the innocent safe?"

Her hazel eyes sparked and shone with anger as her chest rose and fell in shallow pants. She was magnificent. She was David to his Goliath, and if he wasn't careful, he would suffer the same fate. He breathed her in. This time she wasn't able to hold back her emotions. Her anger was sharp on his tongue, and he winced at the intensity of it, but he pushed away the guilt. He was the reason she was so angry, but he had to keep her away from danger. Elijah did not play by the rules. He would slink out of the shadows, and she would never see it coming. The thought of her bright fire being extinguished pained him. He could not, would not, let that happen.

An errant curl fell across her face and rested on her plump lips. Lips that had the capacity to warm up the coldest winter day when she turned on her megawatt smile. Lips that pushed him to the edge of madness with her incessant questions and thirst for knowledge. When her tongue darted out to moisten her lips, heat flared through his body. What would they be like to taste?

When he realized where his mind had taken him, he flinched and released her. He took a painful breath. He had no right to be thinking of her in that way. She was Joshua's granddaughter and Ryan's daughter.

He rubbed his aching forehead. "I'm sorry." He willed his heart to slow down. What the hell had he been thinking? "I got so angry at the damage you're doing to yourself. I don't want to see you hurt like that."

Unable to look her in the eye, he stared out the window. How could he have disrespected June's memory like that?

Bollocks.

He reached for the door and was out of the car in an instant. He was supposed to be investigating another death, not arguing with Kaitlyn over her stupidity, or worse, wanting to kiss her.

When he rounded the Cadillac, Kaitlyn slammed the passenger door so hard the car rocked. Her eyes narrowed and she glared at him. "What I do in my free time is my business."

His muscles tensed. She wasn't going to continue down that path, was she? Perhaps he should have thought about putting her over his knee instead of kissing her. Perhaps that, at least, would have knocked some sense into her. He ground his teeth together and checked the oncoming traffic before striding across the road to the crime scene. How could one woman be so annoying?

He was half way across when he muttered under his breath, "Stupid Humans."

She huffed. "I heard that."

SIXTEEN

A Rose by Any Other Name

Kaitlyn stared at Murphy's back as he jay-strode across the road. How did he, with so very little words, get her sprawled all over the emotional map? Her pulse was still racing.

She lifted her fingers to her lips. For a moment, she could have sworn he was going to kiss her. She bit the inside of her cheek just to make sure she wasn't in some bizarre sleep state and mentally shook her mind. That would be ridiculous. It was just another show of strength. She glanced at the purple mark on her arm and pulled her sleeve down to cover it. Why did he get so angry at her bruises? He was the one who kept insisting she was weak.

Garcia and Saul's squad car pulled up behind Murphy's Cadillac. Garcia jumped out and jogged toward her while Saul followed at a slower pace.

Garcia nodded at the police barrier blocking the path to the alleyway where their vic had been found. "What do you know?"

She shrugged. "Nothing. We just got here."

Saul waved his umbrella and craned his neck to look up at the sky. "We is going to have ourselves a good old-fashioned downpour of biblical proportions. I can feel it in my arthritis."

Garcia scowled and muttered something intelligible as he hurried across the road.

Her skin prickled, and she arched a brow. "Still a bundle of joy, I see."

For the past week Garcia had two settings: his normal flirty self or irritated beyond belief.

Saul rolled his eyes. "Something's gotten up his craw. Every time I try to talk to him about it, he cuts me off. I suspect it's got to do with that mob bust that went south."

A rolling boom cut across the ominous dark clouds.

Saul glanced up. "We'd better get a move on, it may be morning, but that sky's just going to get darker once the rain hits."

She stared at Garcia's retreating back and frowned as the hairs on her arms once again bristled. Maybe Murphy was right. He had been uneasy around Garcia all week, adamant the detective was hiding something from them. Coupled with his change in mood, she had to agree with him. The question was what?

A bolt of lightning flashed from one of the darker clouds and disappeared just as quick. She hurried after the team.

They found Murphy deep in conversation with Dr. Swanson, the Medical Examiner. Crime scene techs hovered on the outskirts of the inner barrier and waited for the ME to release the scene to them. The photographers, the only ones able to do any evidence gathering, were taking photos from where they stood.

She nodded at Dr. Swanson and scanned the immediate area. Her gaze rested on their vic, and she had to look away and swallow the lump in her throat. She had been prepared for a dismembered body, but it took a moment for her to readjust to a mutilated, intact one. Seeing the woman in this light made it more tragic. Blond, matted hair, a halo around her once pixie-like face, made her look far younger than she probably was. A face that, while bruised, had escaped torture from Elijah's blade. The woman's body had been subjected to a multitude of lacerations, though not as deep as their other victims. Her clothes, torn to shreds but still clinging to her, exposed deep gouges across her lower body caused by an animal. A large wolf to be more precise.

She shuddered at the thought of what the woman had gone through. How desperate she must have been in her final moments. If her fingernails were anything to go by, she had put up a good fight. Which was another difference. Elijah had not attempted to hide her identity.

Garcia jotted some notes on his pad. "Are we sure this is the work of our perp?"

The ME let out a surprised yelp when a sharp crack of lightning lit up the dark alleyway, quickly followed by a boom of thunder as it rolled across the sky.

"The teeth marks on her thighs are consistent with the others," the ME said. "The lacerations are not as severe, but they are similar enough. I won't know for sure until I get her back to the morgue." She picked up her medical bag. "Sorry I can't give you time to inspect the body, but if that rain comes down we might lose evidence." She nodded to her assistant, who stood a short distance away with a gurney.

Murphy snapped on gloves and nodded to the crime scene techs. "You heard her, the scene's ours."

He quickly assigned tasks, and she and Murphy divided the scene, while Garcia and Saul headed inside to interview the staff on duty the previous night. When they were out of earshot, she looked over to Murphy and arched a brow. His micro nod confirmed any doubt she may have had. This was Elijah's work.

Murphy was as frustrating as hell—overbearing and grumpy, but they worked well together, and she was beginning to appreciate the very thin line he was walking between her world and his.

She crouched down and pushed aside a half squashed empty soda can to reveal a broken gold chain and a wet and torn business card melded to the concrete. Her stomach tightened when she recalled a similar alleyway not so long ago. After his demonstration outside Abe's nightclub, she had been stunned by her primal reaction to his closeness, but also by the pure power that radiated off him. She had vowed the next time her guard would not be so lax.

And look how that turned out.

She called out to one of the techs for a marker and took the opportunity to gauge how far Murphy was through his quadrant. As usual he was sniffing the evidence. The intense manner in which he searched their vic's handbag echoed the way in which he dealt with just about everything. But his belief that she wasn't capable of defending herself still played on her mind. He was proving his point. Maybe a little too thoroughly, but it meant she needed to up her game. Train more and train harder.

She shivered as the temperature dropped. The intermittent drops of rain changed direction as a flurry of wind rushed between the buildings, dragging a high-pitched whine behind it. Discarded paper spiraled in mini tornadoes which swept up loose dirt on the pavement and tossed it into the air.

Murphy's voice boomed over the chaos. "Tag it and bag it people. We're running out of time."

She frowned and darted a glance at the others. Some techs were in a mild state of panic, most of which was due to Murphy. She pulled out her phone and filmed the rest of her quadrant. If she couldn't comb every inch before the downpour, at least she would be able to view it later. Not that it would do any good. If she found any evidence, it would be long gone.

When the alley fell quiet, she looked up. The sudden drop in noise was eerie, and the calm that replaced the wind had her stomach lurching. If possible, there was even less light.

Garcia, just returned from interviewing the pub staff on duty, stopped mid stride and glanced around as if expecting the sky to fall. "Is it just me or does it feel like Chucky is about to jump out from the shadows?"

Lightning cracked like a whip and Garcia flinched. He swore under his breath as a gust of wind pushed passed him and tossed more paper in its wake. He squinted and stared a spot on the far side of the scene. The one quadrant they had yet to scour. "What the fuck?"

Goosebumps erupted across her skin, and her heart thumped in her chest as she turned her head. The wind had dislodged a piece of a cardboard box that had wedged itself under a brick. The cardboard wasn't his focus. It was the single rose that, until that moment, had been protected from the elements. A dirty alleyway was the last place she would expect to see a red rose.

The heavens chose that moment to open up, and rain pelted down on them.

Saul, who was closest, opened his umbrella over the flower to keep it dry. "It looks like there's a note under the brick that's holding it in place."

She looked to Murphy. Techs scrambled to keep parts of the scene dry while throwing evidence in waterproof containers. The crime scene was in chaos. Yet he remained the calm epicenter of the storm, his granite walls impenetrable. Her forehead erupted in a fine bead of perspiration. Elijah had left the rose, but why?

Garcia crouched and pushed the brick to one side before retrieving the envelope and flower. "Shit." He looked up and held out the envelope to her. "I think it's for you."

Her stomach churned. Sure enough, her name was written across the once white embossed paper.

This time, Elijah had spelled it correctly.

SEVENTEEN

New Pioneers

Kaitlyn flopped in the Cadillac and slammed the door shut. She was soaked. None of their umbrellas had survived the squall hell bent on wreaking havoc with their scene. They'd rounded up as much evidence as they could. Now they were heading back to police headquarters to start delving into the life of their vic, Patricia Hillside, to determine the timeline for her final twenty-four hours. If they were lucky, it would give them a lead on where or how to find Elijah.

She leaned across to the driver's side and pushed the key into the ignition. Murphy, still in the rain, was giving last minute instructions to the techs. She shivered and looked down at her wet suit. She should have caught a lift back with Garcia and Saul. That way she could put off the inevitable.

Besides, a couple leads needed chasing down. Her investigation into Tania Potter, their first vic, had unearthed some interesting information.

Her throat ran dry, and she groaned inwardly. Provided Murphy kept her on the team. He hadn't passed comment on it yet, but she could well guess his intentions. The moment the rose was uncovered, the vein in his neck stood out and threatened to burst. A tell-tale sign he was holding back a tsunami. Elijah had, once again, singled her out and totally screwed with her life.

She seethed inwardly as she struggled with clicking the seat belt into place. If she detested Elijah before, it was nothing to the hate that brewed within her now. Leaving that flower was a cowardly act. Was he so threatened by Murphy he had to resort to taunting him?

William Shatner's pants. What if her mom heard about it? She'd freak.

She was still working on ways to keep the press from getting wind of the rose when Murphy returned to the car. He got in without saying a word and checked his phone before tossing it in the middle console.

Her heart raced. She was positive he was about to cut her from the team. But over her dead body. She wasn't giving up without a fight. She braced for impact. "Don't even attempt it, mister. I'm staying on this case."

Murphy brushed a hand through his short hair to shake it dry. "Wasn't even going to try."

"He's just baiting us." She crossed her arms over her chest. "That flower was a decoy to have us on the back foot. If he was serious about getting to me, it would have happened already."

He turned the key and let out a deep sigh. "I told you, I'm not taking you off the team."

The wind went out of her sails. She was prepared to argue the point. In fact, she had a train load of arguments. She frowned as she stole a glance at his calm exterior. Even the angry vein in his neck wasn't pulsing out of control. Try as she might, she couldn't work out what he was up to. He had caved too fast. "What's the catch?" she said when they were halfway back to headquarters.

Murphy shrugged. "No catch. Elijah is taunting me by targeting you. You want to stay on the case, and it's my responsibility to keep you safe."

She let out a groan. Her invisible security detail had just increased. "Fraggle rock. How many more?"

"Enough."

Her lips pursed together. "No, absolutely not. This is ridiculous. I can look after myself. We've been over this."

"You won't even know they're there."

She sat back in her seat and silently fumed. "Yeah. Right."

It wasn't as though she could complain to anyone. What would she say? "Hey Doug, would you get Murphy to call off the Pioneers who are under the delusion I'm in danger from a psycho Pioneer who happens to be on a killing spree in Boston."

The sooner they caught Elijah the better.

After a fast shower and change, she stashed her wet clothes into the trunk of her car and headed up to the fifth floor. Her spare suit included a shirt with extra-long sleeves. This day was already a nightmare, she didn't fancy having another run in with Murphy over her bruises.

Anika pounced on her the moment she walked into the office. "How are you? Do you need me to get you anything? Are you sure you should be here? When they told me about the rose, I couldn't believe it. I mean you read about that sort of thing, you don't really expect to experience it. Don't worry though, we think we've enough DNA evidence on the envelope to track him down. How are you feeling though? Did you need anything? Hot chocolate? Cupcake? Some of those red liquorish thingies you like so much?"

She rubbed her forehead. Could this get any worse?

Murphy was standing outside the door talking on the phone to Daniel. Right now, she didn't know what concerned her more, listening to him arrange for extra minders she didn't need or Anika having a panic attack.

At the top of her voice she said, "Enough."

Saul and Garcia whipped their heads around. They, too, had been acting weird. Well, Saul was acting weird, Garcia's mind was elsewhere. Anika slinked back to her tablet and pretended to work.

She tapped her foot and glared at them. "In case you have all been living under a rock instead of doing your jobs, you would know there has never been an instance where a serial killer played a genuine cat-and-mouse game with an officer of the law and subsequently attacked them. Serial killers target the weak and those who can't defend themselves. This is the last I want to hear on this matter. The psycho is just trying to screw with our minds."

She turned to Garcia, who had clearly gotten up on the wrong side of bed this morning, and was still snapping at everyone. "How about we change the subject?" She nodded to the Boston Globe he was hiding behind. "It's all over the news. I hear the bust went well, so what's eating you Gilbert Grape?"

Garcia grimaced, folded his paper and tossed it on the table. "The bust was a fucking disaster. The papers only know half of it."

Anika looked up from her tablet and pulled on her braid. "The way I hear it, heads are going to roll, but it's a little sketchy on why."

Garcia rubbed his jaw. "We were executing two major drug raids with the DEA at the same time. One a shipment of cocaine for the Columbian Cartel and the other, a drug den for the mob. We managed to seize two tons of the Columbian's product, and made twenty-five arrests."

She frowned. "Why aren't you celebrating? That's a great outcome."

Garcia ran a hand through his near perfect hair. "When we raided the mob's warehouse, it was empty. They were tipped off."

"How can you be so sure?" she said.

"The warehouse wasn't totally empty. A body with a single bullet to the back of the head was left behind. It was the informant that gave us the intel."

She grimaced as she sat at her desk. "Ouch. Tough break."

Garcia's face turned sour. "Tough break, alright. All that work down the toilet."

She turned back to her laptop and unlocked her screen just as Murphy entered the office. "Well, the mob seem to have their fingers in every game in town these days. I think there's a connection between our first vic, Tania Potter, and the mob," she said

"No way," Anika said.

Garcia choked at the news. "Wait. There's nothing on file to indicate that."

"Yes, but after work last night I decided to head out and canvas the neighborhood"

Murphy scowled. "You what?"

She ignored his daggered stare. "While you were following up your own leads, I did the same. Anyhow, it didn't take long to find people who borrowed money from Potter. Reading between the lines, it looks like organized crime funded her activities."

Garcia leaned back in his chair. "No loss, then. It just means one more shithead off the street."

Saul reached for his empty coffee mug and stood. "Not for long, they're like roaches, squash one, and a bunch more appear." He wandered out the door proclaiming retirement couldn't come soon enough.

Murphy gave her a glare that told her he wasn't going to let her solo investigation go without comment. Her shoulders slumped. She might have had a breakthrough, but even the knowledge of Potter's connection to organized crime didn't get them closer to finding out what Elijah was up to. He was after something. But what? And why didn't he want them identifying the victims, yet he left this new vic intact and identifiable?

She had the sudden urge to bang her head against her desk.

Anika clicked her fingers. "Oh yeah, that's right. Got some results that you'll wanna hear. I came straight over when I found out. Maggie said I should just message or phone you, but it's not really something that can be done over the phone." She wrinkled her nose. "I suppose I could have emailed you with it, but that's just so impersonal, don't you think? It came back a lot faster than I thought it would, but I think that's because I contacted them every day. They must've jumped me straight to the front of the queue. That was nice of them, don't you th—"

Anika stopped when she finally noticed Murphy's dark scowl. "Oh. I suppose you want to know what I'm here for?"

He folded his arms over his chest. "That would be nice."

She beamed up at him and wrung her hands together. "We got a hit on the DNA swab from the last victim."

"Thank fucking Christ. It's about time we caught a break," Garcia said.

She had to agree. Elijah knew exactly what he was doing. They were hitting brick walls at every turn.

Anika turned back to her tablet and tapped the screen. "Just sending you the details now."

Their mailboxes pinged at the same time.

She scanned through the information. "According to this, our vic was a Desmond Crispin. Thirty-eight, divorced, and owned a laundrette with his estranged wife." She let out a tiny snort to keep from laughing. "Get this, Desmond was married to Desdemona. No wonder the marriage didn't last."

"Convictions?" Murphy said.

"Just checking that now," Garcia said. He scanned through the police database. "A few arrests in his late teens and a possession charge, for which the judge gave him probation. Apart from that, nothing."

Murphy came to stand behind Garcia. "Is he a known associate or does he go under an alias?"

"I'll check the FBI database," she said.

Her search proved futile, but just before she logged out, a thought struck her and she brought up a new search. This time, she focused on the ex-wife's information. "Bingo."

She read the details out loud. "Mrs. Crispin is suspected of money laundering, but there's never been enough evidence to even approach her. According to this, the ex-husband is a silent partner but has no dealings with the business."

She looked up at Murphy. "This may be the break we have been waiting for."

Murphy grabbed his keys. "Let's go talk to her."

Before they had a chance to move, Saul rushed through the door. "You seen the latest? It's a goddam media circus."

"What's happened?" she said.

Saul wiped a bead of sweat off his forehead. "Kid got mauled by a wolf last night and it's gone viral. The media is saying the Boston Wolf Killer has lost control of his accomplice."

Anika tapped furiously on her screen. "Give me a sec, and I'll bring it up."

She swiped up when she found what she was looking for, and a video projected to the large monitor on the wall.

The images were grainy, but it looked like a college frat party in full swing. A blur flew out of the darkness and landed on one of the partygoers. The girl taking the video moved closer, but nearly dropped her phone when the wolf snarled and snapped his sharp jaws at the student under attack. The wolf's razor-sharp teeth sank into the kid's midriff. It pulled away, leaving a gaping hole in the screaming boy's side. The wolf took a step back before flying at his victim again.

Anika pulled in a sharp breath and her hands flew up to cover her mouth. "Oh my god."

The wolf's jaw locked onto the teenager's thigh and yanked at it with a feral growl.

Her eyes widened and she flinched at the unnatural guttural sound. Had Elijah finally been caught on camera? She leaned forward to get a better view but even that didn't help. Between the unsteady hand of the camera operator and the minimal light, she couldn't see the wolf's face, let alone its eye color. The animal let go of the boy's leg. Even the hazy video couldn't hide the volume of blood pouring from the open gash. The screams from the boy intensified as the wolf once again savagely tore into his leg. Thank goodness the image was grainy, otherwise it would give viewers, many of whom would be children, nightmares for months.

The news anchor came on and outlined several theories, including the general consensus that the wolf belonged to the Boston Wolf Killer. Whether it was under its master's command or had escaped was anyone's guess, the anchor said. Full blame was being leveled at the police and the FBI for sleeping on the job. The anchor ended with the question: how many more of Boston's good citizens would have to die before the authorities did something about it?

The room fell quiet.

Anika turned off the monitor. "How do you think he trained a wolf to attack like that?"

Murphy snorted. "You can't. A dog mauls a student and media turns it into a circus to sell more airtime."

"You don't think it was a wolf?" The doubt in her voice was clear.

Saul threw himself into his chair. "I don't. The tool with the phone camera had taken one too many runs to the packie for the kegger, he can't see straight. That video's so dark and distorted you can barely make out the boy, let alone know what type of animal attacked him. The only thing we know for sure is the media is out for blood. Ours."

"We need to put an end to this before he strikes again," Murphy said. He turned to a solemn-looking Garcia and Saul. "Find the link between Haladlo and Potter. I don't care what you have to do, just find it."

Garcia's face scrunched into a confused frown. "But boss, what about today's vic? Surely that should be our priority? It's still fresh, we might get a break."

"Today's vic was just a red herring. It's not going to tell us what he's up to. Focus on the connection between our vics with no id left behind." He glanced at her and nodded at the door. "Let's go."

She managed to make it all the way to the elevator before she posed the question uppermost in her mind. "Was that Elijah?"

"No."

"You're sure about that?"

As the doors closed, Murphy handed her his phone and played a video similar to the one they had just seen. This time, it was taken before the wolf attack.

"Wait. You knew about the attack?"

He pointed to one of the partygoers. "Keep your eye on this kid here."

She watched as the boy was attacked, not by a wolf, but by another college student.

She raised a brow as the camera panned to follow the aggressor when he raced away from the scene. "That kid definitely has some anger issues."

Her eyes nearly fell out of their sockets when a wolf came into focus, entering from the same direction the student left. "Oh my god. That kid's a Pioneer."

He pocketed his phone. "What's worse is that it looks like he's freshly turned. Taking his age into consideration, this is a volatile situation that we need to contain. And quickly."

"Wait, what does his age have to do with it?"

"Think of it this way. He's a hormonal teenager pumped up on adrenaline. His wolf is young, reacting on instinct and emotion."

"So how would it be different if he were born one?"

He pressed the subbasement button and she resisted the urge to roll her eyes. How could he possibly think that would make it go faster?

"We spend years teaching our young how to control their emotions, how to work with their wolf when it first emerges."

She massaged her temples. A headache was coming on. "So, this kid has just turned into his worst nightmare, is probably scared, alone, and thinks he's having a psychotic break?"

He nodded. "That pretty much sums it up. Elijah has been busy biting people to turn them."

Her stomach constricted, and her headache intensified. "Are you sure about that?"

"Darian, the 911 supervisor you met the other day, monitors emergency calls. Last week he took a call and recognized the signs of an imminent forced turn. That job was routed to Wendy, one of our ambulance operatives. When Wendy turned up, she confirmed Darian's guess and enlisted Tim's help to get the man to the nearest pack before his turn."

"Is he okay?"

"Yes. But his life will never be the same again."

The elevator dinged their arrival and the doors slid open.

"What about the kid in the video?"

"Tim and the others are trying to find him now."

They exited the elevator to the parking garage.

"Why is Elijah going around randomly biting people?" she said quietly.

He paused before answering. "That's the thing. It's not random." He sighed. "Only those with a dormant wolf gene can be turned. And even then, only by a pure Werewolf."

This fact, she was already aware of. But something cold clutched around her heart as she considered the ramifications. "Then how does he know who to target?"

"That's what we need to work out. That, and we have no idea how many more he's bitten."

"The wolf on the freeway?"

"It's looking more and more like he was newly turned." He opened the driver's door to his Cadillac. "In addition to taking out Elijah, our priority is to find these newly turned Werewolves before they expose us."

She got in and stared at the windscreen. "Who maimed those students? The wolf or the boy? He can't be left to run free. Especially since one of his victims is not expected to survive."

"That will be up to the council to decide."

She dropped the subject, partly because she wasn't sure whether she'd like the answer, and partly because the thought of multiple frightened new Pioneers terrified her. "What about the videos? The more people look at them, the more they might realize something else is going on."

He cleared his throat. "We have someone working on that."

She returned Murphy's phone to him. "Why do you think Elijah hid some of the bodies, while others he left out in broad daylight?"

"That's what I am trying to work out. He has a greater plan in play here. The question is: what?"

His answer did nothing to alleviate her fears.

EIGHTEEN

Family Ties

Kaitlyn tamped down her irritation and pointed to the four photos on the counter. "Mrs. Crispin, can you please take another look to see if you recognize anyone. It may help us understand who killed your ex-husband."

As with the two other times she asked, Desdemona Crispin ignored her. It was as if Kaitlyn wasn't in the room.

Instead, Desdemona ran her finger's down the lapel of Murphy's suit jacket. The blood red of her long nails was a direct contrast to the jacket's dark fabric. "You know, I have extensive experience handling this level of quality. I would be more than happy for you to sample my skills."

Kaitlyn nearly choked at Desdemona's not so veiled proposal. Hello. I'm standing right here.

From the moment they stepped into the dry-cleaning store, Desdemona had latched onto Murphy and completely ignored her. This was her third attempt at getting Desdemona to look at the photos. She took a deep breath and kept her irritation reigned in. While Desdemona wouldn't acknowledge her, Murphy was another story.

Murphy took a half step back. His body was stiff and his expression priceless. "Ma'am, if you could just take a look at the photos?"

Desdemona reached up and plucked invisible lint off Murphy's outer breast pocket. "I told you before. Call me Desdemona." She winked at him. "Tell me, Murphy, where do you keep your gun? I bet it's a big one."

Kaitlyn shook her head and held back a grin. She'd never seen Murphy squirm before. His scowl would have a blind man backing off. Not Desdemona. The woman was a dog with a bone. But she had to give him credit. He managed to remain impassive despite Desdemona's overt suggestions, and her constant need to touch him.

Not that she blamed the woman. Her partner did turn heads. But after Desdemona ran her hands over Murphy's suit jacket one too many times she had to bite her tongue before a retort spewed from her mouth. They needed answers, and their horny money launderer appeared to be more than happy to talk to Murphy. Exclusively.

Murphy caught Desdemona's hands before they slipped under his jacket. "The photos?"

Desdemona threw him a sultry gaze. "For you, anything."

Oh God, she was going to be ill.

Kaitlyn glanced up at the sky as they exited the laundromat. At least the rain had stopped. For now.

"Did you get the feeling she's a little too rehearsed and slippery?" she said as they headed back to the Cadillac. She threw Murphy a sly look and arched a brow. "Or were you otherwise occupied, sweetie?"

When Murphy let out a low growl from the back of his throat, she grinned. He clearly couldn't see the funny side of it. "What did your Spidey sense tell you when she looked at the photos?"

He handed her the folder. "She knew four of the other vics. But she was being truthful when she said she didn't know why her ex-husband was being targeted. She is nervous about something. My guess is Elijah got the wrong Des."

She didn't have his superior hearing or sense of smell, but she had come to the same conclusion. "We can safely assume Elijah's after something, or someone he believes these people can give him. The question is, did he get the information and then kill them? Or did he kill them because they couldn't give him the answers?"

"I suspect the latter with the late Mr. Crispin," Murphy said.

She nodded at the card poking out of Murphy's pocket and held back a laugh. "You going to call her?"

His expression did not alter, but he seemed a bit confused

She hopped in the passenger seat and pointed to the white business card. "She put her number in your pocket."

He pulled the card out, glanced at it, and to her surprise, appeared to be caught off guard. His expression soured as he glared at her. "You were enjoying that."

She grinned. "You betcha."

Murphy ignored her and pulled the Cadillac into traffic. When they stopped at a red light, he suppressed a yawn.

"When was the last time you slept?"

Based on her conversations with Joshua, every night since the freeway incident Murphy had patrolled the streets of Boston with very little rest.

"I don't need sleep."

She raised an eyebrow and threw him a pointed stare. "Everyone needs sleep, even grumpy Pioneers. It's bad enough with Garcia being moody. And don't give me any schtick about how superior you are. I've spoken to Joshua. You can survive on little sleep, not no sleep. And based on my calculations, you haven't slept in a week."

Murphy's lips set into a grim line. "We have a killer to catch, and who knows how many newly turned Werewolves. Or had you forgotten that?"

Ebenezer Scrooge, the man was frustrating. He always had to have the last word. He constantly berated her about taking better care, but he ignored his own advice. She stared out the window and held her tongue. He was right, they had two problems on their hands, both of which needed to be resolved. A wolf going around biting people was one thing, but if the Human world found out the wolf was actually a man who could change … She shuddered at the backlash. Pack mentality would definitely—

Her pulse quickened as an idea hit her. She tapped her fingers on the armrest while her mind sifted through the possibilities. Unable to keep it to herself any longer, she turned to Murphy. "The only way to turn someone is to bite them, right?"

He nodded. "Only the transfer of saliva into the bloodstream can turn a Human with the appropriate gene, and it can only be done in wolf form."

"How deep would the bite need to be?"

Murphy frowned. "Deep enough to cut through the skin and draw blood, I guess."

She turned to stare out the window. She chewed on her thumbnail. It might work. But how would she get the information without people asking questions?

"Out with it," Murphy said.

"With what?"

"Well, something has those wheels in your head turning a mile a minute."

She bit the inside of her cheek and hesitated before clearing her throat. "Massachusetts laws are such that we're more likely to seek medical treatment after an animal attack than any other state. And all attacks are reported to the Department of Public

Health. If we can get our hands on that information, it might narrow down our search."

She sighed and pinched her lips together. "Except—"

"You're worried about how we're going to explain why we need the data?" Murphy said.

She nodded. "We could spin some story, but it will be sketchy at best."

"I know someone who may be able to help. She's already on the case trying to bring those videos down. I'll put you in touch with Parker. But you'll need to refrain from asking her how she gets the information, and you shouldn't use your work phone to contact her."

"Why not?"

He sighed. "For you, the world and the law is black and white. For the rest of us, it's anything but."

She resisted the urge to push him further. While it irked her, at this stage she had no choice but to accept any help to get the information, even if it was strictly outside the law. This might be the only way to track down the poor souls from the freeway and the frat party.

Murphy's phone beeped. He growled when he checked the message.

"Problem?"

He pressed his foot down on the accelerator. "I'm being summoned to the police commissioner's office. He wants me there five minutes ago."

She flinched. "Ouch. That can't be good."

Murphy slammed the button to the elevator a second time. As usual, it was slow to arrive, and he was late. "I need you to build a timeline for Crispin's last twenty-four hours. Talk to everyone he came into contact with. See if any of them crosscheck with our other vics. If you have to haul his ex-wife in, threaten to send out uniformed officers. She won't want that, it's not good for business."

She glanced up at Murphy. His face hadn't changed, but he palpitated with anxiety. "How long do you think you'll be?"

He checked his watch. "It's going to take a while. Don't hang around on my account."

The elevator dinged, and the doors slid open. He stepped in before her.

"Okay. I have a training session booked for seven. If you need me back after that, let me know."

Murphy growled as he swung around to face her, his face stormy. "I thought I already told you you're wasting your time with the training."

Taking a leaf out of the Murphy O'Neill playbook, she ignored him and stepped into the elevator.

When the doors closed on them, he let out a sigh. "If you insist on such a useless endeavor, you should at least learn skills that might actually help you."

She clenched her fist and her nails dug into her flesh. "And where the hell am I going to find that? Because the last time I checked, there's no Fight off a Pioneer for Dummies book at the library."

Murphy glared at her. Standing her ground, it took all of her will to meet his unwavering and furious gaze. Why won't he just let it go?

He closed his eyes and grunted. "Fine. I'll teach you."

"P-pardon?"

When they arrived at the commissioner's floor, he stepped out. "You heard me. My place, after work. Now shut up, will you? We have work to do."

She stared at his retreating back, her mouth open. He had just offered to teach her how to defend herself against Pioneers. Her mind raced. What had prompted this sudden change? And what exactly was he going to teach her? She sighed. His motivation didn't matter. She was never coming from a position of weakness ever again.

The day passed in a blur. Garcia and Saul weren't having any luck finding a connection between Haladlo and Potter, but they did find a confirmed link between Potter and the mob. And Anika, who had been assigned the daunting task of finding fingerprint matches across all the crime scenes, was doing no better. Literally thousands of full and partial prints had been lifted from each scene.

She ignored Anika's messages. Her friend was full of enthusiasm, but it was sometimes draining. Instead, she made a start on warrants for their new vic and attempted to write up her case notes while she waited for a response from the DA's office. Not her favorite aspect of the job, but considering she now had more than Doug breathing down her neck to get the paperwork done, ignoring the reports wasn't an option. She'd even offered to head over to the Massachusetts' State Police Crime Laboratory with Anika to assist her in her fingerprint search to avoid paperwork. Not that she could actually add any value, but anything was better than sitting at a desk and typing up reports.

By the time she left for the day, Murphy hadn't returned. That couldn't be good. From rumors floating around the office, the director was also involved in Murphy's meeting. On her way to Groton she finally had a chance to call Parker Johnson.

When Parker answered the call, she hesitated. From the smattering of Murphy's and Joshua's conversations she had overheard, this Parker person was Daniel Locke's mate and the pack's second alpha. Was there some sort of protocol she was supposed to follow when addressing a Pioneer alpha? Your alphaship?

She cleared her throat. "Umm … Hi, Ms. Johnson, my name is Kaitlyn Quinn. I work—"

"With Murphy. I know, I was expecting your call. And please, call me Parker. Now, Murphy wasn't very clear on what you need."

She relaxed. Parker came across as warm and friendly. "Yes, well with him less is more."

Parker laughed. "That's Murphy alright. But they're not all like that, I promise. It'll take you time to wrap your head around the whole different, but not so different, race that lives among us."

"You make it sound like you're Human," she said.

"That's because I am. For now."

Her fingers tightened around the steering wheel. "Wait. What?" She must have misunderstood. She distinctly remembered Murphy and Joshua referring to her as an alpha.

"Jesus, Mary and Joseph, I understand Murphy not telling you, but clearly your grandfather has Murphy's disease as well." Parker sighed. "I suspect you've questions back up into next year."

She groaned. "Next decade you mean."

"How about we sort out what information you're after, and we can arrange a time one night this week to skype. You are going to need a bottle of something and a lot of … what's your weakness, chocolate or ice cream?"

She grinned. "Most definitely chocolate."

"I'll bring the ice cream, and hopefully the missing bits of information on this bizarre world you've stepped into."

The tightness in her chest lightened. "You are a god send, I thought I'd go insane trying to get answers from Murphy." She paused and remembered the reason for the call. "Speaking of which, I understand you can help us narrow down some information."

When she got off the phone, her body was buzzing with a sense of achievement. She and Parker had spoken for most of the drive. With very little explanation of what she needed, Parker had understood exactly what she was after, including ways in which she could narrow down their suspect pool. Looking into the medical records of the people attacked by animals would give them a more accurate list, but only so much information was available on the public health database. She wasn't about to question how Parker was getting the information. All she cared about at this point was finding anyone who could be in danger.

All that was good, but being able to speak with someone openly about her sudden immersion in a world of Pioneers had her almost giddy. Parker alleviated some of her fears and their next call would most probably put an end to the rest. As long as she had enough chocolate and Pinot Gris for their Skype call, all would be good.

When she pulled her Prius behind Joshua's rental a short while later, she wasn't surprised to see her grandfather appear from around the side of the house and wave to her. She got out and waited for him.

"Murphy said to expect you," he said.

She gave him a hug and grabbed a bag from the car. "He's going to do a bit of training with me."

Joshua raised a brow. "So I hear. He's running a bit late, said he needed to pick up something for your lesson."

She glanced down the long drive way. The gray sedan following her the entire trip from the city was nowhere to be seen. But she knew her minders were there. To give them credit, she had taken a while to catch them out.

They walked into the house as she brought him up to speed on the case. "How's the tracking going?"

"Well, it's zero for two, now three. We're trying to track the new Werewolves around the clock, but so far, nothing. We tracked the Freeway Wolf to Thirteenth Street but then lost him."

"What do you think happened?"

Joshua's phone rang. "I think he was picked up in a car. There's no other explanation on why the trail ran cold." He glanced at the screen then put the phone to his ear. "Molly, sorry I didn't get back to you earlier."

He fell silent as the person on the other end spoke. "Thanks, but you don't need to fuss, Liam has more than enough to do without worrying about my vegetables."

He nodded a few times then smiled as his eyes darted to her. "Good. She's with me at the moment." Joshua frowned. "Uh, I don't think that's a good idea."

He cringed, holding the phone away from his ear. Whoever he was speaking to wasn't happy about something. "Okay, hang on, I'll put her on."

He handed the phone to her. "It's for you."

She reached for the phone. "H-hello?"

"Honey, to be sure you don't know me, but our families go way back," a woman's voice with a distinct Irish brogue said. "I knew your da well. Ah, but Ryan was such a sweet lad. There's not a day that goes by we donmiss'im." The woman sighed. "I confess, I shed more than a tear or two when I heard you were finally part of our Joshua's life again. He tells me you've grown up to be a fine young wan. He's so proud of you."

Her eyes flicked to Joshua. The woman sounded genuine, warm even, but so did stone cold killers when they were trying to declare their innocence. "Umm, thank you. I'm sorry, but you are?"

"Oh child, you must think me mental. I'm Molly. Molly O'Neill. Murphy's me son."

Her heart thudded to a halt, and her brow rose. Murphy had a mother?

Joshua nodded in confirmation.

She wasn't sure why she was surprised. He couldn't have been chiseled from granite, even though he came across hard as rock. She cleared her throat. Why wouldn't Joshua, or even Murphy, have mentioned this? "I'm afraid he's not one to really talk about himself."

Molly laughed. "What? You mean that eejits never spoken about his Da or me? That's not *Craic*, but I'm not surprised. For years, he and Liam have rarely spoken, not since Elijah's escape."

"Oh, I'm sorry."

"Ah, don't be. He's like his Da that way, stubborn and pigheaded." Molly sighed. "There's no point crying over spilt milk. I just wanted to say hello and let you know if there's anything you need, just give me a cooee. You've had a big shock, and sometimes a woman's perspective can give clarity. Ah, if it's okay, Joshua will give ya me number. And if you need anything, anything at all, I'm just a call or message away. You might not know it yet, but you are part of our pack, and a pack is there for one another."

She was at a loss as she ended the call. While she had come to terms with Murphy and Joshua not being like her, it was taking a little longer to accept that there were a lot more out there like them.

Joshua pocketed his phone. "Sorry about that, Molly can be a bit forceful at times."

She pressed a hand to her stomach as if that would ward off her uneasy realization. Parker's comment on Pioneers' personalities being the same as humans suddenly had far more meaning than when she first heard it. "You know what, it's not a problem. It's actually comforting to think that Pioneers are just like the rest of us. They even have dysfunctional families." She hesitated. "What did Molly mean when she said there was some friction between Murphy and his father? What happened?"

"You'll need to ask Murphy that one. I'm afraid it's not my story to tell." Joshua pulled out his phone again. "Speaking of which, what's taking him so long?"

When his call to Murphy went straight to voice mail, he fell quiet and stared into the distance. After a time, he huffed and stood. "No answer, he still has his link closed. How about a drink out on the verandah while we wait? Beer okay for you?"

She nodded, and when he returned with a Corona, she asked, "What does a closed link mean?"

Joshua sat down and studied the beer bottle. "Well, some Werewolves can communicate telepathically."

She blinked, not sure she had heard him correctly. When it became apparent he wasn't joking, her hand shot up to her chest.

The implications were horrifying. "Wait, so you can read minds?"

He raised his hands to calm her down. "No, nothing like that. It's more like a telephone call. Someone attempts to communicate, but the receiver has to accept the call. It takes a while to learn the skill, and it's only used when there is a considerable amount of trust."

At his reassurance, she relaxed slightly. "Okay, I guess that makes sense. But what does a closed link mean?"

"Well, in the case of Werewolves such as Murphy, they have the ability to disconnect from the network, so we can't find where to direct the link. Does that make sense?"

She took a sip of the beer, needing a moment to digest the information. "You're telling me he can switch his Bluetooth on and off."

Joshua chortled at her analogy. "That's exactly what he does. Over the past decades he has very rarely turned it on. I hear tell Daniel is the only one who's gotten through to him." He glanced down at the bottle in his hand. "I must say I was a little caught off guard when he started to open it again."

His expression turned reflective. "You see, Katy, sometimes in the heat of the moment people say and do things that, well, in the light of day they probably shouldn't have."

Before she could question him further, Murphy's Cadillac drove up.

Joshua dropped his voice and leaned forward. "I'd keep the call with Molly to yourself. There's no knowing how he'd take it."

Murphy appeared shortly after and disappeared into the house. When he reappeared a few seconds later, he called out to her gruffly, "Ready?"

She jumped up. "Yes."

"Follow me."

She looked at Joshua for advice, but he shrugged his shoulders. "Don't ask me, I have no idea why he agreed to do this." He shooed her out the door. "But I suggest you hurry before he changes his mind. I'll get dinner started." With that, he headed inside.

She hurried after Murphy. "How was the meeting with the commissioner?" she said when she caught up to him.

Murphy let out a low growl. "He's an idiot who has too many ears floating about. And I think I know what Garcia is hiding. He's got to be the commissioner's informant."

She nearly tripped over her feet. "What?"

"The commissioner had information that wasn't in the reports to him. Garcia is bucking for a promotion, and this is how he intends on securing it."

She took a moment to digest the information. Could flirty Garcia really be a mole for the commissioner? "What are you going to do?"

"Not much we can do about it. I'll need proof first."

They walked the rest of the way in silence and ended up in the middle of the large clearing where she had first seen his wolf. The sun was low on the horizon, presenting a stunning backdrop, and the polar opposite of the last time she looked out over the forest. Her cheeks heated up as she remembered Murphy's state of undress when he stepped onto the verandah that night. Sweet baby cheeses, would she ever get that image out of her mind?

She dropped her head in case Murphy saw the flush on her face.

Murphy exhaled loudly. "You will never win against a Werewolf. The sooner you realize that, the sooner your life expectancy increases."

She folded her arms across her chest but held her tongue. She wasn't about to look a gift horse in the mouth, even if it was a grumpy one.

He pulled out a rectangular metal object from the waistband of his jeans. "Do you know what this is?"

She nodded. "A Taser."

He handed it to her. "This will give you a better chance than a gun. Fifty-thousand volts will temporarily stun most Werewolves long enough to allow you to run."

"What's wrong with a gun?" She inspected the weapon. It was a lot larger than the ones she was used to.

"A bullet, if you even manage to fire it, will sting a little, but won't do the damage you'd expect. The only way to kill us with a gun is a bullet through the eye socket. And even then, it doesn't always work. Weres are faster than Humans. If you are close enough to hit an eye, you won't even get the gun out of the holster."

She stifled a gasp. Surely, that couldn't be right. Nothing living could ever be that fast.

Ignoring her obvious shock, he took the Taser from her and placed it a short distance away. "I am going to come at you. I want to see how you handle yourself."

Murphy circled her. The way he was sizing her up and finding her weaknesses was unsettling.

He threw a roundhouse kick at her head. She ducked, sliding between his legs on her knees. Jumping to her feet, she aimed a swift kick to his back. She expected he would stumble forward, but he stood his ground as if nothing had touched him.

He spun around and landed a blow to her shoulder. A sharp pain shot through her, and she winced. She ducked instinctively, and his arm missed the strike aimed at her head.

She responded with a flurry of punches and kicks, varying her target from Murphy's head to his torso and back again. He blocked each blow while increasing the speed and velocity of his own attacks.

Beads of sweat ran from her brow. Her shirt was soaked, her pulse racing, and her breathing uneven. Murphy looked as though he had just been for an uneventful walk around the park. Nothing about him indicated he had just spent thirty minutes trading blows with her.

He held out a bottle of water. "At least you can hold your own against most Humans."

"Gee, thanks," she said, then took a long drink.

"But you are still delusional if you think you have any chance against a Werewolf."

Tossing the bottle on the ground, she placed her hands on her hips. "I told you, I was unprepared last time. You won't get a chance to do that again."

In the next instant, Murphy materialized behind her. One arm snaked around her midriff, holding her arms in place. The other was around her neck, holding it firmly in the crook of his elbow. Any attempt to struggle out of the steel vise was fruitless. With each attempt at resistance, the grip around her neck tightened and breathing became harder. And right now, she needed to breathe more than ever. The feel of his body against hers was doing some odd things to her stomach and other places, if she were honest.

His lips brushed lightly against her ear. "You were saying?" His voice, low and thick, sent goosebumps down her body as his warm breath fanned the side of her face.

Her shoulders dropped. The thought killed her, but she was coming to the conclusion that maybe ... perhaps ... she was no match for those of his race. Certainly, it seemed like she was no match for him. Physically, at least.

Murphy's very masculine scent sent shivers down her spine as his hard and unyielding body pressed against hers. The warmth spread out from the pit of her stomach and touched every nerve ending as his whiskers brushed against her face.

What the hell was the matter with her?

Wanting to put distance between them, and quickly, she admitted defeat. "Fine, okay you're stronger and faster than me. Happy now?"

He released his hold. She turned to face him only to discover he was removing his T-shirt.

Jumpin' Jesus Jones.

Her face heated up when he revealed his well-defined chest in all its glory. "W-what are you doing?"

He threw his shirt on the ground. "I'm showing you the only way you might have a chance to get away from a Werewolf."

Her imagination was bombarded with an astounding array of possible reasons why Murphy was standing in the middle of his backyard, half naked, jeans riding sinfully low on his hips, dirty blond hair and his usual three-day growth framing his onyx eyes. She studied him from beneath her eyelashes. He was perfectly proportioned in every sense of the word. The contours and muscles of his upper body were as sinful as his eyes. He had the body of someone used to physical exertion and hard work, but he wasn't bulky or overdeveloped. From their brief physical contact, she knew his body was pure masculine power. But nothing had quite prepared her for her reaction to his physical form this close up in broad daylight.

Good lord, were they all like this?

Murphy's smooth, whisky voice broke into her wayward thoughts. "Are you okay?"

She cleared her throat. Embarrassed at being caught ogling, she quickly looked away. "Yes, no problem." Her voice came out croaky and suspicious, even to her ears.

Wrangling control of her erratic thoughts, she moved her focus back to the reason they were here. "What exactly are you going to show me?"

"Werewolves' bones are denser and can bear a lot more pressure than Human ones. We have more strength, stamina, and speed. Our hearing and eyesight are far superior."

She raised an eyebrow at him. "Are you bragging, or is there a point to this?"

He ignored her tone. "So far, you've been thinking about how to match us in the very thing we are naturally better at. You need to learn how to strike us at our weak points."

She snorted in a very unladylike fashion. "According to you, you don't have any."

Murphy crossed his arms over his chest and narrowed his eyes.

She held up her hands in surrender. "Okay, I'm sorry, please continue."

"I'm going to teach you how to strike at some of our vulnerable pressure points. With the limited force you can inflict, you won't be able to disable a Werewolf, but you should cause enough pain to halt him temporarily. Enough to give you a chance to run."

"And how, exactly, will I do this?"

"You'll need to target precision strikes at certain groups of muscles. Provided you perform them correctly, the muscles around the lungs will contract violently, sending pain signals to the brain."

She listened intently. This was something she could do. This was her chance to level the playing field. Forgetting her agitation with him, she gave him all her attention.

Murphy closed the distance between them. "The first combination you need to learn is strikes to the brachial plexus and trachea."

He grabbed her hand and placed it on his chest, over his collar bone. "Feel here," he said putting pressure on her hand and fingers, then moving it slightly. "And here. Apply enough pinpoint force, and it will cause the nerves to send the desired signals to the brain."

Monkey butters.

As if she wasn't already hot and bothered from the workout, now this. His skin, smooth and warm, sent tiny shards of energy up her arm with each touch. Under her fingers his sinewy muscles were hard and unyielding.

"Can you feel it?"

"What? Pardon?" She cleared her throat, hoping it might help clear her brain, too.

"The nerve area you need to concentrate on?"

She pulled her attention away from his hot physique and refocused on the lesson. Her eyes flew open wide. Wait. Since when did she start thinking he was hot?

Murphy demonstrated the optimal way in which to hold her hands when striking each group of muscles. Once he was satisfied she understood, he had her practice on him.

"But won't that hurt you?"

Murphy gave her a look that clearly said he had no confidence she would come close to hitting anything that could affect him.

Determined to prove him wrong, she concentrated her energy.

He growled after they had been at it for what seemed a lifetime. "Faster, you need to move faster."

Her arms were sore and heavy. Her hands were in agony, like she was hitting a brick wall.

Seeing her flexing her fingers, Murphy grabbed her hand and began to gently massage the tension from her fingers and wrist. "Once you hit the nerve, you need to make contact with the trachea an instant later. Any longer than that and it won't have the desired effect."

The sensations from his touch sent another round of warmth through her body. Each time his thumbs placed pressure on the back of her hand in a circling motion, her insides churned in time to his gentle but firm touch. She was positive a horde of deranged butterflies were trying to escape from her stomach. Jumpin Jesus Jones, get a grip.

She looked up to find him gazing at her with a strange expression. One she had not seen before. The gentle soothing movements against her skin ceased, and they stood transfixed, neither speaking or moving. She found herself caught in the pull of his dark gaze, unable to look away and not really wanting to.

"Dinner's ready!"

The moment was broken, and they both took a couple of steps back, as if stung. Unsure of what to say or do next, she bent down and grabbed her Taser. By the time she had retrieved it, Murphy had his shirt on and was heading for the house.

She headed in the same direction, but the back of her throat ached and she had difficulty swallowing. Perhaps this wasn't the best idea. At least with her mixed martial arts trainer she could keep her mind focused. With Murphy, her emotions were dangerously close to the surface. She needed to keep her feelings bottled up. He was her partner and a means to avenge her father's death and make Elijah pay for the damage he had caused. Nothing more.

She clutched the taser and scowled. Something told her that might be easier said than done.

NINETEEN

Who Let the Dogs Out?

By the time Kaitlyn arrived at work the next morning, she had spoken to Parker multiple times. The woman was a genius. Not only had she narrowed the list of possible new Pioneers down from over two thousand to two hundred and fifty names, but she had also cross-referenced the list against the Department of Motor Vehicles database.

Now they needed to work out how to further reduce the number. Elijah had deliberately bitten people across three states. Although a ploy to keep them occupied and distracted from discovering his primary goal, she couldn't help but feel some responsibility for the victims. How many more would surface to create havoc? And what, or who, the hell was Elijah really after? It must be important for him to screw with so many people's lives.

She walked in the door and her stomach clenched. Garcia had already arrived. She checked the time and frowned. He never got in this early. So much for pouring through the names Parker had given her.

Garcia popped his head over his newspaper and smiled. "Morning."

"Good morning, how did it go yesterday?"

"Good. We got a breakthrough, found the link between Marke and Haladlo."

Her brows knitted together, and she swung her chair around to face him. "Wait, Marke? Our second vic, the high school teacher?"

Garcia nodded. "We were just as surprised. But it does support our theory that Marke was in the wrong place at the wrong time."

Before Garcia could elaborate any further, Murphy arrived. Once he was caught up to speed, Garcia continued.

"Marke's car was finally found yesterday. We canvased every store and business in the vicinity and discovered that our school teacher made a last-minute appointment with a nearby dentist. Turns out, the reason he got in on such short notice was because another client cancelled."

"Haladlo?"

Garcia sat back in his chair and nodded. "Yep. Our psycho took out the wrong patient."

Murphy stroked his chin. "That explains why the contents of his wallet were strewn across the scene." He paced. "But we still have no idea why he was targeting Haladlo, Potter, and Weiss. We need to find that link."

Garcia stood and made his way to the victim's board. "I had to leave early yesterday. Saul was following up on another lead. Maybe he's found something,"

She turned her head toward the door. Saul and Anika, who was talking his head off, were heading across the main bull pen. "Speak of the devil."

Saul ambled into the office and pointed behind him. "You do not want to go out there."

She craned her neck. The floor they were on housed the Boston PD's communications department. To her, it looked as chaotic as it normally did.

Anika flopped on a small couch in the corner. She rested her head back and closed her eyes. "Do you blame them? We were all ripped out of our beds at three a.m."

Her ears pricked. "What happened? They're external comms, they don't get woken up for a crime scene."

"They do when it's about to get crazy AF. Last night nine bodies were found, each one with a single gunshot wound to the back of the head. Everyone's freaking to the max."

"I heard they all have ties to the Sinaloa Cartel," Garcia said.

She frowned. Fighting within the organized crime factions had bumped their case off the front page and that was a good thing, but the turf war was in danger of spilling over to innocent people. "Who do they think is responsible?"

Garcia lowered his voice. "According to my source, the evidence is pointing to a rival Mexican cartel."

Saul snorted as he logged into his computer.

Murphy cocked an eyebrow. "You disagree?"

Saul shrugged at Murphy. "I've been around a lot longer than the rest of you wet-behind-the-ears pups. This all started when the bodies that washed up on shore a few months ago turned out to be the boss, underboss, and lieutenants of what was left of the Winter Hill Gang."

He was right. The gang war traced back to that unsolved incident. "Do you think this is a retaliation for those killings?"

Saul shook his head. "No, I'm saying that was the start. Law of the jungle. They took out their oldest rival first."

She cocked her head. That didn't make sense. "But Winter Hill was a threat to no one. They were small-time drug dealers who haven't had any power since the '70s." Her brows flew upward. "Wait, so you think the mob is behind this?"

Saul leaned back in his chair and rested his hands on his portly stomach. "I'm positive it's them. By the way, Mildred said to thank you for that pot roast recipe."

Garcia snorted. "You blame everything on the mob, including why the Red Sox haven't won a world series in five years."

Saul gave Garcia a side-eye. "Those bodies last night prove it's a mob hit. Single bullet to the back of the head."

"But that's not what killed them," Anika said.

All heads swiveled toward her. She opened her eyes and lifted her head from the back of the couch. "Their spinal cords were severed. According to the ME, they were shot postmortem."

"That doesn't mean it wasn't them," Saul said.

"Shots fired." Anika sighed and pushed herself up from the couch. "You salty lot continue fighting among yourselves. But I just dropped in to let you know I've been temporarily pulled off this case. Last night's slaughter has now taken top priority. These dudes aren't known for their forgiving attitudes. The mayor is getting antsy at the thought of a backlash. He's got the commish in a tizz and all resources are being diverted."

When Anika left, Saul turned back to his monitor, grumbling. "Retirement can't come soon enough, I only recognized five of her words."

Kaitlyn swallowed the sour taste in her mouth. She glanced across to Murphy. What was his reaction? If she were a betting person, she'd say Anika wouldn't be the last team member reassigned. As usual, his face was unreadable. But the dark shadows under his eyes concerned her. His lack of rest was becoming obvious.

She shot out of her chair. "I'm going to get coffee for everyone. My treat. Murphy, I'll need help carrying them back."

He understood coffee meant, we need to talk, and got up without questioning her bizarre demand.

As they walked down the corridor, she looked closer. The beginning of fatigue was definitely setting in. "Any luck?"

He shook his head. "No."

"Did you get any sleep?"

He shot her a scowl that told her it was none of her concern.

She pursed her lips. "You know you can't keep this up. Even Pioneers need sleep. You'll be no good to anyone."

He ignored her and stabbed at the down button.

The elevator opened and they stepped inside. They were no longer alone, and she had to bite her tongue. When they exited and headed for the front entrance, she lowered her voice. "Fine, ignore me all you want. While you've been out all night galivanting around the city searching for Elijah and the freeway wolf, some of us have been actually trying to help your sorry ass."

She finally had his attention. "Parker has come up with a list of names."

"And?"

She grimaced. "Do you want the good news or the bad news first?"

He tightened his jaw.

He didn't seem in the mood for lengthy discussions so she hurried on. "There were over two thousand people who sought medical attention after an animal bite during the past three months."

"Was that the good news or the bad news?"

She hid a smile. Was that an attempt at humor? "Parker narrowed that list down to two hundred and fifty possible victims."

He rubbed his jaw. "Is there a way to cross-check that list with anyone involved in the freeway accident?"

"Already done."

Murphy scowled at her. "So why didn't you start there?" He pulled away and placed their order.

She cocked her head. "Didn't we get up on the wrong side of the bed this morning? Oh wait—that's right—we're attempting the world record in sleep deprivation."

"I heard that."

They were headed back with three coffees and a hot chocolate before Kaitlyn continued the most important part of the conversation. The part that should definitely not be overheard. "One of the names from the list of animal bites came back as a match to Mark Dyson, the registered owner of a vehicle involved in the freeway pileup. Based on the police report, Mark was not there. According to the report, his wife was the only one in the car. But what's the bet he actually was there when all hell broke loose?"

Murphy glanced down at her with his usual unfathomable expression, not giving her any indication of what he was thinking. "Only one way to find out. We pay her a visit."

He pulled a coffee and hot chocolate from the tray then headed to the elevator. "I'll bring the car out front, get the address and I'll meet you outside in five."

While she couldn't always read his expression, his faster gait was a sure indication the news had energized him.

"I have an idea," she said after they had cleared the city limits and were on the freeway. "About how to speed up your search for the wolf on the freeway."

She took no-grunt to mean it was okay to continue. "The way I see it, you can't keep going on like this night after night, wandering each city grid to see if you can detect Elijah or the freeway wolf."

Murphy let out a low growl. "If you have a faster way of doing it, I'm all ears."

She grimaced, not sure how he would take her suggestion. "That's the thing. I have an idea of how we can, I just don't think you are going to like it."

Murphy narrowed his eyes and glanced at her. "Which means I'll hate it."

She ignored her racing heart and leaned forward. "Just hear me out. Your sense of smell is far and away more superior to a Human's."

"And?"

"And as a wolf, it's exponentially increased."

"You are aware that I don't have a death wish or any inclination to be the next wolf caught on camera that goes viral, aren't you?"

"With the increased police and animal control presence, I realize it's risky to wander around in wolf form." She gulped. Now or never.

She outlined her plan.

He slammed on the breaks to avoid hitting the vehicle in front of them and threw her an accusing glare. "You've got to be kidding."

"Look, just think about it. It makes sense. You can roam the streets unimpeded. And if anyone spots you, no one will think anything of it."

His body stiffened, and he stared out the front windscreen. "I'm not going to dignify that with an answer."

She crossed her arms over her chest. "You know I'm right. I've even spoken to Parker, and she agrees this is the quickest and most efficient way to get the job done."

He ground his teeth together. "Oh, she does, does she? Well if that's the case, she can bloody well get Daniel to do it. Because I'm not."

"You know I'm right."

"I won't do it. And I don't want to hear anything more about it."

The remainder of the drive was in silence. She let the matter rest. For now.

They pulled up to the address listed on the car's registration. A long wheelbase van emblazoned with A1 Plumbing was parked in the driveway. The license plate confirmed this was the vehicle caught up in the freeway disaster.

They were about to ring the doorbell when a shrill voice called out. Turning, Kaitlyn spotted an elderly neighbor waving at them.

"If you're after Mark and Theresa, they're not home."

Kaitlyn walked over to the woman. She pulled out her identification and held it up. "Ma'am, I'm FBI Special Agent Quinn, and my partner over there is Senior Supervisory Special Agent O'Neill. We are here following up on the freeway accident from a few days ago."

The woman squinted and inspected her card and badge. "Ma'am's my mother. Call me Ethel. I heard about that horrid accident on the news. My heart goes out to those poor families, what a dreadful thing to have happened." She clicked her tongue and took a step backward, nodding her head in sympathy.

Kaitlyn pointed toward the house. "Do you know when they'll be back?"

Ethel shrugged. "I'm not sure. They left in a rush early this morning. Both were quite upset about something."

"Do you have any idea where they went?"

Ethel shook her head. "No. But they were going on about having to evict something. They were in a complete state. But then that nice priest turned up, and they seemed to calm down a bit after that."

She froze, and her chest constricted. She looked over to Murphy, who was still inspecting the damage to the van. Their eyes locked, and she knew he had the same feeling of dread.

The old woman patted her arm. "Are you okay, dear? You don't look so well."

She gulped and cleared her expression to keep the panic from showing. "Ethel, the priest … Do you know who he is, or which parish he belongs to?"

Ethel frowned and her lips pursed, twitching as though that would trigger her memory. "I think one of those big ones in the city, but I can't be sure."

"Do you know how to get hold of them?"

Ethel shook her head. "Sorry. Theresa said they weren't going to be contactable while they were away. She just asked if I could clear their mail."

She thanked Ethel for her help and handed her a business card. "When they return, can you please let them know I need to speak to them?" She pointed in the direction of the damaged vehicle. "If it's okay with you, we'll just take a look at the van and then be on our way."

Ethel looked over to Murphy, who was peering into the back windows of the van. "I don't think I'd mind riding around with him all day." She gave Kaitlyn a sly wink, her long-distance vision obviously better than her short. "He's quite easy on the eye, isn't he dear?"

Knowing full well Murphy could hear every word, she shrugged her shoulders. "Meh, if you like that sort of thing."

She hid a smile when Murphy stiffened and stopped his search. After thanking Ethel for her assistance, she walked over to him. "So what do you think?"

He took another glance at the plumber's work vehicle. "It's him."

"You're sure?"

Murphy nodded. "My guess is he had his first change in the back while they were on the bridge. His wife was driving, and she was trying to get him to the Boston Medical Centre."

She headed back to the Cadillac. "The question is, where are they now?" She lowered her voice. "Because if the priest thinks he's going to perform an exorcism, I think he's in for one hell of a shock."

Ethel waved as they drove past, and she smiled at the old woman. She sat back in the seat and chewed her lower lip, sifting through all the possible scenarios on how this impending disaster could play out. "We need to find them."

Murphy's hands tensed on the steering wheel. "You don't think I know that?"

Her earlier idea returned. Their current situation gave it more credence. In her eyes, at least. She turned to plead her case.

"No."

How in cheese sticks did he know what she was going to say? She finger-tapped the armrest. "You know it's the best idea we have."

"I said no. End of discussion."

Where was he?

She bit her thumbnail and paced her living room. Coming full circle back to the window, she again peered through the curtains. Night had fallen.

He probably changed his mind. She couldn't believe he finally agreed to her plan. And she was far from certain her plan was a good one. What if it didn't work? What if it backfired? How in blue blazes would she get them out of it? Her pulse skipped a beat when the door buzzer rang. She wiped her clammy palms on her jeans and pressed the button to let him upstairs.

Murphy stalked in a few moments later, a less than pleased expression on his face. "I have no idea why I agreed to this hairbrained scheme."

This had better work. "Because we are up against the clock. And it's the best chance we have. You know it, or else you wouldn't be here."

Murphy let out his usual unhappy grunt. "I'm going to change."

A mischievous grin popped out as she pulled two leather straps from a paper bag and held them up, one in each hand. "Before you go, I need to know which one you prefer, black or red?"

A menacing growl reverberated through the room and she gulped.

"I don't need a collar."

She shook her head. "But that's where you're wrong. This will only work if you are on a lead, and people think we're just a typical, extra-large dog and its owner out for a late-night walk. Besides, it's the law."

Murphy glared at her as though she was speaking in an alien language.

"And ..." She reached into the bag and dragged out the matching lead.

Murphy's brows rose, and a look of pure disgust washed over his face. He pointed to the plastic dog bone dangling from the lead. "What the hell is that?"

She cocked her head and winked. "Oh, that. Doggy poop bags. The law is very clear. I'm responsible for making sure you don't litter on the clean streets of Boston. Especially near churches."

His expression of horror was too much, and she burst out laughing.

He scowled at her. "You're enjoying this."

She attempted to look contrite, without success. "Never. But you didn't say which you preferred?"

Seeing his blank look, she held up the collars again.

"Black," he muttered before turning and marching into the other room.

She held her stomach and swallowed the hysterical laughter threatening to bubble over when he grumbled, "And you couldn't have found ones without stupid studs?" as he passed through the doorway.

She pushed down the laughter and reached for her small backpack to rescan the map of Boston City churches while she waited for Murphy's wolf to appear. They had meticulously planned the optimal route required to cover most places of worship. If they were lucky, Murphy's wolf would be able to detect the presence of the freeway Pioneer from the street. Problem solved. Disaster averted. Or at least one of them.

She didn't need to wait long before Murphy's magnificent wolf entered the room. His coat, an unusual shade of golden brown, glimmered as the ceiling light shone directly onto his powerful body.

He walked over to her, his massive paws making no sound, and came to stand directly in front of her, not once breaking eye contact. The wolf, whose giant body came up to her waist, tilted its head and moved another step closer. She froze. Coming up with the plan was one thing, but it was another thing entirely to actually see it through. And now that she was looking the giant Pioneer wolf in the eye, she was not so sure she had made the right decision.

The wolf sniffed her. Not daring to move, she allowed the creature to circle her, his massive head nuzzling her every now and then. She cursed for not finding out more about the wolf from Murphy. Maybe this was how their Wolves became familiar with Humans? After what seemed an eternity, the wolf stood back and sat down on its haunches. A tongue lolled out of its powerful jaws and he looked up at her, as if waiting for something.

She stared at him until she remembered. "Oh, your collar."

She raced to retrieve it. The wolf let out a growl as she made her way to him, collar in hand. Oh oh. She spun on her heels and picked up the black collar instead of the red one.

It took four tries for her to get the leather collar on Murphy's wolf. When it was done, she stood up and inspected her handywork. "Ah, don't you look lovely."

The wolf bared its teeth, stood, and stalked her. As he passed her, he bumped his large body against her legs. The unexpected movement toppled her over, and she sprawled on the floor in an undignified manner.

She got up and dusted off her butt. "Very funny."

Murphy's wolf headed for the front door and barked.

She grabbed her backpack off the bench, clipped the lead onto his collar, and opened the door. She'd only gone two steps before she was thrown backwards. Murphy's wolf wouldn't budge.

"What?" She yanked on the lead. "Dogs aren't allowed out in public without their leads. Don't blame me, it's the law."

The rumble from deep within his chest was a clear sign he was not pleased with the situation.

She shook her head and sighed as she led him out the door. "It's going to be a long night."

Perhaps this wasn't such a good idea after all.

TWENTY

The Devil Made Me Do It

"How could you turn your back on us? You of all people?"

Paul cringed as his sister's high-pitched voice echoed off the walls in the church. No parishioners were present to overhear the bizarre conversation, and that was saying something, considering he had been privy to a range of strange and unusual discussions over the years.

He held his hands palms up and attempted to bring her volume down to an acceptable level. "Theresa, you need to understand, I'm not ignoring your plight, but I don't have the authority to do what you are asking."

Theresa held out the Bible she had been clutching all day and shook it in front of him. "Matthew 17:18—And Jesus rebuked the demon, and it came out of him, and the boy was healed instantly."

Paul Myers, Father Paul to his parishioners, slumped over and dropped his head in his hands. His elbows, which were digging into his knees, added to his overall discomfort. But mild discomfort was preferable to the situation he now found himself in. He loved his sister, but there were times when she tested the patience of a saint. And though he was a Catholic priest, he did not come close to that level of patience.

He said a quick prayer for guidance, took a deep breath, and sat up to face his sibling. Her eyes, red and swollen, were fixed on him. He glanced across the church at his brother-in-law and considered his options. Mark, who was sitting a short distance away, was not the same man. His brother-in-law was usually brash, confident, and outgoing. When he had arrived at his sister's house after her desperate cry for help, the person residing in Mark's skin was a shadow of his former self. He'd spent most of the day trying to break through to the man he knew. Both of them were traumatized from recent events. The fact that they were present during the aftermath of the much-publicised freeway accident only added to their combined hysteria. But even considering his beliefs, he had a hard time accepting what Theresa was telling him.

"Theresa, you have to admit, this is an extraordinary story you are asking me to believe."

Theresa burst into tears. "It's not a story. His body is possessed by the devil. You have to cast him out."

Paul fought to not roll his eyes. Instead, he reached over and squeezed her hand. "You need to calm down. Help me understand what you think has happened. How long has it been going on?"

Theresa clutched the Bible to her chest, her pain evident as she studied her husband. "Mark's not been feeling well lately, but the doctors said it was just a virus. He was moodier than normal, but I put it down to the effects of the medication."

"Tell me about the night the devil emerged." He was astounded he had just used those words, but with any luck, his sister would not detect his disbelief.

"I-I … We haven't slept since. It's killing us. Those poor people. The devil killed those people, and he forced Mark to be the deliverer of death."

Paul groaned inwardly. Here we go again. Fixing his sister with a no-nonsense look, he attempted to get her to focus on exactly what had occurred. He needed facts, not her fanciful interpretation. Not hysteria. "Theresa, the freeway. Tell me what happened on the freeway."

Theresa fidgeted with her rosary beads. Her voice came out quiet and somber. "He was in agony and I couldn't take it anymore, so I decided to drive him to Boston General. I managed to get him into the back of the van, so he could lie down. We were halfway there when I heard—" She stopped mid-sentence, her eyes manic as she looked at her husband.

"Go on."

Just when he thought she was about to quote Bible verses again, she surprised him by resuming her tale.

"The noise, I will go to my grave with that-that sound haunting me." Her voice croaked. "It was as though every bone in his body was b-breaking." She squeezed her eyes shut. "I couldn't see what was happening. But before I knew it, the devil's eyes were…" She flinched. "They were staring at me in the rearview mirror. I panicked and lost control of the van."

Paul frowned as her eyes widened and her pupils dilated, the look of pure terror etched on her face.

"By the time I'd crashed into the barrier, the beast had gotten free and …"

His heart broke as he watched his sister caress the smooth rosary beads. She was suffering under a great weight. "So why did you say nothing to the police?"

Theresa faltered and shrugged. "I-I don't know. I left as soon as I could and went straight home."

"What about Mark? How did he get home?"

"He came back the next morning, dirty and bruised. He said he'd woken up naked under some bushes just before dawn. H-he'd stolen clothing from someone's line and caught a cab home."

His rational mind couldn't believe he was about to ask the next question. He cleared his throat. "And has he turned back into this wolf since then?" His words sounded wrong on so many levels.

His sister bobbed her head and burst into tears again.

Her pulled her into his arms. Mass hysteria, that's the only thing that could explain this. But what had triggered it, and how could two perfectly sane and rational people be convinced this was happening to them? His sister was high-strung and prone to emotional outbursts, but this was a bit much, even for her. He sought to find a way to push past her rantings. "And how do you think the devil gained entrance?"

Theresa's eyes flashed and her expression hardened. "He was bitten by one of the hounds of hell." she said and began quoting verses from the Bible again.

Our Father, who art in heaven … Paul recited the Lord's Prayer to give him the strength to not snap at his sister. He proceeded to calm her down, yet again, but he was getting tired of it.

"A few weeks ago, Mark had an emergency callout. When the job was finished and he was packing up the van, one of the devil's creatures attacked him," Theresa said.

He ran his fingers through his hair. "Facts, 'Resa. I want facts, not your interpretation. If you thought there was a problem, why didn't you come and see me then?"

"Because the devil was disguised as a … as some kind of dog." Theresa halted and let out a small whimper before continuing. "Mark went to the hospital to have the bite treated. We didn't think anything of it at the time."

Paul sighed. Time to get tough. If she couldn't prove it, she would have to realize she needed help. "Can Mark force this wolf to appear?"

"It won't come."

Paul turned to face Mark. It was the first time today his brother-in-law had spoken without being prompted. He was careful to keep his tone neutral. "What won't?"

Mark stared at his hands. "It—the voice in my head. It said it won't come out 'cause it doesn't think it should."

They were finally getting somewhere. Mark was hearing voices.

He was no stranger to mental illness. As part of his ministry, he often visited with patients at a local hospital that catered to the needs of those with emotional issues. From his experience, he knew he needed to tread carefully. One wrong word could close them off and push them over the edge. He tried to think of the best person to help his sister and her husband. With medication and the proper help, they could put this behind them and move on with their lives.

"What about on the freeway. Did it tell you to turn into a ..." He hesitated, still not believing he was having this conversation. "A wolf."

Mark, still downcast, shook his head. "No. Neither of us could control what happened that night."

Theresa pulled at his sleeve and pleaded with him. "You need to cast him out."

"I can't. You have to have special permission to perform an exorcism. The only thing I can do is conduct a prayer of deliverance," he said.

She pulled her hand away and clutched her Bible. "You just don't want to help."

Enough. He raised his voice. "'Resa, you know I would if I could."

He broke out in a cold sweat when Mark's tortured voice cried out. "Stop. Stop arguing. I can't take it anymore."

Both he and Theresa swung to face Mark, who'd jumped to his feet. Mark's arms crossed over his stomach, and he doubled over as if in pain.

Paul watched in horrified fascination as the world he thought he knew crumbled around him. He couldn't tear his gaze away as he witnessed the strange and unnatural contortions of Mark's body. He crossed himself and pushed Theresa behind him. The sound of breaking bones scraped at his ears like nails down a blackboard. He understood Theresa now. Calculating how quickly he could get the bishop to agree to an exorcism, he was rooted to the spot as Satan burst forth from the body of his brother-in-law.

TWENTY-ONE

Yappy Rats

To casual passersby, Kaitlyn was out on a night jog with her dog. Her very, very large dog.

They developed an easy routine to circumnavigate the city in the quickest possible time, and before long they had covered twenty churches in Longwood, Kenmore, and Back Bay. The majority of the churches within the Boston City opened directly onto the street. She would feign a minor injury, hobble to the door, and open it to allow Murphy's wolf to sense if their quarry was inside. Once the wolf was satisfied the new Pioneer was not there, they moved on.

They had just crossed Arlington Street Church off their list and were heading north to Church of the Advent when her phone rang. A warm smile spread across her face as she pushed the answer button. "I wasn't expecting a call from you this evening."

"What? I can't call my granddaughter whenever I want," Joshua said. "You sound a bit puffed."

"I'm taking the dog for a walk."

"Sorry, I was actually after Murphy, but I can't reach him. I thought perhaps you knew where he was?"

She raised an eyebrow and glanced at her companion, who was listening to the conversation intently. She hesitated before speaking. "No. Yes, maybe."

"Well, which is it? Do you know where he is?"

She looked to Murphy's wolf for guidance on how to answer. She glared at the animal as it continued to passively stare at her with its head cocked.

Great help he was.

She made a face at the wolf. "Yes, he's, um, with me at the moment."

"Why isn't he answering his phone? I've left a dozen messages."

"He, err, must have left his phone behind."

She cringed when Joshua asked her to hand the phone to Murphy. "He's not … He's not really in any condition to take a call right now."

"Why not?" The line went quiet. "Hang on. You don't have a dog."

"I don't?" She grinned at Murphy's wolf, who let out a low growl.

"What the hell are you two up to?" Joshua said. "Don't tell me you're out in public with Murphy in wolf form."

She grimaced. "Okay."

"Okay, what?"

"Okay, I won't tell you."

His anger seeped through the phone. "Kaitlyn, you're running the serious risk of people recognizing him as a wolf."

They made their way through the park as she reassured her panic-stricken grandfather. They had almost cleared the park when a dog's yip cut through the night air. She tensed and looked around for the source of the high-pitched yapping. From out of nowhere, a small Jack Russell broke through the undergrowth and ran up to Murphy's wolf.

The small animal was unperturbed by the size differential and was yapping and dancing frantically around the wolf's legs.

Her brain froze. The deluded dog was attempting to assert dominance over the wolf. She wasn't sure who was more shocked at the sight. Her, the wolf, or the Jack Russell's owner when he burst through the thick hedge calling for his dog.

From the owner's repeated chants, the dog answered to Tyson, but the man stopped short when he spotted a beast the size of a small bear towering over his pet.

Diffusing the situation seemed a good idea. "Phone you back," she hissed, then rounded on the unsuspecting dog owner. She narrowed her eyes and wagged an angry finger at Tyson's owner. "You really need to keep that vicious creature on a leash. He's frightening my poor Benji."

With that, she reached behind her and pushed against Murphy's wolf, hoping he would get the hint.

The surprised owner looked between the two mismatched animals and his jaw dropped open. "He's what?"

She gave Murphy's wolf a sly kick to get him to focus on her rather than looking at the Jack Russell like it was his next meal. She shooed the small dog back to its owner. "I'll have you know Benji is a sensitive animal, not used to ill-behaved and unruly dogs."

Murphy's wolf took the hint, and let out a pathetic procession of scared whimpers as he cowered behind her.

She resisted the urge to roll her eyes at his overacting.

The man clipped a lead onto his dog's collar and struggled to pull Tyson away, still looking nervous and a little doubtful as he did so. The Jack Russell continued its high-pitched yapping without taking a breath. And to give him credit, Murphy's wolf continued whimpering as if he was scared of the bolshie dog.

She raised her chin. "Get him to stop that incessant yapping. Don't you know how to control your dog? Really, what is this city coming to? I swear they will let anyone have a dog license these days."

With that, she tugged lightly on Murphy's lead. "Come, Benji, let's get you away from this riff-raff. I think a chamomile bubble bath and some Nom Nom Now may calm your nerves."

She strained not to break into a sprint. Her heart was racing a mile a minute, and sweat was pouring off her forehead. She continued to console Murphy's wolf as if it were a small child. Before they turned the corner, she glanced back to discover a very shocked and confused man still rooted to the spot they left him in, and a small yapping dog pulling on his lead in an attempt to chase after them.

Her pulse returned to normal, and she breathed a sigh of relief as they cleared the next church and were on the move again.

"What?" she said, when she noticed Murphy's wolf walking stiffly.

He threw a look over his shoulder that let her know, in no uncertain terms, he was not thrilled with their close call.

She waved her hand at him dismissively. "Oh pfftt. Who's he going to remember tomorrow? The gigantic dog not dog or the bitch of an owner?" She shrugged. "Besides, your overacting didn't help."

That was it, she couldn't hold it in any longer. She burst out laughing, only to find herself sprawled on the pavement an instant later. "Hey, no fair." She scrambled to regain her balance, still hampered by her laughter.

The wolf stepped closer so that they were eye to eye. One onyx sparkle and she knew he was up to no good. Before she could react, a huge tongue emerged from his powerful jaws and licked the entire side of her face.

She squealed and wiped the saliva off. "Eww." She swatted him with as much strength as she could muster. "You great hairy brute, that's disgusting."

The wolf ignored her, and waited patiently for her to stand up and get on with their mission.

This was not happening. How and why had he agreed to this farce in the first place eluded him. His wolf, on the other hand, was pleased with this hair-brained scheme. The bloody gobshite of a beast thought her plan was a stroke of genius. To make matters worse, his wolf was having way too much fun roaming the streets with Kaitlyn. They could have covered the churches in half the time if they moved faster. She was more than capable of picking up the pace. What had gotten into his wolf to blatantly ignore everything he had to say? He needed to take control of their body, otherwise who knew what his wolf would end up agreeing to.

She called us Benji, and you have nothing to say about that? he grumbled.

His wolf snorted. *She got that rat away from us. Don't care what name she gives us.*

If there was a wall to bang his head against, he would do it. Traipsing across the inner-city streets of Boston was one of the worst cockamamy ideas.

Her pace slowed. "Uh, late night jogger at twelve o'clock. Let's cross over."

She pulled out ahead and checked the road before crossing. His wolf followed and kept pace a few steps behind.

You should be in front, setting the pace. Not lagging behind. Let's get this over with.

But it's such a nice behind, don't you think?

Whether because he was tired or distracted, it took a moment for him to work out what his wolf was referring to. *Give me strength.*

You're blind. Not dead. Or did you forget who licked her?

His wolf's self-satisfied smirk poked at him, and he swiped it away in irritation. *It didn't mean anything.*

His denial rang hollow, even to his own ears.

She tugged on the lead. "Why are you slowing down? We've still got a way to go to the next one."

His wolf picked up the pace and trotted beside her.

She glanced down at him and grinned before turning back to focus on where they were going. "You're still not fixated on that Jack Russell, are you?"

He groaned inwardly remembering his actions after their narrow escape. *What the hell was I thinking?*

After his wolf pushed her to the ground, she sat in the middle of the pavement, eyes bright with mirth and relief. Her laughter reached somewhere long forgotten. The joy on her face was too much for him to take, and instinct took over. An overwhelming desire to kiss her overruled his self-imposed isolation. For once, his wolf conceded to him, and he did the next best thing.

He licked her.

But it meant nothing, despite what his wolf thought. He was just making sure she was okay. *Come on, move faster.* The sooner they got this night over with, the better.

His wolf didn't respond and seemed content to follow Kaitlyn's lead.

They had cleared seventeen more churches and were in South Boston, headed along East Fourth Street, when his senses flared and his hackles rose. His wolf stopped and his muscles tensed, ready to pounce. It was faint, but he could just make out the scent from the plumber's van. Just to make sure he lifted his muzzle and sniffed again.

His wolf body quivered. *We have him.*

His wolf tugged so hard on the lead it slipped from Kaitlyn's hand. He willed his wolf to full speed.

It's about time. If we find him, at least this night's not a complete disaster.

TWENTY-TWO
Hail Mary

"Jumpin' Jack flash."

Kaitlyn shook her hand to curb the burn on her fingers as Murphy's wolf took off. Her pulse, already elevated, kicked into high gear. From his single-mindedness, she guessed he had found what they were after. Show time. She pulled her Taser from her backpack and sprinted after him.

A woman's scream cut through the deserted city street, and she stopped short to gauge the direction. When she caught up with Murphy's wolf at the church, he was dashing from door to door, a low growl reverberating from his chest.

She scowled and lowered her voice. "Keep it down. This is the last place you want to draw attention."

She glanced up and down the residential street to make sure they had not been seen or heard, then sprinted up the stairs to the Gate of Heaven Church and tested the large doors.

Murphy's wolf emitted a low whine. He stood up on his haunches, and his sharp claws scratched at the paneled wood.

"I'm hurrying, I'm hurrying." She yanked at the wrought iron handles. "The doors are locked. So much for a church being available to those in need."

She raced around the other side of the building and spotted a smaller door. Yes.

Before he could snag it on something, she unclipped the wolf's lead and sprinted down the path along the side of the church. To her relief, the side door was unlocked. Murphy's wolf pushed past her when she opened the door and raced into the church. She checked for any nosy neighbors, entered, and immediately locked the door behind her to make sure no unsuspecting parishioner accidently wandered in. When the door closed, she froze. The room was pitch black. Now blind, she took a moment to allow her eyes to adjust. Her shoulders relaxed when her vision returned. Dim shapes took form and gave her a vague path across the room.

Mindful of any obstacles, she raced toward the dim light seeping through the half-opened door in the north transept. Her gaze ping ponged around the church. At night, with no light streaming through the stained-glass windows, the church was large, empty, and downright creepy.

William Shatner's pants. Where the hell did he go?

She clutched her Taser tighter. She should have brought her gun. What if there were more newly turned Pioneers in the church? Could Murphy take on one Pioneer, let alone more? A cold shiver raced up and down her spine when she realized just how unprepared she was. Murphy could be injured or worse. She cursed. Why hadn't she asked more questions? No one should go into a possible hostile situation unprepared.

When the scratch of nails on a hard surface echoed through the church, she inched forward. Too late for overthinking it now. He might be in trouble. White stone pillars that reached high into the vaulted roof obscured her view. She peered around the corner. A half-balding, middle aged man and a woman, not much younger, stood between the marble table that served as the altar, and the knee height marble railings that separated the Chancel from the remainder of the Church.

Her pulse raced. Shit. No Murphy. But also, no Mark, the Pioneer she had expected to see. The dark shirt and clerical collar gave away the man was the parish priest. The woman stood a short distance behind him clutching a well-worn Bible and fingering rosary beads as she mouthed something unintelligible. She craned her neck in an attempt to decipher the words, but the woman's lips were moving too fast.

The priest held out a crucifix in one hand and what looked like a silver baby's rattle in the other. His voice, full of fear, was chanting a prayer she didn't recognize though she understood its meaning. The idiot was attempting to ward off the devil. The priest tossed violent sprays of holy water from a silver ewer into the congregation area.

Low, savage snarls ripped through the priest's incantation. Two wolves stood a few feet apart in the nave, glaring at each other. Both bared fangs and uttered feral growls. After searching half of Boston, they had finally caught up with Mark. And from her distressed murmurings, the woman hovering near the priest gripping her rosary beads was Mark's wife, Theresa. Her already elevated heart rate skyrocketed, and terror clutched at her chest. Murphy could easily take on a human without breaking a sweat, but she had no idea how he would fare against a Pioneer.

Although Murphy's golden wolf was much larger, the smaller gray one was holding its ground. And from its determined stance, it was not going to back down any time soon. The gray wolf snarled and snapped his jaws at Murphy's wolf and her stomach dropped when she saw the whites of its eyes. He was manic, almost crazed. She recognized that look, the same look as psychotically-agitated criminals. This was not going to end well.

Murphy's wolf took a step forward and bared his sharp fangs. He looked terrifying, but the gray wolf did not flinch.

She rechecked her surroundings. She needed to help Murphy. From her experience, they had no chance of getting through to a person in that state. She didn't imagine a Pioneer would be any different. Instinct had taken over. He was running on pure adrenaline and beyond reason.

She glanced down at her Taser. Frack. Adrenaline tended to trump Tasers.

When Mark's wolf snarled and took a step toward Murphy, the woman's sobs rose above the low growls. "Paul, do something."

She swung around to face the priest and woman and immediately regretted it. They both had turned up the volume and frequency of their prayers, and seemed not to realize how much danger they were in. Theresa had moved beyond lip-syncing the rosary to attempting a new world record for the most Hail Mary's within the shortest length of time. Each iteration was louder than the last.

She groaned when the priest, not to be outdone, took three steps down from the sanctuary and continued his chant. He doused holy water on the supposed servants of Satan, asking them to return from whence they came.

The wolves looked ready to strike. No matter how deluded Theresa and the priest were, it was her responsibility to keep them safe. "Father, you need to get her out of here. You're both in dan—"

Theresa's eyes flew open wide, and a hand shot up to cover her mouth.

The hairs at the back of her neck stood on end, and she swung her head back in time to see Mark's wolf lunge. It flew at Murphy, its jaws open wide.

Before she could call out a warning, Murphy's wolf darted out of the way. With nothing to stop his momentum, Mark sailed into the front of the church. As it landed, the gray wolf missed a step and crashed into a table laden with unlit candles. The candles scattered across the room and into the alcove. The priest was now standing between her and Mark's wolf.

Frack. Blood pumped through her veins. Any faster and she was sure to have a coronary.

The gray wolf stalked out of the alcove and stared at the priest like he was his next meal.

She raced to the priest. "Move, Father. Get out of the way." If he wouldn't get himself to safety, she would have to physically move him.

The priest sought refuge behind the altar rails, though he continued his incessant chanting and holy water tossing. Chaos had taken hold in the once peaceful church. The combination of the chanting, wailing, and growls that echoed off the high walls of the church was further exacerbating Mark's wolf's panicked state of mind. Saliva dripped from his sharp teeth as he bared his fangs. The snarls, deep and menacing, meant business. He was after blood, and it did not matter from where.

A muscle on her neck twitched, and for once she was unsure of her next move. No matter how much she mouthed off at him to the contrary, she was out of her depth when it came to Pioneers. She had only scratched the surface when it came to understanding who and what they were. Murphy was her cornerstone into this new world.

Murphy's wolf emerged from the pews and moved across the opening between the nave and altar. Their gaze locked, and her raging pulse leveled out. The man might be grumpy as hell, but she trusted him with her life.

He indicated the front of the church, and she nodded. This was his show. He would deal with the newly turned Pioneer. She would deal with the human side of this disaster. With Murphy distracting Mark's wolf, she focused on the priest and Theresa. She had to get them out of the church before it was too late.

The two wolves circled each other and bared their teeth in an attempt to stare each other down. She was itching to move, but needed to wait until Murphy's wolf stood between her and Mark. She willed Murphy to move faster, she needed to secure the scene and get the wife and priest well away from danger before they added to the victim count.

When her gaze fell on Mark's wolf, her jaw clenched as the reality of the situation hit her. The same could be said of the new Pioneer. He was as much a victim in all this as the others. Mark may have been the cause of the freeway disaster, but he wasn't responsible. A knot tightened in her stomach. None of this should be happening. Theresa and Mark should be home, getting ready for bed after a hard day at work. The priest should be doing whatever priests did at that time of night. And all the people whose lives were lost on the freeway should not be ashes or buried six feet under waiting for nature to pick the flesh from their bones.

She squeezed her fingers into fists to stop the rage that swept through her. This was all Elijah's doing. Never before had she hated someone so much that she saw red. He had deliberately bitten and turned an innocent man knowing what it would lead to. Joshua and Tim's barely restrained panic when they realized what Elijah had been doing now made more sense.

The growls from both Pioneers echoed through the church and rattled the stained-glass windows. Murphy swatted Mark with his claws and thrust him to the floor. Blood rushed from an open gash on Mark's flank, soaking into his matted fur. Mark's wolf, now more enraged than ever, flailed his hind legs. Murphy nipped at Mark's ear and barked out a warning.

She hauled in a breath when a lucky swipe from Mark's hind claws cut into Murphy's foreleg, opening up a considerable-sized gash. Murphy ignored the flow of blood and rolled more heavily on his opponent. After a flurry of bites and slashes, Mark caught Murphy off guard and reversed their positions. A moment later, Murphy broke free and they again flew at each other. Rather than slowing down, everything moved in double time.

The wolves smashed into lecterns, destroyed flower arrangements, candles, and anything else in their wake. The sound of breaking glass and furniture cracking added to the cacophony of growls, backed by the increasingly delirious prayer chants from Theresa and the priest. When Murphy's wolf finally blocked Mark off from the center chancery, she rechecked the layout of the church from the priest and Theresa's position, and mapped out an escape route. When the path with the least risk to her charges presented itself, she briefly closed her eyes. Now or never. She inched her way closer to the priest and Theresa and managed to get as far as the pulpit before stopping beside a plinth holding a statue of Mary looking up to the heavens.

The two wolves, in the throes of battle, rolled across the floor, near to where she stood.

She tossed an irritated glance at the priest as she shrugged off her backpack. "I'm sorry, Father, but your prayers are no use here." She pointed to the two wolves. "Both those wolves are creatures of God, whether you want to believe it or not. They have as much right to walk this earth as you or I do, and no amount of praying is going to change that. What might help is trying to calm Mark down, rather than setting him on edge."

She ignored the disbelieving looks from the priest and Theresa, unzipped the front pouch on her bag, and pulled out her phone. She scanned through her contact list until she found the name she was after and pushed the call button. It didn't take long for it to be answered. "Tim, it's Kaitlyn Quinn. We've found him, but we have a problem."

She quickly relayed their location and situation. Murphy would probably kill her later, but she wasn't about to leave him without knowing he was going to be okay. He was too important to her to take any risks. She rubbed her forehead. What she would give for a gun or rifle about now.

She turned her attention back to the unfolding battle. Murphy continued to hobble the other wolf. Each time Mark's wolf lunged, Murphy's wolf swiped a powerful paw across his leg or chest area. Blood poured from his cuts leaving splatters in his wake. Murphy was the superior fighter. If she had to take a guess, he was prolonging the battle to wear out Mark's wolf.

She pressed a palm to her stomach at the relief that flooded her body. If they got out of this mess in one piece, she was going to kill him for making her worry needlessly. She headed back to the nave and beckoned to the priest and Theresa. "Follow me, we need to get you out of here."

She stepped out into the nave, turned back to check her charges were following, and groaned. They were still in the same spot, still chanting and wailing up a storm. The matter of the new Pioneer, the priest, and the wife was going to be a problem, of that she had no doubt. She groaned aloud. That sounded like the beginning of a bad joke.

When Murphy let out a sharp whine, she froze. Mark's wolf's jaws were holding onto Murphy's neck for dear life as Murphy attempted to dislodge him.

Fear clutched at her chest, and her blood ran cold. Oh no, dear God, no. She'd seen videos of wolves fighting to the death before. This could easily turn fatal. She would be damned if she didn't do everything in her power to help. Kaitlyn reached for her Taser.

She had only taken two steps when Murphy dislodged Mark's jaws from around his neck and put some distance between them. In less than a heartbeat, Mark's wolf leaped into the air and flew toward Murphy. At the last minute, Murphy's wolf ducked, and Mark hit the stone floor with a thud, then rolled in her direction.

She moved to get between the plinth and the altar rails.

The gray wolf smashed full force into the plinth, toppling it over, and with it, the statue of Mary. The air left her lungs in a painful whoosh as the plinth knocked into her chest. She rolled over as the statue toppled, but her foot caught between the base and the altar rails. She cried out and held her arms over her head as the heavy statue came crashing down and pummeled her into the floor. A sharp pain radiated out from her head like lightning. Her world swam with dizzying lights and sound.

A deafening roar ripped from a wolf, and her vision cleared enough to see Murphy's wolf pin the gray wolf to the floor, his massive jaws latched around its neck.

Oh my god, he's going to kill him.

She knew Murphy, and she needed to stop this before he did something he would regret. She scrambled up and gripped the wall to steady her swirling brain. "Stop! Please. Mark, you have to submit. We're only trying to help."

She frantically searched for a way to stop Murphy's wolf before he broke Mark's neck. She grabbed her Taser off the floor and checked the setting. It was a risk, but what choice did she now have? She pointed it at Mark's wolf and closed her eyes for a second. Could she get through to him? "Murphy, I'm going to fire. Let him go."

Murphy's jaws released, and an instant later, fifty thousand volts coursed through Mark's wolf. His muscles convulsed violently as the Taser took effect, and he emitted a high-pitched howl.

Oh my God. It worked.

She moved closer. "Mark, it's okay. You need to calm down. There are more like you. You're not evil or the devil. You were just in the wrong place, at the wrong time. We're here to make sure you get the help you need."

Murphy's wolf brushed alongside her and placed a barrier between her and Mark. A low growl rumbled in his chest, and he nudged her hand.

She sunk her fingers into his pelt and gave him a reassuring squeeze. "I'm fine. I've called Tim. He should be here with a cleanup crew any moment now."

Murphy stood his ground, but turned his attention to Mark's wolf. His stance clearly showed he wasn't taking any risks, and she wasn't getting any closer to the downed wolf. The church was eerily quiet. Theresa and the priest were huddled together, watching the unfolding scene, unable to tear their eyes off Mark.

Her vision went in and out of focus, and her head pounded. Instead of letting go of Murphy's wolf, she kept contact with his warm coat and turned back to Mark. "You aren't alone in this, but we need you to change back. There are some people who will help you through this. Really, it's not as bad as you think."

She paused to gauge his reaction, but the priest began chanting and broke the silence. This time, she was in the wake of the holy water. She threw him a withering look. "Seriously, if you even think of dousing me with water again, I'll arrest you." She held up her Taser. "Or better yet."

Her pounding head appreciated the newfound silence.

Something wet inched its way down the side of her face. Thinking it was holy water, she wiped it off, but when she pulled her arm away her fingers were covered in red. She gingerly touched the skin on her forehead. Pulling her hand away, she was greeted with more blood.

Where the hell did that come from?

The church dimmed and closed in on her. She reached out to grasp something, anything before the dizziness overwhelmed her. A warm and solid something broke her fall.

Wait … who turned out the lights?

TWENTY-THREE

First Aid

Murphy frowned and shook his head. Kaitlyn had taken three attempts to unlock the door to her apartment. "You should have gone to the hospital like I said."

The uneasy tension in his chest tightened. He'd not eaten in forever, how in hell he had acid reflux was beyond him.

She turned the key and stepped through the doorway. "I'll be fine."

He sighed and ignored the ache moving up his stomach. He wasn't so sure. After Tim and the others arrived, it took hours to clean up the mess. And no matter how much he argued with her, she refused to leave, despite being pale as a ghost. He closed the door and headed for the kitchen.

She flopped on the couch and closed her eyes the moment her head met the pillow. "Do you think they're going to be okay?"

He stopped to take a closer look at her. The gash on her forehead looked deep. Why didn't she have that looked at? Not to mention she probably had a concussion. His stomach churned. Bollocks, what the hell did he eat? "Only time will tell."

"What about Father Paul and Teresa, what will happen to them?"

He rubbed his forehead. Even with blood caked across her face and a concussion, her brain ran a mile a minute. "I honestly don't know. We haven't had much success with people involved in organised religion in the past, so I'm not sure how this one will turn out. We might be lucky. The priest's love for his sister could outweigh his conditioning."

"What about Mark?"

He dumped her backpack on the breakfast bar. They'd had trouble getting Mark to change. It had taken some convincing, but in the end, the frightened wolf allowed Mark to reemerge. He let out a deep sigh. "I had a hell of a time to get him to open up to me. He's wracked with guilt over the deaths on the freeway, so it's going to take a while, but I think he'll get through it."

Her voice wavered. "Do you think he'll end up like Brian, that college student?"

His pulse skipped a beat, and he swore under his breath. Either Joshua or Tim must have told her. They tracked down the teenager who had turned during a frat party and attacked a fellow student. Brian had taken Propofol to try and forget what he had done, but he took too much and overdosed. The poor kid died alone and frightened.

He studied the floor before meeting her worried expression. He wished he had a better answer for her, but he didn't, and as much as he wanted to shield her from the pain of knowledge, she deserved to know the truth. "I honestly don't know. It's going to take time. A lot of time."

She fell quiet and stared up at the ceiling.

He had a sudden desire to pull her into his arms and reassure her that everything was going to be okay. Catching himself before he acted on it, he pushed the dangerous thoughts aside. He'd been having too many of them lately. Far too many. And training with her hadn't helped. The entire lesson was a study in self-restraint. Every curve from brow to ankle was distracting.

What was the matter with him?

He suppressed a yawn and ran a hand through his hair. Fuck, he was so tired he couldn't remember the last time he had a good night's sleep. Kaitlyn had been at him all week about sleep, and he'd ignored her warnings that his reaction time would be compromised. The fight with Mark's wolf should have been a walk in the park. He'd made some stupid mistakes which nearly got her hurt, all because he was tired. But it would take a month of Sundays before he'd admit she'd been right.

She made a motion to stand, but she groaned and sank back into the couch.

He rushed to her side. "Where's your first aid kit?"

"In the bathroom. Why?"

"Stay there, don't move."

He needed to clean that cut and assess the damage. If it was more serious than she was making out, he was taking her to a hospital. Even if it meant carrying her kicking and screaming the entire way. He winced when his chest tightened again. Maybe she had something for his bloody acid reflux. After finding what he was after, he sat on the coffee table facing Kaitlyn and rummaged through the oversized first aid box.

"What are you doing?" she said.

"Where's your Tylenol?"

"I didn't think Pioneers got headaches."

"Well then, they've never met you," he mumbled.

He tipped the contents out on the table and found what he was after. He popped two capsules into his hand, grabbed the glass of water from the table, and gave them both to her. "Here, drink these down."

She made a face. "I don't need it. I'll be okay."

An inadvertent growl rumbled in the back of his throat. "Take it, or I'll force it down your throat."

She huffed at him, but took the two capsules without further argument. He watched her like a hawk to make sure she swallowed them both. Once she'd finished, he picked up a damp cloth. "Now lean forward."

She looked at him suspiciously. "Why?"

He sighed. Damn, she was a pain in the butt. "Are you going to question everything I say? Just lean forward so I can clean your cut."

She shuffled forward to give him better access to her injury.

He hesitated for a second. "This might hurt a little."

He gently cleared away the blood that was caked in her hair, across her forehead, and down the side of her face.

She squirmed whenever he touched her skin.

He unearthed an angry purple bruise beneath the dried blood. The cut wasn't as deep as he expected, but the massive lump and bruise concerned him. "Are you sure you won't let me take you to a hospital?"

Her steely look gave him her answer.

His wolf, who had been hovering the entire time, settled once it was evident her wounds weren't as bad as first thought. As he tended her wounds, his mind went into overload. How had she convinced him to run around the streets of Boston on a dog leash? Thank the gods above no one else saw him or there went his reputation. He never would have lived it down. He held back a smile. To give her credit, they found Mark. Something neither he nor the others had managed to accomplish in nearly a week of trying. And to be fair, he hadn't minded it up until the point she forced him to submit to that bloody Jack Russell.

"I should thank you," he said gruffly.

"For what?"

"Your idea. It was stupid, but it worked."

She smiled. "Yeah, well. It only worked because you agreed to do it. I could have done without the Blessed Virgin falling on me."

She chuckled half-heartedly, but he couldn't see the funny side. His chest clenched at the memory of the heavy statue as it toppled onto her, each moment experienced in agonizing slow motion. When the statue hit the ground, emotions he thought long-extinct surfaced, and he had reacted in such a primal way it shocked him to his core. He'd wanted to tear Mark's wolf limb from limb for putting her in harm's way.

His teeth ground together. No one was to hurt her. Ever.

She is strong. She can look after herself.

He had to agree with his wolf. In his rational mind, he knew she could look after herself. She was strong and resilient, for a Human. But a question burned at the back of his mind. Why had he reacted that way?

I can't tell you what you already know.

Murphy stiffened. *What in shite's name are you talking about?*

No response.

He cleaned her wound, careful to keep his outward appearance calm. He applied a medical strip to fasten the edges of the cut together and assessed his handiwork. "I think that about does it."

She sighed. "Thanks. It hurts like hell, but the Tylenol is kicking in."

She reached out and lay her hand on his.

He faltered. The trust reflected in her expression nearly crippled him. His throat ran dry, and he was suddenly unsure of what to say or do next. Ever since he had been partnered with her, he'd been running the gauntlet of emotions. Emotions he thought discarded years ago. Emotions that brought nothing but pain into his life. He averted his eyes. His thoughts were headed into dangerous territory. "If you need anything stronger, I can run out and get it."

His obsession with her lips was getting out of control. Too much time had passed since he had been with a woman. A crack in his armor was all his baser instinct needed. This was his wolf's fault.

We are supposed to fight this together, why have you gone rogue? he said.

No response.

She squeezed his hand gently. The warmth from her touch shot up his arm. "The Tylenol should do. Although it's the first altercation I've had with a religious statue, it's not the worst injury I've had in the line of duty."

His stomach lurched. She was vulnerable. With her headstrong ways, she was more so than others. A bloody miracle she had gotten to this point in her life in one piece.

She bit her bottom lip. "About two years ago a bullet ricocheted and hit me in the arm. It was a through and through. But it still hurt like a bit—"

Mac soith.

In one fluid movement, he cupped her cheek with his hand, pulled her to him, and gently brushed his lips against hers. His need to touch her was greater than his will to resist.

She smelled divine.

It was his last coherent thought before she whimpered, and her fingers came up to rake through his hair, setting his scalp on fire. Her soft lips parted and her tongue playfully caressed his lower lip. He moaned and deepened the kiss. How could he not when she asked so nicely? Their tongues roamed at will, searching each other's limits as they danced and played together. She tasted better than he thought possible. Both sweet and savory. Challenging and yet compliant.

When she tugged him closer, heat flared through his body, sending him over the edge. And into what? He didn't know. And frankly, at this point he didn't care. Kaitlyn's kitten moan was music to his ears. She was as affected as he was. He reached for the back of her neck and pulled her closer. The need to devour her was primal. He emitted a guttural moan when she bit his lip. She tentatively flicked her tongue into his mouth. Teasing. Seductive, yet innocent.

What had taken him so long to do this?

He edged her onto the couch. Their breath intertwined and their pulses spiraled out of control. His heart thumped against his ribcage when her hand reached under his shirt and edged its way up his torso, snaking around to rest on his back.

Fuck.

When she ran her nails across his skin, he moaned again. This was torture. Exquisite, but torture nonetheless.

An insatiable need to feel her skin on his pushed his desire to fever pitch. He slid his hands under her top and roamed his fingers over her soft skin. Electricity shot through him with each touch, and the fire within him raged. When he cupped a hand over one of her breasts, she sucked in a sharp breath and her body released a flood of pheromones. He took in her heady scent and squeezed harder.

It took all his strength to slow down, when all he wanted to do was undress her and sink himself into her inviting body. When he shifted his position to give them more room, his head bumped into her and she cried out in pain. His blood froze and he pulled away. "Bollocks, did I hurt you?"

She closed her eyes for the briefest of moments before meeting his gaze head on. Her pulse was as erratic as his. She shook her head. "I'm all right, that spot is just a bit tender."

He checked her forehead. Satisfied he had not inflicted any further damage, he settled back on the couch, tense and unsure. "I'm sorry."

He should run, but right now, this was the only place he wanted to be. He searched her face for a hint of what might be running through her head.

She grinned, her lips plump and red, and he relaxed. "For what?" She raised a brow. "For hurting me or for kissing me?"

He tried to work out the best way of answering. "The first. I am most definitely not sorry about the second."

She studied her hands then raised her head. "Neither am I."

He moved her into a resting position and lay on the couch beside her. "You need to sleep."

When he was sure she was comfortable, he brought his hand up to caress her face and play with her curls.

She closed her eyes. "I'm not going to remember this in the morning, am I?"

A part of him was happy at the possibility they could forget this had happened. "Probably not."

He kept vigil until the gentle rise and fall of her chest let him know she was asleep. When he was sure she wouldn't wake, he carried her to her room. After the night she'd had, she needed the comfort of her own bed. He tucked her in and stood for a moment to watch her sleep. She turned over, and he eyed up the bed. It was big enough for both of them. His instinct was to climb in beside her and keep vigil, but his more rational mind was dead-set against it. They were partners on this case. They couldn't be anything more. When he killed Elijah, he would be gone without a backwards glance. Anything else between them would not be fair. He would only end up hurting her.

This was why he worked alone. No complications.

I'm not so sure this complication is unwanted, his wolf said.

He frowned and ran his hand through his hair. "What have you done to me, Kaitlyn Quinn?"

His wolf cocked his head. *Made you a little more Human?*

He phoned her invisible minders and let them know they wouldn't be needed, then turned off the lights and returned to the couch. She could still experience aftereffects from the head injury. He tossed, trying to find a comfortable position. He would stay only until dawn. By then, she should be fine on her own.

After all, like it or not, she was his partner. And that's what partners did for each other.

TWENTY-FOUR

The Art of Deception

Kaitlyn's eyes were closed, but that didn't stop her from squishing her lids tighter together. Perhaps if she ignored the alarm, it would go away.

The infernal racket became louder as the seconds passed. Without opening her lids, she flung her hand out from under the covers and hit the snooze button. With more effort than expected, she sat up, grimaced, and groaned aloud. "Oh God. My head hurts."

She struggled to clear the cobwebs and glanced at the time. It was six a.m. So why did she feel like she'd just fought ten rounds with a bulldozer? A glass of water and two Tylenol caught her eye. Her head was groggy, and she couldn't remember why. She downed the drugs and sat still, waiting for the pain to subside. It took a while, but as her senses cleared, her memory returned in fits and starts.

Technicolor images from the chaos in the church were the first to return, and the image of Mark's wife as they drove away lingered. She would never forget the look on Theresa's face as she struggled to hold it together. She was the epitome of a woman torn. Torn between the love she had for her husband, and the creature she now believed was taking over his soul. Despite what had happened, Theresa still clung to her faith to guide her. Unfortunately, there was nothing in the Bible that would help her through the paradigm shift her world had taken. Hopefully the faith Theresa had in Mark was as strong. They were in for a bumpy ride until they came to terms with what had happened to him.

Father Paul, on the other hand, was a different kettle of fish. She shook her head. The clergyman was Theresa's brother. Now that was one for the books. How they were going to explain the sudden disappearance of a Catholic priest from a high-profile church was a mystery, though Tim had assured her they had a procedure in place for a God Squad Revelation. She shuddered. She didn't know what she should be more worried about—that they had forcibly taken a man of the cloth, or that it had happened enough times they had a name for it.

Murphy's gruff dismissal of her concerns had alleviated some of her misgivings. The priest would be treated with the utmost respect, provided he agreed to certain terms. There would not be enough holy water in the city for the clergyman once he was educated on the reach of the spawn of the devil.

She groaned at the memory of the falling Virgin and held her hand up to her head gingerly and winced. That statue was heavier than it looked. Luck had definitely been on her side. A cut and a couple of bruises would heal. She sighed. Her heart was another story. She touched her fingers to her lips. A shiver swept up and down her spine. And despite the uncomfortable pain in her head, a flush of desire rippled through her core.

The kiss.

Her hands flew up to cover her face. Just the memory of it elicited a physical reaction. Who'd a thought he was a champion Olympian kisser?

She scoffed. But what did she know? It had been so long between drinks, she'd think a wet fish was a good kisser. Never had she been so completely and utterly swept away by the moment. She desperately wanted to meld to him like a second skin. Every touch from him torched a new set of flames, fanning out through every nerve ending. She was so lost in passion all reason had flown out the window. She closed her eyes at the implications. She was adult enough to admit it. Had pain not ripped through her body from the accidental bump, she would have willingly followed him down the rabbit hole. She fanned her hot face. Oh, the magical things his talented fingers and lips were capable of.

No. It was just a kiss, and that was where it ended. Nothing else happened. She had fallen asleep on the couch in his arms, feeling safe and protected. The couch. Her eyes darted around her bedroom. How did she get to bed?

A moan escaped her lips when the thought of being carried by him flared another response from her body. Frack it, this had to stop.

She drowned in his ebony eyes. The longer she knew him, the more hypnotic his eyes became. Even his—. She froze and suddenly had difficulty swallowing. Her hands flew up the her face the moment she realized where her thoughts had taken her. She was totally screwed.

She threw back the covers and swung her legs out of bed. She needed to stop this right now, before she became any more emotionally involved with the overbearing, demanding, and moody man. She yanked open a dresser draw and rummaged through the contents. He was way too grumpy for her liking. The problem was, she knew there was more to Murphy than the persona he presented to the outside world. He kept it hidden and secure, but it was surfacing more often lately. And she was powerless to resist the man he truly was. But she had no future with him. And if they continued, she would be the one coming out broken beyond repair. She bit her bottom lip and headed to the bathroom.

No, getting emotionally involved with him was a bad idea. They were partners and maybe friends. Nothing more.

She forced her mind to think more rationally, and suppressed her erratic thoughts as she turned the shower on. If she didn't hurry, she would be late for work. But what about when she saw him? Act like nothing happened? After all, last night they were both on a high from the church scene. Neither of them had been thinking straight.

Her brows rose, and a twinge of pain shot through her forehead.

Yeah, sure. That was it. Adrenaline gave her the most mind-blowing kiss she'd ever experienced.

That and the head injury.

When she arrived at work, Saul's smile froze. "Ouch, that looks nasty."

She avoided looking him in the eye and threw her bag under her desk. "Stupid accident at MMA last night. I wasn't focused, tripped, and ran headlong into a wall." To get him off the subject, she nodded at the new stack of brochures on his desk. "Mildred still got you choosing a retirement holiday destination?"

"Yep, but I'm ignoring them for now." His lips formed a grim line. "I might be on to something with a connection between Haladlo and Potter."

She cocked her head. This was news. "You never said anything yesterday."

Saul rubbed the back of his neck. "Yeah, there's a discrepancy with some of the evidence, and I have a thought as to why." He shrugged and turned back to his notes. "But until I'm sure of my suspicions, there's nothing much to talk about."

She frowned. Something in his tone didn't sit right with her. Before she could question him further, Murphy arrived. She filed Saul's information away for later.

He came over and placed a cup of hot chocolate on her desk. "Are you sure you're well enough to be here?"

She reached for the cup and forced a smile on her face. Pretending nothing happened last night wasn't going to be easy. "I'm fine, just a bit of a headache, that's all." She snuck a glance at Saul who had gone back to pouring through his notes, then leaned closer to Murphy and lowered her voice. "How's, um, you know, the friends you were helping with their little problem. Everything's a little hazy after my accident at training."

Murphy raised a brow. "It is?"

She nodded and took a sip of the hot chocolate without looking him in the eye. "Yeah, I think I hit my head a little harder than I thought."

Murphy stared at her a good long moment before he opened his mouth to speak, but just then Garcia ambled through the door. He snapped his mouth shut and headed to his desk.

"Morning," Garcia mumbled as he made his way across the room staring at the floor the entire time.

She swung to face him, surprised to discover he looked decidedly worse for wear. "Are you alright? You don't look well."

Garcia sat down and placed his head in his hands. "I don't feel it, either. I haven't felt this crappy since college."

Saul closed his folder and grinned at Garcia. "Did your uncles and cousins drink you under the table again?"

Garcia poured himself some water and dropped two Berocca tablets into it. The tablets sizzled as they dropped to the bottom of the glass and dissolved in a flourish. He took a long drink before answering. "Yeah. Pop's birthday always gets a little loud."

Saul swung his chair around and crossed his arms over his chest. "You chickened out, didn't you?"

Garcia groaned. "I don't want to talk about it. Why don't you pick on Kaitlyn? She looks as good as I feel." He turned to her and asked, "What happened to you, by the way?"

Saul's mouth split into a wide grin and he held out his hand. "She has a good excuse. You don't, so pay up."

Garcia's shoulders slumped, and he reached in his pocket and pulled out a twenty.

She looked from Saul to Garcia. What was up with these two?

Garcia slapped the money into Saul's outstretched palm. "I'm named after my father. My uncles tend to drink a little too much at these gatherings and start referring to me as second—second-string, secondary, and any other derivations of the word second they can think of. It was sort a funny when I was a kid. But now, not so much."

Saul chuckled. "I bet him that he wouldn't have the balls to put them in their place. Looks like this peacock's all show and no substance."

Garcia threw his partner a withering glare. "Yeah, and you're full of substance, you are. Have you told Mildred you hate those fad diets she puts you on?"

Saul shrugged. "Alright, kid, you got me there. Looks like both of us bow under pressure from family." He glanced at a glowering Murphy and cleared his throat. "And that's enough chit-chat team, back to work."

Although Murphy seemed focused on his computer, she knew better. Nothing escaped his notice.

Garcia gulped down another glass of Berocca. "Any word on the forensic results yet, boss?"

Murphy shook his head. "No, and we shouldn't expect anything soon. There's a lot for them to sift through."

Garcia sighed. "At least he's given us a break."

Murphy narrowed his eyes. "While our unsub hasn't struck in a few days, it doesn't mean he's done. We still need to get him off the streets, one way or another. And with resources redirected to the organized crime war, we have no chance of getting help. We'll need to follow up every lead ourselves."

Saul and Garcia squirmed in their chairs at Murphy's sharp tone.

Murphy grabbed his keys, nodded at her, and headed for the door. "Let's go."

She frowned. "Where?"

"To follow up on a lead."

Just act normal. Just act normal. Pretend last night didn't happen. She chanted her mantra the entire way down the corridor. By the time they reached the elevator she had managed to nearly bowl over old Edna from accounts, drop her phone twice, and plough her face into Murphy's back when he stopped to let the mail cart cross the hallway.

"Are you sure you're alright?" he said as he poked the elevator down button. "I knew I should have taken you to the hospital."

"Don't fuss, I'm fine. It takes more than a statue falling on me, a lump the size of the titanic, and a hazy memory to keep me away from work."

Murphy grimaced when she climbed into his car and slammed the door behind her. "Why do women feel the need to be so heavy-handed with car doors?"

She clicked her seatbelt into place and glanced across at him blandly. "Probably the same reason men feel the need to leave the toilet seat up. So, what's this lead?"

He handed her a printout. She scanned through it and groaned. She'd seen this list when she'd handed it to Murphy the day before. It contained all the people who had been bitten by a canine in the last few months. She sat back and rested her head against the headrest, thankful she had pocketed some extra Tylenol. This was going to be a long day.

"How many more names?" Murphy said.

Kaitlyn glanced through the list. "Three." They didn't need to interview all two hundred and fifty of the possible new Pioneers themselves. In addition to the local Pioneers she'd met after the freeway incident, the pack in New York state had also sent reinforcements to help.

So far, between the different teams, four of the two hundred and fifty bite victims were confirmed Pioneer cases.

She crossed her fingers and hoped none of the remaining three had been turned. Of the people they had visited today, they'd found the second victim on their list alone and scared in her apartment. She'd had a fever of one hundred and five and was writhing in agony. With no medical insurance, she had nowhere to turn to.

From Murphy's assessment, the woman was hours away from her first turn. Confused, isolated, and unable to fathom what was about to happen to her, they'd had difficulty convincing her this wasn't part of some elaborate prank.

Her throat grew thick. "How do you think she's doing?"

"Wendy knows what to do, the girl will be okay."

"Violet. Her name is Violet Carozza. But what about the people Elijah attacked who didn't go to a doctor?"

She closed her eyes. Her jaw clamped tight. Eleven people died when Mark first turned on the freeway. Who knew where and when the next would occur. They'd gotten lucky with tracking down the names on the list, but this was not over. How many more were out there? Blood rushed to her ears and rage bubbled back to the surface. How many more lives were going to be destroyed before Elijah was stopped? "We have got to stop this madness."

His lips formed a thin line. "Just what do you think we've been doing?"

Her phone rang and she reached into her pocket. "No, I mean we need to get Elijah off the street. Too many people have died because of him—" Her stomach plummeted. "Oh, fudge nuggets."

"What is it?"

"My mom."

"Answer it, then."

She was not going to have a conversation with her mother while Murphy was anywhere in the vicinity. Who knew what he would overhear? She tapped out a message. "No, I was supposed to return her call last night and I forgot. I'll phone her back later."

He shot her a look that told her he knew she was hiding something, and she squirmed.

"Right. Well, who's next on our list?" he said.

She pocketed her phone and scanned the list. "Frank Giordano. I think we're wasting our time with this one. It looks like the wife contacted the public health service to complain about a dog who bit her husband. There's nothing reported through a medical facility or doctor, which means it wasn't serious enough to warrant a doctor's visit. Probably just feuding neighbors."

She gave him directions, pulled her phone back out, and put it on mute.

Molly had also been in contact. After their initial conversation they'd spoken twice, and messaged each other at least a half-dozen times. She hadn't mentioned it to him because she wasn't sure how he would react, considering he wasn't on the best terms with his father. From what she could tell, they weren't exactly fighting, just more like a Mexican standoff. Both men refused to speak to one another unless forced. The reason was still unclear, and although she'd tried to get him to talk, Joshua had been no help. It would be just her luck to get a call from Molly. And he would know.

She refocused and reached for Murphy's tablet. "I'll see what I can dig up on Mr. Giordano."

By the time they pulled up outside an impressive colonial style two-story home in Lexington, one of the more prestigious and upmarket suburbs of Boston, she had a little information on who they were about to interview.

"He must make a killing selling houses," she said as they got out and headed up the narrow path to the front door. She lowered her voice. "According to what I found out, he's one of the big hitters in the industry. I was actually expecting something a little grander."

She rang the doorbell and took a step back just as her phone vibrated. She ignored it.

"You're not going to answer it?"

She heard a movement from inside and pulled out her identification. "Nope."

"It's probably your mother."

She remained still. It wasn't her mother's call she was worried about.

"You know she'll only worry if you don't answer," he said gruffly.

She rolled her eyes. "Yes, Dad."

He responded with a low growl from the back of his throat.

A woman opened the door and stood in the doorway.

She plastered a disarming smile on her face and flashed her badge, careful to keep her finger on the letters FBI. She pocketed it before the woman had a chance to take a proper look. "Hello, I'm Inspector Quinn, this is my colleague O'Neill. We're special investigators for the district attorney's office. We were wondering if we could speak to Mr. Giordano?"

The woman's smile faded and she stiffened. "He's at a real estate conference at the moment. I'm his wife, Linda. Can I help you?"

"We can't divulge too much information with regards to an ongoing investigation, but the DA's office has been looking into some criminal activities involving a particular dog breeder here in Massachusetts. We understand your husband was a victim of one of his dogs."

Linda relaxed and nodded. "He was. And let me tell you, it gave all of us a scare. I thought it was going to kill my poor Frankie. They shouldn't be allowed to breed dogs like that."

She ran through the list of questions they had repeated all that day. "And is your husband well? Sometimes bites can turn infectious."

Linda opened the door a little farther and nodded. "He's perfectly fit. Even upped his training for the Boston Marathon."

She smiled smugly. She'd called it. As expected, they could cross Frank off the list.

"Although, that virus he had a few weeks back put him behind for a while, but he's back to his regular training now. I was so livid, he had already had a setback with that bite. It took forever to heal. I blame the dog owner. That beast should have been tied up, not let loose to wreak havoc on us all."

Or maybe not. She resisted the urge to hit her head against the door frame.

Murphy took a half step closer. "Mrs. Giordano, since you were there and witnessed the event, would you mind if we ask you some questions? It might help us in ensuring that the breeder is brought to justice."

Linda stepped back and opened the door fully. "Not a problem, Inspector. Anything to stop those sorts of attacks in the future. It could so easily have been my children who were attacked."

They stepped inside the Giordano residence and followed Linda into the lounge. "Take a seat why don't you, and I'll fix an iced tea for us all."

As soon as Linda disappeared into the kitchen, she glanced around the room. It looked like a typical upper middle-class house. From the photos the Giordano's had two boys, both of whom were into hockey. Many of the photos on the mantle featured the boys holding up one trophy or another.

She turned to Murphy and raised an eyebrow, nodding at the photos and then toward the kitchen.

He picked up on her unvoiced question. "She's Human, but I can scent a Werewolf in this house. It's strong, although it hasn't been here in a few days."

Linda was back before he could say anything further.

"What exactly did you want to know about the attack on my Frank and the others?"

The air suddenly became so thin she found it hard to breathe. Others? She pretended to consult her notes. Others, as in there were more. Her heart thumped in her chest as she considered the best way of handling the interview. They all couldn't have been turned.

"Could you tell us in your own words your version of the events," Murphy said.

She swung her eyes toward him. Could they?

Linda handed her and Murphy their iced teas and poured herself one before speaking. "Well, the burial had just finished, and everyone was paying their last respects to Uncle Pete. The cathedral was so packed, and there were ears everywhere so it was difficult to talk. You know how it is." She sat down on the couch across from her and Murphy. "A few of us were chatting about how lovely the service was. The Archbishop stayed focused for once, and out of nowhere, this dog attacks my Frankie. Well, it attacked Briana and some of the other cousins before it bit Frank, but it must have mauled over half-a-dozen mourners before it ran off." Linda sniffed and raised her chin. "You think it would have the decency to take a bite out of the reprobates lurking in the background, but no, that mutt tried ripping Frankie and his cousins to shreds instead."

Linda reached for her glass. Her hand shook, and she quickly steadied it with her other hand. "I kept on worrying that the beast might have rabies. It was just so vicious, you see."

"If you were concerned, was everyone treated at the local hospital?"

Murphy's expression remained passive, but from the small tells she was now able to read, he was analyzing not only Linda's responses but everything else about their surroundings.

Linda winced and reached out to straighten an already flat lace doily. "No, but everyone had shots within an hour. We had more than enough doctors in the family to make sure everything was taken care of." She shrugged. "Still, we waited on tenterhooks for fourteen days to confirm they hadn't contracted rabies."

She gave Linda her best sympathetic demeanor. "I can't imagine the pressure it must have put on your family." She took a sip of tea, placed her cup back on the table, and cleared her throat. In addition to Frank, at least five others were bitten. Surely the odds they were now Pioneers was remote? Even so, they needed to be certain. "Linda, could you reconfirm the names of the others who were bitten that day? We want to make sure we have correctly identified all of the victims. It will help with the case against the breeder."

She picked up her pen and looked expectantly at Linda.

Linda waved her hand in the air. "Oh, you probably won't have their names. I told them all they should report it, but they didn't want to make waves. But that's Frankie's family, obsessed about appearances. This time I just couldn't take the injustice so I complained on their behalf." Linda stood, walked over to the piano, and reached for a photo. "This is from my Frankie's fortieth. Most of the others who were bitten are in it." She tapped a finger against her lips and frowned. "Let me see ..."

Linda was a fount of information. She was more than happy to provide them with the details, names, and her own opinion on each family member who was bitten. Kaitlyn spent the next twenty minutes jotting down copious notes that she would be sure to pore over later.

When Murphy excused himself to find the bathroom, Linda didn't drop a beat as she continued to voice her concern at one of the cousin's choices in clothing at a recent charity event. Apparently last season's Stella McCartney was a definite no-no. By the time Murphy returned, her writing hand was sore, and she'd almost run out of paper.

"When do you expect Frank to be home?" Murphy said as they were leaving. "Just in case the District Attorney has any further questions."

"Oh, he's due back tomorrow sometime." Linda's eyes flicked around restlessly. "I don't really think we should mention this to him or the others. Like I said before, they are very private people.”

Murphy’s gaze bore through Linda before he spoke. “As you wish. If we need anything further, we’ll contact you.”

The tension in Linda’s expression relaxed.

She lowered her voice as they headed away from the house. “Do you think she knows?”

“Not a clue.”

Her brows furrowed together. “Then why was she so nervous?”

“That’s what I want to know.” He climbed into the Cadillac and stared out the window.

“What are you thinking?” she said.

He tapped the steering wheel. “Every person Elijah attacked at the cemetery was a blood relation. If Frank was turned, we can assume the others were, too.”

“That’s what I was afraid of.”

“But how did he know to be there that day, and who to go after?”

“Perhaps he got lucky?”

He grunted. “No one gets that lucky. And it can’t be a coincidence that Elijah started butchering those humans a week after Frank and the others were bitten.” He turned the engine over. “We know the date and the cemetery. Find out who was buried there that day. Linda’s hiding something, but it’s not the fact that her husband is a Werewolf.”

She grabbed the tablet. By the time she brought up a browser, they were on the main road and headed to the city. When she found the answer, she groaned. “Shuzbutt. I know why Linda was a bundle of nerves at the thought of us contacting her husband or the others.”

“Why?”

She hesitated before replying. “The uncle being buried was Peter Gionelli. The Peter Gionellii.”

"The previous head of the New England mafia?"

"The one and only. Now I know who the reprobates were that Linda was referring to. The FBI must have had a team on the ground to try and work out who the baton had been passed to." She sat back and shook her head. "What the hell was Elijah doing there? You can't tell me with his enhanced Spidey senses he didn't know the area was under surveillance."

He turned on his indicator before pulling into the fast lane. "Nothing Elijah does is without reason. My guess is he either knew his victim was going to be at the funeral, or he knew Gionelli had the gene and went to the funeral to turn as many relatives as possible. Either way, he discovered a goldmine of possible victims to turn, and took advantage of the situation. What I can't work out is why he started butchering Humans a week after Frank and the others were bitten."

A cold chill ran down her spine. "Judas Priest. Frank and his cousins are related to the previous mafia don."

"We've already established that."

Her chest tightened as she reached for the tablet and reentered her password to access the FBI database. "No, don't you see, this is a disaster. It's possible he's turned someone from within the New England mafia into a Pioneer."

Disaster was probably understating it. Elijah had turned someone with very little regard for human life into a Pioneer with super strength and enhanced senses who would live for hundreds of years. A career criminal who now could literally outrun and out fight anything law enforcement threw at him.

She ran each name Linda supplied through the database, but came up blank.

"Anything?"

"Nothing. None of the names are suspected of being part of the organization. According to the files, they're all on the cleared list. They just happened to have the misfortune of being born into a family with ties to the New England mafia. In addition to being reasonably successful business people, they run a charity to improve literacy. They distribute books to libraries, schools, hospitals, and prisons all along the east coast."

"They're wrong. Frank is mafia and so are the others who were bitten."

"How do you know?

"Linda. The woman was ready to have a heart attack each time we brought up the subject of meeting her husband or what he did for a living. And she had a minor stroke when you asked about what the cousins did for a living. You do not have that sort of reaction if you have nothing to hide. That and on my way to the bathroom I accidently got waylaid in Frank's study and noticed an invoice on the desk from Findlay, Scott, and Rossi."

"The law firm?"

He nodded. "You don't pay a lawyer a two hundred and fifty-thousand-dollar yearly retainer if you're clean."

She gulped at the amount. Where did Linda and Frank get that sort of money? They lived in a swanky part of town, but a quarter million-dollar retainer on a lawyer?

"And what's the bet if we checked, Findlay, Scott, and Rossi would also have the rest of the family on retainer as well?"

Her brows shot up. "You seriously think Elijah has turned a bunch of mafia bosses?"

"That'd be my guess. When Gionelli gave up the reins, no one knew who took charge. The old captains were retired and new management took over. You heard Garcia, the authorities have no idea who's running the show, and that includes the upper echelons."

"But that doesn't explain why Elijah is torturing humans. He's turned the worst possible criminals into Pioneers, you'd think he'd have his hands full with that."

"You're assuming he knows where they are."

She stared at him while the words sunk in. Surely not?

He glanced at the rear-view mirror. "We already know some of Elijah's victims had connections to organized crime. If he's lost his target, what better way to find him again than through a network of people who may know who and where to find him. It makes sense and the timing is right. He's working his way up the network."

She frowned and bit her thumbnail. As far-fetched as his theory sounded, it was the only one they had. "Who would be so important that Elijah would want to ..."

He took his focus off the road for a moment and their eyes locked.

"Oh my god. He's bitten the new don of the New England mafia." She slumped in her seat. Her worst nightmare. "And you think he found him?"

He punched the aircon up higher. "The lack of bodies lately tells us he has."

"But we're still none the wiser. We've got no idea who the don is."

He shrugged. "That's easy, Linda told us."

She waited for him to finish the sentence. He remained quiet, and she squinted at him. "You know what else is easy? Tasering a Pioneer who's full of his own self-importance."

The corner of his mouth twitched. "Ambrose."

"Pardon?"

"The cousin she mentioned, Ambrose. He's in charge."

"How do you know?"

"I told you, she told us."

Her eyebrows rose. "Umm, and where was I at the time?"

He shrugged and she held back the urge to shoot him.

"Right there, sipping iced tea. Did you not see the change in tone and posture when she spoke of him? Ambrose is at the top of the family tree in power, so it would make sense that he'd also be the one in charge of the family business."

Maybe today wasn't such a disaster after all.

He let out a deep sigh and nodded to the now well-worn list. "We still need to mark the last two off. After that, the real work starts. Where to next?"

TWENTY-FIVE

Raw

Kaitlyn glared at her laptop screen and held back an acute desire to hurl it across her living room. Instead, she massaged her temples to dampen down the headache that wouldn't shift. She hissed and sat back in her chair. It was near midnight and still nothing. "I can't believe there's no address for him. Everything's listed against post office boxes or his company's offices."

She looked over at Murphy, who stood in silence after ending his phone call. "What did he say?"

"Daniel is alerting the council. He agrees with my assessment and is going to contact the packs on the eastern seaboard to send in more reinforcements once we've confirmed the location."

She wrinkled her brow. "Why? You didn't need help bringing Elijah down before."

He ran a hand through his hair. "It's not Elijah that's the issue. We now have an unaligned pack given birth by a deranged Werewolf. We have no idea how many new Werewolves he's turned, or how protective they are of Elijah."

She hesitated. While his outward appearance was as staunch as ever, his tone was concerned.

"If this isn't handled properly it could get out of control. The New England mafia was increasing their reach and power before their change. As Werewolves they have a new advantage, which they're using without mercy to decimate the other mafia families," Murphy said.

She briefly closed her eyes. Of course, he was right. She had been so focused on putting the pieces together, she had lost sight that they were now facing a more serious issue. Assuming they were correct, and Elijah had turned members of the mob, the ramifications were of biblical proportions.

Damn it. How had she missed that?

The mafia was bad enough, but pumped up with Pioneer abilities? She shuddered at the thought. To find Elijah they first had to track down Ambrose. Without the help of the FBI. She held back a nervous laugh. The FBI had teams of people trying to work out who had taken over and turned a once minor player in organized crime into a powerhouse. She and Murphy knew the answer, but their hands were tied. How would it look if she walked into Doug's office and told him she had the answer to the FBI's current holy grail but there was a snag? She knew who, but didn't know where he was. And oh yeah, he was no longer fully Human and was protected by the elusive psychopath who killed her father.

He sighed and rubbed his forehead before heading to her kitchen. "You know we have a bigger problem at play here."

"You're telling me, Elijah's going to be much harder to get to."

He reached into her fridge and pulled out a bottle of Guinness. "No, you misunderstand my meaning. Elijah is involved but he's not following his usual pattern." Murphy twisted off the bottle cap. "By now he should be escalating his kills. Taunting the police with their inability to capture him, not completely disappearing off the map."

He took a couple of gulps then shook his head. "I doubt that he's calling the shots. Provided it's Ambrose Giordano in charge, Ambrose's the one using his newfound abilities to his advantage." He paused and studied the label on the bottle. "Somehow he's managed to get Elijah to go along with him, and he's managed to keep him under control at the same time."

The hairs on the back of her neck bristled. "You make it sound like you admire the man."

He crossed the room to her. "You have to admit, it's no small feat for a newly turned Werewolf to control someone much stronger and older."

She nearly fell off the breakfast bar stool. "You've got to be kidding me. You do know what the mob does, right? Drugs, prostitution, trafficking, and racketeering are just the tip of the iceberg. I could go on for days." She crossed her arms over her chest. "We've got to bring these guys to justice."

"And how exactly do you think that justice, in this case, will be served?"

Her jaw tightened and her heart pumped faster. What rock did he just crawl out from under? The mob had no moral compass and killed on a whim. "Just because they are victims of that psychopath does not mean they get a free pass. Like Elijah, they need to be locked up and taken off the streets."

"Kaitlyn, I think you're forgetting one major issue with that scenario. Ambrose Giordano is no longer Human. He will expose us if he's incarcerated."

Her blood was now almost at boiling point. "So what, we just let him and his family of criminals continue breaking the law?"

"I didn't say that." He held up his palms in mock surrender. "All I'm saying is the council will decide their fate outside the law."

She scowled. A bunch of the worst possible degenerates had just gotten a free pass, and she couldn't do anything about it. She stared at her laptop's screen and worked to bring her temper under control. How had everything she ever stood for, everything she ever believed, become so complicated?

Black and white had gone out the window the moment Murphy entered her life. He was right. If the FBI ever managed to catch up with the new don and his captains, they could never take them in. And if by some miracle they did, it wouldn't be long before their Wolves forced a change and exposed the Pioneer race. But at least they would spend the rest of their days rotting away in Pioneer prison. Her shoulders slumped, and she closed the lid of her laptop. She was so tired of hitting brick walls, and only one person was to blame for all this mess. It was all that rat weasel's fault.

She swung around on her stool and looked over at Murphy, who was perched on the back of her sofa, studying her with an intent expression on his handsome face. His obsidian eyes gave nothing away. "And what about Elijah? What fate will the council decree on him?"

His expression wavered. A flash of pain washed across his face and disappeared just as quickly, only to be replaced by an icy glare. "He won't live long enough for the matter to be put to them."

She shivered involuntarily at his tone. She never wanted to get on the bad side of him.

He placed the empty bottle on the breakfast bar and glanced at the window as his guard once again dropped. His expression was raw and, for once, vulnerable.

Her chest ached. She recognized the look. It was the same one that marred her mother's face when she was thinking of Ryan. The desire to reach out and alleviate some of his pain was overwhelming. But he had lived with it for so long he seemed unable to separate it from other emotions. He was still tied to June, and according to Joshua, he always would be. Pioneers only had room for one love, and the spot in Murphy's heart was already filled. She blinked away the sharp sting behind her eyes. They had all lost far too much. What she wouldn't give to turn back time and make things right.

Get a grip girl, he doesn't want or need your pity.

Mindful that he could turn around and catch her unguarded, she glanced down at her hands. Elijah had caused so much destruction over the years, he deserved whatever was coming to him. Many people besides her wanted him held accountable for what he had done. Wanted him to pay for the hollow ache that would stay with them for the rest of their lives. But Murphy's single mindedness was not the answer. She couldn't heal his pain, but the path he was headed down wouldn't heal it either. That much she did know. "How many people has Elijah killed over the years?"

He reached for the second bottle of beer he'd left on the counter top. "Too many to count."

"And I'm assuming June wasn't the only Pioneer he killed from your pack?"

His fingers tightened around the bottle. "How did you know?"

"Joshua."

He sighed and shook his head. "No, he's killed others from my pack."

"There are others, like us, who want Elijah to pay for his crimes?"

His brows knitted together. "Where are you going with this?"

She paused before continuing. He wasn't going to like what she had to say since his argument about justice and the mafia Pioneers clearly did not extend to Elijah. She was skating on thin ice, but the path he was headed down wasn't the answer. "What makes you so special?"

His eyes narrowed and a low growl reverberated from deep within his chest.

She had clearly hit a nerve. "I just mean, why do you get to be his executioner? What about the other lives he destroyed? Don't they have as much right to challenge him or witness his punishment?"

His jaw tightened, and his lips narrowed into a thin line.

Knowing what was at stake, she pressed on. She needed to talk him down from the ledge. "Isn't that your job? You took on the task of tracking him down and bringing him to justice. But you're not looking for justice, you're looking for revenge. Would you deny all those countless others closure, or at least the chance to look Elijah in the eye and ask why he destroyed their lives?"

The low rumble increased in intensity. His icy exterior warned that she had crossed the line. She ignored her initial reaction to flee and stood her ground. Things had to be said. "Don't get me wrong, I want him dead just as much as you do. And given the chance, I'd like to kill him, too. But from what I understand about how packs work, the needs of the collective are paramount." She took a breath. The next part could get her in hot water. "Weren't your father and the Alliance trying to heal the damage Elijah did by giving all those affected the chance to face the monster who took their loved ones?"

She mentally crossed her fingers. Hopefully, he would assume she knew this information through Joshua. If he ever found out about her lengthy conversation with Molly, there would be hell to pay.

His hand clenched tight around the bottle he was holding. The glass, under the intense pressure, let out a series of barely legible snaps as it struggled to remain in one piece. "I would be very careful about what you say next, Kaitlyn. You ..." He jabbed his finger at her chest. "You have no idea of what I've been through, of what I've lost."

She winced. That was going to leave a bruise, but she stood ready for the impending storm. This was a battle between her and his inner demons. No matter the outcome, she needed him to see reason and stop the cycle of pain he was lost within. It nearly drowned her mother. She'd be dammed if she didn't try to pull him to safety. "My father's death wasn't as important as June's? She was more worthy than my dad? Is that what you are saying?"

Murphy towered over her. She didn't know what was darker, his mood or his eyes. "That's not what I said."

"But that's exactly what you meant. Elijah has destroyed countless lives, and that's just the people who were left behind to pick up the pieces. He took my father and a brother I never had a chance to meet. But even so, I'm not selfish enough to lay claim to being the most injured by what he did."

"Selfish?" He turned away from her and slammed the cracked bottle on the breakfast bar. "You're Human, you'll never understand."

How dare he try and pull that BS card. She threw her hands up in the air. "And now we are back to that old chestnut. You, strong and powerful Pioneer. Me, weak Human."

Murphy rubbed the back of his neck. "No, there you go again, taking what I say out of context."

She crossed her arms over her chest. "Then, please, mansplain it to me."

Half expecting him to stride out the door, she was surprised when he froze and his storm wavered. She stayed silent. She had pushed as far as she could. The rest was up to him.

He inhaled, then slowly let it out again. "June was my mate. It was my responsibility to keep her safe. She wanted …" Murphy's eyes flicked to her, and for a moment she was certain she saw cracks in their ombre depths. "She wanted me to go with her that day. I said I was too busy, so she went alone. Don't you see …"

He stopped. His expression was one belonging to a broken man, and her heart ached. If he wouldn't close down at the slightest touch, she'd reach out to him. "It was my fault. She died because I failed to protect her. If I had only gone with her, she'd still be here."

Pressure pushed at her shoulders, and for a moment she, too, struggled under the vast weight of his decades of pain. She had never seen him like this before. Raw, open, and vulnerable. Had he really been blaming himself for June's death through all these years? No wonder he seemed so tortured.

She took a step toward him, willing her voice not to crack. "You're wrong to blame yourself, but you're too blinded by your grief to see it."

He shot her a pointed stare.

"Don't you dare growl at me," she said.

She pulled at her earlobe, thinking, not quite sure how far she could push this. "When it happened, did you know Elijah was in town?"

"No."

"And you always went shopping with June?"

"No. I hate shopping," he said gruffly.

How was he not seeing this? He was trained to recognize this in others. Why couldn't he see it in himself? One wrong step and he could shut her out forever. "Don't you think, then, that this is just survivor's guilt talking? Is … is that why you broke contact with your family?"

He jerked his head back and glared at her as if she had suddenly sprouted an extra head.

Hands on her hips, she waited for the storm.

"My relationship with my family is of no concern to you."

Another raw nerve.

"If you say so."

She rubbed an eye. Her head still throbbed, and it was well past midnight. Murphy's relationship with his parents would have to wait. She'd already pushed her luck and come out relatively unscathed. She reached for the bottle of Tylenol. "Look, it's late, and we need to be at work in a few hours. While you might be the mighty Pioneer, this weak Human needs her sleep."

He eyed the pills in her hand. "I told you, you need to see a doctor."

She glared at him. "And I told you, you're not to blame for June's death, so we're even." She got up and stalked to her bedroom. "I'm going to bed. The couch is yours, if you want it. Otherwise lock the door on your way out."

How could one man spend nearly half a century blaming himself for something he wasn't responsible for? They would catch Elijah, of that she had no doubt, but after that, would he disappear to wallow in his self-imposed prison for the rest of his days? After seeing her mother suffer through grief and depression, it would be a cold day in hell before she allowed someone else she cared about be trapped that way.

She yawned. She was damned tired, but her brain was too active to sleep. Her thoughts kept drifting to Molly. While she had never met the woman, Murphy's mother came across as loving, warm, and outgoing. The rift between Murphy and his father was slowly killing Molly. Couldn't they see what they were doing to her?

She turned over and closed her eyes. Would Murphy ever see sense? He needed to heal. He needed his family. But most of all, he needed to forgive himself for not being the one to die that day.

TWENTY-SIX

Bargain with the Devil

New Hampshire

Ambrose was getting restless. Or at least the voice in his head was.

You can fucking wait until I'm ready. You've already had a run today, and I have shit to do.

He ignored his agitated wolf and focused on the phone conversation with Junior. "And you're sure no one suspects we're behind it?"

"Positive. There's a rumor of a shake up, but nothing that points back to us," Junior said.

Briana leaned forward and glanced at the phone on loud speaker. "I'm hearing the same things from my end."

He steepled his hands and tapped his jaw. It looked like Elijah's bold plan was in play. They now controlled Illinois, New England, and Massachusetts. A few weeks ago, they wouldn't have been able to take on the Chicago outfit, but after flexing their newfound collective Werewolf muscles, they were expanding their power in leaps and bounds. "Make sure we keep it that way. This is only going to work if New York don't know we're coming."

The side trip to Chicago was like taking candy from a baby. While not as strong as they once were, Chicago still had a good-sized crew loyal to Salvatore DeLaurentis. After taking out the entire upper management, he had left Frank to mop up and contain the fall out. The takeover wasn't sanctioned and New York wasn't happy. Not that he cared any more about seeking their permission on anything. Once the next batch of family had their first turn, he was setting his sights on the Big Apple.

Brianna frowned. "We might be fine on that front, but our own back yard is a mess. What are we going to do about him? He's getting a little out of control."

His eyelid twitched, like it was prone to do whenever Elijah came up in conversation. Which meant he had more hours of twitching per day than not.

"You got that right," Junior said. "There's only so many bodies I can cover up. You need to keep Elijah on a leash. The cleaners are demanding double their normal fee. He's leaving a blood trail that is going to bite our motherfucking asses sooner or later. We control Boston lock stock and barrel, but there's only so many people on the payroll willing to turn a blind eye."

His jaw tightened, but he held his temper in check. Elijah, the madman, had been both a blessing and a curse. "In case it missed your notice, he's a whack job with more than twice our strength. The last time we tried to best him, he tracked down Dino's mother-in-law and slaughtered her in front of his wife and kids."

"That hasn't missed my notice, boss. I was the one who cleaned up the fucking mess." Junior paused. "We need to do something. While that looney's out there doing his shit, we're all at risk."

Brianna shuffled in her chair and nodded timidly.

Ambrose sighed. Elijah freaked her out so much she was skittish whenever she heard his name.

"With Haladlo gone, we're short a man at the port, too," she said. "None of the other crews we've taken over have anyone we can use. Word about how he died is out on the street, and we're finding it hard to get a replacement. Next month's shipment is in jeopardy. I don't need to remind you how significant that transaction is."

He rubbed his forehead. This was a fucking disaster. Brianna had been on his case all week. She was responsible for the international and national logistics for their product, whether it was drugs, weapons, or people. Normally the answer was simple: get rid of the problem, one way or another. He reached for his Perier-Jouet limited edition anniversary fountain pen and fingered the gold nib while he considered their options. He frowned at the unfamiliar texture under his fingertips. When he mulled things over, he would normally distract himself with his favorite Montblanc Boehme Papillion, but Elijah had rammed the $250,000 pen in one of his lieutenant's eyes, and he couldn't quite bring himself to touch it after that.

Unfortunately, killing Elijah wasn't an option.

In the short time since his first turn, he'd become less and less tolerant of the Werewolf who had sired them all. Though Elijah had given them the one thing they never thought possible, he had made himself too at home. Too prone to walking the thin line between what was reasonable and what was a psycho with a blade.

He pinched the bridge of his nose and groaned. "We have worked far too hard to get our family on top to just let this piece of shit destroy it all."

"If we can't overpower him, why not hit him with a massive son-of-a-bitch missile? We've got enough lying around," Junior said.

A headache was coming on. If only it was that easy. "We can't. That would be signing our death warrant."

The line fell silent.

"What do you mean?" Junior said.

He glanced up at Brianna. She was his second in command, and like Junior, she was family.

She closed her eyes and sighed. "If he dies, we die, too."

He nodded. It didn't surprise him that she'd worked it out. Even as a child, she'd had a sixth sense.

It took Junior a moment longer for the words to sink in. "Wait. What?"

He groaned. Life used to be a lot simpler. "If he dies, everyone he's turned dies, too. It would be suicide."

Junior choked. "You've got to be fucking kidding me." He whined. "Ambrose, tell me it's not true."

He sat back, and his shoulders drooped. "That's what he said."

"A-and you believe him?"

Brianna played with the Fabergé egg beside his box of Cubans. "You're telling me you'd take that risk?"

Junior swore. "And to think two minutes ago I was pissed you wouldn't let him turn me yet."

He frowned. "We've been over this before, you're too important where you are for us to pull you out just yet."

"What are we going to do?" Junior said.

He thrummed his fingers on his desk. He'd been asking himself the exact same question. "The entire city is looking for Elijah, or rather, the Boston Wolf Killer. Stop that and we have the streets back under our control."

Brianna's forehead crinkled. "Just how do you plan on doing that?"

No matter how he looked at it, there was only one course of action. "The only thing we can. The police need to think Elijah is dead, and we are going to need his help to make it look convincing."

"And how are you going to break it to Mr. Congeniality?" Brianna said after the call with Junior ended.

This wasn't something he was looking forward to. An involuntary chill ran down the back of his neck. Who knew how the lunatic would react? "Let me worry about that. I need you to work out how we're going to get that shipment in and past border control. In the meantime, I think you should put your suggestion in play."

Brianna raised a brow. "You sure you want to go down that path? It's one thing to sanction a targeted hit, but to give him a free ticket to slaughter, and for us to roll the body into an oven to get rid of the evidence is asking for trouble."

He sighed. They had clawed their way to the top by playing the long game. Their branch of the family was the strongest it had been in decades, and that was before their change. "Can you see any other way around this?"

Her lips tightened into a thin line. "Not really, but I don't like it." She paused. "Before this all goes to shit, we need to get him to turn more of the family. We have eleven more candidates. That should bring our numbers up enough to take on New York and the Russians."

He stood and headed to the door. Based on the plan he and Elijah had put in place, those numbers would give them the manpower to take out the Mexicans, Columbians, and the Triads. "I'll organize it. In the meantime, find someone at the port we can buy. That shipment has to come in."

"On it."

He closed the door behind him. The office was one of the only soundproofed rooms in the house. The only place where Elijah couldn't overhear their conversations. If the fucking madman was staying long term, he'd have to look at sound-proofing everything. He tilted his head and listened. The only other soundproofed room was in the sub-basement. Unfortunately, that one only worked if the door was closed. He scowled when the noise repeated. How many times did he need to tell Elijah they didn't shit where they slept? The whispers of a guttural moan could only mean one thing: Elijah had brought home a play thing to fuck, torture, or kill.

He grimaced. Let's face it. It was all three.

Having to listen to Elijah's version of fun was not something he'd ever anticipated, but he was slowly learning the benefits of his new life. He was more active, stronger, and faster.

He did not require as much sleep as before. His eyesight was sharper, he no longer needed to wear reading glasses. Every part of him burst with life and youth.

But his new way of life needed some getting used to. He hadn't thought he would live through his first turn. Toward the end, he had begged Elijah to kill him. The pain was beyond anything he had ever experienced or ever wanted to again. By the time it was over, his throat was hoarse, bleeding, and raw from screaming.

His new self-appointed Consigliere was of no help throughout the ordeal. The only advice he'd received was, "You'll get over it. It's normal."

What he had become was anything but normal. Normal had pivoted to the opposite side of the universe. And Elijah, for all his unpredictability, was frighteningly sharp when it came to discussing battle plans. Which only made him more unpredictable. One moment Elijah was savage and sadistic, the next he was a malevolent genius. His twitch went into overdrive. He needed to work out how to regulate Elijah's mood swings. There was no telling just how far their empire could reach in this new world order.

He pivoted on his heels and headed outside. Even now, the strain on his body to change was unbearable. His wolf wanted out. It didn't give a shit that he needed to run an empire and control a psychopath with superman strength. He clenched his fists and gritted his teeth.

I'm going. Give me a fucking minute. I can't just strip down in the middle of the house and transform.

Ambrose returned from his run in time to hear an ear-piercing, high-pitched scream reverberate up from the cellar and echo through the house. The blood-curdling sound sent him racing down to the basement. It was loud enough to reach the north wing. With Elijah's arrival he'd given up most of the servants, but he refused to give up his chef and kitchen staff, who were confined to the north wing.

What the fuck was he up to now? He needed to teach that motherfucker how to close a goddamn door.

Despite his anger, the moment he entered the room, he regretted coming to the basement. His stomach churned and convulsed. He was used to death. In his line of business, it was commonplace. But this was too gruesome even for him. Standing rooted to the spot, he now understood why the madman had insisted on repurposing the basement for his playroom. This was what happened when a fucking lunatic was left to his own devices.

Like a slab of beef, a man hung from a giant hook bolted to the ceiling. His arms were tied above his head with thick rope. Blood seeped from slices cut into the man's flesh. Elijah had used the man's body like a canvas, and his ever-present knife, dipped in the man's blood, was his brush. Chunks of flesh hung by threads from sections of his torso. Several of the man's fingers lay discarded on the floor.

He squinted, trying to work out what hung from the man's face, but the victim's head had fallen to his chest, obstructing his line of sight. He looked closer and the queasy feeling in his stomach intensified when he recognized what it was.

An eyeball hung out of its socket.

The victim's chest rose and fell weakly. Shit, the poor bastard was still alive. He took a step backwards. The hair at the back of his neck stood on end when a weak, tortured whimper from his right caught his attention. He'd been so distracted by the sight of the bloody man, he had failed to notice anything else in the scene. He turned toward the whimper, and his heart jumped into his throat. A second victim.

Briana chose that moment to investigate. She stormed into the room. "What the hell is going on down here? It sounds like—" Her eyes settled on the nearly dead man, then flicked to the second victim. She brought her hand to her mouth to stop her gagging, and her face lost all color. She turned, raced out the door, and he was treated to the sound of her retching in the hallway.

He watched in abject horror as Elijah continued torturing his second victim, unbothered by his audience.

The woman was strapped face down on a table, her arms pinned to the top by a blade through each of her hands. Her feet were only just able to scrape the floor. Barely conscious, she cried out in pain with each slice Elijah carved into her naked back. At least she tried to cry. Her tongue had been cut out and placed on the table beside her. A cold chill ran down his spine.

When Elijah noticed his presence, he sneered. "I don't share."

He held back the bile pushing its way up his throat and counted to ten. He needed to get used to this. At least here he could contain the fallout. Briana's suggestion was becoming sounder by the minute. It would be costly, but if dead bodies kept piling up in his basement, he needed a way to dispose of them. Commercial ceramics were in his future.

"We need to set some ground rules," he said.

Allowing his wolf out for a run had settled his otherwise turbulent mind. Before he was turned, he would not have entertained the thought of challenging the madman's actions. But his newfound body had also brought with it the balls to speak his mind to the bringer of their bad tidings.

Elijah, now done with his prey, snapped the woman's neck, ending her misery. "What?"

He closed his eyes and pinched the bridge of his nose before he spoke. "You know exactly what I mean. I'm running an organization that can only exist because we are not seen or heard. You are reaping the rewards of that organization, not to mention living a lifestyle that can only be maintained if we are beyond approach. You are far too visible. You're a liability to our operations. That has to stop."

Elijah let out a menacing growl. His face contorted into something feral. "I suggest you consider your next words carefully, half breed."

He pulled himself up to his full height. His jaw tightened. "I didn't say you couldn't continue your extracurricular activities, just that they need to be out of the limelight. We need the cops off the streets."

Elijah reached for his pet knife. He was never without it. For most people, it was a phone, for this fucking lunatic a knife. He wiped the flat side of the blade against the dead woman's buttocks to clean off the blood, then moved toward him, blade twirling in his hand.

He stiffened. The way the madman was playing with that knife made him uneasy. If Elijah made a move, he doubted he would survive. A bead of sweat dripped down his forehead.

Elijah stopped directly in front of him, his lips curled into a mocking smile. "And how do you propose to do that?"

He stood his ground. He needed to make Elijah see reason. Unless the lunatic agreed to his plan, they were doomed. It didn't matter how powerful and strong they were in their Werewolf bodies, their entire legacy would collapse like a house of cards. Everything he and the others had worked for would be worthless. "We need the cops off our backs, and you're going to help us do it."

TWENTY-SEVEN

Soul Food

Kaitlyn pressed the Accept Call button and the music from the car's radio immediately muted. "Hey, Mom."

"Hi, baby. Did I call at a bad time?"

"No, just on my way to a combat training session."

"That sounds ominous."

She heard the concern in her mom's tone. "No need to stress, I'm just doing some refresher training with Murphy."

"Oh, that new partner of yours? Is it a work thing?"

She shook her head and checked the rearview mirror. The gray sedan with her supposed invisible minders was now five cars behind. "No, Murphy's just giving me some advanced training, that's all."

Vivian's tone changed. "I see."

All thoughts of her shadows vanished. "You see what?"

"Nothing, dear. It's just that I get a feeling you've warmed up to this one."

How could her mother even broach that topic? "What could possibly make you think that?"

Vivian chuckled. "Well for starters, I haven't heard you threaten to shoot him once. And each time I ask you about him, you change the subject. That only means one thing as far as I'm concerned."

Her lips set into a thin line. "I do not change the subject. How's the weather, I hear it's been warmer than normal."

"Fine, dear." Her mom paused. "You know, Thanksgiving is in a few weeks' time. If this partner of yours has no plans, maybe you could bring him with you?"

She groaned. "Mom, it's not like that."

"Well, maybe it should be."

"Oh my god, Mom, change the subject already."

"How's the investigation going?"

She rolled her eyes. "You know I can't talk about it."

"Just promise me you won't take unnecessary risks. I have no intention of eating that turkey by myself, which reminds me, is it illegal to hide a fish in an air conditioning duct?"

She pursed her lips. "What have you done?"

"It's not me, dear. I'm asking for a friend."

This ought to be good. "What's Lee up to this time?"

By the time she got off the phone, she wished she hadn't asked that question. She would be so much better off not knowing. Her mom's friend had taken her feud with the non-recycling neighbors a little too far. She groaned as she imagined the putrid smell the neighbors would now spend weeks trying to find.

She dialed Anika's number. Anika had been following the Lee saga with glee. As expected, she was spellbound by this latest episode.

"I have to hand it to Lee, she stands by her principles," Anika said.

She chuckled. "The woman is a hippy vegan who's fixated on recycling. I'm not sure stuffing a dead spotted seatrout into an air duct falls under principled. Breaking and entering with intent maybe."

"You have to give her credit, she does it in style," Anika said. "Any big plans for the night?"

"No. Just a training session, then I was going to do some baking. My neighbors have a party coming up for their two-year-old, and I promised to make my signature brownies."

Anika fell quiet. "But you said I didn't need to worry."

She frowned and glanced at the stereo display with Anika's name flashing across it. "About what?"

"The Boston Wolf killer coming after you. You said there was no chance he was going to do anything beyond leaving stuff at the crime scenes. Did you lie? Is that why you are always doing your super woman ninja turtle thing?"

She rubbed her forehead. Why was everyone freaking out about Elijah coming after her? This was ridiculous. "I told you before, serial killers taunt the agents after them. They don't actually do anything about it. I'm just making sure I'm in shape, that's all."

"Well, at least you have a life outside of the grind. Something I'm longing to return to if I can ever finish analyzing these prints."

"You still wading through them?"

"Yep. Almost ready to give up. We haven't gotten a match yet, and reconstructing partials is doing me in."

She glanced at the clock on the dashboard. It was nearly seven thirty. "Why are you still at work?"

Anika yawned. "Just waiting on Tania to pick me up. We've got reservations at Peaches. Why don't you ditch your session and join us? One night's not going to kill you."

"As much as I would like to, I'm almost there now."

After her late-night conversation with Murphy, she was expecting him to kick her off the case or give her the cold shoulder. She didn't blame him. She was right, but she could have been a little subtler with her opinions and not overstepped.

"Next time, then. You need to get out more," Anika said. "What about your neighbors? Do they have any single friends?"

She sighed. "Haven't we had this conversation before? You're as bad as my mom."

"I'm just saying, life is not all work and no play. Speaking of which, what's it like working with Murphy, hotter than hot, O'Neill?"

In a word? Complicated.

He had been cooler toward her most of the day, but they still spoke when necessary. "He's the same as any other partner. Why do you ask?" Yeah, the same as any other partner who wasn't Human.

She'd nearly fallen off her chair when he had to head off early. Even so, her training session would still start on time.

"No reason. He just freaks me out with those rad eyes of his. And that superpower he has with speaking as little as humanly possible but making the perps spill the beans by just glaring at them. I have to admit, if I wasn't already taken, I'd almost be willing to switch teams."

"Where exactly are you headed with this?"

Anika's smile came through the phone. "Just checking to see if your girly parts are still working. He looks at you like you're his next meal."

What the hell was wrong with people today?

She pulled into Murphy's long driveway, thankful she had a decent excuse to end the call. Anika was like a dog with a bone, and if she showed any weakness, her friend would pounce. Even so, it took the rest of the driveway to convince Anika she really needed to go. In a way, she was thankful for the distraction. Her emotions were all over the place. She was unsure of her reception and despite just phoning her best friend, had no one to talk to about her predicament. Maybe she should have declined his offer. That way she wouldn't be so tied up in knots.

She jumped when Joshua knocked on her car window. "Didn't expect you so soon."

She schooled her features and stepped out of the car. "Left work early. There's only so much paperwork I can put up with in a single year."

After handing him a Tupperware container, she reached into the car for her tote bag.

Joshua cracked the lid open on the Tupperware and smiled. "Brownies. I sure am going to miss your baking once I go home."

Her heart lurched. "Are you thinking about that already?"

"No, you can't get rid of me so easily. I'm staying until this mess with Elijah is over with. Once we know he's gone, and things are back to normal, I'll return to Tudor Falls, and you'll go back to working regular cases."

"And Murphy?"

He sighed. "Well Murphy, I expect, will disappear for good."

Her steps faltered. "What do you mean for good? Surely he'll return to Quantico."

Joshua shook his head. "I doubt that. He's already put in for early retirement. Once Elijah is out of the picture, he can finally lick his wounds."

"Do you think he'll return to Tudor Falls with you?" He didn't answer, and she frowned. "Joshua, what aren't you telling me?"

"Katy, you need to understand, Murphy has been driven by hate for decades. He blames himself for what happened. To everyone, not just June. I ..." He trailed off for a moment before fixing his resolve. "Well, I don't hold much hope of him coming home. And, as much as it pains me, after all this is over, I doubt any of us will ever see him again."

The air left her lungs and she couldn't breathe, but she forced her legs to walk into the house. As much as the news hurt her, Joshua only echoed what she already knew.

He placed the brownies on the bench. "I wouldn't worry. At the rate we're going, it's going to take a while. With your discovery, the council is in a bit of a panic. It was bad enough with rogues and Elise running around. But now Werewolf mafia? That's a new one for the books."

"Still no luck finding anyone who's been in contact with Elijah?"

Joshua shook his head. "He's gone to ground, that's for sure. Tim and I have canvased every Were we tracked down. The stories are all the same. They either haven't seen him, or if they have, it was months back."

"Did any of them know what he was up to?"

"No, but he sure as hell was pissed at Elise."

She glanced around. "Where's Murphy? We were supposed to have another training session."

"He took off."

"What do you mean he took off?"

Joshua pushed his hands into his pockets. "I had to break the news about his parents. And he, um … he didn't take it so well."

Her stomach plummeted. "Molly and Liam? Are they alright?"

He raised his hands. "Yes, it's nothing like that. I had to break the news that they're coming for a visit."

Air raced back into her lungs. "Oh. That's all." She halted. "Wait. What?" She frowned. "Molly never mentioned it when I spoke to her last."

Joshua brows furrowed. "Spoke to her last? Just how many times have you spoken?"

"Umm." She shuffled uncomfortably. "A few. But we mainly text. Why? Is that a problem?"

Joshua let out a low whistle. "My guess is that Murphy doesn't know?"

She nodded.

"I'd keep it that way. Not sure the tree he's been using as a punching bag would survive if he knew." Joshua checked his watch and groaned. "Look, I have to go. Tim and I are tracking down the last two on your list. They're proving elusive."

"Do you think he'll be back?"

Joshua looked out the window and shrugged. "Did he promise to train with you?"

She nodded.

"Well, I've never known Murphy to break a promise. He'll be back. Although, I'd be careful of his mood. Let's just say I'm somewhat relieved to be heading out."

She raised a brow and cocked her head. "So grumpy with a side of broody, then?"

Joshua laughed. "That does seem to be his default position, doesn't it?" He paused. "To be fair, lately he seems to be a little more, I don't know, tolerable."

He grabbed his keys from the bench and headed for the door.

"When are they coming?" she called out to her grandfather. "Molly and Liam, I mean?"

"This weekend."

She headed onto the verandah to wait for Murphy and check her messages. When she found nothing from Parker, her shoulders slumped and she frowned. To be fair, it had been less than twenty-four hours since they discovered who Elijah was after.

Jumpin Jesus Jones. She still couldn't get her head around it. The New England mafia don and most probably all of his captains were newly turned Pioneers. She leaned on the railings and gazed at the tree line. The situation worsened each time she considered the ramifications. While she hated to admit it,

Murphy was right. They could never take Ambrose Giordano into custody. He would decimate anyone who came for him. Not to mention Elijah was in his corner. If the don was captured, they all risked exposure. And that was something the Alliance Council would not allow. They needed the information from Parker. The sooner they tracked down Elijah and his new little army of Pioneers, the better.

A sigh escaped her lips. Finding Elijah meant letting Murphy go. Her eyes stung, and she blinked rapidly. She'd never been more conflicted as she was at that moment. The man who killed her father would finally pay for his crimes, but the day Elijah was brought to justice would also be the day Murphy disappeared from her life. She closed her eyes to shut out the pain. How had he managed to get under her defenses so quickly? They had no future. She had always known. He was here for one reason, and one reason only. Once that was done, he would vanish. So why had her heart not paid attention? Why had it set her up for a fall?

She paced for half an hour, but still no Murphy. Her stomach rumbled. Aside from a half slice of toast that morning, she hadn't eaten all day. Both she and Murphy skipped lunch to track down another lead which didn't pan out, and she'd been too nervous around him to worry about food. If she was hungry, he must be climbing the walls by now. He and her grandfather had ridiculously healthy appetites. Where they managed to put all that food was beyond her.

She wandered into the luxurious kitchen. What she wouldn't do for all the marble counterspace and shiny new appliances. She stared at the brownies, but real food was calling. She peeked into the fridge. Four extra-large steaks took center-stage on the top shelf. She rifled through the cupboards and quickly set to work. Within twenty minutes she had baked potatoes, sliced vegetables, and steaks prepared for the barbecue. Even if he didn't come back before she gave up and went home, at least he and Joshua would have a decent meal.

Once the barbecue burners were fired up, she turned on the radio to a local station, then headed inside humming along to

Adele. A large jug of iced tea in the fridge was calling her name. She poured a glass and headed outside to lean against the railings and wait for the grill to heat. She was a city girl, born and bred, but even she had to admit, a house out here with a huge backyard had a quiet appeal to it. A perfect yard for children to run around in and play.

She suppressed a grin when she spotted Murphy emerge from the tree line. Her timing had been spot on. The food was pretty much done, the steak only needed another minute or two. Likely he'd smelled the food, and his stomach won over his anger at his parents and her.

When he strode into the house without saying anything to her, she snorted. Men. She ignored his mood and piled food onto a plate. Once it was full, she sat down and reached for the salt. "Dinner is on the table. Whether you are going to have it hot or cold, I don't really care, but sulking isn't going to change things."

She poured another iced tea and reached for her knife and fork.

"I am not sulking," Murphy said.

She dropped the cutlery. Murphy stood right by her, less than two feet from the verandah table. How the hell did he get out here without her hearing him? She reached for her abandoned cutlery. "If you say so."

Murphy took a seat opposite her and eyed up his plate. The tension that moments before had marred his face eased. "Has Joshua left already?"

She nodded.

"I suppose he told you?"

"If you mean about your mom and dad visiting? Then, yes."

He cut into his steak.

"Thank you," he eventually mumbled.

She raised a brow. "For what? The food or for not tasering you?"

He let out a low growl.

"Fine, continue to sulk then."

Murphy's fork clattered on the plate "Do you always have to have the last word?"

She tilted her head and glanced at him. "Not always."

Murphy grunted and attacked his food with more gusto. "Have you heard from Parker yet?"

By the time they finished dinner and headed out the back for her lesson, dusk had fallen, and it was pitch black when they finished. The light from the porch provided just enough to see.

She huffed. It still irritated her that he didn't break a sweat during their workouts and yet here she was, looking like a drowned rat. As they headed back to the house, their phones beeped at the same time. A moment later, Murphy's phone rang.

"Garcia, what is it?"

When he hissed and his eyes snapped to hers, the fine hairs along her arm bristled. Whatever Garcia was telling him wasn't good.

"Send me the address." He paused and flicked a glance at her. "Don't bother, I'll let her know." He thrust his phone into his pocket.

Her scalp tingled at his grim expression. "Another body?"

Murphy hesitated before giving her a curt nod.

Her pulse quickened. What the hell wasn't he telling her? "Don't tell me there's more than one?"

"It's not that." His eyes locked with hers. "It's whose body they think it is."

Is It, Or Isn't It?

Murphy put his Cadillac in park and surveyed the chaos. The property itself was well back from the main road. Whatever had occurred here was hidden from prying eyes. His gaze focused on the house that had seen better days. Paint peeled from the warped weatherboards and the cracked tiles in the roof meant the inside would flood with every heavy rainfall. Why hadn't it been condemned by now?

He tapped a finger on the steering wheel as his mind raced. Garcia's call provided more questions than answers. One thing was sure. Those on the scene were under the delusion that the Boston Wolf Killer was dead and by his own pets, no less.

He stepped out of his car and hesitated. Until this moment, he had dismissed Garcia's initial assessment. But Elijah's scent added enough credibility to have him second-guessing.

There was no way Elijah was dead. Was there?

Garcia stood by the front door puffing on his cigarette. Night had settled in, but the mobile lighting kept the dark away. The area was teeming with police cars, the Medical Examiner's vehicle, an ambulance, as well as at least a half-dozen animal control trucks.

He rubbed his forehead. Why the hell did they think they had him? He glanced down the road and let out a low growl. They'd left at the same time, but Kaitlyn insisted on driving her car. He needed her here now, but that roller skate sorry excuse for a car couldn't get past thirty.

As he strode toward the house, his stomach grew heavy, juxtaposing against his frazzled nerves. Elijah's scent strengthened with each step. The area reeked of him. His lips tightened, and he clenched his fists. A measure of doubt pushed through his resolve. But no, Elijah couldn't be dead. He hadn't spent the past fifty years chasing that monster to have it end up like this.

His step faltered when he recalled her words, the ones that haunted him the entire drive over here. He frowned. She'd accused him of being selfish. And as much as he tried, he couldn't shake her accusation. He wasn't selfish, he wanted justice for June.

If he's dead, you have it, his wolf said. *What is it you are really seeking?*

A crime scene tech rushed toward him with a box full of evidence bags. "Excuse me."

Murphy nodded, stepped to one side, and allowed the man to pass.

His feet became heavier with each step closer to the house. To make matters worse, the weight in his stomach increased in direct proportion. He should be elated at the possibility the bastard was dead.

Then why are you angry? his wolf said.

He growled. *Because I was supposed to be the one to end him.*

When his words sunk in, he froze. Was she right?

He thrust his hands into his pockets. She was wrong. Survivors' guilt wasn't what was driving him.

A light breeze picked up, and Elijah's scent intensified. If he was to get to the bottom of this, he needed to focus on the scene. He was headed down the slippery slope of emotion, and that was one place he stayed well clear of.

Two men emerged from the side of the house, each one holding on to a long catch pole. Between them, looped around the neck and under a leg in bandolier style was a snarling wolf. Howls filled the night sky from the animals already caught in the truck. He winced at how neglected the wolves were, presented his credentials to the crime scene manager, and nodded at Garcia. "What do you know?"

Garcia stubbed his cigarette and placed the butt in the Marlborough packet. While he was allowed to smoke, he couldn't leave anything behind that might contaminate evidence. "Neighbors down the road called it in when a wolf ran by their place with blood all over its fur. We found more caged up 'round back."

Murphy looked over to the animal control van. Why would Elijah need wild wolves? It didn't make sense unless there was something different about them. He headed around the back of the house, where with any luck, he'd find answers. The backyard was as run down as the rest of the property. Three wolves were being corralled in a large run, which at some point had been a chicken pen. He shook his head. He had to admire the irony.

Nothing out of the ordinary struck him. He focused on the wolves. Apart from being wild and undernourished, there was nothing that stood out. With no obvious clues in sight, he headed back to the front of the house.

"Finally."

Kaitlyn had arrived. Now they could get in and find out what the hell was going on. As he headed up the stairs, he reached down and pulled gear out of an open crime scene kit.

Garcia nodded at her car. "The bat mobile, it's not."

She glared at him. "Don't you start, too. There's nothing wrong with my Prius."

Murphy handed her a pair of crime scene boots and gloves. "That's a matter of opinion. You would have gotten here faster walking."

Garcia burst out laughing. "You got that right."

She ignored them and glanced around. "Where's Saul?"

Garcia nodded at the house. "He's in with the first attending." He headed inside. "Looks like our search is finally over."

Murphy grunted and followed behind. "That remains to be seen."

The sooner they established what was really going on, the sooner he could set them straight. They approached Saul, who stood to one side of the living room with a uniformed officer.

Saul nodded and pulled out his notepad as the officer continued speaking.

"Someone called in the tip. When we turned up, we found the wolves caged behind the house. The front door was open. No visible signs of forced entry. After calling out, we proceeded into the dwelling where we found the victim. As per procedure, we did a sweep of the house to check for any other occupants. At that point we discovered the basement," said the officer.

"Has anyone disturbed the scene?" Murphy said.

The officer shook his head. "No sir, after verifying no one else was in danger, we exited the house. When the crime scene guys turned up, they did a sweep, but they're waiting for you before processing the scene. The ME's with the victim now."

His nostrils flared. Elijah's scent was strong in the kitchen, almost overwhelming, and as prominent as the stench of blood and death. Just before they walked through the door, he faltered.

His wolf paced. *Worried it is him?*

Ignoring his wolf's pointed dig, he picked up his pace.

Garcia stopped in his tracks. "Fuck me."

Dr Swanson, the city's medical examiner, knelt on the ground beside the body. She looked up. "His pets certainly did a number on him."

The remains of a man lay on the ground, body mauled beyond recognition. Flesh hung from him where it had been ripped off by powerful jaws. Bloody wolf prints covered the floor. Not only had the animals ripped into the flesh on his back, but a large section of his ribcage was also exposed. Murphy exhaled and kept his face neutral, but inside he bounced between relief and confusion. The vic wasn't Elijah, but the poor bastard on the ground was definitely killed by him.

He rescanned the room and his brows drew together. Something seemed off. The scene felt wrong. Why did the local police think this was their killer? He squatted to inspect the body. "Have we got an ID or a time of death?"

"According to his license, his name is Harold Belcher." Dr. Swanson pulled an electronic thermometer from between Harold's buttocks. "Based on his core temperature, I would say at least ten hours."

"What about cause of death?" Garcia said.

Dr Swanson raised an eyebrow and pointed to the lake of blood. "I think it's safe to say he bled out, but I'll know more when I perform the autopsy."

"Nothing more than he deserved, if you ask me," Saul said.

Kaitlyn glanced around the room, then back to Garcia. "What makes you so sure this is our guy?"

He wondered the same thing, especially considering he knew it wasn't.

She darted a pointed look at him and her eyebrow jerked upwards, but he had no way to let her know that the body on the ground wasn't Elijah.

"We know it's him because of what we found in the basement," the first officer on the scene said. He stepped back and motioned for them to follow.

They trailed behind as he guided them through the basement door. "It's what we discovered down here that was the surprise. And you'd better prepare yourselves."

He and the rest of his team made their way down the rickety stairs. A flickering light bulb hung from an exposed chord. As the only light source to guide them, it served to make their descent even more ominous. A putrid odor wafted up to greet them.

Kaitlyn covered her nostrils with her hand.

He grimaced. The sharp stench was like a wall. It took all his effort just to keep moving. When they reached the bottom, he took a moment to let his eyes adjust. Three crime scene techs stood back and waited impatiently for the go-ahead to process the scene.

"That's fucking sick," Garcia said.

He echoed Garcia's sentiment. This was not what he had expected. Even his wolf was surprised.

Kaitlyn headed farther into the room. "God, that's putting it mildly."

One wall of the basement was adorned with knives and tools. A stone bench table dominating the center of the room held a decomposing body. Or, more accurately, pieces of a decomposing body. The room resembled a medieval torture chamber, and the stench of death was hard to miss.

Kaitlyn cleared her throat. "Frack me, are those maggots crawling over him?"

Newspaper clippings covered a second wall. Some had yellowed with age, others were still crisp and fresh. When he moved closer to investigate, the hairs on the back of his neck bristled. Irrespective of age, each article shared a common theme: The Boston Wolf Killer. He scanned the stories. They included not only the most recent killings but extended back to the first set from twenty years ago.

What the hell was going on here?

Kaitlyn came to stand beside him. A pitiful cry emanated from her throat when her gaze fell on the grainy and faded image of her father. He tensed and resisted the urge to pull her away from the pain. Her face lost all color, and at this close up he heard her pulse increasing as she scanned the articles.

He lowered his voice so only she could hear him. "Just breathe."

She blinked, and her walls went up. The scent of her shock evaporated.

He raised a brow. She was getting good at hiding her emotions. Too good.

Garcia opened a small fridge in the corner, stuck his tongue against his bottom teeth and let out a whistle. "We have our man."

He stepped aside and pointed to the contents.

Saul, who was closest, got there first. "That looks like an ear."

"Yep. And check out the jar behind it," Garcia said. "I think we've found our missing fingers."

Saul gulped. "You know what? I think I'll take my retirement a little early."

"Belcher has lived here all his life. He's the right age, clearly fucked up, and to top it off, we have his trophies. I think this calls for a celebration," Garcia said.

The hair on the back of his neck prickled again as he surveyed the room. This was not right.

Saul made a grunting noise from the back of his throat and nodded at a dirty tin vase with a bunch of dead roses in it. "Well, at least you ain't going to get no more love letters," he said to Kaitlyn.

He had to admit, on the face of it, they had their killer. Whoever had staged this was good.

Half a dozen wolves were caged out back. A cut up body was laid out like a prize, which, in all likelihood, would be tied to organized crime. And to top it off, there was evidence of Belcher's involvement. He'd bet they would find his fingerprints all over the fridge and those jars. For the Boston Police Department, this was a slam dunk. The Boston Wolf killer was no more.

And yet he was.

The dead man upstairs was a patsy. To what end, and why Elijah agreed to all this, he couldn't fathom. His mind buzzed. Elijah had given up his keepsakes. What would be so compelling that he would fake his own death?

A chill ran down his spine. Whatever it was, it wasn't good.

Kaitlyn raised a brow at him in a silent question. He glanced across at the others to make sure they weren't looking, shook his head, and pulled out his notebook. It was going to be a long night. They were working a scene that was staged, but to the rest of the team, Harold Belcher was their killer.

And to be honest, had he not known better, he would be inclined to agree.

By the time they'd finished, dawn had broken. And when they walked out onto the road, the media had already gotten wind of what was inside. Although a cordon kept them at bay, it didn't stop them from shouting out questions. They all wanted the scoop on whether the Boston Wolf Killer was finally dead.

Garcia headed to his squad car, dead on his feet.

Saul ambled out of the house and down the path after his partner. "They found some more body parts in the bathroom. Techs are going to bag and tag. Why didn't you tell them there was more evidence?" he said to Garcia.

Murphy's hand froze on the door handle. Whoever staged this scene knew what they were doing. This scene was going to keep the techs busy for days.

Garcia frowned. "How would I know? I didn't go near the bathroom."

Saul halted and a confused expression crossed his face. "But I—you're wearing two cufflinks?"

Garcia chuckled and glanced down at his trademark cufflinks with his initials engraved into the gold. "Jesus, Saul you're sharp this morning. I think, old man, you are in desperate need of sleep."

Saul put his hands into his pockets and a bead of sweat erupted on his forehead. He pulled at his earlobe. "Don't mind me. Just having a senior moment."

Halfway to the car Saul slowed, then turned back to the house. Saul's pensive expression had Murphy on alert. Something was worrying the old detective.

He pulled the car door opened and called out to Saul. "Forget something?"

Saul glanced at him and Kaitlyn, then back at the house. "Nah. It's nothing. Just getting a little jumpy, that's all. Reading things into it that just ain't there."

Murphy shrugged. Whatever was playing on Saul's mind wasn't being shared with Garcia either, if his closed expression was anything to go by. "Go get a couple hours sleep and we'll regroup this afternoon," he called out to them. "The crime scene techs will take care of bagging and tagging the rest of the evidence."

Garcia and Saul nodded somberly, ignored the reporters, and drove off.

Murphy's phone went off, yet again, and his frown deepened. He'd only be able to ignore the commissioner's calls for so long.

"Problems?" Kaitlyn said.

"The commissioner wants answers."

She lowered her voice. "What are you going to tell him?"

He glanced back at the throng of reporters, police, and support staff. He couldn't take the chance of being overheard and nodded to his Cadillac. "Get in."

"You think they're convinced it's him?" she said as she closed the door.

He tapped a finger on the steering wheel. "I lay odds the commissioner will consider it a win and close the case."

She stared down at her hands. "Is that really a problem? Now that we know who Elijah is with, and with Parker's help, we'll track them down." She turned to him. "Was he here? Could you tell?"

His hands tightened on the wheel. "Yes, and he wasn't the only one. I detected the scents of multiple Werewolves all around the house."

"I'm guessing those caged wolves didn't actually kill Belcher, then?"

His stomach clenched uncomfortably at how Elijah and his accomplices had condemned innocent animals like that. "No. Elijah did. But when they compare the bites against the other victims, they will find a match."

She sat back and stared at the house. "Why would he stage his own death? And how did they find a patsy who matches the profile we're after? Odd that they found one the authorities would fall for hook, line, and sinker, don't you think?"

He had been asking himself the exact same questions. "That's what worries me. This isn't something Elijah would do. This has Ambrose Giordano all over it. But I don't get what they're up to, and why."

She sighed and lightly touched the cut on her forehead. "Whatever the reasons, things are going to get worse, aren't they?"

His chest tightened. That cut was his fault. He should never have let her get anywhere near the new werewolf. "Much worse. The mafia lives by a code of commandments, a business model with an overall objective of making money. They don't care how that money is made, and they prey on human weakness. Elijah has now given them an advantage, one they are seizing at any opportunity."

The uneasy feeling at the pit of his stomach returned. The scene was too clinically correct. Ambrose had help ticking all the boxes to make the outcome of the investigation go only one way. Help only a law enforcement insider would be able to supply. He glanced across at Kaitlyn but kept his suspicions to himself. This was something he would need to look into alone. He wasn't about to risk her getting hurt again. He straightened his hunched shoulders. "We need to find out everything we can about not only the New England mafia but all their competition and associations."

His mind flicked through a range of strategies. Ambrose had spent a lifetime building walls in front of walls to keep himself hidden and beyond reproach. This was not going to be easy. He sighed. He had only one option. "I think we need to take a page out of Elijah's playbook. If we can't get to Elijah through Ambrose, we'll have to get to Ambrose through someone else."

"How are we going to do that? The commissioner will close the case, you just said it yourself."

His lips set into a grim line. His plan, while not yet complete, would require Kaitlyn to do something her every instinct would rebel against. However, they had no choice. "We'd better get all the information we can from the Boston PD before the day is through."

Her eyes widened and her brows shot up. "You know that's illegal, right?"

He leaned across the front seat and pushed the passenger door open. "Then you'd better not get caught."

TWENTY-NINE

The Calm Before the Storm

Kaitlyn breathed more easily when safely inside Murphy's house. She'd spent most of the day making copies of everything organized crime-related she could lay her hands on. For most of the morning she worked unimpeded. Garcia and Saul had grabbed breakfast and returned to their precinct to bask in the glory of closing a high-profile case. They wouldn't return to start the closeout paperwork for hours.

Murphy carried the carton of files, and she trailed behind.

"The police department is going to get a massive print bill next month. There were some case files that hadn't been digitized yet so I took copies. The rest are on a couple of USBs."

Murphy's isolated home was the best place for them to work. No possibility of being interrupted or caught working a closed case.

He placed a box down and shook his head. "Better that than learning the truth."

She headed out the door, and Murphy following shortly afterward.

"I've been thinking about what Garcia and Saul mentioned about the raids," she said.

"What of it?"

"Well, every time a big bust was scheduled for a major player, the Boston PD would turn up with a warrant, and the place was already cleared, or they couldn't find what they were after. Saul and Garcia are convinced someone is tipping off Giordano's organization. If that's true, the leak is coming from inside the police department."

He waited for her to catch up. Nothing in his expression indicated he was surprised at her comment. "If we find the dirty cop, we can track Ambrose."

She opened the trunk to her car. "I know it's a stretch, but it's better than nothing. And it gives us another route to Ambrose."

He pointed to what was left in her trunk. "What's all that?"

She looked down, confused at the question. "It's extra linen and bedding."

He growled. "I agreed you could work with me, not move in."

She threw him a withering glare. "God, you can be such an idiot sometimes. It's not for me."

He looked at her blankly.

She let out a disgusted snort. Of course, he would forget. "Tomorrow is Saturday. Your parents are arriving. I noticed the spare room hasn't been set up for them yet, and I couldn't find any fresh linen."

He froze, his gaze fixed on the laundry basket. Much to her surprise, he reached into the trunk and yanked out the basket, a typical non-committal grunt his only response. Without a word, he stomped into the house.

Doing her best to suppress a grin, she grabbed the last box and closed the trunk. Once in the house, she made her way to the spare bedroom, stripped the bed, and opened the windows to let in some fresh air.

The whole while he leaned against the doorframe and watched.

Self-conscious, she blurted out the first thing she could think of. "Are you picking them up from the airport, or are they getting a rental?"

"Yes."

She stopped, confused. "To which option?"

"Both. My mother wants to make sure they get here."

She stuffed one of the pillows into a fresh cover. "Right, because that makes sense."

He righted himself, shoved his fists into his pants pockets, and stared at the floor. "This house is owned by the Mountain Pack and has been used as a safe house or for temporary accommodation over the years. My father was here once in the sixties. He's adamant he can find it again."

She frowned, struggling to understand his logic. "Yeah, still none the wiser."

He shrugged, then pulled his hands out of his pockets and crossed them over his chest. "When he thinks he knows where he's going, my father refuses to consult a map."

Typical male. "But all rentals have a GPS, they can just key in your address and follow the instructions."

He let out a short, sharp laugh. "My father was never a great one for technology. He has yet to send a text message. And according to my mother, he's only recently agreed to carry a cell when he's taking tours into the forest."

"Ah," she said, returning to her task, "I see it now. You're worried about them."

He snorted. "You're delusional."

She glanced at him. Outwardly he wasn't thrilled with the idea of his parent's trip, but she had the distinct impression he was also surprisingly nervous about it.

"Would you like me to come with you?" The words escaped before she could stop them.

The muscles along his jaw twitched. For a brief moment his walls dropped, and his expression showed indecision. Just as quickly, though, it slammed back up. He cleared his throat and stood to his full height. He shrugged, turning to leave the room. "Suit yourself."

She glared at his back, torn between throwing something at him or reaching out and reassuring him that she would help him through the stress of his father's visit. She avoided doing either and resumed making up the bed.

She'd not gotten much further when her phone beeped. A message from Saul flashed on the screen.

>Came to say goodbye but you had already left. It was a pleasure to work with you.

A faint smile tugged at her lips. What a case for him to end his career on.

She tapped out a reply. >Make sure to enjoy your retirement. I'm sure we will bump into each other. Boston's not that big.

By the time she had the guest room sorted, Murphy had pulled all the files out of the boxes. When she walked in, he was briefing Joshua on the unexpected development.

Joshua gave her a hug. "I hear you had an interesting night. Tim said it's all anyone will talk about."

She picked up a file and gave him a half shrug. "If only it was Elijah."

"What did Alpha Locke say about this mess?" Joshua said.

"What can he say? He assured me Parker is trying her best to track Ambrose Giordano and get us that family tree. Until then, we need to see if we can find them on our own," Murphy said.

Joshua checked his watch. "I have a couple of hours before I meet Tim, so I can lend a hand. What do you want me to do?"

"We need to go through all this with a fresh set of eyes." Murphy indicated the massive piles of notes stacked neatly on the floor. He then nodded at the computer. "I've copied the USB data onto the laptop, so take your pick."

The next few hours rolled by in a blur as they came up to speed with all the gangs, cartels, and syndicates that operated out of the Eastern Seaboard. One thing was certain: Giordano started his move against the competition well before Elijah turned up. Their newfound powers only sped up the process.

Murphy tipped his head to the right to stretch his neck. A distinctive crack cut through the silence. "Based on what I've been reading, the mob definitely have someone feeding them information."

She sat back and threw down the folder she had been pouring through. "The only question is who?" She rubbed her cheeks and stood up to stretch the kinks out of her back. "I don't think we're going to find the answers today."

"Go home. We'll continue this tomorrow."

She exhaled and checked her watch. No wonder she was tired. They hadn't slept in nearly forty-eight hours. She reached for her keys and bag. "The only positive thing about this mess is that Elijah won't be slicing up any more innocent people. If they went to that extent to make everyone think the Boston Wolf Killer was dead, he must be done with his killing spree."

He sighed and rubbed the back of his neck. "I wouldn't bet the farm on that."

He trailed behind her as she headed to her car. She turned the key and was ready to close the door when Murphy rested his arm on it.

"Thanks."

"For what?"

He stared at her and a faint smile tugged at his normally stoic expression. "For not taking no for an answer. I've worked alone for so long, I'd forgotten how pleasant talking things through can be."

Floored at his confession, she was, for once, speechless.

Murphy leaned down and lightly touched his lips against hers.

The unexpected action froze her. As exhausted as she was, heat surged through to her core. On autopilot, she brought a hand to his face and deepened their kiss. Heat spread through her body. When he moved his hand around to pull her closer, she nearly burst into flames.

Just as quickly, the moment was over. He pulled away and closed the door.

She pushed back her desire and the intense feeling of loss. She was torn. More than anything she wanted to bolt out of the car and finish the promise of that kiss. But if she did, her heart was done for. Instead, self-preservation kicked in, and she made the fastest escape her Prius could handle.

On the drive home, all she thought about was his lips on hers. He had her so wound up she had no idea which way was north anymore. She jumped in her skin when her phone rang.

Jumpin Jesus Jones.

She was ready to ignore it when she glanced at the caller display. All thoughts of Murphy's kiss evaporated, and her shoulders tensed. She'd heard. "Hi, Mom."

"Is it true?"

Clearly the media coverage of the supposed death of the Boston Wolf Killer had already reached as far south as Florida.

She hesitated before answering. If she told the truth, she'd have to explain why. "The evidence is pointing that way."

Fractures of relief pulsated over the phone, both alleviating and enhancing the guilt of lying. The line went silent.

"Mom?" Her voice cracked.

She struggled to hold back the tears when Vivian broke down in all-encompassing, heart-wrenching sobs. Twenty years of grief and unresolved anger let loose. Her heart shattered.

Elijah wasn't gone. He was very much alive and living it up with the mob.

Eventually, Vivian calmed down enough to ask how she was taking the news.

"I'm fine."

The line fell silent again.

Vivian exhaled. "Kaitlyn, honey …"

She steeled herself at her mom's tone. She wasn't going to like what was coming next.

"I know you don't like going out there, but I was wondering if you could do something for me. Please."

She hesitated.

"Baby …" Vivian's voice quivered. "Would you place a sunflower on your father's grave for me?"

She swallowed in her dry, almost painful throat. She hadn't been out to the cemetery in years. She hated the place. The cemetery had taken away a piece of her mother with each tortured visit. "Of course, I will." It was out of her mouth before she could stop it.

Vivian cleared her throat. "Lee's convinced me to go to a families of homicide victims' support group meeting."

She swerved the car and nearly ran off the road. Vivian had point-blank refused to attend any sort of support group over the years. How Lee had talked her mother into it, she didn't know. Nor did she care. She was just thankful her mom had agreed to it.

"Lee's going to come with me. I-I'm not sure I could do it on my own."

"Mom, you're stronger than you think. But give Lee a big hug for me, will you?" She ached to throw her arms around her mother and Lee.

"You can give her one when you come down for Thanksgiving. You are still coming, aren't you?"

"Don't worry, I'll be there."

"What about that partner of yours, Murphy? Are you bringing him, too?"

"Good grief, Mom. He's going to be well gone by then."

She smiled, but a sharp pain ripped through her chest when she realized the truth in her words. Very soon Murphy would walk out of her life. Forever.

She wrapped things up with her mom by promising to phone her the next day. With everything going on, Murphy and Thanksgiving was the last thing she wanted to discuss.

No matter how much Kaitlyn tried she was too wired to sleep. She gave up trying, marched into the kitchen, pulled out pots and pans, and began cooking in an attempt to create order out of chaos. The outside world believed her father's killer was dead, she'd lied to her mom, and to top it off, she was falling for someone she could never have.

A groan escaped her lips as she pulled ingredients out of the pantry and threw them on the bench. "You have to stop obsessing. It's not healthy."

She yanked open the top drawer, pulled out a sharp knife and waved it at the unsuspecting fruit basket. "You're a bloody adult."

She slammed the knife into the chopping board. "You carry a gun and you're not afraid to use it. In fact, you've even shot someone. So why are you so agitated about a few stupid kisses and an emotionally unavailable Pioneer?"

She opened the fridge and stared at the shelves. "He's moody. And non-talkative when he wants to be. Not to mention he's a Pioneer, and there's definitely an age gap."

Innocent vegetables were slaughtered as she attacked them with furor. No matter which way she looked at it, she had a problem. She was becoming addicted to not only Murphy's earth-shattering kisses but to the man himself. The more she worked with him, the more he let her see behind the wall he'd carefully constructed to shut out the world, and the more she cared for him.

Murphy was locked in a self-imposed prison. One he didn't belong in, nor deserve. And for some reason, he'd let her see behind it. She couldn't deny she was physically attracted to him. That, she had accepted long ago. His body set hers on a constant simmer. She was willing, and if she was honest, more than eager to taste the forbidden fruit.

She sliced a tomato in half with gusto. "We're both consenting adults. So what if things got a little out of hand?" No, she knew what.

Her eyes fluttered closed. She had allowed her heart to get in the way, and that was unacceptable. She could not—would not—feel anything other than a physical attraction to the man. If she allowed more than that, she would be devastated when he walked away.

An onion went flying. "You need to get a grip. You're just tired, and this case has gotten to you. It's just a physical attraction. Nothing more."

Now that she'd schooled her emotions into check, her shoulders relaxed. She finished chopping a carrot, more gently. She had no romantic feelings whatsoever for her very desirable, masculine, and steamy partner, whose eyes bored into her soul and set her on fire every time he got too close.

None whatsoever.

"I wonder if I have enough ingredients for a cheesecake?"

<u>THIRTY</u>

Guess Who's Coming to Dinner?

Murphy studied Kaitlyn as she deposited the third container of food on his bench. Something had her worked up.

Her lips drew into a thin line and she shook her head. "Don't ask."

"Wouldn't dare."

He leaned against the bench, one hand casually tucked into his jeans, the other holding on to his coffee cup. Kaitlyn made three more trips. No wonder she had dark circles under her eyes. What the hell was she doing cooking all night?

His stomach rumbled. He'd already eaten, but he would be more than happy to try out whatever was tantalizing his taste buds. At least it would give him something else to focus on. His stomach had been churning all morning, but that had nothing to do with his hunger.

She wiped her hands on her pants and cast her eyes across the fruits of her labor. "I think that about does it."

He placed his cup on the bench and straightened up. "Yesterday, it was linen. Today, food. I'm just curious about what you'll turn up with tomorrow."

She stopped short and her brows shot up. "Wow. That actually sounded like an attempt at sarcasm."

He grunted, headed over to the cupboard, pulled out an empty cup and poured her a mug of extra hot chocolate with a spoon of salted caramel, just the way she liked it. Unable to stand it any longer, he ruffled through the containers. The aromas were too much for him to resist, but he wasn't sure where to begin.

She sipped her hot chocolate. "Where's Joshua?"

He grabbed a blueberry muffin and took a bite. "He and Tim found a newly turned Werewolf last night, so Joshua is driving him up to the pack in New York State. He should be back later today."

"How many more do you think are out there?"

He'd been asking himself the same question. Elijah had turned more than he'd expected. It was a small miracle they hadn't been exposed yet, but he couldn't guarantee their luck would hold out much longer. "The only way to know for sure is to find Elijah."

She headed for the family room where they had set up a temporary work area. "We'd better get back into those files, then."

"I have a couple of leads."

She turned back to him. "You do?"

"Yeah. I reexamined the files the FBI have on the mafia family connections."

He'd needed to focus his mind last night. He had been too wired, and his wolf wasn't interested in a run. That ornery beast wanted him to wallow in confusion. He ran his fingers through his hair and sighed. He should never have done it. That kiss was wrong on so many levels. But kissing Kaitlyn felt like the most natural thing to do. Given the chance he would not stop there, either. He grabbed one of the files sitting on the countertop and handed it to her. Today, of all days, he needed to stay focused.

She leafed through the pages, the whole while chewing on her bottom lip.

He studied her, hyperaware of his arousal. Guilt reared its ugly head, and just as quickly as it began, his desire ran cold. She was his partner, not to mention Ryan's daughter. He returned his focus to the case and waited for the penny to drop. She had one of the sharpest minds he'd met in a long time. She wouldn't take long to find it.

She frowned. "This doesn't make sense."

He held back a smile when her face lit up.

Her expressive eyes looked up at him, bright with excitement. "How did we not see the link before? According to this, the FBI team suspect Gisela Briana Giordano is well-connected, but they have no proof. There don't seem to be any photos on file, but do you think this might be the same Briana that Frank's wife mentioned?"

"Get an address, we'll find out."

She reached for her bag and headed to the dining room. "I'll see if I can find one."

Her familiar scent settled around him like a warm blanket. He drew in a deep breath. No matter how much he tried, he couldn't recall June's scent. In its place was Kaitlyn's distinct essence. Fresh, spirited, and soothing. She was so different from June. Where June was calm and serene, Kaitlyn was full of fire and energy.

He froze and his heart thudded against his chest, as sharp cuts of shame sliced into him. How could he compare Kaitlyn to his beloved mate? He balled his hands into fists. He had dishonored her memory. Terror escalated along with remorse. He had spent a half century mourning June and grieving for the children they would never have. Loneliness had been his constant companion through the decades, and his consuming need for revenge had driven a wedge between him and his family, his pack, and even his friends.

How could he so easily forget? How could he so easily toss her memory aside?

Of course, he had bedded women over the years, but only to satisfy a primal urge. There was nothing to it. Each time he walked away without looking back. No regrets and certainly no promises. He scratched his jaw and stared at the door Kaitlyn had disappeared through. He wanted her more than he should. His body hummed in her presence. Her insightfulness was refreshing. He enjoyed her company and looked forward to working with her each day, and her cooking rivaled his mam's. That was saying something, considering Molly was considered the best cook in the pack.

A small trickle of sweat ran down the side of his forehead. His life was fucked up beyond control. It didn't matter which way he turned, he was at fault. He had to keep his distance. He would only hurt her. He placed his hands palms down on the kitchen counter and fought for control. Especially today of all days. Kaitlyn might not pick up on his internal struggle, but Joshua and his parents would. How the hell had he gone from self-imposed solitude to being surrounded by people? And not only had they insisted he communicate with them, one managed to slip under his defenses. He needed to push her out before it was too late. He couldn't—he wouldn't—hurt her.

"I have some addresses," Kaitlyn called out.

He squared his shoulders and reached for his keys. He needed to refocus on Elijah. Killing him should be his only goal.

The plan was simple: find Brianna Giordano, follow her, and find out where her cousin lived. A simple plan but her physical location was proving to be just as elusive as her cousin's.

"So, you didn't scent anything?" Kaitlyn said as they got back into the Cadillac.

He shook his head. This was the third address listed for her, and he detected no Werewolf scent.

Kaitlyn glanced down at her printout. "We'll tackle the last four tomorrow."

The dashboard said four thirty. "Why stop now?"

She frowned at him. "There's not enough time. As it is, we'll only just make it to the airport in time."

He grunted and reached for his phone. Maybe they had decided not to come. No message. He sighed and tossed his phone into the console, then turned the engine over. Was it too much to hope for an emergency that required his immediate presence?

"You nervous?" Kaitlyn said as they drove along in silence.

"No."

"Joshua said you haven't seen them in years."

His hands tightened on the wheel. "Joshua has a big mouth."

"You are going to be civil, aren't you?"

He flashed her a look and grunted. This was going to be a long weekend.

They arrived late and sprinted to the arrival's gate. As expected, the area was teeming with people. When his parents exited through the doors, he stiffened. They both looked older than he remembered. Had it been that long?

What do you expect after two decades? his wolf said.

Da was unmistakable. Unless he was surrounded by NBA players, Liam would stick out in any crowd. Ma was the complete opposite. From her short stature, right down to her outgoing and warm nature. Where his da was war, his ma was peace, and he often marveled how fate had paired them together.

Two teenagers pushed through the door, and not looking where they were going, they nearly bowled into his ma. In one fluid movement his da pulled her safely out of their path. Just as quickly, she flashed Liam a smile, pulling away but still holding onto his hand. The new crow's feet on his parent's faces tightened his airways. Twenty years should not have aged them that much.

But stress and worry would, his wolf said.

Kaitlyn let out a gasp. "Blue cheese in a sandwich. I guess that's your parents?"

How did she know?

He threw her a questioning look, and she arched a brow. "Seriously? You're the spitting image of your father, and you have to ask?"

As they drew closer, his stomach became queasy. What was he supposed to say after all these years?

His ma was all smiles. She had always been the peacemaker. But when his gaze moved across to his da, he stilled. From his stony expression, his father wasn't pleased to be here. Mind you, he could be happy, upset, or even have heartburn, and no one would know from his expression. He shifted his weight. Reading his da had always been difficult.

When they were three feet away, they stopped. His ma's happy expression became pensive. She fidgeted with her bag and glanced at each of them. He glanced at the exit. Had the building suddenly become smaller, claustrophobic? All the air had left, and he was struggling for every breath.

Kaitlyn poked him in the side. "I think the customary thing to do here is hug."

His ma's eyes glazed over and she blinked rapidly. She let out a small cry, dropped her suitcase to the ground, and closed the distance between them. When she wrapped her arms around his waist and buried her face in his chest with a sob, his chest tightened. It had been so long, he was unsure of how to react. What did you say after that many years of separation? What words could he use to tell them how sorry he was that he'd failed to protect June and with it, their hope to carry on the O'Neill name.

His arms lifted and he returned her embrace. Strawberries. She still reminded him of strawberries. Summer joy and warmth. "I missed you too, Ma."

He cleared his throat and looked at his da. Liam, as stoic as ever, gave him a curt nod.

Molly pulled away and patted her coat pocket. "My goodness, I told meself I would nay blubber like that. I know how ye hate public displays of emotion, but I just couldn't help meself."

Kaitlyn held out a tissue. "Here."

His mom smiled at her through glassy eyes, took the tissue, and blew her nose. After she wiped her tears away, she smiled gratefully at Kaitlyn. "And ye must be Kaitlyn. It's so lovely to put a face to the voice."

He stiffened. Face to the voice? When the hell had they spoken to each other? His muscles rippled as his teeth ground together. He definitely would be having words with Joshua.

Kaitlyn nodded. "Yes ma'am. Pleased to meet you as well."

His mom snorted. "Firstly, I'm Molly, not ma'am. And secondly, get ye backside over here for a hug, lass."

Perhaps he should have warned Kaitlyn that his ma was a compulsive hugger.

Kaitlyn didn't have a chance to move before his ma had engulfed her in a full bear embrace. When Molly finished squeezing the life out of her, she pulled away and looked her up and down. "I can't believe Ryan's young'un has become such a bonnie lass. I expect ye have to beat your suitors off with a stick."

He stilled and gave Kaitlyn a sidelong glance. His scalp prickled. Was there a man in her life? She'd never mentioned it, but that didn't mean she wasn't dating someone. He scowled. None of his business.

His wolf stirred. *Are you sure about that?*

Kaitlyn chuckled. "No, no. There's no one like that at the moment. Chasing Pioneers around the tristate area doesn't leave much time for a social life."

He glanced away to hide his inward smile. Her confession gave him far too much satisfaction.

Molly frowned. "Pioneers? I thought ye were working together on catching that evil no good degenerate, Elijah?"

He groaned. How she still couldn't refer to his race by their name was beyond him. "*Waswolf,*" he said, using the Gaelic term. "And don't ask."

His ma tucked her arm in the crook of Kaitlyn's. "And how's our lad treating you? It better be decent, or he'll have me to answer to."

Kaitlyn grinned. "You know Murphy, if he's not growling at something, he's grunting at something else."

Molly waived her free hand at his father. "Oh, you have 'im to blame for that."

Liam's eyebrows shot up, and he growled.

Molly winked at Kaitlyn. "See? I call it their caveman language."

Kaitlyn stifled a smile. She once again held out her hand. This time, her expression was more reserved. "Pleased to meet you, Mr. O'Neill."

The hairs on the back of his neck stood on end. Why would he be concerned about what his da thought of her? Technically, being Joshua's granddaughter, she was pack. His da, being an Elder of said pack, knew that. Liam had no choice but to accept her. He let out a breath when his da shook the offered hand, nodded, and said nothing. If he was dead set against her, he would have ignored her.

Kaitlyn glanced around the busy airport. "We'd better get out of people's way. How about we get your rental sorted and then we can get you back to the house. You must be tired."

She and Molly headed through the crowd toward the Budget Car Rental counter, chatting the entire way.

He stood with his father. Despite the noise around them, their small bubble was deathly quiet. Neither said a word. The awkward moment stretched out and Murphy slipped a hand into his jean pockets, struggling to find something to say. Unable to find anything, he reached for his mom's suitcase. "We'd better follow them."

When his father strode off without saying a word, he clenched his jaw. His chest tightened as he watched their retreating backs. Why he expected his father to change was beyond him. The man was as grumpy as hell, thought he knew best, and failed to listen to anyone else's opinion but his own.

They arrived home close to seven. He was thankful they were in separate cars. He could not have survived the trip with his disapproving father glaring at the back of his head.

"I knew this was a bad idea."

Kaitlyn reached over and placed a hand on his arm. "Give it time. You've not seen each other in years. It's bound to be awkward at first."

The comfort in that small touch sent a rush of warmth up his arm and across his chest. He resisted the urge to place a hand over hers to drag out the momentary peace. She calmed his frayed nerves even after he'd barked at her the entire ride home. How was it that she had more empathy and feeling than his own father? How was it that after all these years his father still made him feel like a child? He ran a hand through his hair.

This is not a pity party, his wolf said.

A moment later he was out of the car, his expression as cold as stone, the walls back up.

Joshua sauntered out the front door and headed for his parents' car. "Well, well, well. Look who the cat dragged in."

Joshua opened the front passenger door and grinned. "I see you managed to tear Liam away from Tudor Falls. How on earth did you do it?"

"She arranged for Gilda to take over the café while we're away," Liam said.

Joshua choked and laughed at the same time. "You'd rather face flying than listen to Gilda, huh?"

Liam shrugged his shoulders and headed to the trunk. "Woman talks too much."

Joshua grinned and slapped Liam on the back. "My friend, a deaf-mute talks too much as far as you're concerned. But even I would agree with you there. Gilda is pretty heavy on the ears."

Molly threw her hands on her hips. "Hush now, both of you. There is not a thing wrong with her. She's just a little high-strung, that's all."

Liam glared but said nothing.

He reached for the first bag his father pulled from the trunk. He had no idea who they were talking about. A measure of guilt needled him in the gut. His life had stood still, but he shouldn't be surprised when the world around him carried on. The pack had grown over the years. Perhaps she was new? He had lost touch with a great deal when it came to his own pack.

Joshua picked up the second bag and indicated the house. "Let's get you sorted, then we can catch up."

"Aye, but I'll have no more words of ill against poor Gilda," Molly said. She reached out for Kaitlyn, who had remained quiet. "Now dear, tell me how your mother is doing. Joshua tells us she's in Florida."

Kaitlyn and his mom wandered to the house, deep in conversation.

He wasn't surprised about how well Kaitlyn blended in with them, but why did it make him so happy? Perhaps because she made an awkward situation relatively painless. Yes, that was it.

Joshua chortled as the women walked away, then lowered his voice to whisper to Liam. "You made the right call. Gilda would've been in your ear twenty-four by seven." He shook his head. "No matter the reason, you're here now. And to mark the momentous occasion, I even got you some of that tar you like to drink."

Liam growled. "Guinness."

"Bless you."

Liam headed towards the house. "Don't you ever get tired of that joke?"

"Nope," Joshua said as he raced to catch up. "The classics never get old."

"She wouldn't have worn me down, by the way."

"Sure, she would have. Have you met your mate?"

Liam glanced sideways at Joshua and winked. "There are a lot of ways to distract her. How do you think I got away with accidently burning a hole in her family quilt?"

He stared at their retreating backs. Since when had his father developed a sense of humor?

He showed his parents to their room and left them to unpack. Joshua was on the verandah with his feet up and a beer in his hand. He nodded to a small chiller box in the corner. "Help yourself."

Murphy glanced around the verandah. "Where's Kaitlyn?"

"In the family room, something about files needing to be tidied up."

He stalked back into the house before Joshua detected his relief that she was still there. "I'll go see if she needs help."

The files had been spread across the table and parts of the floor, but in a matter of minutes she'd tidied them up, and they were piled into five stacks on the buffet unit.

"That should give you guys some space. I'll be back in the morning, and we can visit those last addresses. I've a good feeling about it." She reached for her bag and lowered her voice. "They're really nice. You should lighten up."

His gaze flicked toward the door, and his stomach clenched. Of course, Kaitlyn would have an opinion. He grunted.

She shrugged. "Be that way then, but you're not doing yourself any favors. Both your parents are alive. They're good people. Trust me on this. Once they're gone, they're gone. You have one chance to get things right, there's no such thing as a do over."

A hollow ached filled his empty stomach. He pushed his hands into his pockets and looked anywhere but her face. She was right. But he wasn't going to let her know that.

She placed her hands on her hips. "This thing with your dad needs to end. As much as you hide it, this rift is killing you."

He stiffened. He was trying to avoid the subject, not enter into a bloody conversation about it. "This has nothing to do with you," he ground out between clenched teeth.

Kaitlyn snorted and rolled her eyes. "Men."

She headed to the verandah where his parents had joined Joshua. He trailed behind, mulling over her words.

"I'll leave you guys to it. I'm sure you have a lot to catch up on." She turned to him. "Don't forget you just need to reheat the pepper steak casserole on low."

Molly frowned. "Aren't ye staying for supper?"

Kaitlyn shook her head. "The four of you haven't seen each other in a while. You don't need an outsider making things awkward."

Molly waved her hand dismissively. "Nonsense. It's getting late, you must be starved. Besides, I would hazard a guess that you made that casserole. Joshua can't boil water, and my lad is nay much better."

He resisted the urge to correct his ma. His cooking skills weren't half bad. Living alone he had no choice but to learn.

Kaitlyn fished in her bag and pulled out the keys to her roller skate of a car. "No, it's fine. I don't want to intrude."

Molly turned to him, placed her hands on her hips and frowned. He cringed. This wasn't going to go well for him.

"Murphy, where are your manners? I raised ye better than that."

His wolf nodded in agreement.

He ran a hand through his hair. "Ma, you can't force people to bend to your wishes. That's not the way it works."

"Liam and Joshua don't mind." She glared Liam and Joshua. "Do you?"

Instead of replying, both men grunted without looking up. For some reason their beer bottles held an intense fascination.

Molly smiled and turned back to Kaitlyn. "See, it's settled. You're staying. Now dear, where is this casserole you were talking about?"

At what point did he lose charge of his own home?

His wolf snorted and grinned.

Traitor.

Knowing he was beaten, he reached for a bottle of Guinness, and stalked to the far side of the verandah, the farthest distance from his father.

Joshua threw his hands up in the air when the silence became deafening. "This is ridiculous. Would someone please say something? Anything. Even Gilda would be preferable to this."

He picked at the label on his beer bottle. Kaitlin's word repeated in his mind. This was uncharted territory for him. What could he say after twenty years?

Joshua reached for another beer and smirked. His eyes squinted with a twinkle of mischief. "How about I start? Murphy, tell your parents the story of when you traipsed around Boston at the end of a dog lead?"

He glared at Joshua. He could kill him right now.

By the time Kaitlyn and his ma had dinner on the table, Murphy was ready to climb the walls. He'd managed a few words with Ma. That was the easy part. But unless his da made the first move, there was no way on earth he'd start first.

How five adults could have a conversation with two of them not speaking to each other was beyond him, but they'd managed it through dinner. The conversation was stilted, but a conversation nonetheless, helped on by Joshua and Kaitlyn for the most part. Much to his disgust, they even managed to find the Benji story funny. After the fact, it was mildly amusing, but he wasn't going to admit it.

He had just taken the last forkful of food when Molly placed a napkin on her lap. "I think you better tell us about who Elijah has hooked himself up with."

Shite. Careful to keep his expression neutral he forced himself to stay calm.

I was wondering how long it was going to take for the conversation to move to Elijah, his wolf said.

Not long enough.

Joshua let out a small growl. "The sooner we find him the better."

Liam cut into his third steak. "The council is in a panic over who he's gotten into bed with this time. Aren't they just a bunch of hoodlums from Sicily?"

He glanced across at Kaitlyn. Her brows knitted together at Liam's question. He often forgot she had no idea how removed from Human current affairs his people were. This was why he wanted to stay away from the Elijah topic. That bastard was the one who had created the rift with his parents.

Molly looked across the table at him and raised a brow. "Do they really put horses' heads in people's beds?"

He held back a groan. "No Ma, that only happens in the movies."

How did he make them understand just how serious this was? He took a stab. "If anything, the council is underplaying it." He reached for his beer as a heavy weight pressed down on him. This was going to take a while.

After dinner, he and Joshua cleared up the dishes while Kaitlyn and Molly took a walk outside. As expected, the more his mother found out about the people Elijah had aligned himself with, the more upset she became. His father, on the other hand, had not said much. He'd asked Joshua direct questions but ventured no opinions. These would come later, once he'd digested the information.

Joshua stiffened and let out a low growl as he looked out the window. "Something's wrong."

Kaitlyn. His wolf pushed close to the surface.

Both he and Joshua raced out to the verandah, then stopped cold. Kaitlyn and his ma were fine, standing a short way off. Kaitlyn was on the phone. The churn in his stomach dissipated. They were both safe.

When he looked closer at Kaitlyn, though, his heart stopped. She had her hand over her mouth, and her head shook from side to side like she was in pain. He bolted down the stairs. By the time he reached her, the call had ended.

"What's happened?" His voice came out gruffer than intended.

She blinked tears away and he had to hold himself back from reaching out to her.

"T-that was Anika." She cleared her throat. "It's Saul and Mildred. They were involved in a hit and run."

A rock plummeted to the bottom of his stomach. He knew from her tone, before she'd even said the words.

"Saul, he died at the scene. Mildred is not expected to survive the night."

THIRTY-ONE

The Spy Who Came in from the Cold

New Hampshire

Ambrose waved at Junior to enter. A vein in his forehead twitched. The call had already gone on too long. "I don't care how much it's going to cost. I want it done."

He pinched the bridge of his nose to hold back the irritation. He was getting nowhere with this conversation.

When Elijah wandered in behind Junior, his headache intensified. He was trying to run a multi-billion-dollar business, not a zoo.

He clenched his jaw. "Give him till noon tomorrow. If he doesn't play ball, cut a hand off one of his mistresses, then remove something else every hour until he does. I don't care if you have to whack his entire family." He slammed the phone on his desk. "Motherfucking judges, they think they call the shots."

Junior wandered over to the wet bar and poured three glasses of bourbon. "Wheatly will break. If he doesn't, it'll just be a warning for the next one. It's a win-win if you ask me."

Junior handed him a glass and took a sip of his own. "How did you do in New York?"

He reached for the drink, then cradled the cut crystal glass in his hands. "They didn't know what hit them." A quiver ran through the length of his body. In fact, it had gone very well. The five families were down to two. His power and reach was growing in leaps and bounds.

The dismissive snigger from Elijah set his teeth on edge.

"And if you'd listened to me, we could have taken out the rest while we were there," Elijah said.

He cringed. The smug tone grated on his nerves. He took a gulp of his drink and welcomed the burning sensation. Pity he couldn't deal with Elijah the same way he dealt with judges, lawyers, and the occasional congressman. "I told you already, if we take on too much too soon, we won't be able to control them."

Elijah ignored him and took up a prime position on the leather couch. He swung his feet onto the small table and whipped out his knife to inspect the blade.

Fucking psycho. Ambrose's fingers itched to do some form of damage. He ground his teeth together and fought to reign in his temper. He was already pissed at Junior, he didn't need more stress, or he wouldn't last the year with his sanity intact.

He turned back to his cousin. Junior remained quiet and avoided direct eye contact, most probably working out how to break the news to him. He shook his head. After all these years, how Junior would think he didn't already know was beyond him. "I hear you had a little problem."

Junior's pulse kicked into high gear. Another side effect of his new power. One that came in handy.

The Adam's apple on Junior's throat bobbed. "I didn't have much choice. He was getting too close."

He slammed his glass down on the mahogany desktop. "Killing fucking cops is not the way to solve that problem, and you know it."

Junior held up his hands. "Chill out, boss. It's not going to come back to us. I made it look like an accident."

Elijah caressed his blade, and looked at it lovingly. "Next time, let me deal with it. Accidents are too fast. You need to learn to savor the kill."

He white-knuckled his desk and fought not to charge at Elijah. The sardonic grin marring Elijah's features had his hand itching to remove it permanently. "How you've eluded this Alliance of yours is anyone's guess," he muttered.

"Oh, they've all tried. The Alliance, the police, and the FBI. That smug, self-righteous O'Neill masquerading as a Fed has shadowed me for half a century, and I haven't been caught."

His white-hot rage evaporated into a cold chill that smashed into him. Ten pounds of chain settled in his stomach, and his gaze moved to Junior. His cousin's face had lost all color and his eyes were the size of saucers.

"Who?" they said in unison.

"Who what?" Elijah shifted his feet from the table to the floor, and ran his blade across the Laliqui Cactus Table.

He cringed. The crystal table was worth over a hundred grand. And that fucker just made it worth less than something on sale at Ikea.

The damage to his prized coffee table only served to make the dread in his stomach more painful. Surely he heard wrong. It couldn't possibly be the same O'Neill on the FBI task force? He leaned forward. "Who did you say was after you? The name, what's his name?"

Elijah snorted. "Murphy O'Neill. Why, what's it to you?"

The knot in his stomach turned to heavy lead. "And this O'Neill person. He's like you—us. He's a Werewolf."

Elijah snarled. His blade flew through the air and buried itself into the back wall. "Yes. But a pathetic one at that." Elijah leaned back on the couch. "He thinks he can best me. He got lucky when he caught me the last time. I won't be letting that happen again." He smacked his lips and rubbed his loins. "And his partner, Quinn, is going to get the same treatment as O'Neill's mate."

Ambrose tensed. The cold chill leaked through to his arms and legs, and the weight in his stomach was heavy enough to bore a hole in it. He had big plans. Fuck. This couldn't be happening. It wouldn't take long for O'Neill to find the connection to him and bring down everything he had worked for.

Junior let out a half whistle between his teeth. "What do you want me to do, boss?"

He rubbed his forehead. What he wanted to do was kill the motherfucker who put him in this mess. He clenched his fists to stop from doing anything that could kill them all. Instead he focused on the one thing he could control. "We need to find him before he finds us. I want a team on both O'Neill and his partner. Get Frank onto it, ASAP."

Elijah's fist came down on the Laliqui. The force nearly knocked the lamp over. "Let him come." He paused. "Or perhaps I should go find him, for old times' sake."

White-hot rage shattered the ice, and he let out a low growl, his anger finally boiling over. "You will do no such thing. This could end us if you bring the FBI here. Don't forget who's taking care of your rubbish."

Elijah stood and strode across to where his blade was embedded in the wall. "I would watch how you talk to me, half-breed." He yanked the knife out. "I could end you in a heartbeat. Where would your little family be then?"

Elijah held his blade to Junior's neck before he could blink. "Maybe I'll show you firsthand what it's like to fillet a Human."

His throat ran dry. A thin line of blood seeped from where the blade had cut through Junior's skin. His cousin was as white as a sheet. The scent from Junior's terror blasted out like a detonated dirty bomb and enveloped the room.

He attempted to reign in his now out of control pulse. He had to diffuse the situation before it got even more out of control. "You do that and O'Neill will be the first person I call."

Elijah snarled. "Let him come. He's no match for me."

"That may be so, but I suspect he'd come with reinforcements. How do you think you'd fare then?"

Elijah glared at him for a long moment before removing the knife from Junior's neck. He wiped the blade on his jeans. "Like I said, let them come."

With that, Elijah sauntered out of the room as if he had not a care in the world.

He stared at the empty space Elijah had vacated. There wasn't a hole deep enough for that motherfucker.

Junior's shoulders slumped, and he began to breathe again. He brought his hand up to his neck to touch the cut, then pulled it away to inspect the blood. "What do you want me to do?"

He rubbed his forehead. So much for them taking on the Russians and Columbians. They might need to take on this Alliance, as well. "You? Nothing. You need to lay low until this thing with Saul Ruby dies down. A dead cop is more dangerous than a live one. I'll get Frank onto this."

For a long while after Junior left and Elijah disappeared into his subbasement, he stood staring out the window. His jaw ached. And his blood pressure was sure to be through the roof.

It doesn't rain. It fucking pours.

His wolf stopped pacing. *You must deal with this O'Neill. If you can't get rid of him, you need to find a way to control him.*

He rested his head on the glass, contemplating what needed to be done. The cold, smooth surface on his forehead barely registered as his mind filtered through this turn of events. He didn't need this wrinkle in his plans.

Elijah, mad and insane as he was, he could deal with. But this Alliance and Murphy O'Neill was another matter entirely. From his conversations with Elijah, they would not look favorably on his activities, especially in light of his new gifts and abilities. His wolf was right. He needed to contain the threat. Fast. Before it had a chance to fuck up his plans.

He stiffened as the answer came to him. With a rush of adrenaline, hope raced through his veins. He stood up and straightened his shoulders. Why hadn't he thought of it earlier? A broad smile creased his face. Often the tried and true methods were the best. The partner, Quinn. She still had two hands. For now.

THIRTY-TWO
Family Tree

Kaitlyn jumped when her phone went off. She'd been deep in thought. Not a great state of mind when she was driving. She glanced at the caller display and grimaced.

Frack. She forgot Anika wanted an update.

She pressed the answer button on the steering wheel and braced herself. "Hey Anika."

"How is she? You promised to get back to me, and I'm still waiting. You should know, I don't take waiting well."

She sagged against the car seat. From her tone, Anika was more upset than angry. "There's no real news. I tried getting in to see her but she's still in ICU."

She had spent the better part of the morning at the hospital with Garcia. As they weren't family, the doctors wouldn't release much information until Saul and Mildred's children arrived, but the fact she had survived the night was a good sign.

"Garcia was headed to the airport to pick up Saul's daughter, so there was no point in hanging around."

Anika let out a defeated sigh. "I can't believe he's gone. Only a few weeks before he retired." Anika's voice caught in a sob.

Her heart ached. She hadn't known Saul long, but he was a good cop and from all accounts, a wonderful family man. He didn't deserve to go out the way he did.

Anika sniffed and blew her nose. "It just shows you, I guess. Life is way too short. And I was only just saying to him yesterday he shouldn't be so worried about nothing that trivial. But I suppose it doesn't matter now."

The hairs on the back of her neck stirred. "What doesn't matter?"

"His stuff didn't arrive. Saul phoned me yesterday morning. He had some evidence he wanted me to take a look at, but he didn't want anyone to know about it."

"Do you know what the evidence was?"

"No, but he seemed worried about it." Anika paused. "Now that I think about it, he was a bit nervous and he was uber insistent this was between us."

The hairs on the back of her neck bristled. His death and this missing evidence couldn't be related, could it? Regardless, she should not let Anika know her suspicions. "It's probably nothing. But if it arrives, let me know, okay?"

Anika sniffed. "Will do."

Kaitlyn pulled into Murphy's driveway and parked behind Joshua's car and tried to ignore the sick feeling in her stomach ever since the conversation with Anika. She couldn't shake the suspicion that Saul's accident may not have been an accident, after all. It just didn't add up. How did a driver miss two people crossing the road in broad daylight? According to the report, a car ran a red light, and even more chilling, there were no tire tracks from sudden braking. Something wasn't right in the state of Denmark.

She reached for her bag. Maybe Murphy knew more.

The back door was open, so she went straight in. Not seeing anyone, she headed to the family room. By the time she had powered up her laptop, Molly entered with two cups. She held out one of them. "Here ya go. Murphy said you like your chocolate extra hot with a wee bit of milk and caramel."

She gratefully accepted it. "Thanks."

"How's that poor man's wife?" Molly said.

She studied her drink. While she had never met Mildred, her heart went out to her and her family. This was the time she and Saul were supposed to start living for themselves. "It's still touch and go."

"I'll keep her in my prayers."

Despite trying to focus on the task at hand, the idea that the accident was deliberate kept returning. Who could possibly have an axe to grind against Saul? He was a threat to no one. And what the hell evidence was he nervous about?

"Where's Murphy?" she said.

Molly nodded at the back door. "Out on the verandah. He's on the phone with Alpha Locke. Liam is eavesdropping from the garden."

She rolled her eyes. "They've still not had a direct conversation?"

The smile on Molly's face faded, and she shook her head.

Kaitlyn's heart went out to her. It couldn't be easy living in the middle of a Mexican standoff. She reached out and rubbed Molly's arm. "If you want, I can put a bullet in their stubborn butts."

Molly let out a small laugh. "Bless you child, but it's going to take nothing short of a miracle to get those two dunderheads to actually speak to each other." She sighed. "Them arguing would at least be something, and they'd get it out in the open. It's this silence between them that kills me."

Her phone beeped. She hesitated before reaching for it. She had been ignoring Doug. On the other hand, she hadn't heard from her mom in a couple of days so it could be her. But what if it was Doug? He was going to want to know when she'd get the paperwork done. As she scanned the message, her shoulders relaxed and a measure of hope rushed through her.

"Good news?" Molly said.

"The best."

She reopened her laptop. Her fingers itched to get the promised information. "It's from Parker. She's put together the family tree for our mobsters."

"I'll leave you to it then, lass." Molly bustled out the door.

Parker and her team had even managed to find the Pioneer link in the mafia family tree through a family historian who was commissioned to come up with the tree for Elise. Their hypothesis that Elijah had already known who he needed to target was correct. A little money had changed hands between Parker and the historian, and Kaitlyn was now in possession of the entire list of progeny for Giuseppe and Marianna Roma.

She scrunched her nose when she read Parker's other discovery. One of Ambrose's cousins had an unusually large number of properties for a dead man, some of which were acquired after he was six feet under. He had been dead fifteen years, his taxes were up to date, yet probate had not been lodged. Now all they needed to do was hope one of the branches would bear fruit and lead them to Ambrose, the elusive mafia don, and by default, Elijah.

She scanned through the information and shook her head. The family tree only went back five generations but was extensive. It was too large to make sense of on a small screen. She pressed print and eyed up one of the walls.

Forty-two pages later, she stood back to admire her handiwork.

"Well, if he's still alive, I would hate to see his Christmas list," she said.

What made the list so unusually large was the fact that the Pioneer had sired five children with a Human woman. She clicked her pen.

A deep. gruff voice broke through the silence. "Giuseppe did take a shine to the lass."

She let out a small squeal as she spun round to face Liam.

"Don't do that," she said. "I may not live as long as you do, but I don't intend to go before my time."

"Sorry," he replied, his gaze not wavering from the name at the top of the tree.

Molly rushed into the room. "I heard a scream. Is everything okay?" She stopped as soon as she saw the papers fixed to the wall and her brows shot up. "Goodness, you have been busy."

Liam beckoned her over and pointed to the name at the top.

Molly stood beside him and studied the wall, then shook her head and tsked. "I hate to say it, but it doesn't surprise me. He missed the old country, and really, he couldn't adjust. In some ways I think Marianna reminded Giuseppe of home. They came from the same region."

She did some quick math. "Is he still alive?"

Murphy walked in. "Is who alive, and what the hell have you done to my wall?"

"Parker just sent through our mobster's family tree."

Molly took a closer look at the family tree. "No one knows if he's still alive," she said. "But if I hazarded a guess, I'd say no."

As Murphy's parents recounted what they knew, Kaitlyn studied the various branches. They must be Catholics.

Instead of each generation producing fewer children in alignment with the rest of the population, the families were consistently large. The names were familiar, too. It looked like a who's who of both Sicilian and American mafia. *Messina, Buccola, Lombardo, Giordano.* She let out an audible sigh. It was going to be a long day.

"Kaitlyn, wake up."

Her eyes fluttered open and she yawned. Murphy had opened the passenger door and was gently shaking her awake.

She sat up and looked around. "Sorry, must be more tired than I thought."

The Cadillac was parked in Murphy's driveway. From the lights in the house, the others were back already. She reached for her bag and rummaged for her car keys. "I swear to God when we find him, I'm going to shoot him just for making us drive from one end of Connecticut to the other."

They had divided up the list of most likely addresses. Tim and Wendy took New Hampshire, Joshua and Danny Massachusetts, while she and Murphy had scoured Connecticut. To be fair, the entire day hadn't been a complete bust. At one of Ambrose's dead cousin's properties, Murphy scented Pioneers. It was faint, but more than one had been there within the past few days. When Joshua confirmed the same thing with another of the deceased properties, they decided to focus on the remaining twelve before venturing back to the alive and kicking garden variety mafia.

"Where the hell are my keys?"

She stifled a yawn and pushed the car door open farther. "There was another address in Concord. It's a bit off the beaten track, but I'll swing by on the way home."

He pulled her out of the car. "Joshua may have already covered it. We'll regroup in the morning to work out what we still need to cover." When she was clear of the door, he pushed it shut. "Besides, you're not going nowhere, missy. You'd fall asleep before you reached the bottom of the driveway. That roller skate of yours would be wrapped around a tree before you could find the brakes."

He herded her toward the house.

She pulled from his grip and let out an impatient snort. "So how do you expect me to get home? I'm not made of money. The cab fare would cost me a small fortune."

He crossed his arms over his chest. "Quit your complaining. You'll stay here the night. You can have my room, and I'll bunk in with Joshua."

She faltered. Her throat constricted and a shiver ran down her spine. His suggestion made sense. So why did she feel breathless about the idea of sleeping in Murphy's bed?

Get a grip.

She was too tired to drive. And it wasn't as if they were alone. Her grandfather and Murphy's parents were in the house. Still she hesitated. "Are you sure I won't be putting you out?"

Molly poked her head out the window. "Hurry up you two, the natives are getting restless. I wouldn't let them eat until you got here."

Murphy waved. "On our way." He turned back and looked at her pointedly. "I'm not about to let you risk your life. I can survive one night with your grandfather's horrific snoring."

Her lips tugged upward in a half-smile. "Mom always said Dad inherited it from his father. Looks like she was right."

"Don't get me started on Ryan's snoring." He placed his hand on the small of her back and guided her the rest of the way.

Fried green tomatoes. Heat fanned out from the spot where his hand rested to every part of her body. She was suddenly not so tired. Hot and bothered maybe, but not so tired.

Murphy chuckled. "They haven't yet invented ear plugs to drown out his unique decibel level."

She still had a smile on her face as she crawled into bed. From the stories Murphy told, he and her father had been close. He'd refused point blank to talk about their time together twenty years ago, but their friendship before that was a different story. Even Liam had surprised her with one of the fond memories he had of her father. While neither Murphy nor Liam spoke to each other, they had stopped the silent, broody glares. Which, in her book, was progress.

After dinner, Molly insisted she head off to bed, her endless yawns giving away the extent of her tiredness. Too tired even to check on her mom, she slipped between the sheets and relished the scent of Murphy. Even the freshly washed t-shirt he'd lent her to wear reminded her of him. As she turned over and pushed her face into the pillow, it dawned on her how much she had begun to take his presence for granted. She looked forward to seeing him each day. She enjoyed teasing him, arguing with him, and, God help her, she even thought his broodiness was charming, to a degree.

What was most disturbing was the way her body responded to his. Like he was due north and she felt an unconscious gravitational pull toward him.

His parting words, "Sleep well," still played on her mind. How was she going to sleep well when she was in his bed? Her overactive imagination wouldn't let her. She brought her fingers up to her lips. If she asked him to tell her a bedtime story about her father, would he kiss her when he was done? Heat rushed through her face as her mind wandered into forbidden territory. She needed to stop this. It wasn't healthy, and it would only serve to make it worse in the long run. Murphy would disappear as soon as he found and killed Elijah. He had already lost the only woman he would ever love.

Her vision blurred and she blinked rapidly. A sharp pain cut through her chest. They had no future. No matter which way she looked at it, she was going to come out of this more scarred than she came in. She wiped away the single tear that slipped out of the corner of her eye.

How did she allow herself to fall in love with a Pioneer who was out of her reach?

THIRTY-THREE

One Call too Many

Kaitlyn stared out the window of the diner. "I still don't understand how that much property can be in the name of a dead person."

Murphy took a gulp of coffee before answering. "There's nothing against the law about it. And it's a loophole Ambrose has been taking advantage of."

They had confirmed a fourth property where one or more Pioneers had been within the last week. But still no sign of Elijah.

"What are we missing? There has to be a reason they faked Elijah's death. Maybe if we can work that out, we can narrow our search."

Murphy placed his coffee mug on the table. "I agree, Ambrose has something up his sleeve. But I'm more concerned about what Elijah is up to. To be honest, it's worrying me."

"What are you saying?"

"I can't put my finger on it. There's a bigger picture at play here that we're missing, and the sooner I work it out the better." He glanced around the diner and nodded to a waitress. "Let's order, I'm hungry."

She hid a snicker. Yeah right—because a half slab of bacon, a mountain of grits, and two tons of waffles wasn't a healthy enough breakfast. How did they pack in so much food? She shrugged and closed her menu.

Once the waitress had taken their lunch orders, she thrummed her fingers on the table. "What other reason keeps him hidden? It doesn't make sense—"

Her phone rang and she fished it out of her bag. "Sorry, I have to take this, I'm waiting on a call from my mom."

She raised a brow when she saw the name. "It's Anika." She pressed answer. "Hey, how was your weekend?"

"Babe, way too short, but iconic. Went to the Muna concert with Tania and some friends Saturday night. Did lunch with the olds yesterday, then played a bit of Counterstrike, which I totally ruled. So did not want to get out of bed this morning. Adulting really sucks sometimes. And don't forget you promised to come with me to my cousin's wedding. I sent you a calendar invite and you haven't replied yet."

She dropped her head onto her hands. Anika was actually going to make her go.

Anika's voice lowered. "Uh-oh. McKrusty's floating around, he's been complaining I talk too much and slow everyone down in the lab. Do you think I talk too much? See? Of course, you don't."

She tapped her fingers on the tabletop. "You need to stop calling him McKrusty. His name is Rusty, and God forbid you slip up one day and call him that to his face."

Anika giggled. "Whoops. Too late."

Murphy's lips twitched.

She glared at him and mouthed, 'Stop eavesdropping."

He picked up the dessert menu and pretended to focus on it. The waitress took that moment to bring over her order.

She smiled at the woman as she set down her bagel. "Did Saul's evidence ever turn up?"

"Oh, yeah, this morning. The ear in the jar they found at the Boston Wolf Killer's house."

The uneasy feeling she had yesterday returned. "Why would Saul send you that?"

"Beats me. He wanted it dusted for prints."

She leaned forward. "And?"

"And what?"

"What did you find?"

"Oh, nothing. I haven't had a chance to look at it yet. Was just about to—" Anika let out a small squeak. "Crap McKrusty's blowing a fuse. Gotta go."

Murphy's jaw looked like it was about to crack under the strain. "Was she talking about the jar they found in the bathroom cupboard?"

She swallowed and nodded. His eyes were crinkled slits, but the ebony gave away his barely repressed rage. He wasn't taking Elijah's fake death very well. And it didn't help that they'd found another turned Pioneer outside of Ambrose's family tree. They'd been too late to help him. Convinced he'd lost his mind, he took his own life rather than hurt his children.

They fell silent when the waitress returned with Murphy's food. Kaitlyn took the opportunity to reread the message from Tim. He'd included a family photo of the man, his wife, and three-year-old twin boys. Sadness flowed through her veins. They would never know the sacrifice he made for them.

Once the waitress left, Murphy picked up his fork. "Finish your lunch. Joshua is dropping your car off at your apartment, and we'll regroup after that."

Something in his tone made her fingers tingle and her head shot up.

McNuggets.

To the outside world his veneer was impenetrable. He was stoic and detached. She knew better. His dark eyes pierced her with barely repressed fury. His chiseled face was so rigid it could cut rock. She reached over and placed her hand on his. If she had any brains, she'd run in the opposite direction. Instead, she ran directly into the path of a supernova. "Just breathe."

His jaw tightened, and he spoke through clench teeth. "It's my fault. Those deaths are on me. I should have caught him when we rescued Parker."

Ever so slight, but she detected a waver in his voice. A dull ache tore at her chest. She hated to see him in so much pain. He wasn't the untouchable iceberg he worked so hard to portray. His armor had cracked enough for her to peek inside. She squeezed his hand again and willed her strength and support through the touch. The weight he carried had finally buckled under the strain. He was torturing himself. Blaming himself for their deaths.

She scanned his face. "It's not on you. It never was."

Her first instinct was to wrap her arms around him. Tell him she was there for him. Tell him she loved him, and they would get through this. Together. Tell him they would get justice for June and her father.

A two-ton boulder slammed into her chest. She must never let him know how she felt. He trusted her as a partner and perhaps, with a push, as a friend. Her lips tightened. No. She needed to focus both of them on the task at hand. Not wallow in their own personal hells.

She raised her chin and pushed down her pain. She would dwell later. Right now, they had a single purpose. "You are giving yourself too much credit. You're not the one at fault here. Elijah is, and don't you damn well forget it." She pulled her hand away, squared her shoulders, and reached for her bagel. "Eat up, we've got a certified psychopath to catch."

She'd managed to get in a second bite when her phone rang. Her grandfather's name flashed across the display. She swallowed and reached for it. He'd probably dropped her car off at her apartment already and was checking in. "Hey, we're having lunch at Vera's Diner. How far away are you?"

Molly's shaky voice came over the phone instead of Joshua's. "No, love, it's me. Something's happened."

Murphy's head jerked up. "What's wrong?" he said before she could reply.

Something in Molly's tone had them both on high alert. She leaned nearer to the table so he could hear better.

"Well, we're at your place, but when we came upstairs, we found the front door broken."

A cold chill ran down her spine. Surely she heard wrong. "Broken or left unlocked?"

"The door was smashed open, and it's off its hinges. I hope ye don mind, dear, but we peeked inside. Don't fret, we were careful not to touch anything. They were long gone by the time we arrived."

Murphy tensed and leaned close to the phone. "Ma, are Da and Joshua with you?"

"Yes. They told me to wait in the apartment while they checked the building." Her voice dropped. "But Kaitlyn, someone's made a right royal mess of your flat."

She shook her head, dreading what condition her place was in. "Does it look like they took anything?"

"I can't say for sure, but Joshua thinks whoever broke in was not after ye stuff."

Her brows crinkled. "Why does Joshua think it's not an everyday B&E?"

"It doesn't take three Werewolves to rob someone," Molly said.

Her blood ran cold and her gaze raced to Murphy's. What the hell was going on?

"We're on our way." He ended the call, then rubbed the back of his neck. "They know."

She had to agree with his assessment. Ambrose, and most likely, Elijah knew they were getting closer. They had lost the element of surprise. Her stomach churned. She felt a cage closing in, with no way of escape. Had she tempted fate when she declared Elijah wouldn't come after her?

Murphy called for their bill and reached for his wallet.

She rubbed her temples. They still had no idea how to find Elijah. "But how? We weren't followed. Why would they break into my apartment? What were they looking for?"

She shot out of the booth. "Oh, God, Anika! Do you think they might be after anyone involved in the case?"

Her phone chose that moment to chime. She glanced down and frowned. It was Lee, her mother's friend. She was about to reject the call when pinpricks of anxiety danced across her skin, and she thought better of it. No doubt Lee was doing her mom's bidding and phoning to make sure she was coming for Thanksgiving. The woman was a dog with a bone. She would phone every five minutes until she got through.

"Hi Lee, I'm in the middle of something. Can I call you back?"

"Oh, thank goodness you're answering. Would you tell your mother to turn her phone back on? I've been trying to reach her all day. The power went out at her place and I don't know—"

Her pulse skipped a beat and her mouth ran dry. She cut Lee off. "Why would you be phoning me to speak to mom?"

She felt every second of the deathly pause before Lee answered.

"Because she flew up to Boston early yesterday morning," Lee said, her voice clearly confused at Kaitlyn's question. "Your mother decided that she needed closure. It was going to be a surprise. Haven't you seen her yet?"

Kaitlyn froze. The diner went in and out of focus. Something was pressing against her chest making it hard to breathe, and her vision was turning dark at the edges. She sat down.

Murphy caught the phone as it fell out of her hand.

His lips were moving, but she couldn't hear what he was saying. The words were jumbled, like he was a million miles away. Only one coherent thought stuck in her brain, and it terrified her. Her hands shook, and she closed her eyes against the black spots swirling in front of her.

Elijah had already taken one parent. Had he now made her an orphan?

THIRTY-FOUR

Falling Apart

Kaitlyn's panic rose with each red light they encountered. Murphy had run a few but had to stop when the traffic grew heavy. She clenched her hands, one over the other until her fingers turned white. Her chin and lips trembled.

Please no. Don't let it be true.

Her heartbeat echoed in her ears. It beat so loudly it seemed it wanted to escape her chest. This wasn't happening. How could it be? Her mother was safe. Lee was mistaken, and her mom was home. In Florida. Thousands of miles away from Elijah. She had to be. She blinked rapidly and glanced at the dashboard.

When did the Cadillac shrink? The car doors and windows were closing in on her, making it hard to breathe. She touched a hand to her forehead. Like the rest of her skin, it was clammy. She checked her watch. Why was time moving so slowly? Her hands shook as she dialed her mom's phone for the hundredth time.

Answer, damn it.

For the hundredth time it went straight to voicemail.

Her mind sifted through every scenario, but each time, it ended with the same outcome. She let out a whimper and squeezed her eyes shut.

Please no. Don't let it be true.

Murphy reached over to clasp her hand. "We don't know for certain she was even there. She could have gotten caught up anywhere from Florida to here."

She clutched at the thought like a drowning woman. She could be stuck at an airport. Maybe she only just told Lee she was coming here and went on a mini break instead. Somewhere not here. She reached out to hold onto the door handle as Murphy stepped on the accelerator to run another red light. All she could hear was the sound of her heartbeat thrashing in her ears.

Please no. Don't let it be true.

Clutching onto hope, she repeated it like a mantra. The next two minutes were the longest of her life. She was out the door before Murphy came to a full stop. She sprinted up the stairs, through the main doors, and made a beeline to the stairwell. The elevator would only slow her down.

Please no. Don't let it be true.

Joshua caught her before she entered her apartment, concern etched on his face as he held her back. "Wait. I need to warn you before you go in. It looks worse than it actually is."

She ripped from his protective embrace, but stopped the moment she cleared the doorway. Her eyes locked on a blue suitcase, and she let out an anguished cry. Everything else in the room dulled. The people, the noise, everything. The only thing in her universe was the upturned bag with a lime green scarf tied to its extendable handle.

Her legs gave way.

A pair of strong arms caught her. Murphy turned her to him and rested her head on his broad chest so that she could no longer see the evidence that her mom had been there.

"I gave her that scarf for her birthday." Her voice cracked as Murphy held her even tighter.

Full body tremors wracked her body. She couldn't take losing another parent. Not this way. Not to the same killer. She clutched Murphy for dear life. This was on her. If she hadn't insisted on being on the case, her mom wouldn't have been taken. She let out a sob, and buried her face in Murphy's shoulder. "This is all my fault."

She lost track of time and slipped into a bubble of despair. The last thing she'd done was lie to her mom. She knew Elijah wasn't dead. She should have told her the truth. Now her mother was at the mercy of Elijah and who knew how many others. Desolation and grief consumed her. Waves of it washed over her, engulfing her mind, body and spirit. She held tighter to Murphy to stop from drowning.

The shock ebbed away piece by piece until she became aware of her surroundings. Her shaking subsided. With a deep breath, she pulled away from Murphy and squeezed her eyes shut. This couldn't be happening. It wasn't real.

But it was.

When she opened them again, she took stock.

Liam, in the middle of replacing her broken lock, halted what he was doing and shifted his gaze between her and Molly. Molly rose from the couch and wrung her hands together. "It's not so bad luv, we'll help ye put it all back in place. Sure enough, they've made a bit of a mess, but nothing a bit of elbow grease won't fix."

Murphy's voice was soft with concern. "They've taken Vivian. She flew up to surprise Kaitlin yesterday." He nodded to the upturned suitcase. "That's her bag."

Molly's hands flew to her mouth. "Don't say it's so."

"Are you sure?" Joshua's voice cracked.

Murphy murmured something so low she failed to hear what it was. The room fell silent. The air was heavy. Waiting. It was like she was inching along an upturned blade. One wrong step and she'd be done for.

Molly's eyes glazed over, her expression a cross between shock and sympathy.

Kaitlyn hauled in a deep breath. Her lungs burned at the effort. He's got her. Her legs threatened to give out again. Terror filled her chest, but she made an effort to pull herself together. She couldn't help her mother in this condition. They had to find her. They had to get her back. She wiped her eyes and gazed at her upturned apartment.

Joshua, who had been hovering nearby, reached out and squeezed her arm. No one spoke. But from the furtive glances, they were communicating a mile a minute. Murphy guided her to the couch and took a seat beside her. Worry lines etched his forehead. Her grandfather took a position on her left.

"Maybe, maybe she needs a cup of tea?" Molly fussed as she rushed to the kitchen.

Liam frowned as he resumed fixing the front door. "I suspect she needs something a little stronger."

She jumped at the sound of the kettle being turned on. Her teeth bit down on her bottom lip. Molly had said there were three Pioneers. Maybe there was a chance he hadn't gotten to her yet. Why three? Was Elijah one of them? Manic energy swelled in her body. Her brain began to re-engage, and her lethargy fell away. Maybe there was time. She shot up and headed for the hole where her door once was. "We need to find her. Now. We can't wait."

Two sets of arms pulled her back down, and Murphy blocked her path. "I promise you Kaitlyn, we'll get her back. But first we need to make sure Anika is okay, and then we have to work out where they took your mother."

Kaitlyn pressed her lips together. Where the hell was he? What was the point of having a building manager if he wasn't around?

Murphy's hand rested on her shoulder. "No one's in. It doesn't matter how many times you knock on that door, or how loud. There still won't be anyone in there to answer."

She shot him a disgusted look and rested her head on the cold, impersonal door with a dull thud. The metal numbers 2A pressed into her forehead. She had been ringing, buzzing, and banging on the wooden door for ten minutes. "So, where the hell is he?"

"Probably doing his job."

She yanked her phone out of her pocket and redialed, hoping against hope that this time it would not go through to voice mail. They needed to confirm who had taken her mother, and the quickest way was to get their hands on the building's CCTV footage. Joshua and the others were currently working their way from floor to floor, trying to track down the building manager.

Her phone vibrated. Joshua. Her shaking hands almost dropped the phone as she pressed the accept button and thrust it against her ear. "Did you find him?"

"He was in the dumpsters out back of all things. We'll meet you in the foyer."

Thank god. The tension released and she was out the door and flying down the stairwell before the call terminated.

It took a little convincing, numerous flashes of their FBI identification, and a lot of cajoling before Harvey would let them take a copy of yesterday's recordings from the foyer and Kaitlyn's floor.

"I'm not sure I'm supposed to be letting you have a copy," he kept saying.

A part of her was shocked at how many laws she was breaking. Harvey was correct. Without a warrant, they had no reason to compel him to hand over the recordings. Her lips pressed together in a thin line. Warrant be dammed. Her mother's life was on the line. She didn't care how many felonies they committed.

Harvey stopped short when Murphy towered over him, held up an FBI badge, and let out a menacing growl. "How would you like me to take you into custody for obstructing an investigation?"

Harvey's eyes opened wide. "B-but, don't you need a warrant?"

Murphy leaned closer to Harvey, who looked like he was about to wet his pants. "A woman's life is in danger, and you want to waste time with a warrant?"

"I-I guess not." Harvey switched on the monitor and reached for the blank thumb drive she handed him.

She checked her watch. A million fire ants were crawling under her skin, and tearing at her from the inside. How long does it take to copy two measly files? "Can't you go any faster?"

Harvey unplugged the device and she tore it out of his hand, then rushed out the door followed by Murphy and Joshua. Molly and Liam trailed behind as she climbed the stairwell to her apartment. Her heart was pounding. She had no time to waste. She plugged in the thumb drive and started up the program. She bit her thumbnail and jiggled her foot. The fire ants were wreaking havoc with her skin. She swallowed hard. Did she want to see the footage? What if—

Molly's arm wrapped around her shoulders, and she gave her a light hug. "Be strong, luv. Ye won't do Vivian any good if ye pass out."

They all crowded around the small laptop screen. Residents and delivery people rushed in and out of the building. The faces blurred as she increased the speed. Molly took a step closer to her the moment she tensed, and placed a hand on her shoulder as they watched Vivian stroll in through the front doors, her suitcase and scarf billowing behind. She was so focused on her mother that she failed to notice two men wander through the front doors as Vivian stepped into the elevator.

"Can you get a zoom in on those faces," Murphy said.

Her brain collided with itself when she realized what she had missed. She grimaced and fumbled with the mouse, dread filling her every pore. If she didn't focus, she'd be no help to her mom. She enlarged the area Murphy indicated.

He pointed to one of the men. "The one on the left is Frank."

The air grew chilly and she shivered involuntarily. She couldn't go through with this. It was one thing to imagine the horror of her mother being abducted or worse, k … She swallowed.

She couldn't do this.

Murphy lowered his voice and rested a hand on her shoulder. "If you don't think you can watch the next part, let me take over."

She glanced up at him and gave him a faint, but grateful smile. She was thankful he was there. So much for being a kickass FBI agent. That all went out the window when it was your loved one's life on the line. "No, I need to do this."

Her stomach twisted tighter as she double-clicked the second file. The one from the camera that covered the entire length of the corridor on her floor. Her insides churned, and her throat felt raw like sandpaper. Knowing the exact timecode from the previous file, she keyed in the numbers and waited.

On cue, her mother exited the elevator and made her way down the hallway to her apartment. Vivian fumbled in her satchel, then pulled out a set of keys. As she began to sift through them, the keys slipped from her fingers and dropped to the floor.

Kaitlyn reached out and touched the screen. "I gave her a set of keys and the disarm code. In case anything happened to me." Her heart skipped a beat. "Oh, god, I never expected she'd be the one to …"

Her mom picked up the keys and fumbled with them. She found the right one and put it in the lock. Once the door was open, she disappeared through the doorway. The corridor was empty for all of thirty seconds. When Frank and his offsider emerged and kicked in the door, her heart shrank in fear. She recoiled and covered her mouth. She knew what they were going to see next, and it terrified her. She had seen it countless times in her job. But this time, it was different. This time, her quirky, innocent mother was being abducted, not a stranger.

Less than five minutes after the door splintered inward, her mother was hauled into the corridor. Kaitlyn winced when Vivian fought back and one of them elbowed her in the face. "This is my fault. I lied to her, and she thought it was safe."

"It looks worse than it actually is," Murphy said gently. "If they wanted her dead, they wouldn't go through the effort of taking her."

Every limb in her body trembled. "But where is she? Where the hell have they taken her?"

She held her palm up to her forehead and considered her options. She needed to focus. She needed to work out how they were going to get her mom back.

Murphy reached for his phone. "I'm going to mobilize the team and get Parker to trace Vivian's phone."

The minutes dragged by so slowly she was ready to burst by the time Parker phoned back. She wanted to get out there and get her mother back. But where did they begin?

Murphy put Parker onto speaker.

Kaitlyn's stomach dropped at Parker's frustrated sigh.

"I can't find any trace of Vivian after they took her," Parker said.

Murphy paced. "How about traffic cams? Tap into the system, and see if you can track him that way."

"That might work, and I think I can modify an existing program to speed up the recognition routine. I'll get the team on it. Give me an hour to set things up, and I'll phone you back with an update. And, Kaitlyn, hang in there, we'll do everything we can to find your mom."

She stared at the phone. A cold chill raced through her arms, and she rubbed them. Trolling through thousands of cameras in the greater Boston area was going to take time. A lot of time. Time they didn't have.

"There has to be another way," Molly said.

Murphy stood by the window and looked out over the street. "It's going to come down to who's behind the abduction. Elijah or Ambrose."

"What's the difference," Molly said.

He hesitated before answering. "If it's Ambrose, he'll be after leverage. We can negotiate with that."

His answer hung around her neck like an anvil. No one asked the outcome if Elijah took her mom. They knew. With the number of victims he had amassed over the years, she'd have to be delusional not to understand his unspoken words.

Murphy was behind her in a heartbeat. He grabbed her hand to stop her from watching it again. "Don't. It's only going to make you more upset."

She pushed him away. "I need to do this. There might be something we missed. You heard Parker, it's going to take a while before she has any answers. I can't just sit here and do nothing."

Murphy's eyes bored into the back of her head. She appreciated his concern, but even one clue was worth the agony of watching it again. And again. Anything for a tiny detail that might indicate where they took her.

Murphy sighed and sat beside her.

Her resolve faltered as she watched her mother's abduction. But Murphy stayed with her, although he grumbled louder each time she replayed the video. With each viewing, more of her fear dissipated and was replaced with frustration and anger. How dare they involve her mother. What level of coward would sink to that depth, knowing they involved a woman who had no connection to them and who could not possibly fight back?

As her wrath increased, so too did her clarity. Her heart skipped a beat when she honed in on her mother's reaction to being elbowed. Vivian's hand had come up to cradle her injured face. From her mom's expression, the pain was intense. She fixated on the tiniest portion of the screen. Every nerve ending vibrated with hope. She paused the video and whispered, "Oh my God."

Four heads whipped around to face her, each one wearing the same questioning expression.

She let out a slow breath. The theory was remote, but not impossible. She mustn't get her hopes up before it was confirmed. Her hands shook as she opened a browser. "Mom took up cycling a while back," she said as she tapped away on the keyboard. "Because of her high blood pressure, her doctor suggested she use a fitness band to monitor her heart rate and oxygen levels."

"Oh, Gilda told me about those things," Molly said. "They look like a real watch, but they tell you your heart rate and send information to your phone or computer."

"That's right. Mom found one with a cycling app that also collects information on the speed, time, and distance of her training, along with monitoring her health."

Murphy pulled out his phone. His expression said he understood what this meant.

Joshua glanced at Murphy and then the screen. "But why would a watch be so important?"

Her knee shook uncontrollably. Please let this work. "Because it's GPS-enabled. We can't track them, but we might be able to track her." Her fingers flew across the keyboard. "Provided I can get into her online account."

"Do you know her login details?" Murphy said.

She brought up the login page. "My mom only has one email address, and she's used the same password for as long as I can remember."

As she typed in the details and pressed the button, the air in the room thickened. Time stood still. No one moved as the please wait message popped up. Kaitlyn almost wept when it successfully loaded. Then her jaw set. This didn't guarantee they could find her.

She clicked the map. "God, please let her have the GPS turned on."

As the page slowly loaded, she sank into the chair, and her heart pounded in her chest. A tear pushed through her resolve and ran down her face. She closed her eyes and forced her trembling muscles under control. Her mother's Garmin was on and transmitting its current location.

Murphy tapped on Tim's number and held the phone up to his ear. "Concord. We're going to need backup."

He pulled her to a standing position and tipped her chin up to look directly at him. "This is not the time to fall apart. She needs you to be strong."

She was trapped in Murphy's piercing gaze. His black eyes were granite. His stance mirrored his determined expression. To anyone else he resembled Mars, the God of War as he rained down his fury on earth.

"Get your service piece," he said. "Let's get her back."

What was he up to? This was too easy. Why didn't she have to argue with him to go along. Not that she would have listened. This was her mother, and she wasn't staying here. She searched his face. Something was off. She just couldn't work out what. Or was she reading too much into his acquiescence? No matter what happened, he would go to the ends of the earth to find her mom. To keep her safe. Once he made a vow, he carried it through. His determination seeped into her skin and fired up her battered soul.

She placed a hand on his chest. Her fingers pulsed against his beating heart. Her breath caught the moment the rhythm of her heart beat in time with his, and a ripple of warmth settled around her like a soft blanket. He tried to convince those around him he did not have one, yet here it was, ready to go into battle for a woman he had never met.

She squeezed her eyes shut for a second. If she had to have her heart broken by someone, at least it would be broken by a man whose allegedly missing heart and soul were good. "Thank you."

They needed to go. She pulled out of the security in his arms and raced into her bedroom. Her traditional work suit wasn't optimal for what they were about to do. She changed into dark track pants and a hoodie, unlocked her safe, and pulled out her gun. After grabbing two extra clips and attaching the gun to her holster, she was ready. Both physically and mentally. They were going to get her mother back, and with any luck, Murphy would kill Elijah, and they would finally know peace.

Joshua was pacing the small lounge, his usual relaxed expression now strained and worried. The lines etched into his face had aged him in the short time since her mother's abduction. Across the room, Liam and Molly huddled together. From their intent expressions they were communicating telepathically.

Murphy stood and nodded at her before heading for the door. He stopped in front of Joshua. "You can ride with us, mom and dad will need your car to get back to the house."

"We won't be doing that, son."

Liam's curt reply halted Murphy in his tracks and had Kaitlyn doing a double take. In fact, it stopped everyone in the room. She glanced between father and son and gulped hard. This was the first time Liam had spoken directly to Murphy since he and Molly arrived.

"We're coming with you." Another direct address.

Her eyes bulged. Liam's tone was absolute.

Murphy's eyebrows shot up. "Pardon?"

Liam reached for Molly's hand. "You heard me. We're coming with you."

Murphy blinked. "Why?"

"I hope I didn't raise an eejit." Liam drew his shoulders back and stood tall. "I would have thought that obvious. The last time you went up against Elijah, I failed to support you. Had I been a better parent I would have ignored the council's decision. I won't make that mistake again." Liam paused and his gazed flicked to Molly. "We will get Vivian back and take Elijah down together."

Molly reached out to Murphy. "June was not just your mate, she was part of our family. She was pack." Her voice broke. "Just as Vivian is part of our pack, part of our family. She just doesn't know it."

"There's a reason our pack motto is *nihil prius familia.*" Liam took a step forward. "Somewhere along the way we lost sight of the meaning." He held out his hand to Murphy. "We can do this together, if you'll let us."

Her throat constricted as she watched the two men face off. They were so similar in every way. Liam's heartfelt plea couldn't help but affect her. His black eyes, the mirror of his son's, were projecting a silent and raw plea for forgiveness.

She glanced at Murphy to gauge his reaction and stumbled. His walls were bolted in place, and he was deathly still. The only indication he was still alive was the turbulent vortex of his irises. She resisted the urge to reach out to him for fear she would be singed. A war was raging inside him. Her heart beat raced. After all these years of isolation, Murphy was battling with himself, with his father, and with the world. The battle was being waged internally, but the outcome was going to be far reaching.

Let it go. She crossed her fingers. He needed to put an end to the rift that kept his family apart for decades. God, Murphy, let it go. Let go of the rage. The seconds drew out and her heart thumped in her chest. He was going to reject the olive branch.

His expression was still as unscalable as Mt Everest, but she felt the shift when he made his decision. Whether it was a micro movement in his body or she guessed it, she wasn't sure. But he'd come to a decision and made peace with it, no matter the outcome.

She held her breath.

When Murphy reached a hand out to his father, Molly's tears fell, and she brought a hand up to cover her mouth. Instead of taking Murphy's offered hand, Liam embraced his son.

Molly let out a small whimper as she brought her other hand up to her mouth.

Kaitlyn's throat dried, and the back of her eyes stung as she fought to keep the tears at bay. What she would give to wrap her arms around her mom right now. She turned her back on them and reached into her pocket for her phone. She took a moment to steady her raw insides. Murphy had his family back. Over time the wounds that kept them apart would heal.

Joshua rubbed his eyes. "That's enough girly hoo-ha," he said from the door. "We need to be going."

She stared at a photo of her mom. Please be alive. She froze. Frack. Why didn't she think of it before? Tiny goosebumps erupted across her skin and began to tingle as she tapped on her phone.

"What is it?" Murphy said.

"Mom's watch has an inbuilt phone chip to send data back to the server. The GPS tracker works separately from the rest of the functionality. We just looked at the location, not her vitals. I'm downloading the app to see if I can get the rest of the data."

She shook her phone when the app took forever to install. An eternity later she logged in and waited for the data to download. An error message popped up on the screen. She swore under her breath. "Crabapples, it says cannot connect to the server."

Murphy pushed her out the door. "We'll keep on trying on our way there. Let's go."

They raced downstairs, their focus on rescuing her mom.

She clutched her phone to her chest. Her stomach heaved and she felt physically ill. Would they be too late to get her mother back?

Mistaken Identity

New Hampshire

Elijah raced up the steps, two at a time, and strode through the front door just as Ambrose's booming voice carried to the marble entryway. While not as palatial as he was used to, his new home had grown on him. So what if they ate off Royal Dalton instead of Noritake, drank from Waterford rather than Baccarat, or drove SUV's and sedans when they could afford Bentleys and Bugatti's? Ambrose was far too concerned with keeping them out of the limelight. Something he would need to remedy.

"Don't you motherfucking think I know that by now?" Ambrose said, his voice loud enough to wake the dead.

He raised a brow and headed to the library where Ambrose conducted most of his affairs. What had Junior done now? When Ambrose let out a string of curses, he sighed. His children were a handful, though for the most part they did what they were told. To his joy, his army was growing in numbers. It helped that Ambrose's family business was littered with more than enough blood relations. And their recent jaunt to Chicago, then New York, gave him an indication of the army they would eventually turn into. However, they were still finding their feet with some taking longer than others to adjust to their new way of life. But not fast enough for his liking.

"Who is she then?" Junior said.

She? Now he really was curious.

"Turns out those imbeciles took the mother. We're now caught between a fucking rock and a hard place. We can't let her go, and I've got no idea what the repercussions would be if her body was found. We're trying to stay under the radar, not have a fucking target painted on us. Could this day get any worse? Added to this clusterfuck, your cover may have been blown to shit. All this just as Briana and I have to head to New York in two hours," Ambrose said.

He paused at the door to the library. New York? They must have found someone in the Gambino family willing to sell information. His pulse sped up. Finally. Ambrose had finally found his balls. They were finally making a move on the last two families. With all that power, neither the Alliance nor the Human authorities would dare come near him. He could do as he pleased, when he pleased. If only that bitch Elise could see him now.

Yes. Things were falling into place. And when Elise's plan succeeded, he would be well protected behind his army.

"Are you thinking a trade? What does Elijah have to say about it?" Junior said.

He pushed open the door. "Say about what?"

He looked expectantly at them.

Ambrose threw him an angry glare. "This is all your fault. If you had a little more restraint, or even any, we wouldn't be in this shit right now."

He held back a grin. Just like a defiant teenager, Ambrose was flexing his newfound powers. "So, whose mother is she?"

"No one," Ambrose said a little too quickly.

He couldn't help the smirk that tugged at his lips. He headed to the large window facing the back of the property. "You expect me to believe the woman you have locked upstairs is just some random female you grabbed off the street? And you're all running around in a panic for no reason." He picked at his teeth. "Sounds plausible."

Ambrose raised his chin and glared at him. "Who she is and what she is, is of no concern to you. You keep away from her."

This ought to be interesting. Time to remind them who was boss. He swung around to face Ambrose. "Or what?"

Ambrose clenched his fists. "Or you will have to deal with me."

He burst out laughing and turned back to the window. "You have quite the sense of humor, don't you? I think you forget sometimes who you are talking to." He reached for his blade and ran the tip down the pane. The sharp hiss as it cut a fine line through the glass broke through the silence. His face hardened. "Or maybe you need reminding."

He turned and made a step toward Junior.

Ambrose sprang up from his chair and raced around to act as a barrier. "Stop. You've made your point. We were going to take Quinn for leverage, but Frank fucked up and got her mother, Vivien Quinn, instead."

A pang of disappointment washed over him. He hadn't had any fun in days. His children needed to be punished so they would think twice the next time they got out of line. He sighed. But killing Junior would only provide him with a moment's pleasure. Junior, while not yet one of his children, soon would be. And what an asset he would be. Junior had no qualms about killing. What a thrill it would be to see him tear an Alliance watchdog to shreds.

He cocked his head. "Quinn. As in Kaitlyn Quinn, O'Neill's FBI partner?"

Ambrose nodded. "I need to sort out the mess upstairs before I leave. I don't fancy the Fed's turning up to spoil my trip to New York."

His heart thumped in his chest and a shiver of excitement raced up and down his spine. This was just too serendipitous.

He reached for his knife. While it wasn't Quinn the partner, it was a close enough connection to put another nail in O'Neill's coffin. There were so many choices. Should he macedoine, slice, julienne, or parallel cut? He shifted his gaze to the door. "Perhaps ..." He headed for the stairs. "Perhaps I could try them all."

Ambrose raced after him. "Don't touch her. We need her as leverage!"

Vivien Quinn's mouth had been taped, her hands tied behind her back, and her feet secured to the chair. Her dark brown hair was in disarray and a large purple bruise on her right eye was spreading across her cheek. She must have put up quite a fight when Ambrose's men took her. He approached her with a look of interest. Her terror-stricken eyes darted to the door. He had to hand it to her. Even with knowing this was the end, she was hoping for a rescue.

He towered over her and trailed his knife down her neck. A trickle of blood followed its path. He inhaled the metallic scent. Red was such a vibrant color against the skin of a beautiful woman. Her muffled whimper ignited his desire. Even with the bruising, she was certainly fuckable. Maybe it was time to show Ambrose the right way to treat a woman. He had so much he wanted to teach his favored son.

He smiled and kissed the drip of blood that pooled in the shallow dip of Vivien's collar bone. Flicking his tongue across his lips, he shivered. "Shall we have some fun?"

THIRTY-SIX

Ready

Kaitlyn shook her phone again and held it up at roof level. "Why the hell is this thing not working?"

They had cleared Boston city limits in record time and were on the I-93 heading north west toward Concord. Joshua, Liam, and Molly were in the car behind, while she rode with Murphy.

Murphy glanced across at her. "Yelling at an inanimate object is not going to make it go any faster."

"But it is making me feel—" Her neck and shoulder muscles locked. "It's connecting."

When the data loaded her eyes watered, and she fought the urge to break down in tears. "The last reading was from fifteen minutes ago. She's still alive. It looks like it uploads new data every thirty minutes."

She scanned the tiny charts. At first, her relief blinded her to what the gauges, dials, and red blinking icons meant. When it sunk in, her blood ran cold and hot at the same time. She let out a whimper and looked to Murphy. "Her pulse is at 140 and bp is 170 over 110. She's under a lot of stress. We have to go faster."

"Any faster and we'll take off." He dialed Joshua and gave the car behind them an update.

Murphy glanced in the rear-view mirror. "Daniel is sending reinforcements, but it's going to take three hours for them to get to us."

Joshua and Murphy talked tactics, but the words failed to register. The fire ants were back in full force. Scratching at her from the inside. Every part of her begged for relief from the pain. Right now, they were crawling up her throat and making it hard to swallow. Her mom might not have three hours.

Murphy ended the call. "We'll regroup outside of Concord and put a plan together."

She refused to take her eyes off the heart and blood pressure monitor. Her mom's body was reaching hypertensive crisis. Only one thing would put her body under that much pressure.

"Elijah." The name came out in a tortured whisper.

"You don't know that."

Her eyes fluttered closed, and she shook her head. "What else can it be? The data from her Garmin shows her pulse and blood pressure all over the map for the past hour."

"How much longer until the next reading?"

"About five minutes"

They were the slowest five minutes of her life.

When the next reading came through her shoulders relaxed, and her head fell back on the headrest. "One thirty over ninety, and her pulse has come down."

Her mom was out of danger, for now.

Fifteen minutes later they pulled off the road just outside of town and waited for Tim and the other Pioneers to arrive. Just as they stopped, the next reading downloaded and moved her mom back to normal levels.

Tim and Danny pulled up behind them.

Tim was the first to get out. "We did a quick drive-by. The estate is heavily gated, and we couldn't see the house from the road. No visible guards at the entrance, but I'd bet they're there."

Murphy rubbed his jaw. "We can't make a frontal assault, then. We need the element of surprise." He pulled out his phone and brought up a map of the area. "The house backs onto a forest. We'll come in from there." He glanced up and down the road. "But first we need somewhere to lay low until we've taken a closer look."

He turned back to Tim. "Notice any for sale signs?"

"Two. Different agents," Tim said as he reached for his phone.

Her brows furrowed together. "What do real estate agents have to do with anything?"

"It's an old Werewolf trick," Murphy said. "In more affluent areas such as this, when houses go on the market, they tend to be vacant. The agents leave the key in a locked box so others can take clients through without having to worry about who has the key."

"Got one."

Tim showed them a photo from a local agent's website. The house bordered the same forest as the estate where her mother was being held prisoner.

Within ten minutes, they had deftly opened what she had considered, until that point, a safe key box, parked their vehicles in the large garage, and taken over the house. She rolled her eyes at the lax security. The alarm code for the house had been attached to the key ring.

Once they secured a base in the vacant house, she set up her laptop and paired it with her phone.

Murphy took over and brought up an aerial photo of the surrounding area. He frowned at the scan and zoomed in on the property. "There are no obvious positions that will give us the best cover. I'll need to go in and take a closer look."

She had to agree with his assessment. There was too much space between the tree line and the large house. They would be exposed and lose any element of surprise.

Murphy stood and glanced around the room. Dusk had settled and with no light, the room was shrouded in murky gray. He pointed to the front of the house looking out to the road. "Joshua, Tim, take up point positions with eyes on the road. I'll scout out back. We go in when Daniel's men arrive."

The two men nodded and carefully made their way to the front of the house.

Murphy strode to the patio doors that looked over the dense cluster of trees on the other side of the back fence. He remained silent as the rest of them stared at him expectantly. His body was still, a statue for all the movement he made.

Just when she thought he had turned to stone, he turned his head so they could just make out his profile. "Da, I need you to protect Ma and Kaitlyn. Promise me you'll shield them from what's coming."

Her initial reaction turned to confusion, and her forehead crinkled as she looked over to Liam and Molly. His words didn't make sense. What was coming?

Before she could ask, he unlocked the patio door and slid it open. "Danny, you take point on the right of the property. The neighbors on that side are too far away to notice anything amiss, but we need to make sure we're not seen. When Wendy and Jose arrive, they need to protect the inner perimeter."

Danny nodded then headed down the corridor to the other side of the house.

She turned her head back to Murphy. He was looking directly at her. Her skin tingled in waves across her cheek. An invisible hand caressed her face, and she leaned into it. Reason returned with a vengeance and she glanced around her. No one stood near her. No one had physically touched her. Yet, she felt something. And that something was Murphy.

In the dark, with the moon as the only source of light, his face was hidden from her. She couldn't guess his thoughts, nor gauge his mood. His eyes had melted into the shadows playing across his features.

A moment later the door was closed, and he strode away from the house.

The skin at the back of her neck prickled. Something wasn't right. The man could clear a room in three words or less. Why did his instructions to them come out soft, almost broken? He did not do soft. Ever. He was titanium, granite, or carbon steel. None of which was soft, and certainly not broken.

What the hell was he up to?

She pulled out her gun and checked her clip, placing it back in her holster as she headed after Murphy. She lowered her voice and glanced across at Molly and Liam. "I'll be back in a minute."

She edged the sliding door open and stepped into the night air. The gnawing at the back of her mind had finally worked out what he was planning. Her nostrils flared. Heat flushed through her body, and her hands curled into a fist. That demented idiot. To say she was angry was the understatement of the century. She gritted her teeth together. This time she would put a bullet in his ass.

She raced to the small gate in the fence that gave the house direct access to the forest and was through it as fast as she could move. With his speed, he could be miles away already. The moment she was through the gate she stopped short. Murphy stood a short distance away and spun around the moment she opened the gate.

He traversed the distance in the blink of an eye. "What are you doing here? I told you to stay inside."

Ignoring his menacing tone, she threw her hands on her hips. "How stupid do you think I am?"

"I don't know what you're talking about."

His hesitation said otherwise. She poked him in the chest, nearly breaking a finger in the process. "Do you seriously think you can take on Elijah and who knows how many Pioneers by yourself?"

"I'll have more of a chance on my own. The rest of you will just slow me down."

She gritted her teeth. The man was frustrating. "That's bullshit and you know it. I don't know about your father, but Joshua, Tim, and Danny have trained for this. So have the team Daniel is sending. This is what they do. You're not invincible Murphy O'Neill. And you certainly can't take on an army by yourself."

"Go back inside. I am not going to be responsible for any more deaths."

She groaned aloud. Murphy amassed guilt like Imelda Marcos collected shoes. "Is that what this is about? You think their deaths are on you?"

"Don't you see, it's my fault they're gone. If I'd just been a better mate, a better friend, they'd be with us today. I'm not going to let history repeat itself."

Her chest tightened at his raw pain and grief. Why was he torturing himself like this? She placed a tentative hand on his chest, and her voice softened. "You're allowing your misguided guilt to crush you. Punishing yourself like this is not going to bring June back, nor is it going to bring my father back. If they could speak to us, they'd be telling you the exact same thing."

"You don't know what you are talking about." His face wore a grim mask. "I told you to go back inside."

Her hand curled around the cloth of his shirt. What would it take to get through his thick skull? "You cannot do this on your own. It's a suicide mission."

She indicated the house behind them. "Every person is in there because they want to be. Because it is who they are."

He remained silent and turned his head to face the dense trees. His heart thudded under her fingertips. The man was stubborn as a mule. She sighed and admitted a truth she had only recently come to accept. "My father knew what he was doing when he went in without you. His death is on him. Not you. He had a choice. As much as I hate to say it, he chose wrong. He should have waited for back up. He didn't and you've carried the weight of it ever since. It's not on you, it never was."

She reached up and gently turned his face to look at her. "You have to stop shielding us from danger. You've spent too many years in a self-imposed purgatory. Instead of punishing yourself, you've just ended up punishing everyone who cares for you. This has got to end."

Still he remained silent, but this time he didn't look away. She caught her breath at the weight of his stare as it bore into her. How could one man say so little? What the hell was going on in that head of his? She'd been able to see through his façade and interpret every micro expression he hid from the outside world. But now, when she really needed that skill, he'd closed up and she was back at square one.

"We are coming with you. End. Of. Story." She dropped her hand and rested it on her holstered gun. "If you try and go on your own, I'll shoot you, and tell everyone what you tried to do. No one will blame me. Well, maybe your mom, but only because she couldn't smack you around the head first."

On at least two occasions she was sure his wolf was pushing to the surface. His mesmerizing inky black eyes had swirled to amber and back again. With the exception of his eyes, nothing in his expression changed. The cracks that had begun to appear were now safely drywalled. The silence dragged out as they faced off against each other. She wasn't willing to back down. It was against his nature to do so. Another Mexican standoff.

"Do you ever stop talking?" he said, eventually breaking the impasse. His voice was gruff with only a hint of anger.

She grinned. "Not when I'm trying to make a point."

She was standing so close to him. In her anger she had gone toe to toe. Literally. Not wanting to back down, she lifted her chin and willed herself not to look away. Not that she could. She was trapped in his gaze.

"And that is?" The anger had dissipated from his voice. In its place was smooth honey whisky. Raw with a subtle aftertaste.

Her stomach quivered. She was breathtakingly aware of just how close they were. Each exhale had her breasts close to making contact with his chest.

"You're not in this alone. We're coming with you." Her voice hitched as she began to drown in the fiery depths of his brooding gaze as it turned into something far more dangerous.

His hand enveloped the hand that rested on her holster. In quick succession her other hand was trapped, and both twisted and held behind her back. Her breasts were now pressed up against his chest.

He ran his free hand down the length of her arm. "And what if I said no."

White heat scorched everything in its path. Her legs were about to give out as sudden desire gushed through her body. Her gaze found his lips, now soft with a hint of a predatory smile. She sucked in her bottom lip. Her mouth and throat had gone dry.

How she wanted to taste those lips.

His head lowered at an agonizingly slow pace, and her stomach quivered. Her body flooded with desire as his lips grazed hers, and his warm breath caressed her as he nipped her bottom lip.

Oh God. She let out a low moan. It should be a sin to taste that good. To have lips that made her forget her own name when they drew close. His tongue skimmed her trembling lips and began to dip and swirl as he deepened the kiss and became more urgent, more demanding. The need to touch him was too strong, and she reached up to cup his face. His ever-present whiskers were soft under her fingers as she explored his chiseled features.

He raised her palm to his lips and sent tingles up her arm and down to her core as he tasted her.

A charge of excitement shot through her as he let her hand go, and his fingers reached under her shirt and feathered across her skin. Their eyes locked, and she was undone by the desire and tenderness reflected back at her.

She wanted this handsome, hypnotic, and powerful man. But her inner demon rose to the surface and questioned her ability to come out of this in one piece. They had no long-term future. He would be gone before Elijah's body was cold, and she would be left heartbroken.

Frack.

As much as she wanted to continue this to its natural and most probably earth-shattering end, she had to stop. They were groping each other like teenagers on date night. She put all her effort into pulling away from him. They were not randy teenagers. They were adults. Adults who, right now, needed to get her mom out of Elijah's clutches.

She cleared her throat. "We are coming with you. You're not doing this alone."

He raked his fingers through his hair, and she took a measure of satisfaction with how their kiss affected him. He gazed into the woods and gave her a curt nod. "Fine. We'll do it your way."

He pierced her with a determined look. "But when this is over, we are finishing what we started."

Goosebumps erupted across her skin, and her palms grew clammy. She didn't know what to be more hopeful for. The fact he was confident of a successful assault on the mafia Pioneers and Elijah, or his confidence on just where that kiss was leading.

Murphy stared at Kaitlyn and struggled to keep his erratic emotions under control. Blood surged through his body. Every nerve ending felt—alive. It was as if he'd woken up from a long sleep.

Why did you stop?

He left the question hanging in the air. He knew the answer, he just needed more time to digest it.

Without making a comment, Kaitlyn spun on her heels and headed back to the house. Her torn expression told him exactly what he wanted to know. She wanted him as much as he wanted her. Just the memory of the feel of her soft skin under his fingers set him on fire. He pushed down the urge to reach out and pull her back to him. A part of him needed her now. Not later.

He groaned. What if his Ma or Da had come out? What the hell would they have made of the display they were putting on for all to see? His self-imposed isolation had not prepared him for the sudden influx of people and foreign emotions thrust on him now.

He was feared. No one came near him or spoke to him if they didn't absolutely need to. At least that was how it used to be. Now he had lost control and couldn't even leave an abandoned house without everyone knowing what he was up to. He ran a hand through his hair. Was he that transparent?

If you were, the others would be out here, not just her.

He hesitated. His wolf was right. But how did she know what he was about to do?

Kaitlyn reached the small gate and waited for him to catch up.

He followed behind at a slower pace. Confused. Emotions long dead rose to the surface, further adding to his confusion. Who knew what they would find at Ambrose's stronghold? He wouldn't put her in harms way. Not while he could keep her safe. He closed his eyes and sighed. At what point did she take center stage in his universe? At what point did the guilt of betraying June's memory lessen enough for him to allow Kaitlyn through his defenses?

His wolf snorted. *You are an idiot.*

Not wanting to enter into any sort of argument with his smug wolf, he returned to the house, careful to school his emotions before he entered. He didn't need the rest of the world knowing his state of mind. Not before he had fully accepted it himself.

In his absence, Jose and Wendy had arrived and were talking with his Da.

Wendy broke off her conversation and looked at him. "Sorry we're late. I was still on shift and couldn't find anyone to cover me. Some kids took daddy's car out for a joyride and wrapped it around a tree. Then we had an elderly couple whose gas exploded and trapped them in their kitchen, followed by a construction worker who fell off scaffolding and impaled his thigh through a rebar."

Jose shrugged and grinned. "Just another ordinary day at the office then?"

Wendy winked. "Pretty much."

He detected footsteps up the side of the house and stiffened, but Tim's distinctive gait announced him before he entered the house. He left Kaitlyn and Wendy to discuss strategy with Tim on how to take on Ambrose and the mafia Werewolves. Daniel's team would bolster their numbers and give them a fighting chance to free Vivien without too much bloodshed. But without knowing how many Elijah had turned, who knew what they were up against.

Tim was giving him a run down on his earlier drive-by when Kaitlyn gasped.

He was across the room in a heartbeat. "What's the matter?"

She held up her phone for him to see. Her hand shook and he steadied it. Vivian's latest readings showed her pulse had plummeted and her blood pressure was dangerously high.

Wendy reached out and grabbed the phone. Her expression was somber as she flicked through the numbers. "Is your mom on blood pressure meds?"

Kaitlyn shook her head.

Wendy handed the phone back to Kaitlyn. "She needs medical help. I don't want to alarm anyone but nine times out of ten these reading are associated with traumatic injuries and internal bleeding."

"How far away are Daniel's men?" Liam said.

He checked his watch. "At least two hours."

Kaitlyn's hand tightened around her phone. She stared at the screen as though willing the readings to change.

He glanced across at his Ma and his chest tightened. If it where her in Vivien's situation, Daniel's men be dammed, they'd already be there.

His wolf paced, irritated at the lack of momentum. *What are we waiting for then?*

THIRTY-SEVEN

Aim

Kaitlyn's limbs were numb.

While it was dark and the forest was thick with trees, the sentries posted on the roof of Ambrose's mansion would notice any movement. She molded to a large conifer, held on to her modified Barret, and remained silent. She wouldn't be the one to give them away. Her hammering heart was another story. That, she was positive, Pioneers would hear from miles away.

She pulled her phone from her back pocket and checked the Garmin app. Two more minutes before the next download. A small bead of sweat seeped down her forehead. She was caught between hope and fear. The last reading still showed her mother's vitals dangerously low. Her hands shook as she fixated on the time. A plummet in pulse and blood pressure after the extremes it had been put through meant one thing. Elijah. Visions of red swirled through her brain as she recalled how they found Elijah's victims. Her overactive imagination danced and wound itself through the crime scenes. Suddenly, it was her mother's body in pieces on the floor.

She brought a hand up to her mouth to stop the anguished cry that threatened to erupt from the pit of her stomach. Please don't let her be bleeding out. Please let us get to her in time.

A hand lightly touched her on the shoulder. Murphy had completed a circuit of the property, and they were preparing to storm the house.

"Are you ready?" he said, lowering his voice to a gruff whisper.

She clutched the sniper's rifle and nodded.

"Remember, stay here until we give the signal. You need to clear the roof."

His unspoken words were clear. If she didn't succeed, both they and her mother were done for.

She glanced down at the modified rifle. A Nightforce NXS Scope and M110 suppressor added a little more weight than she was used to, but would do the trick. "So no pressure then."

"What pressure? You're the best sharpshooter in the Boston field office." He stopped talking and cocked his head, a sign someone was reaching out to him telepathically. "Everyone's almost in position."

Her phone vibrated. Thirty minutes had passed since her mom's last reading. She pulled it from her pocket and refreshed the Garmin app. Her breath hitched, leaving behind a lump in her throat. "It's still too low. If she's bleeding out, she won't last much longer."

He glanced at the dark silhouette of the house. "You clear a path, leave the rest to us."

She raised her chin. "But—"

His head bent down so their faces were an inch apart. "There's no but's. We agreed. Neither your grandfather nor I will be able to do our jobs if we're worried about your safety."

She pursed her lips. This was ridiculous. That was her mom in there. She wasn't a pushover. She could hold her own, but when Murphy let out a low growl, she refrained from arguing the point. The clock was ticking, and who knew how much time her mom had before it was too late. She picked up the Barrett, rested the butt of the rifle against her shoulder and peered through the scope. They were outnumbered, and Daniel's men were still an hour away. But they could no longer wait.

She focused on the nearest guard through her sight, then picked up some dirt and threw it out beyond the trees. They were lucky. There was virtually no wind to impede her shot. For this to work they needed the element of surprise, but five guards stood at strategic positions on the roof of the two-story mansion. They needed to be eliminated or Murphy and his team would be picked off when they raced across the clearing.

"Are you sure you can do this?"

She glanced away from her sight and nodded. "Just get my mom out of there."

Murphy turned to head back to his position, then stopped and turned back to face her. "Kaitlyn …"

Instead of finishing his sentence he stared at her for five full seconds before spinning on his heel and melding into the darkness.

She stared at the void he'd vacated. The man was an enigma. She didn't know whether to shoot him or kiss him. A flurry of emotions tore through her. After tonight she would have no more opportunities to taste him, to feel his lips on hers, to know the pure unbridled pleasure of being held by him. Provided they survived this, she would get her mother back, but lose a precious piece of her heart.

She fortified her resolve. Her only thoughts should be on getting through the night alive and saving her mother, not wallowing. She could wallow in a pity party later. She focused on the soldier through the rifle's telescopic sight. Mafia soldier number one's attention was on his phone and not his surroundings. If he kept his eyes and mind on Candy Crush, he wouldn't know what happened until it was too late. She placed him in the cross hairs of her scope. With no wind, she did not need to compensate for drift. A twinge of something akin to second thoughts stabbed at her. She was about to kill a living human being without any clear and present danger to her.

She mentally shook herself. These were the barbarians who had her mother. They were aiding and abetting a serial killing madman. They were mafia. They lost any rights the moment they crossed that line. She took turns at checking each of the sentries within range as she went from cold to hot and then back again. While she had been on countless stakeouts and raids, this time things were different. Never before had she been as fearful or restless as she was now. The operation was more personal and every nerve ending was vying for attention. From the pit of her churning stomach to her tightened chest, she was on edge.

She glanced to the other side of the clearing. Somewhere in the darkness was Murphy, her grandfather, Liam, Molly, Tim, and Danny. By now they would have transformed. They were stronger in wolf form, but were they strong enough? Who knew how many thugs lurked inside the mafia stronghold. They were likely outnumbered and outgunned.

Her stomach lurched, and she swallowed not to throw up. There was a good chance they wouldn't get through this alive. A cold flush washed over her body and she faltered. People she cared about were putting their lives on the line to help her. Did she really want to have their deaths hanging over her head? Maybe they should wait.

She checked her phone for her mom's readings and winced. As much as her common sense told her to wait for Daniel's team to arrive, her mom might not hold out that long. They had no choice. She closed her eyes and sent out a silent prayer for her mother and for her rescuers. An owl hooted nearby, and her heart jumped in her chest. No sooner was her pulse under control than rustling leaves caught her attention. Her head swung in the direction of the noise, and she unholstered the gun at her hip. When Molly's wolf appeared, she breathed a sigh and her shoulders relaxed.

She holstered her weapon. "You scared the bejesus out of me," she whispered.

Molly's wolf glanced forlornly in the direction of the others.

"There's still time to back out," Kaitlyn whispered. "This is not yours or Liam's fight."

Molly's wolf let out a low growl and shook its head.

Kaitlyn straightened, took up her position, and braced against a tree. Molly's presence could only mean one thing. They were ready. She took aim and waited. The air vibrated as if it, too, felt the tension from the small band ready to strike.

Molly's wolf nudged her. It was time.

She cleared her mind. For this to work she couldn't afford any emotions or second guesses. One wrong move and the life of someone she cared about would be in danger. The Pioneers were strong. They were not invincible.

One.

The first guard was still playing Candy Crush. If she got the timing right, she could take out all five before anyone raised the alarm. She held her breath then pulled the trigger.

The bullet flew through the air. Silent. Its aim true. The first guard collapsed like a sack of potatoes. Her gaze darted to the remaining ones visible on her side of the house. None of them were any the wiser.

Two

The second man, also hidden from his fellow guards, peered over the balustrade on the roof and scanned the garden below. Unlike the first guard, he appeared to be doing his job. She rechecked the wind then pulled the trigger.

Shit. Instead of crumpling in a heap on the roof his body hung limp on the balustrade. She needed to get rid of the next one before he moved in that direction.

Three.

Taking aim again, she fired. The bullet in his forehead ensured he was dead before he hit the ground.

Four and five were on the other side of the house. Under the cover of darkness, she moved through the trees toward the back of the house. Molly's wolf followed close behind. When she had a clear sight, she set up position and scoped out the two remaining guards.

She felt the blood drain from her face. Crap.

Instead of being in their assigned posts they were together playing a game of cards. If she couldn't take them out in quick succession, one of them would have time to raise the alarm. She aimed.

Four.

She placed her finger on the trigger, but before she squeezed off the shot, shouts erupted from the front of the house. "Do they know we're here?"

Molly's wolf nodded and let out a whine.

Kaitlyn groaned. Someone must have come outside and spotted number two hanging off the roof. She took aim. Four and five had dropped their cards and reached for their guns. A barrage of shots fired from the front of the house followed by guttural snarls. With the element of surprise lost, Murphy and the others must have started their assault. Sweat formed along the hairline of her neck. If the two remaining guards got to the other side before they were across the clearing, they would be slowed down enough to give the mafia Pioneers time to regroup. She re-aimed and fired two shots in quick succession.

Crap.

The first met its mark and the fourth man went down. Guard number five moved at the last moment, and her second bullet missed. She ignored the escalating noise from the other side of the house and took aim again.

Five.

The bullet lodged in the back of his head. He stopped in his tracks, wobbled for a moment, then collapsed.

Her mission complete, she looked to Molly's wolf and stilled. From the wolf's manic pacing, something was wrong. She scanned the distance between them and the house. So far no one had come to the back to investigate. Whatever was happening was around the front. Her insides pulled at her in different directions. Her first instinct was to race in and help. However,

Murphy's warning hung in the air. She had promised him. Sort of.

She placed the strap of the Barret over her head so that it was firmly held in place against her back. It would be of no use in close range. She unholstered her hand gun and switched off the safety. When another scream rang out, she'd made up her mind. Promise or not, she was going in to help. She couldn't stand back and do nothing.

She nodded to Molly's wolf. "Let's go. I can't take this anymore,"

Molly's ears pricked, and she raced off.

"Fraggle Rock." Kaitlyn scrambled up from her crouching position and rushed to catch up with the wolf.

They were careful to stay out of sight while they crept around the house. As they turned the corner that faced the front, pain shot through her chest like a hand was squeezing the life out of her heart. Light lit up the front of the house and garden like a Christmas tree. The front lawn was littered with blood and three bodies. She gulped down breaths to settle the fear and scanned the ground. No fur among the bodies.

Molly's wolf let out a low growl when three wolves tumbled out the front door and down the stairs.

Two against one.

Molly's wolf pushed her into the bushes to keep them out of sight.

Kaitlyn peered through the gap in the leaves, and a lump formed in her throat when she recognized the distinctive markings on the wolf under attack. Wendy the paramedic. The larger of the two attackers snarled, its sharp teeth glistening in the dark. The second, a wiry gray wolf, slinked around Wendy so he and his partner were circling their prey. Wendy's wolf crouched and prepared to pounce. Two large patches of red dampened her fur and a gaping wound ran along her neck.

Kaitlyn's gaze darted between Wendy's wolf and the mafia wolves. "We have to help."

Before she could get clear of the bush they hid in, a shout rang out from nearby, and she froze in place. The shout came from the front entrance to the house. Two men burst through the doorway and raced down the stairs. Both were armed and pointing their weapons at the wolves. One of the men, a lanky red head with far too much gel in his hair, stopped at the bottom and hesitated. "Shit, Vince, I don't know which one is ours."

Vince pushed the other man's gun barrel to point down. "We can't risk taking out one of our own."

"But the boss said we didn't need to leave any of them alive."

Vince kept his eyes on the three fighting wolves. "Dude, he also told us how they'll ID themselves. We just wait to see how this pans out. If the winner doesn't do what's expected, we'll plug 'em through the eye sockets."

Wendy's wolf let out a sharp yelp when the larger wolf faked a lunge, then at the last moment changed direction and clenched its powerful jaws around her hind leg and pulled. The second wolf took advantage of her sudden imbalance and flew at her, bringing her down to the ground.

She tensed. Wendy was no match for her assailants.

Vince let out a scream, and she turned in time to see him plunge to the ground, a huge wolf on his back. She blinked and the wolf's jaw was around Vince's neck.

"Is that Tim?" she said in a whisper to Molly's wolf.

Molly's wolf nodded.

She'd only seen Tim's wolf once, but the missing patch of hair on his shoulder was a dead giveaway. Tim tore at Vince's neck and bit down hard. Vince's hands, which had been clawing at Tim's mane, let go and his arms dropped to the ground like lead.

Kaitlyn jumped out of her skin when a shot rang out. They'd forgotten about the red head. He pointed his gun at Tim and pulled the trigger. Time stood still. When the bullet missed Tim's head but hit him in the side, her muscles let go of the death grip on her clenched fist. Not a kill shot.

Tim's wolf faltered and a menacing growl reverberated from somewhere deep in his stomach.

The red head pointed the gun again. But before he could fire, Tim's wolf flew the short distance to him. She looked away as Tim savagely tore at the man's face and torso.

Wendy's wolf lay on the ground. One of her attackers pulled at her hind leg while the other tore at her foreleg. Unable to stay quiet and out of sight, Kaitlyn rushed from their hiding place and yelled out to Tim, "Help her."

Tim's wolf's head lifted and blood dripped from his muzzle. He bared his fangs and let out a savage growl before barreling into the larger of Wendy's attackers. They rolled a short distance before regaining their footing. Tim recovered faster and was up and curled his lips back to expose pearl-white fangs. The two wolves faced off and circled each other, looking for a weakness in the other's defenses.

Wendy's wolf was still on the ground. The second wolf, seeing no resistance, had taken advantage and tore at her underbelly with a manic ferocity.

Kaitlyn raced toward the wolves. Molly's wolf attempted to block her path. She swatted at her. "Get out of my way. Wendy needs help."

She deftly pushed past Molly's wolf. Her heart hammered in her chest. This was neither wise nor safe. Who knew how many more mafia Pioneers might spring out the house? She'd be a sitting duck. And then where would her mother be? Despite this, she was unable to sit still and was across the lawn in a matter of seconds. She stopped ten feet from the wolf ripping Wendy to shreds, aimed her gun, and rested her finger against the trigger. "Hey, Hannibal."

The wolf looked up.

She pressed the trigger. Once. Twice.

Her heart, still drowning out any other sound, accelerated, if that was at all possible. The bullets through the eye sockets did their job. The wolf was dead before it hit the ground.

Molly's wolf sped over to Wendy's and nudged at her, whimpering.

Kaitlyn spun on her heals and raised her gun. If Tim was overpowered by the other wolf, she would need to defend them. She glanced over her shoulder. "How is she?"

Molly's wolf's mournful howl ripped at her like shards of glass. They were too late. Wendy was gone. Molly's howl was enough to distract the last mafia wolf, and Tim, seeing his moment, went in for the kill. With two bullets, numerous bite marks, and blood pouring from open gashes, whether he had the stamina to finish the job was debatable.

She needn't have worried. The mafia wolf lunged in the wrong direction, and Tim bit down hard on his throat. With a crushed windpipe and no oxygen, the mafia wolf was dead in minutes. The noise from the other side of the house dulled. Tim's wolf's heavy panting was the only sound taking center stage. Everything around them was still while blood from the savaged bodies dripped onto the grass.

Fear punched through her gut. Wendy was dead. Tim injured. How were her grandfather and the others? Was Murphy all right? She resisted the urge to find out. With what she had just witnessed, she was no longer confident their mission would succeed. If they couldn't get to her mom, she would have to try.

Tim limped to the side of the house, determined to get back into the fight, no matter the cost.

"Please keep him safe," she whispered, hoping that someone would hear her prayer.

She squared her shoulders and rechecked her gun. If she got her mom to safety, they could retreat, regroup, and then finish the job when they had back-up. They couldn't allow Elijah and Ambrose's terror to go unchecked.

She called out to Molly as she headed up the stairs. "I'm getting her out. Stay down here out of sight."

THIRTY-EIGHT
Fire

Kaitlyn edged her way to the front door and peeked into the main foyer. It was empty. Her pulse quickened. With everyone outside, there would be only one, maybe two thugs guarding her mom. She could work with that.

She raced inside the house, her gaze darting into every shadow and corner. Outside, the mayhem continued. Inside, the silence reminded her of a funeral parlor. Uncomfortable and eerie. She was halfway up the staircase when nails scratching against marble tiles below stopped her. Her blood ran cold as she pivoted and aimed.

Molly's wolf. Her shoulders relaxed. "You've got to stop scaring me like that."

The wolf raced past her and Kaitlyn sprinted the rest of the way up the stairs following behind. Molly's wolf stopped at each door and sniffed at the small gap between the wood and the floor. With each pass her anxiety increased. The fire ants were back with a vengeance. Where the hell was her mother?

At the fourth door, Molly's wolf let out a whine and scratched at the wood.

Kaitlyn placed a hand on the handle and froze. Was she prepared for what she was about to find behind the closed door?

Her stomach did somersaults as she turned the handle. She nodded at Molly's wolf to follow as she slipped into the room and closed the door. The room was pitch black, and she had to blink to adjust her vision.

Molly's wolf brushed against her thigh and nudged her.

She reached for her phone and turned on the torch. "Okay, okay, I'm hurrying."

The fire ants clawed at her insides when her gaze fell on the outline of a body on the bed. A blanket covered it.

"Stay here," she whispered to Molly. "Guard the door."

Her pulse rushed through her ears, blocking everything out as she reached the bed and pulled the cover away to reveal the darkened features of a woman. One hand cuffed to the bed. Please. Please let it be her. And let her be alive.

Her heart stopped the moment she saw her mom's face. She placed two fingers on her mother's neck to feel for a pulse. It was faint, but she was still alive. "I'm here, mom. You're safe now."

She brought the light from the phone closer to her mother.

What the?

She bit back the anguished cry that threatened to tumble out. From the video of her mother's abduction, she had expected a few bruises, but not this.

No.

She moved the phone down her mother's neck, chest, and stomach, lifting her bloodied shirt to inspect the injuries.

No. No. No.

Terror clutched at her chest, threatening to rip her heart out. God, no.

Only one person would have inflicted this type of damage. "Mom. Oh God, what has he done to you?"

Vivian had been used as a cutting board. Her face was a web of cuts and lacerations, each one shallow enough to not be dangerous, but deep enough to cause extreme pain and damage.

She choked down a sob. From the bandages across the rest of her, Elijah had been meticulous. Blood seeped through the gauze and soaked the white sheets red. As she stroked her mother's hair, rage welled within her, and every muscle contracted. The need to lash out was primal. How could that animal have done this to her? The bastard had taken her father, and now he had taken his sick pleasure with her mother as well. "I'm here now, we've got you."

Molly's wolf nudged against her leg. They needed to get out of here. She wiped her tears and rocked her mother gently. "Mom, mom, you need to wake up."

Her mom slowly opened her eyes. Her pupils were dilated and glassy. She struggled to focus and blinked a few times before she tensed, and her frightened eyes opened wide.

Kaitlyn tenderly placed a hand against her cheek. "Mom, it's me. We're going to get you out of here, okay?"

Vivian let out a shallow breath. "I-he … it hurts."

She helped Vivian into a sitting position. "I know, mom. Don't try and speak."

She rifled in the drawers for something to unlock the cuffs. "Did they leave the keys anywhere in the room?"

Vivian shook her head as if to physically wake up. "I-I don fink show." Her words slurred, and she cried out as she swung her legs over the side of the bed. She reached out with her free hand to steady her shaking body when she almost toppled off the bed. "I can fink straight."

Kaitlyn stopped short when she opened the second draw. She pulled out one of the small medicine vials and held it up. "Mom, did they give you this?"

Vivian squinted as she struggled to stay seated.

She cringed. Her mom must have been given a high dose sedative to be as groggy and unresponsive as she was. No wonder her vitals had shown her nearly catatonic.

Molly's wolf let out a whimper. They needed to hurry. All hell was breaking loose outside.

Vivian pointed at Molly. "What's doggy doin' here?"

"She's helping us escape." She pulled on the handcuff attached to the headboard to test its strength and frowned. There had to be a way to free her mother.

She stood and searched the rest of the room. "Molly, I need to find something strong to pry a post from the headboard. Can you see anything?"

Molly's wolf let out a weak yelp, and scratched at a floor lamp.

"Yes, this just might work."

She unplugged the floor lamp, removed the shade and bulb, and dragged it to the bed. She wedged the base of the lamp between the wooden slats. "Mom, I need you to get on the ground, as far away from the bed as you can get."

Vivian winced as she sank to the floor with one hand still attached to the bed. "S'okay. Go for it," she said, holding up a shaky thumb.

Kaitlyn applied pressure but the slat refused to budge. She glared at the headboard and redoubled her effort. When the wood groaned, she grit her teeth and pushed again. Break, you stupid frankinfurter.

Her palms grew clammy as the noise in the hallway came closer. Crap.

She pushed as if the devil was about to burst through the door. The sound of wood cracking was music to her ears. When it split in two, she threw the lamp stand away and reached for her mom.

Molly jumped up and paced in front of the door while she helped her mom off the floor and unhooked the handcuff from the broken bedhead.

She fumbled with the handcuffs as Molly's pacing became more frantic. Had something happened to Murphy? No, worrying about him wasn't going to get them out of here. She needed to get her mom to safety and then somehow get them to pull back. "Okay, let's go."

Vivian leaned heavily against her as they headed for the door. Kaitlyn's muscles tensed when Molly's wolf yelped, warning them of immediate danger. The bedroom door swung open with enough force to embed the doorknob in the wall. Light from the corridor streamed through the room.

"I told you I heard something," said a faceless male in the corridor, right before two men rushed in, ready to attack.

Frack, they were supposed to be outside.

In a heartbeat, Molly's wolf pounced on the first man through the entrance. He was heavyset with a full beard and looked like he meant business. A feral growl ripped from the wolf as she flew at him, teeth bared. Not prepared for the assault, the man crashed back against the wall. Molly's wolf didn't pause. She clenched her jaws around the bearded man's neck. But before she could bear down to finish him, the second guard, much younger than his partner, roared at the top of his lungs, and lunged at her with a fire poker.

"Watch out, behind you."

Molly's wolf wasn't quick enough, and the poker embedded in her shoulder. Not expecting the attack from behind, Molly's wolf lost her grip on the bearded man's neck and let out a sharp yelp. The younger man pushed the poker farther in, and Kaitlyn shuddered. Molly attempted to dislodge him but he held on with enough brute force to make it difficult.

Kaitlyn reached for her Taser. The way he was resisting Molly's wolf's powerful attempts to dislodge him could only mean he was a Pioneer. She assessed the options available to her. With a metal rod embedded in her, the wolf could hold out only so long.

The bearded man, now on his feet, raced to Molly from behind and clamped his arms around her neck, trying to cut off her airway. Molly snarled and broke free of the younger man's grip on the poker, her powerful claws swiping against his chest as she shook her body to dislodge the bearded man from her back.

Blood seeped from the man where her claws had cut into his flesh. He growled and pulled on Molly's fur, twisting her to the ground. Against two humans, Molly would be fine. But against two Pioneers? A volley of punches to the wolf's ribcage spurred Kaitlyn into action. Murphy's mother was already losing too much blood.

She leaned her mother against the nearest wall. "Mom, stay here and don't move."

"Help the nice doggy." Her mother slurred urgently as she held onto the wall for dear life.

She glanced around the room, searching for possible weapons. The three entangled bodies were too close for her to fire her gun or Taser. Their movements were too fast, and she might inadvertently shoot Molly, who, unable to dislodge the second assailant, was now fending off attacks from both the front and rear as well as attempting to keep the metal poker hanging from her hind leg away from the guards.

Kaitlyn seized the heavy lampstand that had helped free her mother. She lifted the base over her head and charged toward the man on Molly's back. With as much force as she could summon, she smashed the base straight onto the man's skull. The impact knocked him off Molly's back. He rolled on the floor and howled in pain. That was enough of a distraction to allow Molly's wolf to focus on the young Pioneer. A ferocious roar filled the room and she charged for his jugular.

Distracted by the scene, it wasn't until the last moment that she noticed the bearded man fly toward her.

"I'll make you pay for that," he said as he clamped her in an iron grip.

He pushed her backward and slammed her head into something hard. A sharp pain shot through her skull and ricocheted through her neck and down her shoulders. Her vision blurred and her lungs were on fire. Her legs gave way and her body began to shake. She clenched her teeth and clawed at the man's steely fingers. She would not die today. Murphy's voice echoed through her mind, and his training pushed to the forefront. Her hands locked around his arm, just below the elbow. She closed her eyes and her fingers squeezed with all that she was worth.

His enraged scream reverberated around the room. Two precision strikes later, he was on the ground. This time, a Pioneer was unable to breathe.

In a split second, a pair of powerful jaws latched around the bearded man's neck. Molly's wolf tore flesh, cartilage, and trachea from his body and spat the contents on the floor. Blood gushed from the severed artery and sprayed everything in its wake.

The younger man was lying on the ground in a similar condition. She turned back to Molly, who was whimpering and attempting to reach the fire poker with her muzzle. Katlyn raced to her and pulled the metal rod out. "Sheesh, remind me never to get on your bad side."

When she was satisfied the wound was not as bad as it looked, she headed back to her mother. "Okay, let's get you out of here."

The hallway was clear, and they quickly made their way out of the room. A mix of snarls and screams, as well as a dull thumping sound, came from outside. Inside was eerily quiet. As she pulled Vivian toward the stairs, she glanced at the grandfather clock. Her eyes widened.

Ten minutes. How had only ten minutes passed?

They reached the bottom of the stairs, but Vivian slumped against the bannister. "Shleep. Need shleep."

"Mom, no. You need to stay awake."

Vivian scrunched her nose and pouted. When she looked out the front door, her eyebrows shot up. She pointed at a body lying outside the entrance. "How come he's 'loud to shleep?"

She pushed Vivian through the front door. "Because he's dead, Mom."

Vivian craned her neck to inspect the corpse. "Dead, he don' look dead."

Clearly her mom needed glasses. She half carried, half dragged her mother down the entrance staircase.

A body flew from behind the far side of the house and across the front yard.

You have got to be kidding me, what now?

The man, naked as the day he was born, landed on the grass, groaned, and rolled over. She pushed her mother behind her and reached for her weapon. When she realized who it was she gasped. Danny's normally jovial expression was etched in pain. The fight mustn't be going well. His face was covered in blood, and he had a series of large gashes on his body. From the way he cradled his arm, she guessed it was dislocated. How he'd transformed back like that was anyone's guess.

His eyes widened when he saw her. "Get out of here. Run."

Before he could rise, two snarling gray wolves descended on him, quickly followed by a third.

Just how many damn mafia Pioneers were there?

Molly's wolf raced to the third mafia wolf and cut off its path to Danny. Her fangs bared as she snarled. The other two wolves circled Danny. Their jaws snapped and bloodied saliva dripped from their fangs.

Her eyes darted over the scene. They had already taken turns at Danny, and it wouldn't take much more to finish him. He was too wounded to effectively fight back. She bit her bottom lip, torn between getting her mother to safety and evening the odds. With only one arm to fight with, Danny was in a world of trouble.

Frack it.

She couldn't leave him like that. She eased Vivian onto the top stair. "Mom hold on to the banister until I get back, okay?"

Without waiting for a reply, she double-timed it into the battle and grimaced. Where the hell was Murphy? She pulled her gun from its holster and stopped a short distance from the mafia wolves. With more courage than she felt, she called out, "Hey, mutts, two against one is a bit unfair, isn't it?"

The wolf nearest to her swung his mangy head around. He let out a snarl as he lowered his head to the ground and hunched his shoulders, ready to attack.

She squared her shoulders and held her ground, meeting the wolf's stare. Her palms were clammy and her stomach quivered. What she was about to do was stupid and reckless. She could just imagine Murphy's reaction if he ever found out. She would only get one chance, and it wasn't only her life at risk. If she failed, her mother would fall soon after.

The creature pounced, his massive claws reaching out to cut through her flesh like butter.

At the same instant, she raised her weapon, took aim and fired. She discharged a second bullet close behind the first. The ear-piercing crack caught the attention of the other two wolves. They turned in time to see the body of their companion fall, dead before he hit the ground.

She inhaled. Her aim had been true, and both bullets had gone through the wolf's eye socket and into its brain, exploding on impact. Had the bullet hit anywhere else, it would not have stopped him. She heard a growl and spun around in time to see Molly's wolf launch herself at the mafia wolf she'd blocked. Not expecting the attack, the wolf failed to defend himself and Molly ripped out his throat before he knew what had happened.

Kaitlyn aimed her weapon at the last wolf standing and narrowed her eyes. "Feeling lucky, punk?"

Molly's wolf stalked toward the remaining wolf with a menacing growl.

The wolf, now not as sure as it once was, began to back away. But Molly's wolf wasn't about to show mercy. She flew through the air and landed on the wolf.

Satisfied Molly could deal with the last wolf, she raced across the lawn to Danny. "Where's everyone? Are you okay? Is anyone else hurt?"

Danny clenched his teeth and his face contorted against considerable pain. "We ended up around the back. Elijah's nowhere to be seen, but there are a lot more wolves than we thought." He nursed his useless arm. "Those three came out of nowhere."

She attempted to help Danny up. "Can you stand?"

He winced. "I'll be fine as soon as my shoulder is back in its socket." He lay down on the ground on his back. "But I need you to put it into place. I need to change to heal, but I can't in this condition."

She holstered her weapon and her eyebrows knotted. "You do realize I haven't done this before?"

Danny grimaced and braced himself. "I have, so I'll guide you through it. You need to move my arm at a ninety-degree angle. And hurry, I need to get back in the fight."

A shiver ran down her spine as his shoulder moved into place. If she thought the sound of Molly's wolf breaking the wolf's neck was chilling, it did not compare to the sound of a shoulder popping back into its socket.

Danny stood and tested his arm. He nodded toward her mother. "Murphy isn't going to be happy. You weren't supposed to get close to the house."

She averted her eyes. Danny wasn't wearing any clothes, not that she'd noticed before. "Yeah, well, he can take that up with me once we get out of here."

The insistent thumping caught her attention. "What's that noise?"

He grimaced. "They have an underground hideout. Quite a few were down there. I managed to change and barricaded the door before they all had a chance to get out." He nodded to the dead Pioneers. "Those fuckers got to me before I could change back."

He headed to the side of the house.

She raced beside him as she checked her gun. Empty. "How's Murphy, Joshua, and the others?" Not wanting to look at him in case he could read her, she pressed the magazine release on the grip of her hand gun, pulled the empty magazine, and threw it to the ground.

"Liam's got a couple of bullets in him, and Joshua took a bit of a hit as well, but provided we get through this, they'll live. I lost sight of Murphy and Tim just after things got hectic."

Her stomach lurched. They were clearly outnumbered. She took out a full magazine from her back pocket and reloaded her weapon. She pulled back the slide and released.

He glanced down at her gun. "Where do you think you are going?"

"Where do you think? You need help."

He spun her around and pushed her back toward Molly. "Oh no, you don't. My life won't be worth living if Murphy sees you anywhere near the fight. You weren't even supposed to get to the house. No. You get your mom and get the hell out of here."

She frowned. This was ridiculous. She couldn't leave Murphy or the others without backup. They'd already lost Wendy and who knew how weak Tim was after the damage inflicted from two bullets floating around his body. She opened her mouth but closed it again when Molly's wolf pulled at her pant leg. "What the hell?"

Molly glanced toward Vivian and her face grew hot with shame. Her mother had lost so much blood. Her focus needed to be on getting her out of there and to a hospital.

A howl rang out from somewhere on the other side of the house and Danny tensed. "I have to go." He glanced down at Molly. "You get them out of here."

Without saying anything else he sprinted away, likely to change into his wolf before he rejoined the battle. Just as quickly Kaitlyn and Molly headed for Vivien, who had fallen asleep.

Kaitlyn shook her mother awake. "Let's go mom."

She half carried her mother into the tree line with Molly leading the way. Once she was sure they were hidden from view, she set her mother down on the ground and propped her against a thick tree trunk. Her mother fell asleep again. Kaitlyn gazed at the house they had left behind. Somewhere on the other side, a battle was raging. Her old friends, the fire ants, clawed at her insides. Her indecision was tearing her up inside, and the panic was back. If she got her mom to safety, she'd live, but at the cost of Murphy, and the others. If she stayed to help, her mom's life would be forfeit, and she had no guarantee they could defeat the mafia Pioneers.

Something wet ran down the back of her neck. What the hell? She lifted a hand to the back of her neck and pulled it away covered in a dark sticky substance. The sickly metallic scent told her exactly what it was. Her hair was matted with blood.

Frankinfurter. No wonder her head was thumping.

Molly's wolf scratched on the ground to get her attention.

She held her palms up to her forehead as if the action alone would hold back the wave of nausea. She had to ignore it. Her mother needed medical help before the sedative wore off and her pain became unbearable. How the hell was she going to get her to safety? "Molly, I need you to change back into your Human form and get my mom to a hospital."

Molly's wolf took a step back and let out a low growl.

She held up her hands. What if Molly wouldn't agree, what then? "I know that wasn't the plan, but I can't carry her the distance. Look at her, she can't even stay awake. Mom's not getting there on her own two feet. I'm not sure how much longer the drugs will last, and once they wear off, she's going to be in agony."

She crouched beside Vivian and gently touched her mother's damaged face with the back of her hand. Her eyes glazed over and her chest burned. Elijah's damage was extensive. She turned to Molly. "Look at her. You're my only hope of getting her to safety."

At first, she thought her appeal had fallen on deaf ears, but a gruff snort from the animal soothed her. The wolf was giving control back to her Human side.

She was unable to tear her eyes away as the wolf's body lurched uncontrollably and rippled as though something was moving under its skin. Skin replaced hair, and the wolf's forepaws morphed into Molly's Human hands. Once it was over, Molly rose up and stood over her.

Kaitlyn hugged her. "Th-thank you."

"Murphy's going to kill us both, lass."

Molly raced to the spot where they left their clothes and returned fully dressed. She bent down and picked Vivian up with ease. When she righted herself, she nodded her head in the direction of the now brightly lit house. "I suppose you'll be going back in, then."

Kaitlyn nodded. "Mom's safe now. I couldn't live with myself if I didn't try to help."

Through the dark, Molly's eyes burned into her. "Keep safe, my girl. Don't you go taking no risks. You have miles to go before you sleep. And make sure my boy's okay, you hear me?"

Kaitlyn nodded and with that, Molly turned, and headed out. She stopped and turned back to Kaitlyn. "What do I tell her if she wakes up and wants to know why she's being carried by a stranger?"

Kaitlyn smiled and wiped away a tear. "Just tell her you're her guardian angel and to go back to sleep."

Once Molly and her mother disappeared into the thick trees, Kaitlyn sprinted back to the house.

Please, let them be okay.

Would she be too late to make a difference? Her chest ached at visions of what she would find on the other side of the house. Even without Elijah, the mafia Pioneers were stronger in number and might than expected.

Murphy, please be okay.

He had to come through this alive. They all did. She couldn't live with herself if they didn't. They were here because of her. She should have waited until Daniel's men arrived. If they had, Wendy would still be alive.

She reached the base of the stairs that led up to the front door. Even though she was bathed in lights from the house and garden, no one came rushing out to attack her. She took a moment to evaluate her options. If she moved along the side of the house, she might be exposed before she reached them. Inside she had more options. And more risks. She placed a foot on the bottom step and took a deep breath.

Please, let them be okay.

<u>THIRTY-NINE</u>

Betrayal

Kaitlyn's stomach was tied in knots as she edged her way down the massive foyer and through the corridor into the back of the house. When she entered a grand living room, her jaw dropped at the soaring ceilings and cavernous room. Unlike the rest of the house, the room was dark. With only the lights from outside to see her way, she made out the no doubt expensive furniture.

And who said crime didn't pay?

Careful to keep out of what little light there was, she made her way around the room and sidled up to the window, her back against the wall.

A feral snarl from outside seemed a little too close for comfort. She held her gun pointing down with both arms straight. What she wouldn't give for a Sherman tank right about now. She inched her head around the window to look outside. The living room opened onto a large patio that took up half the side of the mansion. She wasn't sure if she was relieved or terrified no bodies littered the jumbled mess of broken chairs and overturned planters, but the distinct noise of wolves fighting was coming from somewhere. She willed her racing pulse to slow down. Now or never. She swung her body out the door and raised her gun to face the left side of the patio.

Thank God.

Joshua's wolf was backing two mafia wolves and one human mafia thug into a corner next to an outdoor fireplace. While she was relieved to see he was still alive, his coat was matted with blood and deep lacerations.

She quashed her first instinct to call out to him. They had a job to do, and any distraction could tip the scales in the mafia wolves' favor. She surveyed the immediate area. Perhaps she had spoken too soon. Unlike the area directly outside of the living room, bodies, both human and wolf, littered the patio and pool. Where was Murphy?

Instead of Murphy, Kaitlyn spotted Liam not far from her grandfather. Liam's wolf limped toward a small group of mafias cowering in the corner. He had chunks of fur missing and exposed flesh on his back. She frowned. Where the hell were the rest of them? Apart from Joshua and Liam, the rest of the team was missing. When her eyes landed on a body by the swimming pool, her heart stopped.

No!

She cried out and ran to Danny's broken body, still in his Human form. The Pioneer policeman had a gaping chest wound that exposed half his organs. Her body shook, as she sunk to her knees and fought to hold back bile. The damage to his chest, coupled with the chunks of torn flesh from his legs and arms, showed that he had put up a valiant fight, but the wolves that shredded him to pieces had shown him no mercy. His lifeless eyes stared back at her. She blinked rapidly to stem the tide that threatened. How many more would she find like this? Unable to see him like that, she closed his eyelids and draped a half-soaked towel over his mangled body.

A low, forceful growl cut through her sorrow and her head shot up. Her fingers tightened around her gun. Murphy?

Something hard hit her with enough force to topple her over. The gun flew out of her hand and slid across the tiles and out of her reach. Pain ripped through her shoulder. She bit her tongue to keep from screaming out and tried to ignore the agony that tore through her arm and down half her body. She jumped up and spun around to face her attacker, her body in full attack position. Flashes of light and stars swam into view forcing her to wince. She would feel that blow for days. If she lived. Her shoulders tightened and she gasped when she recognized the man with a baseball bat in his hand.

Garcia?

But that didn't make sense. Why would he … Her stomach clenched and the air left her lungs. The mole. Garcia was the mole.

"Well, well, look at what the cat dragged in. Or should I say the dogs?" His voice dripped with venom.

Joshua stalked toward them, his head low and his eyes fixated on Garcia.

In a flash, Garcia bent down, retrieved her gun and aimed it at her. "I wouldn't if I were you." He grinned at Joshua. "I couldn't miss at this distance."

Joshua stopped in his tracks and snarled.

Garcia dropped the bat. "You can cut the attitude. You're the ones who invaded us. Not the other way around. Now tell your friend to let my cousins go." He waved the gun at her. "Or I plug two in her gut, and you can watch her bleed out in less than fifteen minutes."

She clenched her fists. How the hell was this the same person she'd been working with? How did she not see underneath his smooth façade?

"Thank god Saul didn't live to see this. He would never have forgiven himself for not seeing who you truly are," she said.

Garcia chuckled. "He knew. He recognized me about a second before I hit him."

She physically recoiled as if a train hit her. No. At first, her brain rejected the statement. She must have misunderstood the words. But when she looked Garcia in the eye, her heart sank. His mouth was curled up in a sardonic grin. His eyes were hard as flint. The civilized veneer he disguised himself behind, fell away. He was a man without empathy or a shred of decency.

How had she not seen it before? Gone was the jovial flirt. In its place was someone she didn't recognize.

Joshua took another step. A sharp crack rang out, and she froze as a bullet flew past her. Her heart beat drowned out everything else. The bastard had pulled the trigger.

"I told you to not move," he said to Joshua's wolf.

Joshua's wolf stopped. He let out a whine and glanced at her.

Kaitlyn gave him a shallow smile. "I'm all right."

Garcia waved the gun toward the mafia wolves Liam was guarding. "Back the fuck up and let my cousins go."

"No."

Crap. Did she say that out loud?

She squared her shoulders and stood to her full height. He was not going to get away with this. Not on her watch. Over her dead body would they let the mafia wolves go free. "Liam, whatever happens, do not let them go. Our country does not negotiate with terrorists and neither do I." She glanced at her grandfather. "I'm sorry, but you know I'm right."

Garcia shrugged. "Fine, have it your way."

He lifted the gun higher and aimed.

Fuck. Her pulse exploded and blood raced through her veins like an angry volcano. He was going to shoot.

His finger pulled on the trigger.

The gun fired just as a flash of golden brown flew between her and Garcia. It fired twice more in quick succession. She glanced down. No bullet holes. The shocked paralysis dimmed, and she regained control of her body. What did he hit? He was too close to have missed her.

Kaitlyn turned her head in the direction the blur flew, and her heart tore open. A golden-brown wolf lay on its side a short distance away.

Murphy.

Murphy had put himself between her and the bullets. She wavered between denial and panic. Like the others, he had gashes across his body where sharp teeth had managed to get beyond his defenses. Not as much as Liam and Joshua, but enough for her see a trail of blood matted in his fur.

Murphy's wolf moved, and she held back the sob that bubbled up and threatened to burst. He was okay. He rose and faced Garcia. His lips curled back to expose razor sharp teeth, and he let out a chilling growl. Blood dripped from his fur where the three bullets lodged in his ribs.

Despite the nip in the night air, a bead of perspiration ran across her forehead. Murphy had said bullets wouldn't kill them, but he didn't say they wouldn't hurt like hell.

She was so engrossed in making certain Murphy wasn't going to die, she almost missed the sound of a warning bark. She turned as Garcia bore down on her, the baseball bat over his head. She screamed, dove out of the way, and circled her leg into a round-house kick. She glanced behind. Garcia was doubled over, clutching his midriff. A pained groan burst out with his exhale, and she grinned. Elijah obviously hadn't turned him yet.

Garcia quickly recovered and broke into a run. "You'll regret that, bitch."

She reached for her gun, but it was too far away. She pulled out her Taser, pointed at her former teammate, and fired. Two probes embedded in his chest, and he dropped to the ground like a ton of bricks. He convulsed as fifty thousand volts coursed through his body. The shock was so quick he had no chance of calling out in pain.

"You know, I don't think I'll regret that for an instant."

She raced over and kicked him in the side. Her lips pressed together in a harsh line. "That's for Saul, you murdering bastard." She kicked him again. "And that's for Mildred."

Liam approached her and whined while he scratched at the tiles.

She glanced at Murphy and then her grandfather. She couldn't be sure, but she could have sworn they were looking at her with pride. Liam pushed her toward Garcia, then attempted to pull at Garcia's clothing.

"Here, let me," she said, getting the hint.

Before the effects wore off, she dragged his still-shaking body over to Joshua and the prisoners. Once he was in Joshua and Liam's custody, she raced back to Murphy. How he could be moving with three bullets lodged in his ribs was beyond her. He was pacing the length of the pool, agitated at something. The hairs on the back of her neck bristled.

His instincts were normally spot on. Something wasn't right. Straining her eyes, she scanned the area between the main house, and the guest and pool house to see what had him so upset. The pitch black of night was edging its way toward dawn, and she was able to make out the silhouettes of bodies, both human and wolf, lying dead on the cold, damp grass.

"No sign of Elijah?"

He stopped pacing and turned his head to face her. Amber eyes filled with an ancient pain stared at her. He shook his massive head and turned back to the darkness.

She reached out and tentatively raked her fingers through the pelt on his neck. A heavy weight pulled at her chest. She knew Danny and Wendy were gone.

"Tim …" Her voice broke and she tried again. "What about Tim, Rachel, and Jose? Would she find their bodies broken and cold out there in the darkness?

Murphy raised his head and a low howl rang out to the night sky. A moment later three separate howls from somewhere in the distance, responded.

She briefly closed her eyes and her knees went weak. They were okay. She relaxed her hold on Murphy's fur. She needed to do something. Anything to keep from being overwhelmed with a deluge of emotions. She retrieved her gun from where it had landed.

When she reached down, her eyes drew to her hands. Blood red. Danny's blood. She had Danny's blood on her hands. Both literally and figuratively. He was dead because she insisted they couldn't wait for Daniel. A sharp pain ripped through her chest. She didn't once ask him if he had a family. Who did he leave behind to mourn him? Was there anyone to remember the sacrifice he made?

Why didn't she ask?

The metallic stench of fresh blood was rife in the air, each breath a new reminder of the carnage that surrounded her. The airway in her throat constricted. All she wanted to do was find her mom, make sure she was okay, and hug her so hard she would never let her go. She bit her lip and a single tear slid down her cheek. That would not be an option for quite a while. Her mom was too badly injured to hug.

"That son of a bitch nearly killed her and he got away with it. Again."

She wiped at the tear with the back of her hand. She couldn't dwell on her hatred of Elijah. Murphy had wallowed in it for decades, and he had once again been thwarted. She needed to get to her mom. Exhaustion washed over her as she made her way to the pool and washed off the blood on her hands.

He struck when she was leaning over the water. Before she could cry out, a sharp blade pressed against the skin at the base of her neck.

<u>FORTY</u>

Last Stand

Murphy urged his wolf to go to Kaitlyn. *She's suffering*

His wolf headed away from Kaitlyn and toward their prisoners. *I know, but she is strong. Resilient. She will survive.*

As much as it pained him, he settled back and allowed his wolf to deal with their main priority. Their prisoners. His wolf was right. Kaitlyn was strong. With time, tonight would be nothing but a bad memory. He would make sure of it. A sense of purpose washed over him. He would help her through it every step of the way. For the first time in what seemed forever, he had a plan for the future. One that had him thinking about the day after tomorrow and the day after that.

It's about time.

More settled, his wolf stalked the prisoners.

He surveyed the damage and the bodies littered across the property. Good thing they were in a secluded area. No nosy neighbors or prying eyes to also clean up.

His wolf snapped his jaws at their prisoners and scratched at the ground.

He opened his link to Joshua and his Da. Lately it was becoming easier to make the connection. It even gave him a measure of comfort. *We need the prisoners back in their Human form. That means we've got to communicate with them.*

Joshua's wolf turned his head and nodded. *I'll change back first. That way if they get out of line you and the others can still handle them.*

He was tired. And sore. The bullets lodged in various parts of him probably didn't help things. But the mafia wolves had put up a considerable resistance. The fact that they were already experienced thugs and fighters gave them an advantage.

We would have gladly taken more, his wolf reminded him.

Garcia.

He had the sudden urge to hit something. How could he have missed the traitor in their midst? He had been so intent on protecting her from Elijah, he had failed to see the obvious. The signs were there.

His wolf let out a low growl then snapped his jaws at Garcia. *He should not be allowed to live for what he nearly did to her.*

On this they agreed. He would make sure Garcia paid for killing Saul. There were probably more he had killed in cold blood, but they only had one confession from Garcia. He shuddered at how close they had come to loosing Kaitlyn. His injuries, on top of his lack of sleep over the past few weeks, meant his reaction time was slower and he had almost not made it to stop the bullets meant for her.

Kaitlyn let out a whimper.

He turned his head and froze. Time stood still.

Elijah stood at the far side of the patio holding a knife at the base of Kaitlyn's throat. A drop of blood seeped from under the blade.

A chill ran through his body. How had he not heard his approach?

Contempt and maliciousness oozed from Elijah. "You? I was wondering when you would turn up."

His wolf lowered his head and drew back his lips in a snarl. This was the night Elijah was going to pay for what he had done. Tonight, he would finish the job he'd started decades ago.

Liam and Joshua's stance mimicked his. His wolf snarled again, a sound that rolled across the distance like thunder before an impending storm, but that only served to amuse Elijah. Elijah's sarcastic laugh grated on his nerves. More than anything, he wanted to lash out, but the knife at Kaitlyn's neck kept him frozen to the spot.

"I thought by now you would be tired of losing." Elijah shrugged. "But you know what they say about the Irish, as thick as two planks." He smirked and pulled Kaitlyn tighter to his body and nuzzled her ear. "Your mother and I had such a lovely time together."

She squirmed.

His wolf let out a threatening growl and prepared to pounce.

He wrestled for control. *No. We need to wait, we could hurt her.*

Elijah's eyes narrowed to slits. "Interesting. I see we are a bit protective of the Human. Don't worry, when I'm done with you, I'll make sure to keep her very entertained. Just like June, she'll be begging me to end her."

Kaitlyn locked eyes with him and curled her fingers into fists. Her silent message was all too clear. It didn't matter what happened to her. Elijah couldn't go free.

Terror ripped through him like a knife. She was willing to sacrifice herself. All that mattered was Elijah's reign of carnage ended now. Her hand slowly reached up and curled around the gun she'd jammed into the waist band of her pants.

His body tensed, ready to attack. He couldn't allow her to do this. An enraged growl ripped from his wolf as he stalked forward, his tail horizontal, his fur bristled, every inch of him threatening. His rage erupted, and his lips curled back to expose his dagger-like fangs.

Elijah chuckled. "My dear Murphy, if you insist." He brutally threw Kaitlyn across the patio and pulled off his shirt.

"But when I take her in front of your broken and dying body don't say I didn't warn you."

Elijah's body began to shimmer and contort.

Without taking his eyes of Elijah, he opened a link to his father. *Get her clear.*

Kaitlyn's adrenaline flooded her body as she scrambled up.

Liam's wolf bolted across the patio toward her and let out a low whine.

She pressed a hand to the base of her throat. The cut was small but hurt like a bitch. "I'm fine."

With more speed that she thought possible, Elijah transformed into his wolf form. Clearly, he had decades of experience over the younger mafia wolves. She glanced at Murphy, and her heart sank. Elijah was fresh and undamaged. Unlike Murphy's wolf, who looked like he'd just gone ten rounds with Tyson, Elijah's wolf was unmarred and at full stamina.

Liam nudged her and she scrambled backward. When she was a fair distance from center stage, Liam raced back to stand guard over their prisoners with Joshua. They both looked concerned, but they stayed back.

One of the mafia wolves inched forward and Joshua snapped at him. The mafia wolf quickly backed away. If either Joshua or Liam went to help Murphy, the prisoners would besiege the other one, and none of them would get out of this alive.

Where the hell were Tim and Jose?

The two wolves circled, snapping at each other in an attempt to gain an advantage.

She tensed as Elijah's wolf rushed at Murphy's, his jaws snapping together with a loud crack. Murphy jumped back, barely making it out of harm's way. Then, almost in unison, they attacked front on, rising on their hind legs to gain leverage. The resulting flurry of parry-and-thrusts was almost too fast for her to keep up with, and her chest knotted tighter.

Elijah's years of combat experience showed. He was smaller, but his wiry frame had the ability to dodge out of Murphy grasp. And with Murphy being already spent, this only gave Elijah more of an edge. For each bite or slash Murphy inflicted, Elijah responded in kind.

Elijah's wolf faked a move and at the last moment spun to clamp onto Murphy's hind leg.

She screamed when Murphy yipped in pain.

With a viciousness that was hard to watch, Elijah's wolf shook his head violently in an attempt to maul Murphy's wolf.

Murphy's wolf twisted around and pounced on Elijah with his front paws. His lethal claws dug into Elijah's backbone, and he took a bite out of Elijah's rump. The resulting yelp gave Murphy enough time to pull his leg free.

A heartbeat later, they were again digging into each other.

Liam's wolf paced back and forth. She knew how he felt.

A yip and a yowl told her Joshua and Liam were struggling to keep the prisoners under control, but she never took her eyes off Murphy's wolf. With no back up, and waning stamina, this could go very wrong for him. For all of them.

One of them would die tonight. She bit down hard on the inside of her cheek. Murphy must not be the one. The battle, half a century in the making, could not have Elijah walking out alive. Could it?

Murphy had to live. Even if he wasn't in her life, her heart couldn't take the pain of him no longer walking the earth. Broody and gruff, but still alive and well. She hauled in a deep breath. Who was she kidding? If Elijah won, they were all dead.

A soft feathery sensation ran down her arm, and the hairs on the back of her neck stood up. The temperature dropped and an ethereal gust of wind surrounded her. She looked around, but nothing had changed and none of the others seemed to have noticed. When a cold hand touched her shoulder, and another wrapped around her left hand, her eyes flew wide. She fell forward as if jostled, cried out and swung to face whoever touched her.

No one was there.

Her brows knitted in a frown. The others were still glued to the action, but the air around her continued to hum, like she was surrounded by people. But how could she be? She was alone. Liam was at least twenty feet from her, and no one else was near her. A heavy weight crushed her body. She nearly buckled under the sensation as every bone and muscle screamed out. She clutched at her stomach as dread poured over her.

Liam's wolf raised his head and let out a howl. Liam's melodic tones were joined a moment later by Joshua.

Her gaze darted to the wolves he and Joshua were guarding. The prisoners were still there. Heart racing, she turned back to the fight. The howling grew in intensity, and so did the feeling she was not alone.

Murphy, after evading another strike from Elijah, lashed out and caught his opponent's underbelly. He tore through the fur and skin to expose a deep gash. Before Elijah's wolf recovered, he struck again. This time, he slashed into Elijah's flank.

The howls from Liam and the pack grew louder and more mournful, chilling her to the bone.

Elijah, not to be outdone, shred into Murphy's muzzle.

She flinched. The cut was to the bone.

"Please, give Murphy the energy to end this. I can't take much more," she whispered.

A gust of wind swirled around them, picking up leaves and dust in its wake. Something squeezed her hand and brushed across her cheek as if lightly kissed. Another chill ran up and down her spine. She was losing her mind. She had to be. No one was beside her. The wind moved across the patio. Liam's and Joshua's howls intensified. The mafia wolves whimpered, dropped to the ground, and rolled over to expose their undersides.

The hairs on her arm and the back of her neck quivered and bristled.

When Murphy growled, she turned her focus back to the fight. He threw himself at Elijah in a graceful leap that defied the laws of gravity. He snapped his jaws in a vice around Elijah's neck. Elijah, bleeding profusely from his wounds, was doing his best to pull out of the deadly grip. With each attempt at escape, Murphy bit down harder, blocking Elijah's airway, and making it more difficult for him to breathe. Liam and Joshua's wolves stopped their howls and slowly inched forward.

In all her time as an FBI agent, she'd never thought the distinct sound of bones cracking under pressure was music to her ears, but it was.

She clenched her fists. Finish it.

A small flurry of wind brushed past her and the very air echoed her chant. Everything stilled as if time itself was pausing. Every nerve ending was on fire.

Finish it.

Murphy's wolf readied for the kill, and she closed her eyes. Visions of her father washed through her, clearer than they had ever been, almost as if he were with her. Justice would finally be served. The monster that had taken her father and her unborn brother was meeting the end he deserved, and she would bear witness. Every victim he had ever taken would be free to move on and find peace at last. She opened her eyes, refusing even to blink. If she was to represent Elijah's victims, she needed to see this.

Murphy's wolf was staring at her, his jaws clenched around Elijah's throat and blood pooled on the ground below. But Elijah was still alive. Just.

Murphy's wolf growled, not once taking his eyes from her.

She let out the breath she'd been holding. The small gust of wind pushed at her shoulders, swaying her forward. She resisted and pushed back.

Why had he not ended it?

Liam left his post and made his way to where she stood. His fast gait added to the urgency of the moment. He pressed his wet and bloodied nose against her and pushed from behind. A tingling sensation scaled the length of her body. What the hell was going on?

"What?" she said as he nudged her again.

She turned back to Murphy's wolf. He continued to hold firm to his prey, but he had not shifted his steady gaze from her. She glanced down at Elijah, then at Murphy. She couldn't shake the feeling that she was being watched by hundreds of eyes.

"I don't know what you—"

A hand tugged at her arm, and she froze. With the exception of Liam, no one was close to her. Liam pushed her again, and she shuffled back two steps, as the realization of what he wanted hit her. Tears prickled behind her eyes, and the lump in her throat made it hard to swallow. He was gifting her the kill. After everything he'd gone through, Murphy was allowing her to be the one who sent Elijah to hell.

Kaitlyn reached for her weapon and slowly made her way across the courtyard. She stood over the two wolves, and looked down at Elijah's fluttering eyes. Her heart hammered in her chest as she squared her shoulders and held the gun with both hands. Her grip tightened. She kept her arms steady as she aimed and steeled herself for the kill. She had no remorse for what she was about to do. This was the only option available to them. She should be horrified at her decision. Instead, an invisible hand rested on her shoulder, and she was at peace.

She steadied her erratic breathing and put her finger on the trigger.

Just as she was about to pull the trigger, Elijah's eyes opened wide. Self-preservation kicked in, and he made a last-ditch attempt to escape Murphy's grip. But before he had a chance to hurt Murphy more than he already had, she emptied the remainder of her clip into both eye sockets.

Elijah's body went limp the moment the second bullet exploded in his brain.

She stumbled backward and watched as Murphy's wolf tore out Elijah's throat. A combination of numbness, satisfaction, and relief spread through her. She wasn't sure if she should laugh or cry.

He's gone. Daddy … we got him.

Murphy's wolf stood to his full height and let out a howl, one much deeper and richer than Liam's. This was a victory cry, one that was quickly joined by the others. Their howls carried on the wind to let the dead know they had been avenged.

She gasped, surprised when even the mafia wolves joined in. A far cry from their whimpering and agitation just before she pulled the trigger. All around her, the air bristled and dispersed. Like a balloon that had popped, her sense of being watched slowly evaporated. The gentle caress of her cheek from the last wisp of pressure calmed her, before the aroma of blood and death overwhelmed her again. A single tear ran down her face. She felt a distant echo of something lost, as if something she never knew she had was now gone, never to return. She wiped her eyes. It wouldn't do to have a mental breakdown, not now. Not until she made sure her mother was well.

Murphy's wolf nuzzled his head along her leg, then looked up at her with large ebony eyes.

She took one last look at Elijah's body, and her shoulders relaxed. "I'm okay," she said in a whisper. "He can't hurt anyone anymore."

He turned on his haunches and headed to where Liam and Joshua were guarding their prisoners.

One problem down. But another world of issues was huddled together, nervously darting glances at a gray wolf standing between them and Murphy, Liam, and Joshua. She pressed her lips together, quickly reloaded her gun, then pointed it at the mafia wolves. "I recommend you take Human form. My friends may change their mind and decide not to let you live."

Her finger twitched when she glared at Garcia. He deserved to rot in jail for the rest of his life for what he had done to Saul. He'd played them all for fools and allowed a bunch of criminals to prosper. Just how many lives were lost from the drugs and guns because he gave a bunch of criminals a hall pass? There was a special place in hell for people like him. Right next to Elijah.

Murphy let out a low growl and took a step forward. The mafia wolves cowered.

"Last chance," she said.

The gray wolf protecting the others glanced behind him, then let out a small whine. He looked Murphy straight in the eye as if trying to assess his odds. Clearly not liking them, the muscles on his body began to contort, and he changed into his Human form.

She raced inside to find clothes for the Pioneers. The sooner they secured their prisoners, the sooner she could get to her mom.

The first rays of dawn edged closer. The new day was almost upon them. She scanned the bodies littering the park-like grounds. In their hastily put together plan, they had not thought beyond freeing her mother and taking Elijah down. Now, in the cold light of day, they'd have to figure out how to deal with the dead. They couldn't leave them for the authorities to find. There would be too many questions.

She took a moment to take stock. They had Garcia and his family secure in their underground bunker with the rest of the survivors. Unfortunately, Ambrose Giordano and who knew how many more were missing. No one was talking and she doubted threats would loosen their lips.

Rachel and Jose stood guard at the bunker, and Liam and Joshua were changing into their Human form. For the first time in what felt like forever, it was quiet enough to think. She pulled out her phone and dialed Molly's number. "Please let them have gotten away," she whispered.

A small sob escaped her lips when Molly answered on the first ring.

"Is it over?" Molly said.

"Elijah will no longer be a problem. And before you ask, Liam and Murphy are fine."

"Thank the lord. I swear I have aged decades not knowing."

"How's my mom?"

"She's fine," Molly said. "She's in with the doctors now. They have her bandaged, and she's been treated for any possible infections or other complications. They don't think there's any internal bleeding."

A huge weight lifted from her shoulders. The relief was so strong she nearly broke down.

"She's asking for you," Molly said.

She rubbed her forehead. "I'll get there as soon as I can."

"Tim will drive you to the hospital," Murphy said the moment she ended the call.

After all the mafia wolves had changed back to Human form, Murphy had followed suit. They all looked as though they'd been through hell and back. At least three times. She nodded to the blood stains Murphy's sweat pants and t-shirt couldn't hide. Garcia's bullets had hit his shoulder and thigh. "Shouldn't you be coming, too?"

Murphy shook his head. "I'll be fine. It's nothing."

She raised her brows. He had to be in pain. Pioneer or not, he was going to feel the battle he'd just been through for days. "What now?"

He indicated the dead. "Daniel's men will be here shortly. We'll clean up here and take them to Colorado. Daniel has facilities to detain them until we work out what to do. Then we'll focus on finding Ambrose and the rest of his pack."

"Where do you think he is?"

He shrugged. "None of them are talking. But it's Daniel's problem now. I've done what I came here to do."

A hand clenched around her heart and squeezed it. This was it. This was the moment she knew was coming. The moment her heart was officially breaking. "I suppose you'll be heading back to Quantico after that?"

The words were out before she could stop them. She didn't want to know the answer. It would just confirm what she already knew.

"I haven't decided. Elijah's gone, and I think my time there is over as well. My priorities have changed."

The hand squeezed harder. He was going to disappear. Vanish without a trace and lick his wounds. She focused on ignoring the painful emotions the way her grandfather had taught her. It wouldn't do to let Murphy know just how much this was killing her. The man she was in love with was about to walk out of her life. Forever. She knew this was coming. He had never hidden his intentions, nor had he made promises.

"Oh."

She cringed. He was telling her this was the last time they would ever see each other and all she could say was Oh.

Tim cleared his throat, and she jumped in her skin. She'd been so focused on filtering everything out, she'd failed to realize Tim hovering nearby.

"Ready to go," he said.

Dark circles ringed Tim's eyes. The image of Tim's friends' broken forms hit her. In her personal pity party, she'd forgotten how much they had sacrificed. This wouldn't sit well with any of the Pioneers.

Not sure what words could convey her sorrow, she felt she had to at least say something. She reached out and touched him lightly on the arm. "I'm … I'm sorry about Danny and Wendy."

Tim nodded and he shuffled his feet as he focused on the ground. "Thanks." He cleared his throat. "They were good people."

"They fought with honor," Murphy said.

They fell silent, and she sent out a silent prayer for their fallen.

Murphy, the first to break the silence, pushed her toward the house. "Get cleaned up and go. You need to get to your mother."

Her breath caught at his touch. She wanted more. More of him, more of his heady kisses, more of how he made her feel.

No, she couldn't do this to herself.

She looked down at her red-stained hands. Like the damage to her heart, she doubted she'd ever truly be able to wash off the blood. She blinked rapidly. She'd break down later in the privacy of her own home. Right now, she needed to pretend that all was well, and she was okay with saying goodbye to him.

She pulled out her gun and Taser and handed them to Murphy. "You better take these. It might start a panic if I walk into the hospital with them."

Murphy grunted in acknowledgement. "I see you finally got to use the Taser."

A faint smile crossed her lips. "Just not on the person I had expected to use it on."

His gaze met hers, and she was a deer stuck in headlights. His intense, dark eyes bore into hers and reached into her very soul. Their fingers brushed as he took the weapons from her. She snapped her hands back as if burned.

"I-I'd better be going." She cleared her throat then held out her hand. "It was an honor and privilege working with you."

His brows furrowed together. He hesitated but eventually shook her offered hand. His grip was strong and gentle at the same time. A burning sensation raced up her arm from their touch. He opened his mouth as if to speak, but unable to bear the torture much longer without breaking down, she ripped her hand out of his grip and readied to leave. This was too hard. It was taking everything she had to hide her real emotions. She needed to get away before the tsunami of grief overtook her.

"Ryan. He would have been proud." His voice was soft.

Her chest tightened at his words. Somehow, she knew beyond a doubt that was true. Her father could finally rest easy knowing Elijah was gone for good. Her mind drifted to the countless others whose lives were taken before their time. They could rest easy. A shadow of a smile played across her lips. Just as it was a closure for her, he too, had been waiting a long time for this. "June's soul will no longer suffer in knowing the person who separated you lives. I think … somehow, I feel you have given her the peace that has eluded her all this time."

Murphy closed his eyes and tilted his face to the heavens, as if deep in prayer.

"And I hope it's given you the peace you have been looking for," she whispered.

For once his stoic mask had fallen away, leaving behind the true Murphy. A good man who didn't deserve what life had thrown his way. Protector. Warrior. A man who loved so deeply he devoted his life to avenge what was taken from him. She reached out to touch his arm, but pulled back her hand. A twinge of guilt pricked at the back of her head. This was quickly followed by shame. She was jealous of a long dead woman.

Tim poked his head out the door and waved a set of car keys at her. He was ready to take her to the hospital. She nodded, and he disappeared back into the house.

A tear forced its way from behind her resolve to be strong, and she pivoted and strode across the patio. He was June's and forever would be. Pioneers only loved once. There was no hope for her, and if she didn't leave now, she wouldn't leave with her dignity intact.

She managed to make it to the top of the driveway before the dam broke. She should be happy. She had fulfilled her promise to her father.

But at what cost?

FORTY-ONE
Still Waters Run Deep

Two Weeks Later - Florida

Kaitlyn reached for the French press before her mother could get to it. "Mom, let me do that."

Vivian swatted her daughter's hand away. "Don't fuss, sweetheart. I love you dearly, but you're starting to get on my nerves."

"You should be resting."

Vivian placed a hand on her hip and frowned at her daughter. "I'm not an invalid. And I don't know how many times I need to tell you, I'm all right. Stop worrying."

She spooned ground coffee into the press and swirled the container to settle the granulated beans. "I'm sorry. I just can't help it."

Vivian closed the short distance between them. She placed an arm around her. "It's over. You need to stop blaming yourself."

She closed her eyes. That was easier said than done. Had she been more careful, the mafia wouldn't have worked out she was onto them, and their foot soldiers wouldn't have been watching her apartment. Moreover, they most definitely would not have taken her mother.

The ten days her mother spent in hospital were a constant reminder of how close she had come to losing her.

She returned her mother's embrace. "I love you, Mom."

They hadn't once talked about what Vivian might or might not have seen. Kaitlyn wasn't sure how to broach the subject. How much did her mom really know? Rehashing memories from the abduction might be too much, so she let sleeping dogs lie. Her mom would talk about it when she was good and ready.

After filling the container with hot water, she placed the lid on the French press and left the coffee to steep.

Vivian made her way to the couch in the living room.

"What would you like to do today?" Kaitlyn said. "How about I take you out shopping?"

Vivian raised an eyebrow and picked up the novel she had recently abandoned. "I'm not a vain woman, Kaitlyn, but even so, there's no way I'm going out to the mall looking like the bride of Frankenstein."

Kaitlyn winced. "It's not that bad."

Her mother made a sound that let her know she thought otherwise. "Even if I wanted to, I can't. Lee's picking up some more oils."

"I could have done that for you."

Vivian shrugged and opened her book.

Her phone rang as she handed her mother a piping hot coffee. "It's work, I need to get it." She grabbed the phone before her mother spotted Joshua's name and rushed outside, closing the ranch slider behind her.

She had contacted Joshua. Even though she was half a country away, she needed to know what was going on.

He briefed her on the current situation. "They have yet to rule on the main charges, but council has given the Giordano family pack status."

She recoiled. "They what?"

"I know that's not what you wanted to hear, but that's the decision."

Her muscles twitched, and she clenched her fist in an effort not to destroy any of her mom's prized garden. "But they're career criminals. They kill and mutilate for a living. For all you know they've killed more than Elijah ever could. They should to be punished for what they've done."

"And that's exactly what Murphy is trying to make the council aware of. They've adjourned till tomorrow. He has one more day to convince them. After that, they will deliberate."

The weight on her shoulders grew heavier. That was probably why Murphy had been phoning her. To warn her about the possible decision. Knowing she would never see him again, and just how fragile her heart was, she had let each call go to voice mail. Childish, but self-preservation could do stupid things to a person. "How much longer are you in Colorado?"

"I'm on a flight back to Boston this afternoon to close down the house, then back home tomorrow afternoon."

Her chest ached. That could only mean one thing. Joshua didn't expect Murphy to return. Her assumption had been right all along. "I guess I won't be seeing you when I get back?"

"Afraid not, hon," he said, the regret palpable in his voice. "I've been ordered home. Molly and Liam already left. The council is taking so long with your mafia friends because they're dealing with another Elise issue. All packs have been put on high alert. But I'll try to get back up to Boston as soon as I can for a visit. I promise."

She sucked in her bottom lip and bit on it to keep from breaking down. In one fell swoop she had lost two people who had become a pivotal part of her life. One permanently, and the other for who knew how long.

She stood staring at her mother's vegetable garden for some time after she hung up. Her heart and mind were not able to return to her new normalcy just yet. Everything ached. She missed Murphy more than she ever thought possible. Like a part of her had died. During the day she kept busy looking after her mother, but at night he filled her dreams.

Her mom poked her head out the window. "Lee's here."

She plastered a fake smile on her face before turning around. "Be right in."

"Are you expecting a call?" Vivian said.

They had finished dinner and her mother was sitting in what she termed her cozy chair, determined to finish the novel.

She stopped wiping down the table and stood up. "No. Why?"

Vivian looked at her as if to say something, then returned to her book. "No reason."

She ambled back to the kitchen to finish cleaning up. A short while later she wiped her hands on her pants. "There, dishwasher's loaded."

Her mother looked up. "When are you due back at work?"

"Next Monday," she said. "Cases are starting to pile up and Doug needs me back."

"This partner you were working with, what was his name again?"

A sharp pain cut through her chest. She placed a wayward glass in the dishwasher and attempted to keep her voice even. "Murphy."

"Will you be teamed up with him again when you get back?"

She suddenly found it difficult to swallow. "Umm, no."

This topic was too raw. She turned away and schooled her features.

"No? From our phone calls, I thought you enjoyed working with him."

"He's already gone. Now the case is over, I doubt I'll ever see him again." Even to her ears, her voice came out strained.

"Hmm … That's a shame." Vivian glanced at her book for a moment before clearing her throat. "And how's your grandfather?"

She spun around to face her mother so quickly the bones in her neck cracked. "P-pardon?"

Vivian's face was buried in her book. Without looking up she said, "You heard me. How's Joshua? I assume the call this morning was from him."

Open mouthed, she sank into the chair opposite her mother without saying a word. From her mother's tone she could be asking for directions or for weather conditions. Not asking after a man she thought dead all these years.

How the hell was she supposed to reply to that?

"I—" She cleared her throat. "I don't know what you're talking about. Are you sure you didn't bump your head when you were taken?"

Vivian put her book on the armrest and looked up at her. "Sweetheart, let's not play games." She took off her reading glasses and placed them on top of her head. "I spotted him as we left the hospital, and then again at the cemetery."

Her brows shot up. "H-How?"

"Pffft." Vivian waved her hand dismissively, a half smile playing on her lips. "There were never any secrets between your father and me. I've always known your father and your grandfather's history, as well as who and what Elijah was."

She dug her nails into the armrest. She couldn't have heard this right.

Vivian blinked rapidly, her eyes glazed over with tears. "I spent the last few weeks in absolute hell thinking that monster was going to take my baby as well. When I heard he was dead and gone I could finally breathe again. But then coming face to face with him …."

She shuddered, and her heart was once again ripped open raw. "Why did you never say anything?"

Her mom shrugged. "Your father and I decided it was safer for all concerned if everyone thought I was in the dark. It allowed us to live our lives without the pack constantly looking over our shoulders."

She shook her head from side to side, still not sure if this conversation was really happening. "You said nothing, even when you knew Elijah was back."

Her mother exhaled. "I assumed you had no idea what he truly was. As far as I was aware, you had no inkling that we shared this planet with another race who were only half Human. Your dad …" Vivian's lower lip wavered and she brought a hand up to cover her mouth. Her face contorted in pain and tears rolled down her cheeks. "How did you find out?"

She blinked. "Find out?"

"About Werewolves."

"Oh, that. I-I accidently saw Murphy transform."

"I see. That would have been a bit of a shock."

She chuckled at the memory. "Oh boy, was it ever."

Vivian dabbed the corner of her eye with a tissue. "If you think Murphy's gone for good, why are you constantly checking your messages?"

She picked at a stray thread on the arm of the sofa. "I do no such thing."

Vivian shrugged and picked up her abandoned book. "If he's anything like his mother, I'm sure he'll be back."

Kaitlyn frowned. "His mother?"

Her mom arched an eyebrow and smirked. "What's with you and repeating everything I say? Yes. His mother, Molly. While we were waiting for you to arrive, we had to talk about something. I told her about you. She told me a little about her son and daughter. I knew she was a Werewolf." She rolled her eyes. "I was drugged, not in a coma. It wasn't until you reminded me that your partner's name was Murphy that I put it together. Your father knew him well."

She opened then closed her mouth. Words eluded her. She was torn between telling her mother everything and denying it all.

"Molly seems like a wonderful woman. I hope to meet her again someday."

Vivian got up and came to sit next to her. She pushed a stray curl behind Kaitlyn's ear. "I am not going to push, but a mother knows when her child's heart is breaking. And I think it has something to do with Murphy. When you're ready to talk, just know I'll be here for you."

She bit back a sob, and tears rushed to the surface, spilling over her lids and down her cheeks. She could hide her emotions from the Pioneers, but that skill clearly didn't extend to fooling her mom.

Vivian let out a deep sigh and pulled her close. "You said your grandfather was stopping in Boston before heading home."

She nodded and wiped her tears with the back of her hand.

"Honey, I want you on a plane in the morning. At least have some closure with him."

She frowned, pulled away, and sat up straight. She wouldn't leave her mom in this condition. "But—"

Her mom held up her hand. "There will be no buts, young lady. I am fine. The worst thing that can happen to me now is Lee starting another argument with the Johannson's."

Exhumed

Boston, MA

Kaitlyn stumbled into her apartment after midnight. She was hungry, tired, and in need of a shower. The four-hour delay for her flight's departure, then the mechanical problem in Atlanta had resulted in her returning home twelve hours later than expected. She had missed Joshua by four hours. The universe was conspiring against her at an alarming rate.

She glanced around her apartment. It looked the same as it ever did. Any damage from the mafia Pioneers was long gone. Liam had fixed the door and Molly set the place in order before they brought her mother home from the hospital.

She tossed her bag in her bedroom then stared at the photo of her father on the bookshelf. What the hell was she going to do now? The apartment was quiet. Too quiet. She was floating aimlessly on an ocean that went on forever, and she didn't know which way to paddle. She swallowed the lump in her throat. Coming back to Boston knowing Murphy was gone for good left an ache in her heart. She had driven her mother insane in Florida, insisting on doing everything. The busy work kept her mind occupied and away from the overwhelming despair of never seeing him again. She knew this was going to happen. The outcome had always been a foregone conclusion. Now she had to accept it.

Her phone beeped and she jumped at the sudden break in the silence. She glanced at the screen. Anika. She shut off the phone. She'd call Anika in the morning. No doubt she was calling to see how she was and give her a moment by moment run down of the wedding. While Anika was disappointed Kaitlyn had to cancel on her, she fully understood that family came first. Her friend was well meaning, but right now she didn't have the energy.

She wandered into the kitchen. Maybe if she cooked something it might settle her. She opened the pantry door and blindly stared at the contents. Her fingers tightened on the pantry door handle. She should not have taken the case, and she definitely should not have gone out to his place that night.

Her vision blurred and her hands shook. She rested her head against the door. The grief became too strong. She let go of her emotions and allowed her heart to take over. A sorrowful cry escaped her lips as the tears fell. Her body racked with sobs, and she leaned against the door. She mourned the loss of something she never had but desperately needed.

Finally spent, she sat in the dark and stared into space. Empty was painful. She reached into her bag for a tissue just as her phone buzzed again. A faint smile flitted across her face as she read the message through her tears. Joshua was back in Tennessee, and he wanted to make sure she was okay.

While he had no immediate blood in Tudor Falls, she knew family surrounded him. She sighed. Maybe family was what she lacked. With the exception of Anika, she had no one in the city whom she could fall back on. She had lots of friends and acquaintances, but none close.

She hiccupped. This was ridiculous. She was a grown woman, used to being on her own. "I'm just tired. With everything that's happened with mom, I'm bound to be a bit flakey."

Her doorbell rang, and she nearly jumped out of her skin. No one knew she was here, and it was after midnight. The hairs at the back of her neck bristled, and her heart kicked into overdrive. She dropped her bag, raced to the kitchen, and grabbed a large knife from the block. She sidled up to the wall beside the door. "Who is it?"

A deep sigh came from the other side of the door. "You don't really think that a knife would hurt a Were—Pioneer, do you?"

Murphy?

She lowered the blade and turned on the lights before scrambling to open the door. Her fingers fumbled with the chain, and it took her two goes to get it unlocked. When she opened the door, her dazed brain found it difficult to accept Murphy was hovering in her hallway.

He frowned and glanced into the apartment over her shoulder. "Are you going to let me in?"

She moved away from the entrance. "Umm ... Yes. Sure." Why was he there?

He strode in and she took a little longer than necessary to close the door.

He placed a small bag on the breakfast bar and turned back to her. "I thought you might like your gun and Taser back."

His eyes narrowed before closing the gap between them. "You've been crying. Is everyone okay? Has something happened?"

He held her by her arms and searched her face.

She averted her gaze and pushed him away. "No, everyone's fine." She wiped her eyes. "I was just a little upset. I missed Joshua. My stupid flight was late."

He kept staring at her, but thankfully chose not to say anything more.

They stood in awkward silence. She was still unsure as to how he could be standing in her apartment. He was supposed to be in Colorado. She'd expected him to disappear without a trace.

She swallowed. "I've just gotten back and was about to make myself something to eat." She headed into the kitchen, hoping he wouldn't see through her lie. "You hungry?"

The earthy way he said, "Always," sent a shiver across her skin. She glanced over her shoulder, but his expression gave nothing away. She concentrated on hiding her emotions the way Joshua had taught her. Thank the stars he couldn't read minds. She'd be screwed.

He leaned against a wall and watched her prepare the ingredients for an omelet. "How's your mom?"

"She's strong. She'll come out of this just fine."

He opened a beer he grabbed from the fridge and studied the label. "Ma pretty much said the same thing."

She whipped the mixture and tried to keep her voice even. "What brings you back to Boston? When I spoke to Joshua, he said deliberations hadn't finished yet."

"They haven't. They don't need me for a few days, and I had to get the house sorted."

Her whisk faltered and nearly slipped from her hand. "I thought Joshua closed up the house."

The room fell silent. He stared at the bottle he cradled in his hands. "He did."

She poured the egg batter into the heated skillet. He was making no sense. "So why are you back? I thought once you were gone, you would be gone for good." She winced. Even to her ears she sounded waspish.

His brows furrowed together. "What gave you that idea?"

"You."

Her hand froze over the skillet, and her blood ran cold. "Something happened didn't it? It's not Joshua, he just messaged me." Her fingers tightened around the handle. "Please don't tell me something has happened to your parents."

He chuckled. "No. They're fine."

Her shoulders dropped, and she returned to flipping the omelet. "Don't scare me like that. So what was so important you had to return to Boston?"

He placed the bottle on the countertop. "There's something I need to do first before I tell you."

Within a heartbeat, he was off the stool, removing the pan from the gas.

She opened her mouth to protest, but before she could say anything, he cupped her face between his hands. His dark eyes scanned her as if trying to memorize every crevice and blemish. "I've missed you," he said, with barely repressed emotion.

His walls dropped, and her heart broke at the torture reflected in his expression. His fingers tangled in her hair and hauled her against his hard body. Murphy's lips pressed against hers in a burning kiss, and the world fell away. The cold taste of corona drifted across her tongue. Combined with his essence, it set her alight. She clutched fistfuls of his shirt as his tongue stroked the fire. Goosebumps erupted and desire raced from the pit of her stomach to every nerve ending. She was this close to heaven with only a kiss.

Too quickly, the kiss ended. He rested his forehead against hers and closed his eyes. "I missed that." His voice came out husky, as raw as earth and fire.

Her body quivered, and she leaned into him. She was the moth, and he was the flame. And if she allowed this to happen, she would be burned beyond recognition.

She pulled away with great difficulty. "Food's getting cold."

To preserve her sanity, she needed to put an end to this. She couldn't put herself through this torture. He needed to go while she still had the strength. To put some distance between them, she pulled two plates out of the cupboard. The mundane activity gave her time to think. She placed three quarters of the omelet onto one of the plates and the remainder onto the other before pushing the larger portion over to Murphy.

He refrained from questioning her sudden change in behavior. Instead, he took his seat and began to eat.

If she had any sense, she'd ask him to leave. She pushed her egg around the plate with her fork.

The room sank into silence.

"Kaitlyn."

Her name on his lips was like melted chocolate. Decadent and addictive.

"Kaitlyn."

This time his voice was more demanding, and she looked up.

He was staring at her. The dark eyes boring into hers made all sorts of promises. The air charged with electrical energy and sent tiny currents through her stomach. He was looking at her like she was his next meal. She fought off the sudden desire that ripped through her core. He couldn't keep doing this to her. It wasn't fair. He was too damn sexy.

"This has to stop."

There she did it. The words were out.

He frowned. "What does?"

"This." She pointed between them. "You can't just show up. Kiss me like that, then disappear from my life. You don't get to do that." She drew in a deep breath. "I think you should leave."

His posture stiffened. "Why?"

"You know why."

He crossed his arms over his chest. "No, actually, I don't. Explain it to me."

"Because I'm not like you. I can't get physical and not get burned. I'm not sure I'd recover. You, of all people, should understand that. I can't be the scratch to your itch."

His lips slid into a sexy, sly grin. "I don't know about that. I'd say we both have an itch. And I'm quite happy to scratch yours."

She bit her bottom lip. He'd dropped his guard and reminded her of a wolf stalking its prey. And right now, she was the prey. Heat surged through her body at his implied meaning. She needed to protect her heart. Right now, she had a chance of surviving. If she gave in to their desire, she would be lost. "That's not going to happen."

"Why not?"

She looked him in the eye. No matter how much it hurt, she had to tell him the truth. "Because when you leave, and you will, you'll leave without looking back. Me, I won't recover. I can't do it. I can't set my heart up for a fall like that. It's best you go now while I can still pick up the pieces and get over you the best I can."

He stared at her, his face hidden behind the granite mask that had bolted back into place. Unreadable and unreachable. "If I'm understanding you correctly, you don't want to be with me because you're in love with me?"

She nodded. When he said it like that she sounded demented. The minutes ticked by in time to the thumping of her heart.

Without saying a word, he strode across to the bookshelf. He picked up the photo of her father and gazed at it.

Her face heated up. She'd done it now, and she couldn't take the words back. If she were a betting person, she'd wager he was calculating the fastest route to Colorado or any of the other fifty states. Anywhere but here.

The silence ticked on.

He placed the photo back on the shelf.

She steeled herself for the inevitable so long, I'm out of here.

He growled and ran his fingers through his hair. "I've spent the better part of the past century as dead and buried as June.

My only reason for living was my need for revenge. And I'll admit I had no intention of living once Elijah was gone. Why would I? There would be nothing for me."

He turned and made his way back to stand in front of her. His large muscular body boxed her into the kitchen bench. She had nowhere to escape. "But then I met this smart aleck woman who drove a skate and insisted on calling it a car. She cooked when she was working through a problem, and was one of the best damn agents I've ever worked with." He tilted his head and narrowed his gaze. "Without even knowing it, I started to look forward to getting up each day. Breathing became easier. I started to remember what happy felt like."

Her heart thumped against her ribcage.

He reached out and caressed a curl. "I'd been so focused on what I had buried that I missed how this frustrating know-it-all brought me back to the land of the living. I was so entrenched with my loss and the need for revenge that I ignored what my wolf knew from the start."

She cleared her throat, not sure if she could find her voice. "And that is?"

He smiled a smile that warmed her very soul.

"You. My world isn't complete unless you're in it."

She struggled to breathe. Or stand, or anything. His unexpected confession played havoc with her brain. She alternated between euphoria and misery, her mind still trying to explain everything away as a fantasy. Was it possible he was expressing his undying friendship? His words could tip the scale either way.

She placed a hand against her stomach. "W-what are you saying?"

In a split second, the confident Murphy was gone. In his place was a man on the precipice of uncertainty. "Kaitlyn, when I told you my priorities had changed, I thought you understood what I meant."

He let out a frustrated growl and rubbed the back of his neck. "I'm fucking this up. I'm not a man used to expressing feelings. It is not who I am, but I want to be clear so there is no confusion." He tilted her chin up so she had no choice but to look him in the eye. "Because of you I am alive again. Because of you, my heart beats again. You are the music of my heart. I want, no, I need you in my life. *Mo shíorghrá*, I am in love with you. Nothing will ever change that, and I don't want it to. Simply put, you are my world. I never expected to feel this way again. But my body, heart, and soul belong to you. If you want it."

Her head spun. Her pulse raced. Did he just say he loved her? The weight lifted from her shoulders and her legs suddenly felt weak. She was a kick ass FBI agent who'd gone up against a bunch of mafia Pioneers, and here she was weak at the knees over a few sappy words.

Her hand reached out and rested on his firm chest. She grinned at him. "You do know that you've just said more in the last five minutes than most people hear from you in an entire day?"

He cupped her head in his hand. His free hand wrapped around her waist and yanked her against his hard body. "You didn't answer me."

She loved this broody, virile man with every fiber of her being. Her fingers moved up to touch his face. "I love you, Murphy O'Neil. Of course, I want your heart and your soul." She grinned. "And especially your body."

She didn't know who moved first, but the onslaught of raw physical desire that ripped through her body was her undoing. His mouth sealed hers, stealing her gasp of longing and need. The taste of him flooded her senses until she had no idea where she ended and he began. She moaned into his lips. He deepened the kiss and pillaged her mouth. Her skin sizzled and her temperature rose. His lips moved down her neck, nipping and biting as they travelled lower.

Her breathing became labored. She needed more. She needed him. Now.

She wrapped her arms around him as he pulled her up so that her knees were clamped around his hips. She pulled him closer, and he groaned.

"If you want to stop you need to say so now. Any more of this and I won't be able to," he said with a growl into her ear.

"If you dare stop, I will shoot you." Her voice came out in a tortured pant.

She molded herself to him as he deftly carried her from the kitchen, their frenzied kisses more potent with each passing moment. Their urgent need for each other took over and they failed to make it to the bedroom.

Kaitlyn woke to Murphy playing with a stray curl. She opened her eyes and smiled. "You're up early."

He propped up on his elbow and winked. "Didn't go to sleep. I've been waiting for you to wake up so I could make love to you again."

She yawned and stretched, and she wrapped her leg around his stone hard leg. "Well, aren't you the energizer bunny this morning?"

He loomed above her. "I wouldn't mind showing you just how long I can last." He dipped his head and coaxed her lips into a searing kiss.

She arched her back when his fingers trailed down her stomach. More than happy for a repeat, she gave in to the liquid heat of desire. This she could get used to.

She reluctantly swung out of bed and reached for her pajama top late in the morning. Her stomach rumbled and she felt her face heat up.

He let out a chuckle. "Sounds like I'd better feed you."

She grinned and made her way to the bathroom. "Well, you were the one responsible for my sleep-in this morning."

By the time she made it to the kitchen, Murphy had brunch ready for her. He had downed half a cup of coffee and was checking his messages as she took a chair at the breakfast bar. She gazed at him over her cup. A small smile tugged at her lips as she recalled how their evening had turned out. She suspected making love to him would be pleasurable. But nothing had quite prepared her for just how perfect they were together. They just fit. She took a sip of her hot chocolate and realized she hadn't once thought of Elijah or the mafia Pioneers since Murphy stepped through her door.

A twinge at the back of her scalp reminded her of what Garcia had done, and her fingers tightened around her cup. "When are you handing Garcia over to the authorities."

"We're not."

She tensed, sure she had heard him incorrectly. "I beg you're what?"

He sighed and clicked his phone screen off. "If we hand him over to the authorities, he'll expose us. We can't allow that to happen,"

Her lips set into a grim line, and she narrowed her eyes. "So, you would hunt down a murderer for decades, but allow another one to roam free."

He held up his hands. "I didn't say he wasn't going to be punished, it just won't be by the human justice system. Garcia's case was an easy one for the council to deliberate. We have a first-hand account of his confession, and his attempt on your life was also taken into account."

Her shoulders relaxed. "What's going to happen to him then?"

"He'll spend the next five years with a pack in Resolute, northern Canada. They are hundreds of miles from any civilization, and the temperature is below freezing year-round. Even if he got away from them, he wouldn't get far."

"And after that?"

"He'll be turned. If he's one of us, he'll be less inclined to expose what he is."

The Werewolves' council had made the right decision. With the exception of his confession, which couldn't be used, she had no proof he'd killed Saul. With unlimited access to mafia funds and the best lawyers, the chance was good he would get the charges dropped. "What about the search for Ambrose?"

"Daniel has a team on it but no word yet. The council is holding off on their final decision on the new pack pending Ambrose's capture." Murphy put his phone down and took the seat next to her. "We've never had a situation where a pack evolved like this. It'll take a lot of debating to work out what they're going to do. It doesn't help they've had another Elise crisis to deal with in the interim."

"What do you think they'll do?"

He considered the question. "There's no doubt Ambrose is an Alpha. If he wasn't, we would have broken his men by now. In all likelihood, they'll be read the riot act and given strict instructions on what they can and can't do as far as Werewolves are concerned. They'll be allowed to go home under close supervision for the next few decades."

She nearly choked on her drink. "How could you say that after all these years in law enforcement? They're into drug trafficking, weapons, and racketeering. You name it, they do it."

He rubbed his forehead. "And you think by removing Ambrose that'll stop? There are others out there with far fewer scruples ready to step in and take over at a moment's notice. Who should we really be worried about? The ones who are after money? The ones who want to wipe US citizens off the face of the earth? The ones who want to eradicate anyone or anything different from them? If you ask me, I'd prefer the devil I know."

She mulled over his words. Her nature and training rebelled against allowing the New England mafia to continue as if nothing had happened. But she had to admit his argument held some logic.

He entwined his hand in hers. "Don't overthink it. The rules you are used to don't work when it comes to Were's. If we were out in the open, perhaps they would. But while a gap divides Humans from the rest of us, things won't be as you expect."

She studied their hands. As much as she hated to admit it, her new normal would take some getting used to. She needed to protect Murphy, Joshua, Molly, Liam, and the rest of the Pioneers she'd met. They were good people. She shuddered at the thought of the government finding out about them. The DOD would have a field day, and Pioneers would become a terrorist threat.

Frankinfurter. Her pulse quickened when she considered the risks.

She squeezed his hand. "How do you do it?" she said. "How do you cope knowing that at any moment you could be found out?"

He hesitated before answering. "You get used to it. That's why we typically live in packs. It gives us the luxury of living as ourselves in a protected environment. We know we are stronger and faster than the majority of those we share the earth with. That's why we've put guidelines in place to make sure we don't take advantage of the situation. Our rules and laws are not just there to protect Were's, they're there to protect Humans as well."

She pulled her hand away and fingered her mug. He just made her argument. "All the more reason to make sure Ambrose and his cronies don't get away with the crimes they have perpetrated. Where is the justice for all those families affected by their blatant disregard for life?"

He chuckled. "Maybe next time, I'll get you to argue the point with the council. That way, maybe we can cut out the middleman."

She sipped her drink then nodded at her taser. "Do you think they'd let me taser them if I didn't like the way they voted."

"I would pay to see that."

She tapped a finger on her mug. He had mentioned Elise. "Should I be worried about this crisis the council is dealing with?"

He frowned. "We don't know. There's been some odd wolf sightings reported in Nebraska."

She cocked her head and her stomach clenched "Odd? How?"

"Well, wolves haven't been seen in the area for the past century, and it's too close to the Airforce base for Werewolves to risk, so there is no local pack."

The uneasy feeling in her stomach increased. She didn't like something in his tone. "Maybe a stray wolf who has somehow gotten lost."

He shook his head. "The reports are of wolf-like creatures walking on their hind legs."

She froze, not sure she heard him correctly. "That can't be right—can it?"

"No. That's why Daniel wants me to head to Nebraska."

"So why aren't you there?"

"You."

He slipped off the chair and reached for her. "I couldn't go until I knew where I stood with you. I needed to know if we had a chance for a future together."

A twinge of anguish shot through her at the realization he would soon be gone again. She couldn't, she wouldn't stop him. He had a responsibility, and he had to go. A smile played on her lips. The knowledge that he would always return to her provided a small measure of comfort. She could live with that. For now.

He bent down and nipped along her neck.

Although every bone in her body was aching from their double marathon, she was ready to fly apart and give in to the sudden flare of desire.

She unbuttoned her shirt, her voice husky. "How much time do we have before you need to leave?"

His dark eyes bore into hers, reaching for the deepest part of her soul. "How long do you need?"

The end. For now.

Acknowledgements

No book is ever written without support. I would like to express my gratitude to the following:

To Sebastian and Dominic for your patience and encouragement. I am so proud of the young men you are both becoming. But please stop leaving empty milk bottles in the fridge.

Debbie, Angela & Heleine, for their unwavering support and cheerleading. I will be forever grateful for you.

A special thanks to the RWNZ Auckland chapter writers. You inspired me to persevere.

I would also like to thank Emma Bryson and Shirley Fedorak, my editors. Ladies, you continue to teach me so much about the craft. I am very much in your debt.

Of course, I can't forget my launch team who helped me get Buried into the public arena. I couldn't have done it without you — thanks:

Naourès, Chantelle, Ana, Debbie, Vikki, Christy, Danielle, Ange, Belen, Marie, Taylor, Kim and Laurie.

And I am especially grateful for you, the reader who picked up this book and gave an author a chance to let her voice be heard.

About The Author

After failing miserably at world domination and surviving many years of producing technical documentation, project plans and test plans that no one bothered to open, M (pron. M) Greenhill decided to create something that might actually be read.

She enjoys creating paranormal stories that takes the reader on a journey filled with intrigue, excitement and more twists and turns than are bugs in a Microsoft update.

M lives in New Zealand with her two Fortnight addicted sons, a miniature schnauzer that destroys shoes, and a cat that lets us think we are in charge. Ever the optimist, she hopes that one day she will own a pair of Louboutin's and that, for once, the kids wouldn't leave empty milk bottles in the fridge.

Connect with M Greenhill:

Facebook: https://www.facebook.com/MNJGreenhillAuthor

Twitter: https://twitter.com/MNJGreenhill

Web: http://www.mgreenhill.com